HELL'S PAWN

Jay Bell Books
www.jaybellbooks.com

Cover art by Andreas Bell
www.andreasbell.com

Acknowledgements

Surrounding me is a team of people, supporting my writing and constantly steering me away from making a fool of myself. There's Linda Anderson, my tireless editor and champion of grammar. Then there are my early readers and safety nets: Katherine Coolon, Kira Miles, Zate Lockard, and last but certainly not least, my mom. I love all of you and couldn't do this without you.

Then there is Andreas, who has done so much for me that I could write an entire book about it. Maybe I will someday.

To Zate – my kindred spirit and fellow wanderer in worlds unknown.

Hell's Pawn

by Jay Bell

Chapter One

The world was a blanket of heavy fog, the San Francisco Bay ahead swallowed up along with the surrounding land. Only the two towers of the Golden Gate Bridge jutted out, like enormous shark fins stripped down to the cartilage. Occasionally the fog would stir, a witch's brew that allowed brief patches of paved streets to be seen. All were hauntingly empty, perhaps closed due to the unusual weather.

John Grey breathed in deeply, wondering if the thick air was to blame for how muddled his thoughts felt. When he exhaled, he half expected to see streams of fog pouring from his nose like cigarette smoke.

"It's quite a sight, isn't it?"

John pushed himself away from the pier's railing and regarded the extraordinarily wrinkled man. Ancient creases deepened as Asian features smiled at him. The stranger's clothes were simple and worn, but clean. The old man nodded in greeting before turning back to the view.

"I never expected to see the Great Wall again," the old man continued in an accent so thick that John marveled at his own ability to understand it. And yet the man spoke perfect English. Not one consonant was forgotten, nor a single vowel pronounced incorrectly. His grammar, so far, had been impeccable. In a way, it wasn't really an accent at all, but more like another language that John could inexplicably understand.

"Great wall?" he responded at last.

The old man nodded toward the bridge. "I spent my whole life trying to escape. The wall cast a shadow over my village, one that caused me to chase the sun all the way to Beijing. I never regretted leaving. I loved Beijing, and yet, seeing the Great Wall again, I feel as though I am looking upon the forgiving face of my father."

John stared, first at the man, then at the bridge. Eventually he turned his attention back to the wizened old man. He seemed amiable enough for someone who was completely insane. Or perhaps he was senile. John looked around, expecting to see a flustered nurse searching for her escaped patient. Aside from a worn-down warehouse, the area seemed deserted.

"A dog! On the wall!" The man pointed to the bridge.

John humored the stranger and gazed across the bay. There *was* a dog. This wasn't as surprising as the fact that John could actually see him. The bridge was miles away, and yet John's eyes didn't strain to focus on the English Shepherd. Not only could he identify the dog's breed, but he could see the hair on its back bristle before it ran from a dog catcher, darting in and out of the fog to escape.

The old man laughed, and John joined him. Maybe they were both mad. That would explain why John had no recollection of how he had come to be here. They cheered as the dog repeatedly avoided capture. The Shepherd would wait until the catcher was near, seeming to pretend to cooperate, but as the catcher came within reach, the dog would race away again. This game continued until both figures were lost in the fog.

John's head was clearing, enough that he began seriously considering his predicament. Where exactly was he? He strained to recall his last memory. Too many weeks in a row had been filled by his drafting table. He had breathed and dreamed nothing but blueprints for the corporate headquarters that was destined to turn forty acres of sleepy countryside into an institution of nine-to-five conformity. John's job as an architectural engineer was to make sure the corporate building was both functional and practical, but his personal goal was to minimize its ugliness for the poor souls who had to drag themselves there to work every day.

Finally, the project ended, but instead of the usual release of tension, John felt knots of stress so tight that he feared they would never come undone. He had retreated outside of the city, seeking a bar where no one knew him, and set about drinking his dinner.

He must have gone on one hell of a binge to cause him to black out, his first since college. Maybe the old Asian man was a new drinking buddy he picked up last night. Surely something more intimate hadn't happened between them. John was pondering the most diplomatic way of asking when the clicking of high heels caused them both to turn.

"I knew two were missing," the newcomer said with no warmth. Her voice, like her appearance, was all business. She wore the sort of power suit favored by most female politicians: conservative trousers combined with a shoulder-enhancing blazer. Her blonde hair was piled atop her head and skewered by a pencil. That last touch was purely for show since the clipboard she held was clearly electronic. She narrowed her humorless eyes at the device. "Lists be damned, you can always feel when unexpected guests arrive."

The woman wasted no time in herding them away from the pier. A quick glance at the Asian man showed John that he had no idea what was going on either. They were guided to the front of a dreary warehouse where a motley group had gathered. Most of them were old. Some were dressed formally while others were wearing bathrobes and pajamas. None of them showed any embarrassment at being over- or under-dressed, nor did they take any interest in the two new members of their group.

Oddest of all were the blue lines of light connecting each person at the waist. The chains of light were as precise and bright as lasers, except they curved and swung like common string. A feeling of unease built within John as he realized that none of the group was moving. They stood perfectly still like sculpture.

"I'm sorry you missed the initial orientation," the woman said, sounding anything but apologetic. "You'll need these, of course." She pulled two bronze triangles from the air and handed one to each of them.

John took his and examined it. The device might have been made of thick metal were it not so lightweight. The design was simple and had no detail aside from a single red button in its center. Naturally he wanted to press it, but he looked first at their host for some indication of if this was allowed.

"Put the badges on your belts," she instructed them in tones that were curiously hard to disobey. "Good. Now, if you'll just push the button, we'll be on our way."

John watched as his companion pressed his button first. This activated a beam of light that connected with the others in the group. Immediately, the old man's eyes glazed over and his jaw went slack. John's unease graduated to full-blown panic. He didn't know what was going on, or how he had gotten himself into it, but he wanted out. John pulled on the triangle, trying to dislodge it from his belt, but it wouldn't budge.

"Here, let me help." Moving with surprising speed, the woman's finger struck like a cobra, pressing the button on John's device.

The world around John dimmed, his limbs becoming heavy and burdensome. What little color the gray morning had contained faded into monochrome. There was a time, shortly after leaving the longest relationship of his life, that John had lost his job and struggled for six months to find work. As the credit card bills grew, so did his depression. The deeper he sank, the less motivated he became. He felt that way now. He knew he should be frightened and try to think of a way to escape, but it was all too much bother.

John didn't notice the crowd of people filing through the warehouse door until he was the last one left. The businesswoman had gone ahead, no longer needing to ensure that he would follow, not with the line from his belt tugging him forward. That his thoughts and feelings were being suppressed was a mercy, for his new surroundings were the last place John wanted to be right now. Instead of a dingy warehouse interior, an endless sea of cubicles stretched beyond the horizon, as if the beast he had so recently finished designing had come to life and swallowed him whole.

John closed his eyes against the stark florescent lights and let the line pull him along. Blind now, the constant hum of the busy office lulled him into a trance. Time and distance lost all meaning as he and the others stumbled along like a heavily medicated chain gang.

Eventually the light through his eyelids grew dark, and cool air brushed against his skin. John opened his eyes to find himself in a large open room. Marble covered the walls and floor, as well as the massive pillars supporting the ceiling. Through the haze, John's engineer training helped him recognize the intent to intimidate—a tactic reserved for first impressions—which would make this reception. In the center of the room, at a blocky desk that faced the spinning door, sat a woman who was almost a twin of their guide except that her brown hair was fashioned in an impossibly tight bun. One by one, the drowsy newcomers approached the desk and were each handed a generic manila folder.

"I just have to register an extra report on our two unexpecteds," their guide told them. "You may look in your file while you wait."

The suppressive blanket lifted from the group, and although

the blue lines dimmed, they didn't disappear completely. Some of the group murmured in puzzlement, but most opened their files to examine the contents. John did as well, but first he assessed his surroundings, specifically the exit. He could see a busy city street outside the rotating door. His mind reeled in confusion. They had started at the bay, and while the warehouse had been large, it couldn't have stretched far enough to reach a densely populated area. How far had they walked while his eyes were closed?

"I have a 263 in charitable deeds," a middle-aged woman said to John, pointing in her folder. "That sounds high. Do you think that's high?"

John regarded her irritably before looking down at his own file. The page he had randomly turned to was cluttered with statistics and graphs. Under the heading of "Reactions in Familial Crisis" was listed:

Fortitude: 154.87
Recrimination: 16.2
Avoidance of Confrontation: 53
Placement of Blame: 120.55
Use of Manipulation: 12.3

The list went on and on, accompanied by charts displaying averages and correlations, predicted responses versus proven, the effect on other incarnate beings, and other endless gibberish. These made as much sense as everything else had so far.

"Is yours so high?" the woman pressed.

"See for yourself," John said, thrusting his folder into her hands.

As nonchalantly as possible, he began walking toward the door, but the blue line halted him. Like a dog on a leash, he could only go so far, no matter how much he struggled.

"Right," their guide said as she returned. "We'll be moving through the city now to the acclimatizing dormitories where you will be residing for your initial period here. One more time under the dampeners, sorry."

John braced himself as the oppressive feeling of depression descended on him once more. Perhaps he was prepared for it, because it wasn't nearly as bad this time. He still let the line pull him wherever he was being led, but he was much more aware of his surroundings as they exited to the street.

They emerged into light that felt as artificial as the office they had passed through. Around them was a thriving downtown area. John, despite resisting the forces pressing on him, still had trouble focusing on his surroundings. Pedestrians passing by in the opposite direction did so in a distorted haze, leaving smudged after-images trailing behind. He turned his attention to the street, which was a much less hectic scene since no car was in sight.

The car. Where had he parked it? A memory tore through his mind, firing through his synapses like a burst of lightning. There really had been lightning. Flash flooding, too. John had guzzled so much alcohol that his breath had tasted like fumes. He never should have gotten behind the wheel, but he had been outside the reach of public transportation and taxis were so damned expensive. He had compensated for his inebriation by driving extra slow, but he couldn't judge how fast he was going without frequently squinting at the speedometer. When he had last looked up from the blurry gauge, the headlights were illuminating a tree, the detail of its bark intricate and beautiful before everything went dark.

I'm dead.

The realization hit John like a cold shower.

I drank too much and like an idiot I tried to drive home. I slammed into that tree and it killed me. Now I am— where? Heaven? Hell?

Wherever he was, John no longer wanted to be there. Ahead of him the rest of the group trundled along like children being led by an apathetic nanny. Whatever hold the dampening device had held over him was gone, defeated by the startling revelation of his own demise. John looked down at the bronze triangle and noticed that the blue line was sparking and snapping. He reached down to break the current, even though every fiber of his being screamed that to do so would be fatal.

John laughed wildly at the idea. As if he could die again! He thrust his hand into the light and felt only a mild shock before the line flickered and disappeared. Stunned by his success, he halted on the sidewalk, the others walking on without him. John didn't dare wait to see if he'd be spotted, so he ducked down a side street and broke into a run.

His vision was no longer blurred, which was good considering the number of pedestrians he had to dodge. Some turned as he passed, curious to know what he was doing, but most ignored him, aside from the occasional grumble when he got in their way. Maybe he wasn't dead after all. Maybe he had been part of some sort of pharmaceutical trial or had gotten tangled up in a bizarre cult. It happened, right? People were brainwashed all the time.

The image of the tree rushing toward him returned, reinforcing the truth. If this weren't proof enough, John had run five blocks and wasn't out of breath. In fact, he wasn't breathing at all. He skidded to a stop and sucked in air experimentally. He *could* breathe or at least perform some imitation of the act, but it was no longer necessary.

Glares and a few muttered curses were directed at him by people not happy that he was standing still in the middle of the sidewalk. What did they care? Where did they have to go? Forty-hour weeks were a thing of the past, or so he hoped. Everyone had the day off now, for all eternity. Defiantly returning a few glares, John continued walking until he found a narrow alley to duck into. He saw no sign of pursuit, but his absence could be noticed at any moment.

Taking advantage of his newfound privacy, John took stock of himself. He was still wearing the stylish suit that he had put on before leaving town, just in case a handsome face awaited him at the bar. A careful examination of the jacket didn't reveal any sign of tearing, blood, or anything else morbid. Next he moved his hands across his face, astounded that he could still detect remnants of the aftershave that conditioned his skin. He certainly didn't feel dead. A quick sweep of his forehead and a tousling of his dirty blonde hair failed to reveal any sign of injury. Since his arrival, he hadn't seen anyone else who looked particularly deceased, either. Maybe this was Heaven after all.

A noise from the entrance of the alley attracted his attention. Running toward him was a bank robber. This was an easy deduction to make because the robber's clothes were patterned with black and white stripes. If this weren't enough, the cloth bag he held had a single, large, dollar sign printed on it. John expected he would have seen the classic black mask as well had the man been facing him, but his head was turned back toward the direction he had come from.

John was so taken aback by this completely generic apparition that he didn't think to move out of the way. The robber collided with him, knocking them both to the ground.

"Mine!" a male voice called out from a few paces away.

John disentangled himself from the robber to see a face staring down at him, one somewhere in its forties that had probably been attractive at one time. Pallid skin, a fiercely stubbled chin, and manic eyes all suggested a person who had enjoyed a lifetime's worth of illicit pleasures within a few decades. Despite this, the black spiky hair was still thick and untainted by gray. Decked out in a punk's leather jacket and a ratty T-shirt, the man's fashion choices hadn't been updated since the eighties. He reached down toward John, his fingers covered in cheap tattoos.

"Thanks," John said, reaching up to him, but the man's hand passed his by and snatched away the bag of money.

"It doesn't matter if you knocked him down," the stranger said. "I chased the bastard all the way here. The reds are mine!"

"Reds?" The term could have been foreign slang, considering the Irish accent. John shook his head, deciding that it was of little consequence. His more immediate concern was getting out from underneath the body on top of him. He squirmed, but the robber didn't budge. "Did you hit him over the head or something? Feels like he's dead."

"Him?" The stranger rolled the robber over with his foot. "He's just a Prop, and anyway, *dead*? Bloody hell, you're a fresh one, aren't you?"

"Yeah." He managed to get to his feet and offered his hand. "John Grey"

The Irishman eyed it wearily, holding the money bag behind his back before finally accepting it. "Dante."

"No kidding?" John snorted. His new companion didn't share his amusement, so John stifled his laughter. "Look, we're dead right?"

"As nails in a coffin, yeah." Dante shrugged, as if it didn't matter to him. "Did you miss orientation? I barely paid attention myself. Took ages to believe any of it until—"

Dante stopped speaking and stared at John's crotch. John was beginning to feel self-conscious when he realized that Dante was looking at the triangular device.

"Now that's something," Dante murmured. "You say this is your first day? Shouldn't you be in the acclimation dorms?"

John tensed and eyed the alleyway entrance.

"No need to run from me, mate. I say fuck the rules. I'm just curious is all."

"I got a little freaked out," John admitted, "broke away from the group."

"They forget to switch you on?"

John shook his head. "If 'on' means being made into a zombie, they didn't forget. I was out of it until I put my hand through the beam and it broke."

Dante scoffed. "Touching the blue is enough to put any soul down for weeks. There's no escaping a dampener."

"Maybe mine was defective."

"Let's see if it still works." Dante made as if he were going to press the button and laughed when John jumped backwards.

"Don't!" John protested. He reached down and tugged at the device until it came off. Dante's eyes widened twice as much as before.

"I don't suppose I could have that?"

"Be my guest." John tossed it to him, happy to be rid of it. Already he had worried it might contain some sort of tracking device. Now it was no longer his problem.

"Well," Dante said after quickly pocketing the dampener and turning to leave, "I have to return this money to the bank. Or give it to an orphanage or something. Whatever gets me the most reds."

"Bank robbery halted."

The voice was high-pitched and monotone and came from the fallen robber. John turned the body over and looked into an empty face. The only details were two black pin pricks for eyes and a slit where the mouth should be.

"Split Reward," the non-living entity continued. *"Dante Stewart: 146 redemption points. John Grey: 146 redemption points."*

"That's just great," Dante spat. "Stupid Props can't even read intention. It's not like you *meant* to stop the robber."

John held up his hands defensively. "Don't blame me. I don't even know why I would need points. You can have mine if they mean so much to you."

"It isn't worth the paperwork." Dante stalked to the end of the alley and held up the money bag. "This one is all mine, got it? Sayonara!"

"Wait! I don't know where I'm supposed to go or what I'm doing here."

"Read your file!" Dante shouted as he disappeared around the corner.

"But I don't have it anymore!" John yelled after him. Silence was the only response.

"Reset complete. Returning for reassignment."

The Prop righted itself, rising from the ground like a puppet on invisible strings. It oriented by spinning in a slow circle before zooming away and leaving John alone in a barren alley somewhere in the afterlife.

Chapter Two

Strolling the city streets, this time without being spurred on by panic, John noticed a number of details that he hadn't before. The sky, for instance. Not a cloud was in it, nor any sign of sun or gradation of light. The heavens were a uniform gray from horizon to horizon. As for the ground, no plants, trees, or even a single weed were to be found. Perhaps vegetation didn't have a soul and thus couldn't be here.

What cities lacked in natural beauty was often balanced out with unique architecture, but the buildings here were as drab as cardboard boxes. John saw no parks, fountains, sculpture or other forms of art. Just square tomb-shaped buildings and the streets that separated them.

The inhabitants of the city were a stark contrast to their monotone surroundings. Walking the streets were people of all colors, wearing every conceivable style of dress. The differing fashions between nationalities provided enough variety, but wasn't the limit. On the busy sidewalk Edwardian frock coats brushed against primitive pelts, delicate kimonos stepped out of the way of suits of armor, while grungy jeans and T-shirts walked next to regal Parisian dresses.

More than once John stopped to stare at the unintended costume party on parade. He suspected that people weren't wearing what they had died in, but what had been fashionable at the time. Most people died in bed, after all, and not while fully dressed. He didn't see anyone in underwear, pajamas, or the buff, which implied a change of clothes was possible after death. As an experiment, John took off his suit jacket and tossed it over one shoulder for a bit before putting it back on again. That he could do so proved it wasn't part of his soul, but left him clueless as to what it was made of.

If there was a place to buy new clothing, John hadn't discovered it. The shops were only for show. They had display windows, prices, and even store names, but never an actual door. Almost every building on the street seemed to have been built that way, apartments included. Much like a Hollywood set, nothing was behind the decorative facades. The city was a hollow shell.

Restaurants and cafes were the exception, seating and serving customers, but most diners didn't seem the least bit interested in their food. Dead or not, John had always appreciated a good meal. Even if sustenance wasn't required anymore, he still desired the pleasure of a rich cake or a good fat steak. His senses, from what he could tell so far, hadn't been affected by being bodiless. John considered stopping to eat, but didn't have any currency.

The financial question was just one among many. Only so much could be learned from wandering aimlessly. John was forced to admit that he would probably have all the answers he needed if he hadn't broken away from his group. What had Dante said? Something about acclimatization dorms? He had also said that his file could help him understand what to do. To get his file, John would have to return to where he had last seen it, which would mean turning himself in. At this point, that would probably be for the best.

He attempted to backtrack along the route he had taken and soon came upon a building of massive proportions with large block letters that declared it was "Administration." The entire appearance of the building reminded John of totalitarian architecture, a style that intimidated through sheer size and a generous amount of concrete. He stared, questioning the wisdom of his actions but unable to think of any other options.

John entered through the spinning door. If he was a wanted fugitive, the woman behind the counter didn't show any sign of it. The same lady who had been there before was still on duty. She was petite, modernly fashionable, and wearing a completely false smile.

"What can I do for you?"

John stared for a moment, realizing that he hadn't prepared what to say. "I don't know what to do," he blurted out.

The woman's smile became even more forced.

"Let's take a look in your file," she said.

As they both stood motionless, John realized that something was expected of him. Another person entered from the street, the footsteps echoing loudly in the hollow room. Soon a line would form behind him, which would only increase the pressure he was feeling.

"I don't have my file."

The smile disappeared. "Residents are required to keep

papers on their persons at all times, must consult them a minimum of three times per daylight period, and present them to any authority figure who requests to see them. Failure to comply can result in identity branding or therapeutic incarceration."

John seriously considered running again. "What if someone loses their papers?" he ventured cautiously.

"Replacement of your file is subject to a 300-point demerit along with another 150-point demerit for processing." The smile on the woman's face returned as if she were beginning to enjoy herself. "I also see—" she glanced down at a screen in the desk, "—that you haven't completed your acclimatization period and are not chaperoned, an offense that is punishable by—"

"Lay off, Nancy," said a voice from behind. "I'll pay for his file replacement, and I'll be his bleeding mentor."

John turned, eyes widening with surprise when he saw Dante. Gone was the safety-pinned leather jacket and Sex Pistols T-shirt. In its place was a finely cut suit that, while a little outdated, still spoke volumes of his status. If the clothing wasn't enough, the scruff was gone from his face and his wild hair was neatly slicked back.

Nancy balked, but soon recovered. "Application for mentorship must be registered in the presence of the official chaperone."

"So punish the original chaperone for failing in their duties," Dante countered. "You can't hold John responsible, seeing how he's not out of his acclimatization period. He hasn't even had the rules presented to him, have you?"

"No, I haven't!" John said, still entranced by Dante's transformation.

"As I recall," his would-be lawyer continued, "in the event that an assigned chaperone can no longer perform his or her duties, the responsibility passes to the nearest authority figure, which would be you."

"Me?" Nancy sputtered, finally losing her composure. "But I have my own duties. Chaperoning is a full-time engagement!"

"Day and night, around the clock," Dante agreed. "Still, he's a quick learner. I'm sure he'll be out of your hair in a few months. Unless of course—"

Dante broke off meaningfully, eyebrows raised and waiting for Nancy to make the next move. It didn't take her long. In a flurry of activity and whirlwind of technical jargon, she handed over papers to be filled out and signed. John felt like a newly purchased appliance as his file was presented to Dante and they were pushed out the door.

Dante Stewart: 1,750 redemption points, a voice manifested from thin air.

"We can spend those right away," Dante beamed. "I didn't know chaperoning paid so well. I wonder if that's a weekly rate."

John stopped in the middle of the sidewalk, intending to demand an explanation, but lost his train of thought when he noticed that Dante had completely reverted to his first guise as an Irish punk.

"I recognize that expression," Dante spoke before John could. "You're on the verge of going off your rocker. You want to know what's going on, and rightly so. Just keep it together for five more minutes so we can do this over a pint, yeah?"

This was the best idea that John had heard all day.

Welcome to Purgatory.

This was printed with a flourish across John's file in a cursive font that wanted desperately to appear hand-written. John stared at it, set the file down, and carefully drained half of his beer. The taste wasn't exceptional, and the brew itself was room temperature instead of ice cold like he preferred.

"You've caught on quickly there," Dante said with a nod. "Downing it is the only way to get plastered in this place."

John shook his head, refusing to be sidetracked by tangents of information. "Purgatory?" he asked.

"Not a Catholic then?" Dante chugged his pint, motioning to the waitress for more while still guzzling from the glass. "Simplest way to put it," he began after a satisfied sigh, "you've got Heaven up above, you've got Hell down below, but what's in between?"

"Purgatory?" John ventured.

"That's right."

"But, why?"

"For all the in-between cases. Say you kill Hitler. Knifing the bastard to death is doing humanity a favor, but it's still murder, right? Or maybe you run a little kid over, and you honestly didn't see the little brat until he was under your wheels."

"Jesus! Keep your voice down!"

"Nothing taboo about death on this side of the curtain," Dante said. "Anyway, you get my point, right? All those trouble cases, the ones too hard to judge either way, they end up here. So what did you do?"

John considered the question while he caught up with his drinking. He had been no saint in life. He had carelessly broken more than one heart, and his teenage years were riddled with the usual self-destructive behavior, but he had long since left his adolescent anger behind. Slowly, over the last ten years, he had grown more considerate of others' feelings and taken responsibility for his own actions. This, when added to his innocent childhood years, meant that he had been "good" for two-thirds of his life. He couldn't remember any morally hazy events in his past, not like Dante had described.

"I don't know. Why are you here?" John asked. "Any idea?"

Dante waited until the waitress set their beers on the table and left before he answered. "Me? I saved a man's life. A good man. One who committed his life to charity, helping others and all that bloody nonsense."

"A priest?"

"No, I said a good man. All priests are good for is putting you to sleep with sermons or breaking in choir boys."

John grinned before considering what was really being said. "So if you only made it here because you saved a man's life, that means—"

"That aside from that one uncharacteristic deed, I was a very, very bad boy."

Dante's dark eyes glimmered wickedly over his glass as he drank to his own decadence. For one brief moment, John wondered if he wasn't actually in Hell, having a pint with the devil himself.

"What did you do?" John ventured, unsure if he really wanted to know. After all, this was his only associate in the afterlife. It would be a shame to become repulsed by his new friend so soon.

Dante shook his head. "Funny. I thought you'd have more questions about Purgatory. Instead you're giving me the third degree."

"Fair enough. Back to Purgatory. So souls here don't fit into Heaven or Hell." John's mind raced, connecting the puzzle pieces of the day's events. "So we play games, earning points to go to Heaven?"

"If you consider foiling fake bank robberies and helping old ladies across the street games, then yes."

As if on cue, a patron at the table next to them began making choking noises while motioning to his neck. John stood to help, but Dante grabbed his wrist.

"Not tonight, kiddo," he muttered. "Sit."

John sat, only able to relax because so many other people came to the choking victim's aid. He watched as an ill-informed version of the Heimlich maneuver was performed by a Native American chieftain. Once John overcame his surprise at seeing the classical depiction of an Indian, he noticed that the choking person's face was just as nondescript and featureless as the bank robber's had been.

"Crap like this happens all the time," Dante complained. "Drives me mental. You can't walk down the street without a Prop setting up a good deed for you."

John's blood rushed, partially because of his buzz, but also out of excitement. "Then it's easy! How long can it take to work off a few paltry sins? I play the game, and before you know it I'm in Heaven!"

Dante shrugged. "If you're so eager to get there. Might as well take a look in your file. I'm going to get us another couple of beers. I think the waitress had her fill of easy reds for the night. That's short for redemption points, in case you're slow."

John nodded distractedly as Dante left, full attention on his file. The first page included a photo of him wearing the same jacket he was currently wearing. The short blonde hair in the photo was messier than he preferred, causing him to reach up and fix it self-consciously. As soon as he did so, the photo changed, reflecting the adjustment he had just made. He thought of Dante's drastic change in appearance at the administration building and realized that this must be for security purposes. If Dante could change from a punk into a cleanly shaven bureaucrat, surely others could also easily adopt disguises. Thus the need for instantly up-to-date identification.

Below the photo were a number of statistics with the qualifier of "upon demise."

Age: 28
Height: 5'11"
Weight: 165lbs
Build: Normal

He skipped down the list, bored with the details that he already knew. Further down the statistics became more interesting. Listed was the fluctuating spectrum range of his aura, the diameter of his psychic field, and even the average pulse rate of his chakras. The numbers listed after each entry were nothing to him, since he didn't have the slightest idea what they meant.

At the very bottom of the page, in large bold text, were the meager 146 redemption points he had earned since arriving in Purgatory. Below that was the amount needed until graduation, which was currently just under 100,000 points. John did some quick mental calculations. Even if he only managed to earn 100 points a day, that meant he would have to spend 1,000 days in Purgatory, somewhere close to three years. That wouldn't be too bad, really. Better than the eternity in the fiery pit that his grandma had always threatened him with.

And that was only the minimum of 100 points. He had already earned 146 by pure chance. If he really applied himself, he would be out in no time. But where exactly was he going? He was sure it would be Heaven, but he couldn't imagine what existence there would be like. Blue skies and clouds maybe, and every pet he had growing up, even the turtles. Relatives too, and angels, maybe even God himself. The thought, or more likely the beer, made his head swim. The idea was too much to consider, so John returned his attention to the file.

He flipped to random pages, noticing that dozens were passing by even though the folder appeared to contain at most ten pages. He played with this phenomenon, watching the pages whiz by until he was sure that they numbered in the hundreds. He stopped on a random page and read:

> *"Despite the promise of paternal assistance to the extent that a specific time and date had been set, subject proceeded to rebuke responsibility, engaging in subterfuge involving the avoidance of communication and intentional deception during three subsequent physical intercommunication sessions."*

John's brow furrowed as he reread this paragraph. He muttered a grunt of gratitude when Dante placed another beer in front of him and sipped it while scanning the text a third time. His increasing drunkenness might partially be to blame for his confusion, but there was no doubting the amount of technical jargon and run-on sentences.

"Find something juicy?" Dante inquired.

"I'm not sure," John responded. "I think it's talking about the time I promised to babysit my sister's kid, and then blew it off."

"If you farted and someone else had to smell it, it's in there. Don't sweat the details. There's no pop quiz at the end of your time here. All that matters is getting reds."

"Seems pretty straightforward."

"It is." Dante's words were beginning to slur. "This is the new system, the humanitarian way. In the old days they used to burn the sin out, or so I hear. Old Jacobi could tell you things. He's been here for ages. Stories that make your skin crawl."

John wasn't particularly sure he wanted to hear them. What he needed to do, once his head was clear again, was to focus on working his way out of Purgatory. Hopefully Dante could help him in this regard, since he was now his chaperone.

"Better drink up," Dante warned. "We don't have much time."

"I'm already tipsy."

"Not for long. Drink! I promise you won't have a hangover."

John drank the rest of his beer, warily sizing up his new friend and wondering if there was a reason for the encouraged intoxication. What did he have to be afraid of? It wasn't like Dante could rob him, and even if he could, John barely had any reds to call his own. Aside from that, he was already dead, so he couldn't be murdered or harmed. Could he?

"So, dead means we're okay, right?" John was struggling to arrange his words. "I mean, you can't get beaten up or anything. Right?"

Dante looked amused and opened his mouth to reply, but a voice from the air interrupted him.

Dante Stewart. Intoxication. 78 point demerit.

"What was that?" John managed to say before the voice spoke again.

John Grey. Intoxication. 78 point demerit.

Instantly and without warning, John was completely sober. He looked questioningly to Dante, who rolled his eyes.

"That's all you get. Half an hour of fun before they cut you off and hit you with demerits. Kind of makes you wonder if we're really in Hell, huh?" He pushed himself from the table. "I'll get us another round."

"No," John said quickly, glad for the sudden sobriety. "Look, what I really want to do now is focus on getting out of this place."

Dante sat back down with a sour expression on his face. "So you want to graduate and go where, exactly?"

"Heaven, I guess. Is there a choice?"

Dante shrugged. "What religion are you?"

"My parents were Lutheran."

"That doesn't mean a thing. Look, I know it's an almost automatic response to think that Heaven is the ultimate destination, but maybe it's not all it's cracked up to be. You think they let you drink up there? You think they have women, poker games, cigars, drugs?"

"I'm pretty sure there are women in Heaven," John retorted.

"You know what I mean. Purgatory might have its shortcomings, but it's damn close to the life we had on Earth. There's no burning in fiery pits or singing hymns to God all day. Graduating will only send you to a prison of another sort. That's not to say there isn't some sense in the idea of *leaving*."

Dante gave a ridiculous stage wink, which John ignored.

"You seemed pretty keen on earning those reds earlier today."

Dante shrugged. "I'm no more interested in going to Hell than I am Heaven. It's a delicate balance. Too much sinful living here, and they graduate you in a different direction."

Before John could respond, the Prop at the table near them starting choking on its food again. Within seconds the other patrons were scrambling to assist and tally up redemption points.

"Time to piss off," Dante hissed as he stood. "I need some fresh air."

As he left, John remained in his seat, watching the Irishman as he pushed his way to the door. He seriously considered not following him, sitting where he was, biding his time until the Prop needed help again. Or maybe he could play waiter for a while. That must be worth something. But the hint that Dante had dropped, the idea that there might be another way out, intrigued him. He hated waiting tables anyway.

Night had fallen in Purgatory, or at least the featureless sky above had deepened into the darkest shade of gray possible. John had never minded the color in life, even had a fondness for it because of his last name, but now he was beginning to despise gray. He wondered how he would feel about it after months, or even years. Dante claimed to appreciate Purgatory, but his irritation with it lurked just beneath the surface.

John cast an uneasy glance up and down the street. Visiting a new city always made him nervous, especially the first night. To him it felt like being in the den of a beast he didn't know the nature of. Even his palms felt sweaty, which was odd now that he considered it.

"I don't feel dead," John said. "Sometimes I even feel my heart beat."

"Habit," Dante answered. "Don't expect to break it either. Girls still gasp, guys still burp, and even though most people don't bother with bathroom stuff, I did meet one guy that couldn't let that go. Your soul remembers what you used to be and that's what you are."

"So we could be anything we wanted, if we put our minds to it?"

"Maybe, but it's human nature to dwell on the past."

Speaking of which, John gave Dante's clothes another once over. "So you've been here since the eighties?"

"No, I'm from the eighties. There's a difference." Dante produced a cigarette from thin air and lit it, rolling his eyes at the announcement of more demerits. "When are you from?"

"2010," John answered.

Dante perked up. "Wow, the future! Been up in space before?"

"No."

"Have a hover car? Or maybe a sexy robot maid?"

"Nope."

"Oh." Dante shrugged off his disappointment. "Well, anyway, the eighties might have been thirty years ago to you, but I've only been here about eight. Time doesn't work the same on this side, or doesn't exist, or something. Ask Jacobi if you want your ear chewed off about it. All I know is that people show up here from all sorts of times." He pointed his cigarette across the street. "You think that samurai over there has been here for centuries? Not a chance. Nobody has been here that long. Even Jacobi only has ninety or so years under his belt."

"And that's who we're going to see?" John asked.

Dante nodded and motioned for him to follow. The streets, despite the increasingly late hour, were still just as crowded as they had been during the day, but without any sense of nighttime revelry. The people of Purgatory were still rushing down sidewalks as if their time was somehow limited. Dante matched their pace, and John had to turn his complete attention to not losing him in the crowd.

They walked for many blocks, but judging their progress was difficult because the streets all looked similar. John began to see a pattern, different arrangements that were used over and over again. Fake department store, fake bakery, two inaccessible apartment buildings, and repeat, like the background of a cheap cartoon.

Eventually the monotony gave way to something slightly different. They entered an open space that, to all appearances, was intended to be a park. Grass was absent, as were any trees, but a playground, basketball court, and tennis court still gave the impression of a recreational area. The park was just as crowded as the rest of Purgatory, but here people seemed content to mill around aimlessly or simply sit. No sports were being played because, as Dante explained, no equipment was available.

They headed toward a pristine baseball diamond. None of the white lines were scuffed and the bases showed no sign of wear. The space inside the diamond was completely empty of people, except for one man standing on the pitcher's mound.

John breathed in deeply as he ventured into this empty area, resisting the urge to spin with his arms outspread in celebration of free space. The man on the pitcher's mound might have had the same idea. His arms were held parallel to the ground and his face turned skyward, but he wasn't spinning. He was standing perfectly still, eyes closed. Long white hair flowed from his head and chin, pouring down both his back and his chest. This alone was enough to make him appear wise, but the pristine white toga drove the point home. John realized with excitement that he may actually be in the presence of one of the great Greek philosophers.

The old man opened his eyes with a gasp and turned his pale blue eyes on John. "I'm the only tree in Purgatory!" he said.

"John, Jacobi. Jacobi, John," Dante said without ceremony, summoning up another cigarette to keep himself occupied.

"It's nice to meet you." John said, offering his hand.

Jacobi ignored it, choosing instead to tug on his beard while his eyes darted randomly over John's person. "He doesn't look like much."

"I agree," Dante said with a wink in John's direction, "but he did have this." He held out his free hand, and where once was nothing, was now a bronze triangle with a red button in the center.

"How do you keep doing that?" John asked, nervously eyeing the dampener.

"Pure memory," Jacobi explained. "In the afterlife, there is no physical matter, only astral material. Forms are shaped by will and held together by memory. Everything you carry with you can be kept in your thoughts until you need it. Your head is a pocket. Mine is, too!"

"In other words, anyone can do it," Dante translated. "There's time for that later."

"But it's important!" Jacobi protested.

"Only if he was telling the truth," Dante countered.

Jacobi squinted in thought for a moment. "You're right. Make him put on the dampener."

"No!" John said, backing away. "There's no way you're getting me to put that thing on again."

"We just want to see you escape from it," Dante said soothingly.

"Why?" John demanded. "So you can figure out how to escape from one next time you get into trouble?"

Jacobi cackled. "He's quick!"

"Not just that," Dante said through gritted teeth. "Listen, *no one* can deactivate their own dampener. It's never been done. If you can, it could mean a lot of things."

John's curiosity got the better of him. "Like what?"

"Like I told the old man, there's no sense in talking about it until we know for sure." Dante held out the device to him. "We have a deal?"

Was there any reason not to? What illicit purpose could they have for wanting him under the dampener's influence? Even if their intentions were malevolent, John had escaped from it once before.

"Okay," John agreed, "but if I can't shake it off in five minutes, then promise you'll push the button and disable it for me."

"Deal."

Dante tossed it to him. John caught it and pressed it to his belt, marveling at how it stuck there without any sign of clip or adhesive. Then he looked into the eyes of both men, weighing how much he could trust them, before pressing the red button. The lethargy descended on him with a vengeance. Despite his intentions, John gave into it, welcoming a departure from the strange world he had found himself immersed in. He was vaguely aware of Dante and Jacobi talking, but was too apathetic to focus on their words.

The peace he felt slowly transformed into panic. This wasn't right. These feelings weren't his own. He was standing vulnerable in front of two strangers, in a world he didn't understand. He needed his wits about him if he was going to survive. Instead he was drooling like an idiot, under the influence of some sort of magical lobotomy that he might not escape from. He threw himself into his panic as he did the first time, letting it jostle him into full consciousness.

John looked down, seeing the line of blue light. This time, with no one to connect to, it circled his waist before joining with itself. Once again his mind screamed that to touch the light would spell his own doom, but he ignored this and used his hand to break the circuit. Time flowed back into the world, the voices of his companions becoming clear.

"Ten minutes," Dante said. "Not bad."

"I said five minutes, you asshole!" John tore off the device and threw it at Dante, who dodged it and laughed.

"Amazing," Jacobi whispered, his pale blue eyes shining with interest.

Some of John's anger waned, replaced by a sense of pride. "Really? No one else can do that?"

"I've never seen such a feat." Jacobi shook his head. "Never, and I've been here a very long time."

"Why me, though? What makes me special?"

"Willpower perhaps," Jacobi mused, again tugging gently on his beard. "As I was saying before, everything in the afterlife is formed and held together by sheer force of will. There is no physical matter, only ether that can be forged by our minds. A realm such as Purgatory is shaped by one willpower, a sort of spiritual dictator that sets the rules. Otherwise we could walk through walls like ghosts or float in the air, for there is no physical law here. Those who reside in Purgatory reinforce its structure by perceiving and interacting with the reality surrounding them."

"Reality here is nothing but a big ball of clay," Dante chimed in, "but knowing that doesn't make it any easier to break out. Otherwise Jacobi and I would have been out of here years ago."

"Out of here, how?" John prompted.

"Well," Jacobi said slowly, "it's just a theory, mind you, but if you can mentally affect a dampener, then maybe you can affect other aspects of Purgatory."

"Like what?"

"Opening locked doors," Dante suggested, "or moving walls that are in our way."

"Something like that, yes," the old man agreed.

"And just where are we escaping to?" John asked. "I thought you didn't want to go to Heaven, Dante."

"He doesn't, and neither do I," Jacobi replied. "I believe there are other options, realms belonging to other religions that might suit us better, but even they don't interest me. Once reunited with the raw material of creation, we can forge our own realm from the ether, one of our own design. We can set rules or live without them! Imagine pure creative freedom, where every whim becomes reality. The clay, as Dante put it, would be in our hands."

Dante nudged John with his elbow. "Once we're out there on the astral plane, we'll be like gods. Anything we desire will be just a thought away."

"In theory," John said.

"It's not all theory." Dante pulled another cigarette from the air, this one already lit. "We can already create here, but only a little. Once we're free, we'll be able to do whatever we want. A keg of beer, a house, a car, even the streets to drive it on. We'll be like millionaires!"

John had to admit the idea was appealing. His niece had been obsessed with a video game that let the player design their own home and characters to fill it with. All day long she would make her characters get up, take showers, and go to work, rearranging their furniture while they were gone. As dull as this sounded, John had tried it one day and ended up wasting an entire week that should have been spent at the drafting table. So yes, he could understand the allure of such an idea, especially since this wouldn't be a simple game.

Except in life, anything that sounded too good to be true usually was. John suspected it was the same here. "How do we know that it isn't the dampener that is defective?"

"We tried it out," Dante replied. "Both of us. We couldn't break free."

John supposed it wouldn't hurt to at least try what they were suggesting. "Assuming I am capable of doing whatever you need me to, what's the plan? Where do we go?"

Now the other men looked uncertain, glancing uneasily at each other. Jacobi spoke first.

"Logically, the way out is the way we all came in. Getting through the administration building undetected would be impossible, but—"

"Wait," John interrupted. "What happens if we get caught?"

"Nothing serious," Dante answered quickly.

"Well, maybe serious," Jacobi admitted. "We could be incarcerated, which means being put under a dampener twice as strong as that one for a few years at least."

Dante rolled his eyes. "Which won't happen."

"Or they could hit us with enough demerits to send us to Hell," Jacobi said thoughtfully. "They might even fire up the old sin burners, which would mean agony unlike—"

"Shut up, old man!" Dante snarled.

But John had already heard enough. He was facing three years, maybe less, in a system that went out of its way to help him redeem himself. As much as he didn't like the idea of being a hamster on a wheel, he was willing to play the game until he could graduate. Unlike his current company, John had no qualms about going to Heaven, and he certainly wasn't going to gamble everything on the schemes of two men with questionable morals. Dante had already confessed to having led an evil life, and as for Jacobi, he must have done something bad to spend so much time here.

"Thanks for the offer," John said, "but I'm going to pass."

Jacobi looked crestfallen, and Dante argued with him, but it was no use. John had made up his mind. He was going to play the game, and then he was going to Heaven.

Chapter Three

Dante wasn't kidding when he said that Props threw themselves at residents for assistance. In just a week, John had earned 2,000 points without having to exert much effort. He had done so by breaking up a fight between two Props, helping a lost Prop child find its Prop parent, and giving money that had mysteriously appeared in his pocket to a Prop beggar. All of these situations had presented themselves to him while he explored the city and tried to get a better feel for life in Purgatory.

John felt he had already seen most of it. In addition to the restaurants, there were banks, police departments, schools, and libraries, but all of these were somehow connected to schemes involving the Props, such as the bank robber that Dante had apprehended. Aside from redemption point quests, these locations had no real functions.

Nor were there any homes. Without physical possessions or a need for sleep, no one needed private space to return to. While the need might not exist, the desire certainly did. The entire population of Purgatory was constantly out on the streets. John could find no privacy, not that he was sure what he would do with it. The only breaks from the monotony were the restaurants, which he suspected existed solely to stave off insanity.

The food, he discovered, was bland and almost flavorless. Entrees tasted either like boiled chicken or white bread. A steak with fries and German chocolate cake became the equivalent of boiled chicken with bread on the side and bread for dessert. Because no one had any need to eat, this may have been intentional torture—which seemed to be a reoccurring theme in Purgatory. In addition to restaurants serving food that couldn't be tasted, the library was full of books that couldn't be opened, and Jacobi's park had sports fields but lacked the equipment needed to play games.

John tried not to let it get to him. He worked one night as a waiter, not so much for the points but to feel more like a real person. The work also presented him with a chance to socialize, which wasn't very satisfying either, since all anyone talked about were the lives they had left behind. There was no current news to share, no gossip from the office, no big story in the newspaper.

Only past lives and an empty present.

During the second week, John began experimenting with some of the tricks he had seen Dante perform. Early on he learned to make his file disappear just by shoving it into his pocket. It always fit, even without enough physical space for it. The pockets were only symbolic. John could pull the file from thin air, just as he saw others do.

He didn't understand how Dante managed to create cigarettes, not that he ever smoked, but John was eager to change his clothing. He asked around until he found someone who knew the trick. By remembering an outfit as something other than it actually was, he could change it. John started with the basics, keeping the same suit but altering the color. The jacket he changed to plum, and to add pizzazz to the drab world he was trapped in, he made his tie electric blue. Occasionally he would find the suit had reverted to its original color, but the flexing of some mental muscles soon put it right again.

The third week he drank. John could no longer stand the predictable games required to earn points any more than he could tolerate another dreary conversation about loved ones left behind. He drank dozens of beers, never feeling full or having to urinate, regardless of how much he guzzled. Sobriety would come—along with demerits—but John didn't pause in his quest for release.

Eventually he tired even of this. Consulting his file, he found that he was back down to 312 redemption points. John walked the streets, thinking that he would get back on track and earn more reds, but he ignored every opportunity that presented itself. He walked faster, enjoying the feeling of needing to hurry somewhere, a false sense of urgency that he had a place to be, people waiting there for his arrival, their lives incomplete without him. He let his mind roam as he rushed along, often thinking of the life he had left behind and how good it had been. He barely realized how he had become one of the crowd, an anxious animal in an unhappy herd, hurrying toward nothing.

During one of these restless wanderings, John found himself in a familiar park. There, still in the middle of the baseball diamond, was Jacobi. He had returned to standing motionless, but now he had adopted a different position. One leg wrapped around the other, he held his hands skyward. They were cupped, as if he expected rain, but Purgatory had no weather. After a moment's hesitation, John approached.

"Today I am a flower," Jacobi said without opening his eyes. "I become the things I miss, the very things I long to see again."

John nodded. The idea would have sounded crazy three weeks ago, but now it was almost appealing. At least it was more productive than pacing the streets. He couldn't help but smile, and found it hard to imagine the eccentric old coot as having been a bad person in life.

"Why are you here, Jacobi? What did you do?"

Jacobi's arms fell to his sides. He opened his eyes to regard John before he answered. "I was a heretic. I spoke out against the authority of the church. I disputed the authenticity of the Bible, and I pleaded with men to listen to their hearts instead of acting on their fears."

"Is that so serious a crime that you can't work off your debt?"

"Heresy?" Jacobi chuckled. "Goodness, no. It's as common as infidelity. I could have left here ages ago, were I not so stubborn. You see, when I arrived they still burned sin out. They called it purging, thus the name Purgatory. The process was very painful, but at least back then there were angels to sing the hurt away at night. I rather liked the angels, but every time they tried to purge me, I would blaspheme some more. It frustrated them to no end, but I outlasted them, didn't I?"

John frowned. Why fight against leaving this place? The purging process didn't sound pleasant, but at least the mindless games didn't exist back then. "What happened to the angels?"

"Gone. Back to Heaven. Purgatory was abandoned by the church, cast away, much like all the souls stranded here. I'd say it was poetic justice, but now life here is even worse."

"I don't follow you," John said.

"The church back on earth made philosophical changes that had ramifications in this reality. You've heard the saying 'as above, so below'? Well, it works both ways." Jacobi tugged on his beard. "The Vatican decided to downgrade Purgatory from being a place to more of an idea. A soul wouldn't actually arrive in Purgatory, they insisted. The idea of a safety net took the fire and brimstone out of their sermons, you see, and so they did away with it. That's when the changes started here, resulting in the parody of reform that exists today."

"How do you even know what the Vatican is?" John asked. "I thought you were from ancient Greece?"

"Oh no," Jacobi smiled. "I'm just a fan. I'm from the sixteen hundreds. Back then the Vatican was known as the Holy See, and it wasn't the best era to speak out against the church. I chose my appearance because I embrace the ideals of the ancient Greeks. Well, aside from the naked Olympics, but that's mostly just because I don't like sports."

John smiled. "If the angels have all gone away, then who is in charge of Purgatory?"

"No one knows. Certainly not the Props. I've studied them, and they don't show any signs of real intelligence. Even those paper shufflers working in administration are merely souls who have been promoted. If they know who they report to, they aren't telling."

"And you're content to stay here for all eternity, doing nothing?"

"Doing nothing requires more effort than you might think." Jacobi sighed. "But yes, I've wanted to move on. My stubbornness faded long ago, and I started to play the game, but then events took an even stranger turn. About five decades ago, all sorts of souls began showing up here. Buddhists, Muslims, Taoists, you name it. Even atheists."

"Where else are they supposed to go?"

"To whatever afterlife they believe in, of course. Or nowhere, or back to Earth to reincarnate. Anywhere but here. They don't belong in a Christian paradigm."

"But neither does Purgatory anymore," John replied.

"Precisely! An astute observation! Now, one could imagine that all the undesirables are being sent here by other religions. Just look at our friend Dante. But not everyone here is as unabashedly naughty as he is. I've spent decades talking to the other souls here. Learning about the times and places they come from has been wondrous, but you know what else I noticed? Most of the people here are good. Oh sure, none of our hands are exactly clean, but not so much that our own belief systems would reject us. Certainly not. So why are we here, and most important, where do they really send souls when they graduate?"

John shrugged. "Maybe Purgatory works for all religions now. The souls who need a little more work come here first before being sent to where they really belong."

"I could ask to see your file, John, but I don't need to. I can read it in your face that you're a good man. Do you really think you're not worthy of Heaven as you are?"

John thought about it. "I once stole a bottle of my grandma's cooking wine. When she noticed it missing, I blamed it on grandpa, and she thought he'd fallen off the wagon and made him go back to AA. Then there was the time I put thumbtacks on my history teacher's chair, but I swear he was an old Nazi." John paused, but Jacobi nodded encouragingly. "I used to shoplift CDs all the time, and who doesn't download music illegally, right? In fact, I'm pretty sure I left my computer running the night I died. It's probably still sharing the entire ABBA discography with the whole world, which is an embarrassing thought. Uh, do you have any idea what I'm talking about?"

Jacobi nodded but said, "Not a clue."

"Well, I might have some reasons for being here, but they don't seem that serious. I've never killed anyone, and I lived a pretty decent life most of the time. I don't know if I belong here or not, but I know that I don't want to stay."

Jacobi gave a conspiratorial wink. "Any good escape plan relies on accurate information. You want answers, and I think I know where to find them, but there are obstacles."

"Obstacles that you think I can overcome." John tried to hide his smile and failed. After three weeks of boredom, he was ready for some adventure, even if it meant damning himself to Hell in the process.

Three men huddled together on a street, examining something at their feet. From an outsider's perspective, it was hard to see what. Through the gaps in their legs, a bystander might spy a bit of concrete or a discarded cigarette butt or two that had likely been dropped by the dark-haired man who was smoking another. The oldest of these men squatted with hands on bony knees, eyes watering in concentration as the fair-haired man pointed repeatedly at the same empty spot.

"You really can't see it?" John asked.

"What are we looking for again?" Dante asked.

"The sewer grate," Jacobi said, squinting his eyes so tightly they were almost shut. "There! I saw it flicker before it disappeared again!"

John glanced back down. For him the manhole was as clear as day. Unless his new friends were crazy, some sort of illusion prevented them from seeing it. Dante couldn't even keep the idea in mind before asking—

"Seriously now, what are we doing here?"

"Try to open it," Jacobi said. "Go on! Before he asks us again. I only spotted it while pretending to be a row of hedges one day, and spent a good hour fighting off the urge to forget it. Anything they don't want us to notice, that tries to erase itself from our minds, must be important, right?"

John nodded. The manhole existed, but how was he supposed to open it without a crowbar? He reached down to hook a finger in the hole where such a tool would normally be inserted. His finger tingled as it brushed against the metal, the sensation similar to the dampeners. John gave a tentative tug to see if the cover would even budge, and was surprised when it provided no resistance. The manhole cover was as light as paper! He flipped it over onto the street.

"Now I can see it," Jacobi said, prodding the discarded cover.

Dante shook his head. "Yeah. Me too. That was weird. The thought kept slipping my mind, no matter how hard I tried to remember. Now I know how Gran must have felt."

Jacobi glanced up and down the street. "Get inside before somebody sees. Quickly!"

A ladder led down into an ominous gray void, but at least it was somewhere new. John went first, on Dante's insistence. The ladder ended ten feet down in a featureless room with a short passageway ahead. Once Dante climbed down, they both turned their heads upward expectantly. Jacobi wasn't following. Instead his worried face peered over the edge.

"One of us has to close this again," he said, "and play decoy in case we tripped an alarm."

"Don't be ridiculous!" Dante said. "Get down here, and we'll all make a run for it."

"If that truly is an exit," Jacobi replied. "Anything could be down there, so keep your eyes open. If you do find the way out, come back for me."

"Have it your way," Dante said, as the cover slid closed. "Old man has been here too long. He's spent so long dreaming of leaving that the idea must terrify him."

John was only half-listening, his attention focused on their surroundings. Walls, ceiling, and floor were all made from the same colorless material, textureless and completely smooth when touched. Walking created no sound, and no variations showed in the material's bland surface. Not even shadow could take hold here. Despite there being no source of light, their surroundings were completely visible.

With nothing to see or do, they moved down the short hallway until reaching a dead end, except for a square hole in the floor. This time there was no ladder, nor could a bottom be seen.

"Ladies first," Dante said.

"What? You expect me just to jump?"

"I promise it won't be fatal."

John scowled at him before considering the opening in the floor again. Jacobi had said that Purgatory was once a series of levels, before all souls had been moved to the surface when the great change occurred. Descending through the old layers might take them somewhere, but John would feel a lot more comfortable knowing where exactly.

"You have to go first," Dante pressed. "If there's some sort of trap, you're more likely to escape it than I would."

"I don't suppose you can create a rope or something?"

"No, but I can make you a cigarette if you want one final smoke before you go."

John wondered if this was the Irishman's version of revenge for having avoided him the past three weeks.

"Or," Dante said, "we go back up for Jacobi and toss the old geezer in first."

John laughed, then braced himself. If he thought about it any more he wouldn't do it, so he silenced his fears and jumped. His stomach lurched, mostly out of habit, as he plummeted down. The wind whipped through his hair and his clothing flapped against him like a flag in a storm as he continued to drop. When the bottom failed to appear a few minutes later, John began to wonder if this was how he was going to spend the rest of eternity.

He heard Dante scream above him, signaling that he had chosen to follow. The scream ran its course, was followed by a thoughtful pause, and then a groan. John was about to shout something smart up to him when he hit the ground, his legs crumpling beneath him.

He felt no pain. He hadn't experienced pain since entering Purgatory. John's legs, still remembering the basic rules of life, felt they should be broken and wouldn't respond to his mind's directives. After some coaxing they accepted that they were still on duty and allowed John to stand. He made it one step away before Dante came crashing down on top of him. After a series of curses and accusations, they took stock of their surroundings.

They were surrounded by wild animals. Still on the floor and tangled up in Dante's limbs, John found himself face to face with a snarling boar, one of its long pointed tusks just inches from his eye. He froze instinctively. Oddly enough, so did the boar.

"A bear," Dante whispered. "There's a flipping bear over here!"

"Is it blue?" John asked.

"Yeah. Sort of."

So was the boar. Its fur was still the russet color that it should be, but the animal itself was glowing with blue light.

"I think they're stunned," John said.

"Then don't touch them," Dante said as they got to their feet. "We don't want your freaky voodoo waking them up."

"Hey, are those elephants over there?"

"Might be," Dante said, awe creeping into his voice. "Could be every animal in existence."

For a moment, they were just as motionless and mute as the creatures around them, silenced by the sheer scale of what they saw. As far as they could see were every conceivable species of animal, all glowing blue, all unnaturally still. Even with the afterlife's strange ability to see great distances, John couldn't spot a wall in any direction. There was only fang and fur, as if Noah had traded his ark for a hangar the size of Texas.

"I've seen something like this before," Dante said. "This guy went off his nut a few years back, started throwing furniture around, hitting people, trying to destroy everything in sight. Some Props went after him, and I don't know what they did, but the next thing you know he's as blue as a Smurf and dead as a stone."

"I thought you said we couldn't die."

"Right, but this is pretty damn close."

"Think people are kept down here, too? Like the guy who freaked out. Maybe they brought him here."

"Hope not," Dante said. "If this is where they put people on ice, then we've gone from bad to worse. Come on."

They chose a random direction to walk in, hoping that if they followed a straight line they would eventually reach a wall. This proved difficult since they were forced to pick their way around animals of all shapes and sizes, although some of the taller species, such as giraffes, they were able to walk under.

"There aren't any birds," John said as they skirted an assortment of cougars.

"What about the huge group of penguins back there?"

"They don't count. They can't even fly."

"They have wings." Dante argued.

"No they don't! Those are—" John hesitated, and in the silence they heard the distinct sound of a dog barking.

John looked at Dante, who shrugged. The barking came again, and they began to cautiously move toward it. The floor was made of the same soundless material as the corridors were, so their footsteps made no noise. They had been so busy watching where they were stepping that they hadn't noticed the wall ahead until now. At least the chamber wasn't infinite. Ducking and dodging between animals, they tried to keep hidden as they progressed. While using the massive bulk of a hippo as cover, the barking became frantic.

Peering over the hippo's body, they saw a Prop dragging a dog along by a glowing blue rope tied around its neck. The dog, a black and white English Shepherd, was resisting, hind legs skidding along the floor in a desperate attempt to brake.

Despite the Prop's merciless yanking and pulling, the dog was putting up a fair fight, causing the Prop to tumble over. The dog dragged it a few feet, growling and whipping its head back and forth. But then the Prop recovered itself, placing the blue rope in the slit that passed for its mouth before changing shape. The Prop's arms and legs split into halves, the body rising off the ground on eight limbs instead of two. Then it slowly began to swallow the rope, looking very much like a spider devouring its web. Fur bristling, the dog was powerless against this new strategy, losing ground until it was dragged within reach. Two of the Prop's arms scooped the animal up as its head descended, fangs now protruding from its maw.

John stood to help, but Dante dragged him down, fixing him

with a scowl that threatened death—or whatever the equivalent was here—should John act on this impulse. The dog yelped. Both men looked in time to see the Prop's mouth enclosed over the dog's neck like a bizarre vampire. Electricity flickered and settled around the Shepherd's form until it was just as blue and motionless as the other animals in the room.

Skin tingling with fear, Dante and John ducked the rest of the way behind the hippo, not moving until the room went silent. Even then they refused to move, wanting to be absolutely sure the coast was clear.

Once they dared to come out of hiding, they found the dog added to the foremost line of paralyzed animals, between a raccoon and a zebra. John knelt down beside it, reaching out to touch, but Dante caught his wrist. John pulled it away irritably.

"I think I know this dog," John whispered, examining it but still not touching it.

"Family pet?" Dante asked with disinterest.

"No. I saw it my first day here. I saw it on the bridge."

Dante had walked away toward the wall and was now inspecting the large number of doors. There were at least ten, all spaced out equally.

"Did you know they could do that?" John asked, rushing to catch up. "The Props, I mean."

Dante shook his head. "Never seen it before, but like I said, they did something similar to that one guy. There were a lot of Props in the way. Maybe they were intentionally blocking the view. I doubt they'd want everyone to know that Purgatory is run by bunch of creepy vampire spiders."

John swallowed. At times in the last month he had come close to flipping out. Had he done so, the Props would have made short work of him. He never would have seen it coming, either. They looked so ineffectual and useless. Now he knew the truth. Countless Props were in Purgatory, intermingling among the souls and playing their silly games when really they were an invisible police force. Should rebellion or riot break out, it wouldn't last long, but John still didn't believe they were the masters of Purgatory. Jacobi was right. The Props were nothing more than mindless tools, but whose?

"Which door?" Dante muttered. "I wish I had seen which one the spider left through. That's the last one I want to open."

John took advantage of his companion's distraction and returned to the dog. Unhindered, he reached out and touched it, expecting his special abilities to instantly break the spell. Nothing happened. He glanced back at Dante, who was systematically opening each door a crack and peeking at what was beyond.

"Come on," John whispered. "Wake up."

He tried shaking the dog, but its body was stiff. Next he wrapped his arms around it, hoping that more body contact would make a difference. The animal didn't stir. John closed his eyes and began breathing, hoping to encourage the dog to do the same. He didn't believe in New Age mumbo jumbo. He'd had no room in his life for crystals, tarot cards, or spirit guides, but he did believe in visualization. Athletes who pictured successfully shooting hoops would perform much better the next day. This was an idea John could believe in. More than once he would imagine a meeting going well before having to face difficult clients. Maybe something like that could help here.

In his mind, he pictured the blue light draining away from the dog, puddling on the ground and soaking into the floor. Nothing. The animal was still as stiff as stone in his arms. Maybe he needed to give as well as take away. John had something in him that made him more resistant to Purgatory's tricks. He pictured this as white light inside himself and, keeping his eyes closed, he breathed out and tried to send as much of that light to the dog as he could.

The furry body squirmed in John's arms. When he opened his eyes, the dog's head was turned toward him, looking confused and somewhat groggy.

"Hey there!" John said. "Feeling better?"

The dog panted happily in response.

"Wonderful," Dante said from behind. "Plan on waking up the rest of the zoo while we're here?"

"Maybe," John answered, although truth be told, the effort had taken a lot out of him. For the first time since dying, he felt tired. He started to yawn but was interrupted by a number of wet licks to his face. John laughed as he fell backward, the dog relentless in its effort to make sure he was drenched.

"Jacobi didn't send us down here to open up a pet store," Dante grumbled. "We need to find a way out of here."

"Maybe Bolo can help us," John said as he got to his feet.

"Bolo?" Dante was incredulous. "You named her?"

"Him," John corrected after a cursory inspection.

"Well, you've had your fun. Put it back and let's get out of here."

John ignored him, addressing the dog instead. "Bolo! Wanna go potty?" he said with an overdose of enthusiasm. "Huh? Wanna go potty? Let's go!"

It worked. Bolo took off toward the doors and began sniffing each entrance. Six doors down he started barking, his tail waving so fast that John worried it might fall off.

"Yeah, all right," Dante conceded. "Having a dog could be good."

John opened the door and Bolo bolted through, ignoring John's calls for him to return.

"Seems like he knows where he's going," Dante said, surprising John by taking off after the dog. John raced after them both, gray corridors whizzing by to either side. Bolo took turns at random, leading them deeper into the labyrinth. John was terrified that their carelessness would land them in an entire nest of Props, but they couldn't stop, not if they wanted to keep sight on their four-legged guide.

The halls gave way to a large open space where fog oozed across the ground, obscuring it from view. The sound of machinery rumbled like thunder in the distance, even though nothing mechanical was visible. They raced across this open space, John catching sight of more spidery Props in the distance, slinking through the low fog, but by some miracle he and his friends went unseen. On the other side of the room, a short hallway ended with a door, and here Bolo waited for them, tail wagging and eyes eager.

John hurried to open the door before the dog could bark. Daylight, or at least Purgatory's poor equivalent, lay beyond. But that wasn't all. The Golden Gate Bridge stretched out in front of them. Bolo quickly disappeared in the obscuring fog, barking happily.

"Deserter," Dante muttered before breaking out into a smile. "This is it! The mutt led us right to it!"

"Across the bridge and we're free?" John asked, excitement overtaking him.

"Bridge? Oh, yeah, I get it." Dante scratched at his stubble.

"Everyone sees something different, just like the rest of Purgatory. I've heard people talk about the Berlin Wall, or a river, that sort of stuff. Whatever you see, it's always a barrier and a border to be crossed."

"What do you see then?"

"The Dublin Ferry. Come on."

What about Jacobi? John thought, but the question went unspoken. He thought of the creatures lurking in the room just behind them and knew they were lucky to have made it across without being seen. They would never find their way back through the maze of hallways, either. John's fear heavily outweighed the guilt he felt for abandoning Jacobi, so he shoved thoughts of the old man away and turned his attention toward the unknown.

The fog swallowed them as they reached the bridge, blinding their vision. Dante had only been a few feet ahead, but already he was lost to sight. Their footsteps echoed eerily, reflecting back at them from all directions and giving the impression they were being chased. John tried to ignore his rising trepidation, but he had lost all sense of direction and didn't know if he was still following the others. Bolo's barks echoed all around him, but they no longer sounded joyous, and each was preceded by a guttural growl.

Through the white cloud that dominated John's field of vision, a shadow rose up before him. At first John thought he had finally caught up to Dante, but then the clouds broke, revealing the minimalistic face of a Prop just inches away from John's own. The scream stuck in his throat as John stared at the protruding fangs dripping with blue poison. From around this gruesome visage, eight spidery limbs shot through the fog and wrapped around John.

Teeth bit into him, and now John found his scream. He fought and struggled as the poison made him sluggish, almost escaping from the Prop's grip, but the fangs stabbed out over and over again. It hurt. Each puncture was the burning cold of ice. John's screams faltered as even his throat muscles went numb. That his mind soon followed was a mercy.

Chapter Four

A face, pristine in beauty, serene. A sculpture made of light. No, not light. Glass. The hypnotic eyes were two perfectly fashioned orbs, glass grapes set delicately inside their sockets, impossible detail carved into each iris. What master craftsman could create such perfection?

The brow above the glass eyes furrowed, shocking John out of his repose. He tried to open his mouth to speak, to ask any number of questions, but he could not. He was completely paralyzed, unable even to blink, his field of vision filled by the beautiful face looking down at him.

The glass head pulled back, bringing into view a neck and chest just as immaculate. John watched in fascination as the glass man put a thoughtful finger to his lips. The gray walls of Purgatory were visible through his transparent body, telling John that his escape had been a failure. But had he been rescued? He saw no sign of the spiders.

"You should be unconscious," the glass man said, each word perfectly formed, his voice ideal in pitch and volume, "and yet, here you are, seeing things that no soul in Purgatory has ever laid eyes upon."

As pleasant as the voice was, it was laced with disapproval. John hadn't been rescued after all. He had been captured.

"Captured?" the glass man said, pursing his lips. "Yes, I suppose you could say that. You were, after all, behaving like an animal, scurrying after a dog like part of a depraved pack. A more formidable man might have been restrained, a dangerous opponent neutralized, but you? Captured. Downed like a mindless beast. But who is your keeper? Who unleashed you and allowed you to run free?"

John silenced the name before it could reach his mind, focusing instead on the image of a solitary tree in a park.

"Amusing," the glass man said. "Normally in these situations I am unable to read minds since my guests are always unconscious, but I do have other methods at my disposal. There is one in particular that I enjoy. I am quite eager to see how a conscious mind reacts to it. Shall we begin?"

The glass man came near, his graceful crystalline hands

poised before him. The beautiful transparent face came close to John's own, as if proposing a kiss, before the delicate hands pressed against John's abdomen. After minimal resistance, the fingertips passed into his body.

Cold! Like the spider's fangs but a thousand times worse. Cold and hard. The fingers slid further inside John until immersed up to the wrist. Glass hands moved through him, opening him up in impossible ways, exposing his insides to air and causing them to ache. Was this what rape felt like? This violation, helplessness, exposure?

The face in front of him grinned, diamond teeth framed by lips made of stars. So beautiful, but the sensations coursing through John's body were of pure revulsion. Like a careless surgeon, the glass man's hands scampered inside of him, but instead of organs and intestines, memories were being manipulated. Dozens of experiences were brought to the surface, all of them painful. The heartbreak of being left by his first love, the crushing pain that came with losing his grandmother, the humiliations he had suffered in junior high, each feeling as fresh as the moment it had happened, but now all were occurring simultaneously. The glass man had found Jacobi's name long ago, but still he played.

Life's brutality came next: his drunken father beating him, or the night he was jumped by three men and became the victim of random violence. He felt everything, the physical pain dim and distant compared to the anger, frustration, and powerlessness that had accompanied the experiences. John longed to moan, but even that release was denied him.

Then it was over. The glass man's lips curved in satisfaction before he spoke again. "There is only one system, John, one path to walk correctly. We try to teach you that in life, to break your insignificant spirit before you come here. You don't realize how generous that is of us. Purgatory was your last chance to learn your place. You're nothing but a rat ungrateful for his cage, when you should be thankful for the shelter given to you. You should have obeyed our love. Disappointments like you don't even deserve to be broken, only discarded. The rest of eternity awaits you, John Grey."

The glass man snapped his fingers and everything went black.

* * * * *

A rainbow of balloons soared into the overcast sky, theoretically breaking through the clouds to the blue beyond. A crowd cheered, and John noticed that he was being carried, hoisted heroically for all to see. His head lolled to one side. He could see Dante to his right, pale and limp, like a fish starved of water. The two Props beneath Dante carried him above their heads like a giant entrée making its way toward the dining room. With a grunt of effort, John rolled his head to the other side to find Jacobi also being carried, his wide eyes full of panic.

"We're graduating!" the old man said. "You have to do something!"

On the contrary, John thought. Heaven, Hell, or whatever came next had to be better than here. He never wanted to set foot in Purgatory again, or to think about the icy hands that had played with his insides as if they were a toy.

John managed a groan as they began ascending a hill. Dante had pointed it out to him once. Here was where every good soul went to graduate, an inaccessible green slope covered in grass that led upward to an ancient stone archway glowing with golden light. Beyond lay the greatest of promises. Heaven, sponsored by McDonald's, they had joked. John noticed with some disappointment that the grass appeared to be artificial.

They passed through the golden arch and the sound of the jubilant crowd ceased. The plastic grass and the hill had disappeared too, replaced by choking fog that suggested they were on the edge of Purgatory again. Why hadn't they been allowed to escape? Their punishment for trying was to be exiled? This was nonsense, but John didn't care as long as he got away. The Props set him on the ground, then transformed into their natural spider forms.

Jacobi began yelling, begging John to "do something, do something, please do something!" Dante was roused from his sleep and panicked, reaching out to Jacobi before the spiders bit them both to silence their screams. John was bitten as well and went still after the first bite, not wanting to earn extra venom by revealing his natural resistance. One of the spiders tensed its abdomen and shot a blue line of web somewhere above before gathering John like freshly caught prey and rising upward.

All around him, other souls were rising into the air, not just Jacobi and Dante. Their expressions of terror or confusion, all frozen in place the moment they had been bitten, showed that they had expected something more from graduation. John almost envied their unconsciousness, the tranquil oblivion that followed the brief moment of fear. Perhaps he should struggle, be bitten more until his mind went blank.

The gray sky slowly faded into blue, but instead of hope John felt only puzzlement. This blue wasn't that of the sky, but the electric, stinging blue he had first seen with the dampeners. Their ascension stopped abruptly, and John was hoisted upward.

Above him was a ceiling that stretched as far as the eye could see, a dome glowing with blue energy that pulsed around the frozen, unmoving bodies that were its bricks. Countless souls were pressed together, their twisted limbs forming a barrier against whatever was beyond. Already the spiders were working the new arrivals into this patchwork, binding with blue web that soon dissolved to become part of the abominable structure.

John was stuffed unceremoniously into the mass of bodies. He wanted to scream, but the thrumming blue energy overwhelmed him, made even worse when more souls were layered on top of him. All he could see in front of him were bodies, souls transformed into corpses, translucent like frosted glass.

Despite his growing claustrophobia, John didn't dare move until the activity behind him had ceased. Then he tried moving his arm, causing a shock to run along his body. He tried again and again, every movement sending another burst of pain that subdued him like the spider's venom had. Wincing with each effort, he maneuvered to identify his neighbors. Jacobi was beside him, the old man's hand reaching down to grasp the hand of someone below. If the spiky hair near John's feet was any indication, it was Dante. Neither of them stirred. Except for John, no one in the hideous barrier was awake.

He reached out to shake Jacobi's arm, but before he could reach it, the repeated shocks overwhelmed him and he lost consciousness. When John awoke some time later, he chose to remain still and think rather than suffer further.

So this was graduation. No Heaven or Hell. Just a bizarre traffic jam of souls with nowhere to go. Maybe that was the truth. Maybe Purgatory was all there was in the afterlife. John's mind drifted, thinking of how Jacobi and Dante had reached for each other before being stung, clasping hands like frightened children.

He wondered how they felt now in their sleep, and whether or not it was a state he could ever attain. John tried his best to join them. When this failed, he grew restless and moved, clambering through the other bodies before passing out, but he was no longer certain which way was up and which was down, or if either held meaning anymore.

John returned for his companions, and found that he could drag them along when he moved. Jacobi was a lifeline linked to Dante, their grip on each other's hand unbreakable. This gave John hope. If there was somewhere to go, he had an eternity to find it. Maybe he could work his way down and drop through the sky back where they had come from. The thought of the glass man's hands made him abandon this idea. Instead he tried moving upward, hoping to find something beyond the dome's barrier.

Time stretched on as he continued dragging his companions along with him, even though it doubled the amount of movement necessary and increased his suffering. The process was slow and painful, like moving through electrified jelly. John passed out countless times, awaking with his will diminished. For how many centuries had souls been left here to rot? Was it everyone who had ever died? Was the pain he endured for nothing?

Days, maybe even weeks, passed like this. Sometimes John would quit, not moving a muscle and preferring to lose himself in his thoughts rather than suffer any more pain. Then he would grow bored and try again.

He shifted, feeling a sting and screaming in response. He continued screaming. No longer needing to breathe meant his screams could continue for as long as he pleased. The sound wailed out of him like a ship lost at sea until it eventually broke into a sob.

A dog barked.

Hope, desperate and tiny, blossomed within John. He screamed again, primal and formless. The bark came again, from behind him. If the bark was coming from outside the barrier, as he hoped, then John had been travelling horizontally through the bodies. He had experienced the same disorienting sensation in the ocean once, when the waves had sent him tumbling below the surface. Only by relaxing and allowing his body to float had he rediscovered which direction up was. The bark came again, setting John into motion. He ignored the pain, only screaming now to trigger another bark that he could hone in on.

Eventually he stopped howling and began calling Bolo's name, for John knew it had to be the same dog. Bolo had been there since the first day. *Maybe the dog is God,* he thought madly as the barks continued to guide him. John still passed out regularly. Each time he awoke he was terrified that the dog might have wandered away, but every time he called out the bark came again.

Thrusting an arm upward for the thousandth time, John was overjoyed when it was greeted not by pain but by a barrage of licks. John laughed joyously and redoubled his efforts. When his head broke through the surface, he felt reborn. Letting go of Jacobi, he squirmed out of the sea of souls and found himself free, moving without pain. Bolo bounded into him, moving through the air like a canine version of Superman. He continued to laugh with joy as the dog licked his face, tears streaming from John's eyes.

Bodies of light, very much like suns, radiated strange vibrations that could be felt across the endless void, swirls of color without names and in impossible shapes. Sounds chased each other across space, noises more haunting than whale song and twice as hypnotic. Sensations travelled in waves, feelings floating along on an invisible astral wind.

John stared, taking it all in, one hand scratching the scruffy fur on Bolo's neck. They were sitting on nothing. They had no gravity, and yet it wasn't like the free-floating astronauts he had seen on television. John could stop and move at will, depending more on his mind than on physical movements. All of this took a lot of getting used to, which is why he hadn't yet freed Jacobi or Dante. He wanted to be sure of his abilities and to regain some of his strength before he even tried. So he sat with his dog and marveled at the wonders surrounding him.

When John felt ready, he turned back to the sobering blue dome of bodies. It stretched impossibly far in all directions, like the atmosphere of a planet and just as beautiful, despite its horrid nature. Bracing himself against the pain, John reached in to where he thought he had left his friends, grabbed a body part, and pulled. What came out of the barrier wasn't Jacobi, but a little old lady. She came to life instantly, gasping as if she had been holding her breath for a very long time. Her face flushed in excitement.

"Can you see it?" she asked with watery eyes.

"Yes," John said, smiling in return.

"It's Heaven! Just like they said it would be. The white clouds, the angels, and Saint Peter's gate. Oh the gate!"

John frowned in puzzlement. He hadn't seen anything of the sort. He was about to turn and look when the woman began to blur as if she was somehow moving. And then she was gone.

John considered what this meant, coming up with a few theories. He liked to think that the old woman had seen Heaven, and that was where her soul belonged. Maybe he had just witnessed a soul gravitating to where it was meant to be. That would be nice if it were true, but maybe the woman's soul had become weak after being frozen in place for so long. Perhaps her soul had extinguished, fading away before his very eyes.

John decided to pull another person free, this time intentionally choosing someone he didn't know. Out came a stocky middle-aged man who glared at him and the realm beyond with disdain.

"What's all this then?" he spat in a thick Scottish accent. "All a bit science fiction, isn't it?"

John didn't know how to respond to this, so he continued to quietly observe.

The man seemed happy to see a dog and was reaching down to pet Bolo when he suddenly stood straight up again.

"Do yeh hear it?" he whispered. "Gabriel's horn! It's a-callin' me. Do yeah hear it?"

Like the woman before him, there was the curious notion of movement along with a blurring before the man disappeared. John felt certain now that the souls were finally going to where they belonged. He realized that he could free them all, dismantle the dome piece by piece. It would take forever, but maybe if he did this, he too would be called away to an eternal reward.

John was careful with his next selection, making sure this time to choose Jacobi. The old man awoke with a start and took in their surroundings with wide eyes. John was looking so intently for any sign of departure that he flinched when Jacobi starting shouting with glee.

"We're free!" he said, doing a little jig. "Oh, by the heavens, we are FREE!"

John laughed. "That we are. Do you feel all right? You don't hear any horns or see any pearly gates?"

"Look around, John! This *is* Heaven!"

But Jacobi must have meant this figuratively, because he didn't disappear. John described what had happened to the other souls, Jacobi listening with rapt attention.

"It could be any number of reasons," Jacobi surmised. "Our souls may still be tuned to Purgatory, since we never truly earned our graduation. That means we are still in balance, not quite good or bad enough to be summoned elsewhere. Or maybe it is a lack of desire or faith that leaves us free to choose our own destiny. Yes, I like that."

"We better be sure before we pull Dante out," John said. "Something tells me he's the ideal candidate for a trip south."

"Nonsense," Jacobi said dismissively. "He's one of us! Purgatory's great escapists! Besides, he always kept his points in balance so he wouldn't be expelled. Let's pull him free. Then together we can decide what to do next."

Still John hesitated, but he couldn't just leave Dante trapped forever. He reached down, grabbed the hand sticking out of the barrier, and pulled.

The Irishman groaned when he was free, muttering something about a bender. He glared at each of them before rubbing his eyes. "I take it we ended up in Hell?"

"On the contrary," Jacobi said. "My theories were correct. We are now on the astral plane. Here we will be able to give shape to the formless, to create a world of our choosing!"

"So which one of you made the train station?"

They looked to where Dante had nodded, but neither John nor Jacobi could see anything but swirls and stars.

"You feel that?" Dante asked. "Like being pulled by an undertow. What is that?"

The Irishman's features began to blur, but before he could disappear, John leapt on him, wrapping his arms firmly around Dante's torso. He wouldn't let him fade away! There was a terrible sinking sensation, and John strained against it until it passed and Dante's features went from blurry to solid again.

"That was a close one," John said with relief.

"Think so?"

A train whistle startled John into letting go. He spun around to find himself submersed in a massive station. Trains from all time periods occupied the platforms, passengers pouring out of each one. There was no sign of Bolo, Jacobi, or the psychedelic lights of the astral plane. All of it was gone, replaced by a train station where everyone seemed to be arriving, but no one was departing.

"Doesn't look so bad," Dante said with cautious optimism as he stepped into the crowd.

John hurried to keep up with him, grabbing his jacket so as not to lose him.

"Dante, what was your standing in Purgatory? How many points did you have?"

"About five thousand."

"Oh. Good!"

"In the red."

John gaped at Dante who was grinning. "Do you know what that means? Do you realize where we are?"

"Yup."

"Then why are you acting so nonchalant?"

Dante stopped, the crowd pouring around him as he turned to face John. "Because for the first time since dying, I feel like I've come home again."

"Well, that's a relief," John said through gritted teeth. "What about me?"

Dante shrugged. "You managed to break out of Purgatory easily enough. I'm sure your superpowers can help you leave here if you want, but I think you should wait. I've been here before. Well, not *here* but the equivalent on Earth, and I think you're going to like it."

They were alone now, the most recent arrivals having dispersed to whatever their destination was. Not knowing what else to do, John followed Dante through a large ornate hall. The exit was blocked by the standard passport control usually found in airports. Even the guard on duty, who appeared human enough, seemed appropriately bored with his post.

"What are we going to do now?" John asked.

"Show them our IDs, of course." Dante pulled a passport from the air. He looked as surprised by its appearance as John did. The passport was blood red and had the word "Hell" emblazoned on it beneath a stylized depiction of a devil's head.

"Where did you get that?"

"I don't know," Dante admitted. "I was going for our papers from Purgatory."

John tried the same trick but came up empty-handed. "Now what?"

"Let's see what they say. If you aren't allowed in, then they'll show you the exit."

Without waiting for approval, Dante strode up to the guard on duty and presented his credentials. He was waved through the barrier, where he waited for John.

"Passport," the disinterested guard droned.

"I don't have one."

"He's with me," Dante offered.

"Get lost," the guard growled. "Next!"

John looked behind him. There was no one else in line so he stayed where he was.

Reluctantly, the guard turned his attention back to him. "I said to get lost, so turn around and go back the way you came. Don't make me sick the three-headed dogs on you."

"Forget him," Dante called. "Who follows the rules in Hell anyway? Come on!"

The guard bared his teeth and stood, readying himself for conflict, but then a look of surprise crossed his face. He placed a finger to one ear and listened, responding finally with a humble, "Yes, sir." Sitting back on his stool, he thumbed toward the barrier, indicating that John could pass through.

"What did I tell ya?" Dante smirked. "No problem. Prepare yourself for some fun, Johnny-boy, because I was right. See for yourself!"

Outside the station was a long stretch of concrete slashed across by rail tracks. Beyond this, an old European city was squeezed in between rows of canals. The buildings, tall and narrow, were covered in ornate detail that had been worn down over the centuries. From behind the station, barely detectable over the typical city sounds and smells, was the scent of a harbor and the occasional call of a seagull.

"Welcome to Amsterdam," Dante said, throwing an arm around John's shoulders and leading him forward.

"I thought we were in Hell."

"Call it what you like, but either way it's paradise to me."

As they made their way around the stationed trams, John read their destinations: Las Vegas, Sodom/Gomorrah, Shanghai, Bangkok. Despite his apprehension, John couldn't help but laugh. So Hell was one big bachelor party?

Dante's earthly visit to Amsterdam must have been fresh on his mind, because he made a bee-line for the old part of the city. Here the cobbled streets narrowed so much that the sky above was almost lost behind the tall, leaning buildings. All around were smoky coffee shops, windows full of blow-up dolls and pornography, and stores offering a plethora of mushrooms and herbs. The streets were stuffed full of people, not all of them entirely human, but John couldn't focus on them lest he lose Dante in the crowd.

Dante led them to a coffee shop on the corner. The smoke was thick inside the dark interior, and most of the stools were filled with patrons not the least bit interested in coffee. David Bowie was blaring over the speakers, singing something about sound and vision, as Dante pointed happily to the ceiling and grinned. John realized he hadn't heard any music in Purgatory. He couldn't imagine going without it for as many years as Dante must have.

They wound through the tables until they found a free spot in the back. Dante left to order from the counter, leaving John to examine the other patrons. For the most part those here were human, none of them appearing particularly seedy despite being in Hell. The rest were demons. He didn't know what else to call them. They had red skin, horns, and tails, the basic criteria for such creatures, but the humans they intermingled with didn't appear intimidated.

Dante returned with a tray loaded with a half-dozen joints already rolled, a plateful of brownies, and a couple of beers. If Dante's grin was any wider it would have severed his head in two.

"I found money in my pocket!" he exclaimed, tossing his change onto the tray after he was seated.

John picked up a coin and examined it. One side was engraved with a sour, fat-faced devil. On the other a pile of bodies engaged in an impressively detailed orgy. "Why am I not surprised that Hell has an economy?"

Dante sparked up one of the joints and took an impressive pull that burned away half its length, something no mortal could have achieved. He then held it out to John with a questioning look.

"No, thanks. I think one of us should keep a clear head."

Dante shrugged indifferently and finished it off in another drag. "You could have a brownie. They're fine."

John rolled his eyes. "I'm sure they are." He left the hashish-laced brownies where they were, but allowed himself a few cautious sips of beer. The draft was cold and tasted even better than the German beer his father used to import.

John realized that he was both literally and figuratively holding his breath. He kept waiting for a little monotone voice to announce demerits. So far their limited experience of Hell had been a marked improvement over Purgatory, which didn't seem right at all.

"If only I had known," Dante said wistfully. "Eight years wasted in Purgatory when I could have been here. Here's to eternity!" He raised his glass and gasped in satisfaction after a hearty swig. Then the music changed, and his ridiculously bloodshot eyes widened. "Hey, who's singing this?"

"Nirvana. They're after your time."

"Man, they're really good! Music is way better in the future."

John thought of the endless boy bands and sophomoric teenage pop stars that had dominated the music scene since the likes of Kurt Cobain had died, but kept his mouth shut. It was kinder to let Dante believe the lie.

"You boys must be new in town," oozed a voice made of silk.

John looked up to see five and a half feet of naked, red flesh. *Demoness* was the first word that came to mind, with *vixen* hot on its heels. Her clothing consisted of a single chain wrapped around her pert breasts, covering nothing more than her nipples. A similar chain circled her waist with a sparse curtain of chainmail hanging from it that left nothing to the imagination. Long black hair complimented the shiny black lips that smiled around slightly pointed teeth. The delicate looping horns that protruded from her forehead silenced any doubt about what she was.

This is it, John thought. *This is where the good times end. Hell has lured us in and is about to make with the torture and turmoil.*

The demoness wrinkled her nose cutely at John as if she could smell his distrust before turning to Dante. The effect on him was instant. He straightened up, like a puppet yanked on strings, his full attention dedicated to the demoness. Even the red from his eyes cleared as if he was shocked sober by his sudden need for sex.

"Do you want a brownie?" he asked stupidly.

The demoness laughed as if he had said something clever. "Aren't you sweet?"

"And aren't you lovely?" Dante responded, taking her hand.

"Mmm, an Irishman! I haven't had one in ages." She held out a black-nailed hand to him, palm side down. "Delilah. It's a pleasure to meet you."

"Dante, at your service." He took her hand and kissed it.

Another demoness joined them, this one blonde with a lighter tint to her red skin. Her face was more angular and her body more petite. Unlike her companion, she was dressed respectably in a summer dress the color of orange sherbet. She didn't waste any time in dedicating her full attention to John.

"Looks like someone could use a tour guide," she said shyly. "I know the first few days here can be confusing."

"Actually, we were doing just fine," John answered coldly.

Dante spared him one glance, accompanied by an expression that said John was crazy, before turning back to the vixen. "I wouldn't mind a little exploration."

"The sun has just gone down over Hades," Delilah said seductively. "Let's have us a night on the town."

"I don't think that's a good idea," John said.

"Oh! Daddy is cranky!" Delilah taunted as she began to drag Dante away. "I'll have him back in one piece, old man. Don't worry."

"And I can keep you company until then," the shy demoness offered.

"It's not going to work on him," Delilah called over her shoulder. "I'll send Rimmon over instead."

"Now she tells me," the blonde demoness rolled her eyes, all signs of timidness gone in an instant. John tried to stand, but the demoness shoved him effortlessly back into his seat. "Let your friend go," she said. "He'll be fine."

John glared at her. "So this is the real Hell. You let new

arrivals think they've found paradise before a demoness drags them away to a fiery pit."

"Hardly," the demoness snorted. "A couple of wet fish like you could never afford a succubus. Not that you'd be interested."

"Then tell me what's going on here!"

"I'll take it from here," a masculine voice purred.

If the afterlife had Calvin Klein ads, the demon standing before him would be their star model. The immaculate physique was blatant below the tasteful black dress shirt and charcoal gray slacks. A face perfect in symmetry was gifted with lips as full as the cheeks were hollow. The half-lidded, golden cat-eyes radiated cool confidence. Unlike the looping demoness horns, his were short and blunt, like those of a baby goat, and could barely be seen under the tangle of messy black hair. John had never heard of a male succubus before, but the demon oozed so much sex appeal that he couldn't be anything else.

"That's not fair," John whimpered.

"He's all yours," the demoness sighed before gliding away.

"My name is Rimmon," the demon said with a subtle smile, "and I'm hoping we can spend some time together."

Sweat broke out on John's forehead as he summoned the willpower to look away from this avatar of male perfection. He succeeded in the end, speaking through gritted teeth. "If you want anything from me, you'll have to turn off your demonic mojo."

Rimmon chuckled, and after a moment the sexual tension dissipated. John looked back at him. Without using the full extent of his charm, Rimmon was merely extraordinary.

"Better?" he asked.

"Barely," John admitted. "Now tell me what you are really doing here."

"You're something different," Rimmon said, his tail curling into a question mark shape behind him. "Very well, since the usual methods won't work on you, I've been sent to show you a good time. Nothing more, nothing less."

"But why?" John asked, trying to suppress the feeling that Christmas had come early.

"Because tomorrow you have a meeting with a very important person, and he wants to make sure you are of an agreeable disposition." Rimmon held up a hand when John tried to interrupt. "I can't tell you more than that because I'm not privy to the information. What I can promise you is that there are no tricks, no deceptions, or anything else that would cause you or your friend harm. You are, in effect, being bribed."

"Bribed? Why? What do we have to offer?"

Rimmon spread his hands in a gesture of helplessness, melting John's heart. "If you really want, I can leave you alone, but it would be a shame. My clients are rarely as attractive as you."

John wanted to roll his eyes, but his face betrayed him by smiling. "Oh, to hell with it. What did you have in mind?"

Chapter Five

The night was warm and the sky clear. The gray clouds of Purgatory held no sway here. The stars were in full view, sparkling rubies rather than the diamonds of old. John and Rimmon walked side by side down the streets of Hell, silent at first as John cautiously observed the local night life. Like Purgatory, Hell's streets were full of people, but they strolled casually, chatting to each other or the demons that walked among them. The first such demon John saw was a woman covered in snake scales from her bare feet to her bald head, her arms full of ordinary grocery bags. Elsewhere, a man who appeared totally human except for leathery wings protruding from his back walked down the street peddling drugs. Later, a six-breasted panther woman passed them by, leading a man on a chain. He wore an expression of pure bliss, even though the chain was attached through hooks in his nipples.

"Sex is Hell's theme, then?" John asked of his companion.

"In Amsterdam, yes, but only to a small extent," Rimmon said. "Drugs are more prominent. The new arrivals often seek them out to help them acclimatize. Eventually one learns that being high is very much a state of mind in the afterlife."

A tram rattled by, taking passengers to a destination that John didn't manage to read. "And the other cities?"

"Each has its specialty. Sex, violence, greed, all the cardinal sins that priests and popes preach against. Until they arrive here, of course. We even have Paris so the gluttons can gorge themselves on food and wine."

"But why Amsterdam?" John asked. "Or Vegas or any of the others? I thought Hell was supposed to be all fire and brimstone."

"Oh, we have that, too," Rimmon said. "There's much more to Hell than resort-themed Earth cities. Hell consists of nine circles, each ever expanding. The outer-most circles, where we are now, are the closest to what you knew in life. The locales become much more unique the deeper you travel toward the hub. Sin and pleasure take on new meaning there, and in many cases are purely intellectual or spiritual in nature."

A boat drifted by in the canal they walked along. The vessel's passage through the water was nearly silent, the gentle waves it caused disrupting the reflection of red stars. The scene was oddly tranquil for a realm that was supposed to encompass eternal punishment.

"So serial killers, rapists, child molesters, they all end up here?"

Rimmon nodded. "A good number of them do."

"Seems unfair. We're taught to live a good wholesome life, but when you get down to it, none of it matters in the end."

"Funny thing, human nature," the demon mused. "More than half of those who come here expect to be punished. They are so burdened by guilt and convinced of their preconceived notions of Hell that there is nothing else to do but humor them."

Rimmon stopped and placed his palm over John's eyes. He was about to protest when the darkness was replaced by a vision. Suddenly John saw Hell as it was classically portrayed.

The materials of this world were fire and stone, metal and lava. Men, women, even children were in varying degrees of dismemberment. Piked heads screamed in unison, all of them eyeless except for one head that had the collection of missing eyeballs crammed into its mouth. Entrails were strung across space like decorative banners, while discarded organs on the floor still pumped, twitched, or beat in an effort to perform their functions. In the middle of all this was one man, directing the monstrosities like the conductor of an orchestra.

John gasped, pulling away and restoring his sight to the much more pleasant scenes of Amsterdam. "That wasn't a demon! The man in the middle of it all, he was human."

"Yes," Rimmon confirmed. "Not all murderers and rapists show up here with a guilty conscience, so we put them to work torturing those who do. We demons have little interest in such activities."

The revulsion John felt left the moment Rimmon placed a guiding arm around his shoulder. He smelled of designer cologne and probably a healthy dose of pheromones from the way John's body reacted. The demon's ability to easily manipulate his emotions made John uneasy, but that suspicion was very hard to maintain when Rimmon radiated comfort. Among other things.

"So what's life as a succubus like?" John asked, hoping for information that might help him resist the demon's charms.

"I'm no succubus," Rimmon said with a laugh. "They are the

female of the species. Incubus is the proper term for me, and I like my life. Especially my job."

He stopped, pulling John toward him in what should have been a romantic scene. They stood on an ancient stone bridge that arched over a canal, the evening breeze teasing their hair. Rimmon's eyes were attentive and hungry as his head came closer for a kiss. But John braced his hands against the demon's chest, pushing away as much as he could. He was already cursing himself for doing so, but his mind wouldn't be silenced.

"But what do you do?" John said. "I have nothing against sex and drugs, and there's even some rock and roll I find tolerable, but is that it? We're supposed to be content with screwing around like a bunch of frat boys for all eternity?"

The incubus sighed, releasing John from his grip. "Already the existential crisis?"

"What do you mean?"

"While alive, humans are completely preoccupied with surviving. Money must be earned in order to eat and pay the rent. Then come the endless health concerns, worries over social status, and memberships to fitness clubs in a fruitless attempt to look sixteen again. Behind all of this, the death clock is ticking out a constant reminder that time is running out."

"I wouldn't say life was exactly like that."

"Once here," the demon continued unabashed, "comes the realization that time is unlimited and that all of life's necessities are now optional. Most people get on with enjoying themselves, while the more cerebral wring their hands and wonder what it all means."

"What *does* it all mean?" John asked, before laughing at himself. "I'm not cerebral. I just want to understand everything."

"Everything? Is that all?" Rimmon's golden eyes sparkled with amusement. "If I teach you everything there is to know, then will I be allowed to kiss you?"

John grinned. "I'll think about it."

"Very well. We'll start with the life of an incubus. After all, with experience comes understanding. You want to know what my life is like? Fine. Let me take you home and show you."

Before John could reply, the world around him shifted and disappeared.

* * * * *

Thick down comforters, warmth, and the scent of sandalwood. John opened his bleary eyes to dim light and a well-organized bedroom. The furnishings and decorations were minimal but tasteful. The dresser, nightstands, and wardrobe shared the same dark wood and silver handles, giving the room a classy yet comfortable ambiance.

A weight shifted next to John. He reached over to feel a handful of fur before suffering an onslaught of licks to the face. John pushed the animal away so he could see.

Bolo! He didn't know how it was possible, but the dog was with him again. Bolo barked happily before hopping off the bed and trotting out of the room. Seeking an answer to his confusion, John forced himself to get up, glad that the suit he wore perpetually these days seemed to be wrinkle-proof.

Two heavy russet curtains blocked either a large window or a balcony door. John moved toward it, hoping to find some hint as to where he was. He remembered Amsterdam, but here the silence was complete, all sounds typical of nightlife gone. John reached for the curtain, pausing to admire its soft texture.

"I wouldn't do that if I were you." Rimmon strode into the room, Bolo in tow. "We're in the fourth circle of Hell now. Your mind wouldn't be able to comprehend what lies beyond. Being dead doesn't mean that you can't go insane." The incubus took John's hand, moving it away but not letting go of it. "Are you all right?"

"Yeah, I guess so. What happened?"

"A simple teleport, that's all. I've never seen anyone react like you."

"How long was I out? Wait, was I sleeping?"

"An hour," Rimmon smiled, "and yes. "Sloth is one of the seven sins after all. Stop that!" The last sentence was directed at Bolo, who was using the demon's tail as a chew toy. "Is this your dog?"

"Uh, sort of, but I don't understand how he can be here. The last time I saw him was on the astral plane outside of Purgatory."

"Animals go where they please. You and I are limited in that regard, but they are lucky."

"I wouldn't say lucky," John said, the image of an endless collection of motionless animals momentarily haunting him.

"You feel troubled. You've been through much since dying."

John shrugged. "No more than anyone else, I guess."

"Well, someone did a number on you." Rimmon traced a finger down to John's stomach and for one instant the painful memory of the glass man burst into vivid detail.

"You can see that?"

Rimmon nodded. "It marks you, vicious and crimson like a wound. I can help you. Take off your clothes. Trust me," he added before John could object.

Rimmon shooed Bolo out of the room as John undressed for the first time since dying. He was relieved to see that everything was still there as he remembered, and still fully functional too, since his body was quickly reacting to the situation. That was curious. John's sex life had always been fairly active, depending on whether or not he was single, but since dying the idea simply hadn't interested him. Not having a physical body meant being free of the influence of hormones and testosterone, but in the presence of the incubus, John felt like a horny teenager again.

Rimmon noticed John's arousal and smiled, but took John's hand like a gentleman and guided him to the bed. At his request, John lay on his back, feeling absurdly nervous. As if he hadn't done something like this thousands of times before! But he hadn't really, since he didn't have a clue if sex worked differently in the afterlife.

"There will be time for those urges later," Rimmon said. "First, let me free you of the suffering you've been through."

Rimmon placed his palm flat against John's skin. The hand was unnaturally warm, but comforting, like a hot water bottle. Starting at John's chest, he brushed his hand downward.

John winced when the demon reached the place where the glass man had toyed with him. His stomach was still tender and sore, a pain he had ignored until now. Rimmon gently rubbed his hand over this spot, humming a strange tune that sounded like many voices harmonizing instead of just one.

Tranquility flowed over John, pouring into the invisible wound and cooling it like a salve. The sound of Rimmon's soothing tune made his mind heavy and calm. Memories from his childhood flooded back. The loving warmth of his mother's arms. The security of being in his father's presence in the years before alcohol had changed him. Lazy summer days spent digging in the back yard with the family dog. All these happy moments came forward to gradually drown away the memory of the glass man.

"Wait!" John cried, coming out of his trance and grabbing the demon's hand. "Not all of it. Don't take the memory completely away. I want to remember. It's important."

Rimmon's eyes widened, but he assented to the request. John's memory of the glass man remained, close enough to be remembered but far enough away to no longer hurt. Then Rimmon slid the rest of the way into bed with John, his body just as hot as his hand had been. At some point he had lost his clothing.

"I admire your willpower, John, and your restraint. I've been trying to match your resolve tonight, but now I am at my limit." Rimmon's words were seductive, whispered into John's ear. "I want nothing more right now than to be myself with you."

"You can be yourself," John said, not understanding what this meant until the incubus released the full powers of his magnetism again.

The lust in John was immediate, and Rimmon responded. In the beginning, they went through the same motions that always accompanied physical pleasure. Rimmon was everything and anything that John needed him to be, responding to every whim almost before John thought of them. They thrust and moaned in an infinite amount of positions, their passion inexhaustible, never tiring as a physical body would. As the hours wore on, this evolved. Sex became the pressing together of two souls, an exchange of energy, even thoughts. The thrumming pleasure of an orgasm was constant, driving them toward becoming one entity. Just as it seemed they would be forever lost in each other—their individual identities stripped away for all eternity— Rimmon pulled away.

Exhausted and yet feeling reborn, John slept.

"Rise and shine!"

John groaned, but only out of habit. He felt magnificent as he pulled himself out of bed. The room was now daylight bright even though the curtains were still pulled shut. Rimmon, dressed in a black silk robe, leaned against the door frame, the smell of bacon and eggs coming from another room.

"You made breakfast?"

"Isn't that tradition in the 21st century?" Rimmon asked.

"Breakfast follows a one-night stand, if I'm not mistaken."

"That, or sneaking out before the other person wakes up," John said.

The demon smirked before leaving him alone to dress. John could get used to this. His body and clothing still smelled as fresh as the day he arrived. He had no need to shave or brush his teeth, no need to pick up clothes from the cleaner. No fuss, no muss, although the idea of a steaming hot shower still sounded appealing.

John wandered through Rimmon's considerable home, vaguely following the scent of food as he poked his head into the different rooms. The rest of the house was just as stylishly decorated as the bedroom. He saw no signs of technology, but did find a number of items that looked rather occult, and many devices that he didn't recognize at all.

Eventually he found the dining room, a narrow space lined with house plants and art. Rimmon was waiting for him at one end of a long, slender table, and nodded to a place set at the other end. Never one for formal dining arrangements, John took the plate and cutlery and moved it to the seat nearest the demon, surprised to find Bolo sitting at Rimmon's side. The dog's entire attention was desperately focused on the table and its contents.

"Sorry about all the drool," John said.

"Easily remedied," Rimmon said, spearing a slab of bacon with a miniature silver pitchfork and feeding it to Bolo. "Eat up, both of you. We'll have to leave early. If you react to teleportation as you did the first time, you'll need extra time to recover."

"Right, the mysterious meeting," John said through a half-full mouth. In addition to the bacon, John found eggs, hash browns, even a side of pancakes. The flavor was outstanding, better than anything he had eaten in living memory.

"You'll be meeting with Asmoday, one of the Archdukes of Hell," Rimmon said, his tone more clipped than John liked. "Despite his status, there are no formal customs you need to observe except for a general degree of respect. In the spirit of full disclosure, I feel I should tell you that I am expected to report to him anything vital that I have learned from you. In fact, I have already done so."

John shrugged. He had nothing to hide, but he did wonder what this meeting was all about. Rimmon had been sent to ensure that John's impression of Hell was positive, but what did they want from him? Was he expected to sell his soul? Could he even do that, considering that's all he was now?

Bolo began whimpering pathetically and pawing at Rimmon's leg. The demon surrendered entirely, piece by piece giving his remaining food to the dog. John sped up his chewing before Bolo could use his charm on him, and sighed contentedly when finished. With his appetite satiated, he turned his full attention to the room's art. The tapestry and paintings were nice, but nothing compared to the sculpture. On a pedestal in one corner was a bust of a heartbreakingly beautiful young man. John thought at first that it might be Rimmon himself, but the features were too delicate and fair.

"My boyfriend," the demon commented when he noticed John staring. "A good likeness, but only a shadow of his true beauty."

"Your boyfriend," John repeated. "Why am I not surprised?"

"Don't worry," Rimmon assured him. "He's aware of my occupation."

"And he's fine with it?"

"I didn't say that." The incubus looked momentarily distraught. "I'm afraid it's a point of contention between us."

"If I had known that last night, nothing would have happened between us."

"Oh, it would have," Rimmon said. "It's my nature, not simply my choice of career. That's precisely the problem. My amorous desire is as instinctual as breathing is to the living. I try to make him understand that I love only him, and that sex is separate from that, but— Well, let's just say he had a conservative upbringing."

John no longer fell in love at the drop of a hat as he had in his younger days, so this revelation didn't hurt him. More than once he had mistaken a one-night stand as being something more. As he grew older, he played the opposite role, having to gently enforce distance in the morning. He understood what Rimmon was doing now, the far-away place setting, the conversation that revolved around business or his relationship with another, and that was fine. John hadn't expected them to get married, but he did hope that he and Rimmon could remain friends, even after the mysterious business of the day was through.

Teleportation didn't make John pass out a second time, perhaps because he was prepared for it. They used the extra time to see more of the city and to stop in another coffee shop, this time for actual coffee. Rimmon's frigid demeanor steadily defrosted, most likely because John was playing it cool and giving no signs of expecting more from their night together.

Sometime during the walk that followed, Bolo disappeared. John called out and whistled to no avail. Rimmon assured him that the dog would find his way back when he was ready. Considering that the dog had followed him all the way to Hell, John didn't find this hard to believe.

When it was time for the meeting, Rimmon led him to the notorious red light district. Even in the daytime the endless lines of windows were still lit with red light; females of all varieties, both human and demon, were behind each glass plane and giving their all to sell themselves. Most of them were beautiful, but none could compare to the two sucubi that had approached John and Dante the night before. Those two were leagues above the women available here, in a class of their own. Equally difficult to imagine was a male hustler who could compete with Rimmon. Hell had given them their best, and John was about to find out why.

After a few twists and turns through the neon alleyways, they reached a window identical to all the others except that it was unoccupied. Nothing but a red glow was visible inside. At Rimmon's touch the door opened. He gestured for John to enter. John's trust wavered momentarily as he pictured himself trapped as a working girl for all eternity, but the idea was too silly for him to truly fear.

Stepping into the dense red light, John found himself in a Victorian study full of leather chairs, dusty books, and unwieldy furniture. The study was exactly the sort Sherlock Holmes would nest in, but the figure behind the desk didn't begin to resemble the famous detective.

This demon's skin was the hue of black cherries. His ample body was stuffed into a tacky, houndstooth-patterned suit, the collar of the white shirt underneath as large and wide as a palm leaf. Below two fat horns and above a considerable double chin was a stern face, its three eyes glaring at him as he entered. John recounted to be sure. There, in the middle of the usual two and beneath the crease of a brow, was one extra eye.

He realized he was staring and quickly averted his gaze. Occupying one of the two chairs before the desk was Dante. The succubus assigned to entertain him, Delilah, stood against one wall with a bored expression. Rimmon instructed John that he should sit before moving to join her.

"Have fun last night?" Dante whispered like an excited school boy.

John ignored him, oddly feeling as though he'd been called to the principal's office. That would make Dante the best friend who always dragged him into trouble. John put on his best innocent expression, just in case, and waited for the Archduke to address him, as Rimmon had coached.

Asmoday examined him a moment longer, his three eyes moving independently of each other. "I trust you have found Hell to your liking?" he grumbled, his voice deep.

"Very much so," John answered. "You have been a gracious host. Rimmon in particular should be commended as a very capable companion."

Asmoday nodded as if satisfied. "And yet, despite your enjoyable evening, you doubt Hell's pleasures will satisfy you in the long run?"

John hesitated.

"You have nothing to fear from me," Asmoday assured him. "Honesty is highly valued, even in the pit. In fact, I think you will find that more truth is spoken here than in any other realm. If I may be as direct with you as I hope you will be with me, I believe we can be of great service to each other."

Here we go, John thought.

"You are not content here because you don't belong here, Mr. Grey. This begs the question of which realm you are suited to, for there are many more than just Heaven and Hell. I can provide you with an opportunity that will allow you to travel to many of these realms. I have no doubt that by doing so, you will eventually find your proper place in the grand scheme of things."

Asmoday smiled, which took John aback since his teeth were as black as onyx. Little wisps of shadow curled away from each pointed tooth, giving the impression that Asmoday was exhaling black smoke. The demonic chompers were meant to intimidate as much as the words were meant to soothe, but John wouldn't let himself be cowed.

"Your concern for me is touching," he replied, "but I don't see anything to prevent me from travelling on my own. Whatever errands you had in mind for me are surely better trusted to one of Hell's own."

Asmoday's middle eye turned to glare at Rimmon. John hoped this wasn't getting him into trouble, but he had no intention of being played like the devil's fiddle.

"Look, just tell me what you want," John said in the form of a truce.

The Archduke leaned back in his chair and snapped his fingers. Delilah rushed over and popped a cigar in his mouth, lighting it with a flame that burned directly from her finger. Asmoday allowed himself a few puffs while studying John. When he spoke again, all sophistication was gone from his voice. "So much for the ol' reach around," he muttered, sounding like he'd been possessed by a New York cabbie. "I can't give it to you any straighter than this. Hell is going to war and we want you to recruit allies for us."

John, to his credit, barely blinked an eye. "War against whom? Heaven?"

"Who else?" Asmoday snarled. "Whose agent do you think you met in Purgatory?"

"The glass man?"

"Ministers of Order, they call themselves. Yeah, there's more than one of them. The damn things are like cockroaches. God's little sparrows were bad enough, but some chump decided angels weren't cutting it. Even we Fallen find them repulsive, and that's saying something. You've seen what they did to Purgatory. They made a dam out of souls just to step on our profits. Not to mention how they scraped the place clean of pleasure or pain. At least in the old days a soul could suffer and rise or give in to temptation and sink. That was a fair system, but now we're out of the loop. Not that I want back in, even if they asked me."

"You're rambling, darling," Delilah said from the wall. "You know that bores me. Either get to the point or shut up."

Asmoday recomposed himself, apparently comfortable with the succubus's insubordination. This familiarity wasn't lost on Dante, who looked somewhat crestfallen.

"These Ministers have been making changes," the Archduke continued. "Hell isn't too pleased with any of them. Purgatory was meant to be a sorting station for tough cases, not a prison."

"Is there something we can do about it?" John asked, his interest growing. He needed a purpose, and while taking on Heaven wouldn't be part of it, he did desire to see the captive souls of Purgatory freed.

"War is the only answer." Asmoday sucked deep on his cigar. "Purgatory is just the tip of the iceberg. The Ministers have made trouble in all the realms, but you're not stupid enough to take my word for it. Let us send you out, just once, and you can draw your own conclusions. Chances are you'll find just as much reason to hate Heaven as you do Purgatory."

John had seen that Hell wasn't as evil as he had expected, and Heaven might not be as good, but that didn't mean that God was a cruel tyrant. Then again, if the other Ministers of Order were all as nasty as the glass man he had met, and if they truly were working for Heaven, then John didn't see how they could be serving any force for good. Asmoday was right. Sitting here wasn't going to get him the answers he needed.

"Where would you send me? Heaven?"

Asmoday snorted. "No! Couldn't even if I wanted to. You don't need to visit Heaven to see what the slimy bastards have been up to."

"Where, then?"

"Asgard to start with, home of the Norse gods. They aren't the brightest bunch, but they know war. While you're there, ask them how they feel about a mutual arrangement. That's all you have to do."

"Why me?" John asked.

Asmoday rolled his eyes. "Does it matter? We're offering you a job!"

"I think it does matter. This sounds important. Why trust a stranger with these duties? Why not a charming incubus or even yourself?"

The Archduke glowered at him.

"Honesty is highly valued, even in the pit," John parroted.

"Oh, he's got you there," Delilah said with a titter.

Asmoday's third eye found her, glared, and stayed locked on her as he answered John. "We've sent demons before you, from ambassadors to smoking hot succubi, and when they came back, they did so in pieces. I told you the Ministers have been meddling everywhere. They have a knack of pinning their dirty deeds on other realms. So many seeds of mistrust have been sown that we're up to our assholes in weeds.

"Thanks to all their conniving and scheming, the realms are more segregated than a Jim Crow toilet. For me to step foot in the Japanese gardens of the Shinto or for a Hindu deva to fly too close Olympus would result in war. The Ministers have us all by our nuts and they won't stop yanking." Asmoday flipped the remainder of his cigar into his mouth, swallowed it whole, and sighed. "Would you want to live in a world painted in one color? Hear only one song for the rest of your life? I miss fucking angels, getting wasted with Vikings, hunting elementals, and losing myself in the raw astral lights."

"I love it when you wax poetic," Delilah breathed, walking over to rub the Archduke's shoulders.

Poor Dante looked positively dejected, but John was too distracted to comfort him. Instead he was weighing the risks against his own desires. He didn't fully understand either, but he knew he didn't want to spend eternity loitering in Hell's decadent establishments or trapped in Purgatory's prison.

"I'm in," he said.

Asmoday smiled, this time keeping his teeth hidden behind his fat lips. "I knew we had the right man. Men, I should say," he added, looking to Dante.

"Me?" the Irishman protested. "Oh, no! Nice try. I already know where I belong!"

"Suit yourself," Asmoday replied. "You are free to go, assuming of course you can pay your debts."

"Debts?"

"The money you've been spending all night on drugs, drinks, clubs, and Delilah. The money I kept magicking into your pockets for your greedy little hands to find." Asmoday leaned forward and treated Dante to a wide, meaningful grin. "Of course, there are other ways you can pay me back. Tasks so miserable that you'll be begging to be let back into Purgatory. Or maybe I'll do them a favor and ship your scrawny ass back there."

A number of expressions played across Dante's face, the last of which was resignation. He shot an annoyed look at John as if this were all his fault.

"Good, good," Asmoday nodded, pleased with himself. "That

just leaves one small matter to attend to."

A ringing in John's ear grew louder and louder until it was all he could hear. Asmoday's lips were flapping, but every single word was lost to John. Not that it mattered since the Archduke was addressing Dante. John placed a finger in each ear, ineffectively trying to relieve the pressure. Suddenly it was over. He looked up. Asmoday had a calculating gleam in his eye, and Dante appeared surprised. Everyone in the room was looking at John. The ringing had been no coincidence. Something had been deliberately kept from him, but now wasn't the time to ask what. He would grill Dante later.

"Your transportation awaits you outside." Asmoday gestured meaningfully to the door before turning in his chair to give his full attention to the succubus. "As for you," he growled seductively.

Dante looked as though he wouldn't mind staying, even if he wouldn't be the center of attention, but Rimmon was hustling them toward the door. They stumbled out into the narrow alley that was now almost completely filled by a vehicle. At first glance it appeared to be an old fashioned, horse-drawn coach, one with a number of curious alterations. Brass tubes sprouted from the back of the elongated coach, as if the vehicle had been rear-ended by a church organ. A hint of large iron gears gleamed from the undercarriage. Just above the rear wheels, partially hidden by black-painted wooden panels, was a massive set of bellows.

"What's that supposed to be?" Dante asked.

"A Gurney steam coach," Rimmon said. "Your transportation."

The demon checked various points of the carriage with an air of efficiency before turning to the driver. The poor man had seen better days. His long blonde hair was matted, his beard missing tufts of hair, and his clothing full of holes.

"Listen to me, Norseman," Rimmon snarled, grabbing him by the beard with unexpected aggression. "We've decided you've suffered enough for your sins."

"You... You have?" the ragged man trembled.

"We have, but Heaven doesn't want you, and we can't stand the sight of you." Rimmon feigned thoughtfulness, his face beautiful even when scowling. "You remember those stories your grandfather used to tell you? About Odin and his bunch of fools? Well, they're all true. Maybe the old gods will take you in, if you think hard enough of them and your grandpappy. Otherwise it's back in the pit with you."

The incubus released his victim and moved to the side of the coach, opening a door and waving John in. "Pull the lever as soon as Dante's in and you'll be on your way."

"What's with the castaway?" John asked, nodding to the Norseman.

"He's your driver and your engine. Remember how you hitched a ride here by holding on to Dante? The same concept applies, except the seating arrangements are more comfortable. Goodbye, John."

Rimmon turned away, walking around the back of the coach with Dante in tow. That was it? A night more intimate than John had ever known, and this was how they parted? Business was business, but a courtesy kiss would have been nice. Or at least one of those pitiful hugs where they patted you on the back.

John waited in the coach, trying as casually as possible to glance out the far window for one last look at Rimmon, but it was only Dante who appeared around the other side, looking pale as he struggled to pull himself up on the bronze step. By the time he was seated, he appeared positively nauseous.

"What's the matter, stagecoach fright?" John asked.

"Ha, ha. Let's get this over with."

The coach was luxurious inside, with two blue velvet benches facing each other. Polished mahogany paneled the interior, and a stylish brass lamp with emerald glass hung from the ceiling. One of the benches was segmented by an armrest, and protruding from this was a simple, brass-tipped wooden lever. Because it was the only lever in sight, John felt safe in pulling it. The coach jerked, propelled forward with a hiss of steam. Their unwilling coach driver began a dreadful moan that soon graduated into a full blown scream as they increased in speed. Furious shouts came from the pedestrians who were rolled over or knocked aside by the runaway coach, which was accelerating at an alarming rate.

John's stomach lurched as the coach rounded sharp corners, maneuvering at right angles with frightening precision. The vehicle slid left, right, and back again, all in a matter of seconds as it wound through the city streets. The world outside was nothing more than a blur when an explosion rocked them to the core. Then came calm. Outside the coach window, nameless colors looped and spiraled, their hues overlapping and mixing when blown by the occasional astral wind. They had broken free of Hell.

Chapter Six

Any sight, no matter how breathtakingly beautiful, becomes routine given enough time. This truth allowed John to eventually pull his eyes away from the entrancing world outside the coach window. He had thought Dante's silence was for the same reason as his own, but the Irishman wasn't looking out the window at all. Instead he was leaning back against the bench with his eyes closed, his skin still pale.

"Are you all right?"

"I'm fine," Dante murmured, opening his eyes with some reluctance. "I just had a long night, is all."

Except that he had been his usually chipper self in Asmoday's office. Only before boarding the coach had he gone green in the gills. Unless a soul could be travel sick, whatever had been covertly conveyed had Dante upset.

"What did they say to you back there? My ears started ringing when Asmoday was speaking to you, which was hardly subtle."

Dante paused a little too long before answering. "They just wanted to make sure—" He hesitated but then picked up speed, obviously running with a new idea, "—that I do right by you. You say jump, I jump. That sort of thing. Asmoday wants to keep me in line, that's all."

"Right."

If that were the case, they wouldn't have bothered keeping John out of the loop. But he thought he could guess the truth. Asmoday wanted someone to report back to him, one of Hell's own. Maybe there was more to it than that, but John suspected that Dante was worse at keeping a secret than a nosey neighbor. He would bide his time and find out sooner or later.

"This is taking a long time," John said. "It took about two seconds to get to Hell."

"Our driver's connection to Asgard isn't as strong as mine was to Hell," Dante said, resting his eyes again. "We'll be there shortly."

John turned back to the window and was surprised to see a familiar shape—a tree, with far-reaching branches that drooped under the weight of its own broad leaves. The trunk was gnarled and twisted, worn by the uncountable years it had taken to grow so astoundingly tall.

The coach veered toward the tree's canopy and began to speed, the driver excited by the appearance of a place he scarcely believed existed. Even Dante came out of his repose to gawk. The branches weren't just burdened with leaves. They supported entire lands along their length: some frozen tundras, others mountainous planes, all dotted with trees of the same species as their gigantic mother. Rivers spilled over the edges of flat worlds, spiraling downward to quench the tree's roots far below.

The coach dipped as if gravity had finally caught hold, the world outside becoming a blur before they jarred to a stop. John didn't hesitate to spring from the coach when he saw what awaited them.

Grass! And trees! And air as fresh and clean as any laundry day in July. John squatted to run his hands through the grass and dig in with his fingers, feeling dirt gather beneath his nails. He had always been a city boy, but the time he had spent trapped in Purgatory's metropolis had heightened nature's allure. The difference was like stepping out of winter and directly into summer, the air suddenly alive with sunshine and bird song. John glanced up to catch sight of the singing avians and stared.

The sky was made of branches. This wasn't poetry. Where they had landed were hardly any trees, just a few scrawny specimens scattered across the surrounding slopes. But where the sky should have been, the endless branches of the world tree splayed out in every direction. He could see no blue beyond, no sky peeking though, and no sign of a sun, yet the day was as bright and warm as any other.

Birds of every species busied themselves in these branches, cheerfully chattering when not swooping from location to location. Some flew in densely populated flocks, drifting like feathered clouds through the air. If there was a heaven for birds, this must be it, a place where tree and sky had become one.

"I'm free!" someone hooted joyously.

John turned to see the Norseman had undergone a transformation. Not only had he freed himself from the coach, but his previous bedraggled appearance had changed. Gone was the singed hair and stained clothing. He was clean now, his body and his clothes, and his cheeks had taken on a healthy hue. The Norseman cast one suspicious glance in John's direction before running away down the hill.

"Good riddance," Dante muttered, his back against the coach. Like the Norseman, his appearance had improved. He was still as scruffy as ever, but the color had returned to his face.

"You sure we don't need him as a guide or something?"

"He doesn't know Asgard any better than we do," Dante said dismissively. "Besides, I'm pretty sure we need to go up. What self-respecting god would reside at the bottom of a hill?"

John regarded the gentle slope where they stood. They were at the bottom near a sparse forest, where the Norseman had already disappeared. Above them, the hill rose until its apex. The hike wouldn't be easy, but Dante was right: Gods were more likely to be at the peak.

As it turned out, the hike was nothing to worry about. Physical exertion was a thing of the past. They reached the top of the hill with little effort and no pain. John wasn't even breathing hard, because he wasn't breathing at all.

Before them, a farm lay on an even plateau. Every field was in full bloom, the crops ripe and ready to be harvested. They stopped to watch a man in the field, picking various items and placing them in a basket as if he were shopping. The man noticed the two onlookers but didn't seem concerned. When he was finished choosing the food he wanted, he returned to a path and walked away from them. They followed, finding a simple road outlined on each side by grooves created from the frequent passage of carts.

They travelled along this road until they reached a village. Rustic buildings crowded together, each crafted from the most basic materials. Most were long with odd rounded roofs reminiscent of hulls, like the Vikings had simply turned their ships upside down when settling on land. The curious roofs were supported from the ground by hewn tree trunks spaced every few feet.

Other buildings were also squat and long, but their walls were made of packed dirt. Like their counterparts, the roof dominated the architecture, but these were made of turf and were green with sprouting grass.

"I have to see inside of those," John breathed in awe. "They're brilliant!"

John had spent countless hours creating blueprints, obsessing over the smallest details to ensure maximum space usage, energy efficiency, visual appeal, and an overwhelming number of other considerations. He relied on drafting tools and the accuracy of computers, and yet the simple practical structures here had been built by hand. No construction vehicles had erected these buildings. They were created by the sweat and muscle of men and women who were unlikely to take them for granted.

"We'll be going in one of them, I'm sure," Dante said. "Most likely in the center of the village and of a size much larger than these."

John was surprised by Dante's confidence in what they needed to do. The conversation he wasn't allowed to hear had only lasted a minute. Could they have really briefed him so thoroughly?

Most of the villagers were dressed in simple but colorful robes, decorated with belts, cords, and primitive jewelry. Like the man in the field, none of them appeared surprised by the presence of two strangers. Apart from initial glances, John and Dante were ignored as they moved through the village.

After travelling a considerable distance, they reached the center of town and found what they were looking for. The hall was so large that it dwarfed shopping malls and football stadiums. Like the buildings they had seen earlier, it resembled a boat turned upside down, but this one had a roof thatched in gold. Light from an invisible sun reflected off its surface, the effect almost blinding.

"Valhalla," Dante said before grinning. "You know what goes on in there, don't you?"

Even John was familiar with this myth. The great heroes and those who had fallen in battle spent eternity in Valhalla, drinking, feasting, and brawling with the gods. There may have been some womanizing with the Valkyries as well, he couldn't quite remember, but there was sure to be booze.

"There's a lot of drinking in the afterlife," John commented.

"When in Rome," Dante said, "or Norseland or wherever."

John shook his head and followed Dante as he strode forward. No guards were at the door, but what sort of deities would need them? Especially when the hall beyond was stuffed with hundreds if not thousands of immortal warriors, drunk, rowdy, and no doubt eager for a good fight. John winced in anticipation of the loud festivities taking place inside as Dante threw open the door.

The hall beyond was completely silent until a cranky voice called out, "Close the door! You're letting in the cold!"

They hurried in, the door slamming shut behind them. The hall was even grander inside. Mythical beasts hung from the ceiling, monsters that had been slain by heroes and stuffed. Swords, armor, and weapons of all kinds were mounted on the walls, each with a plaque declaring who they belonged to and what their achievements were. The most important of these were accompanied with statues of the heroes, each in a noble pose.

A long table ran the considerable length of the hall. The surface should have been covered in steaming bird carcasses, delicious fruits, great slabs of meat, and of course, tankards of mead. Instead it was bare except for some knitting, a number of used handkerchiefs, and something that looked like a bowl full of prunes.

A handful of gods sat at the table. There was no mistaking what they were. Even though they appeared more wizened than expected, they still radiated power. As John looked upon each of them, he knew them by name and reputation. Such was their presence that their stories gathered around them as auras.

There was Baldur the sun god, still beautiful despite his considerable age. His brilliant blue eyes shone with what might have been youth or senility; it was difficult to tell. Next to him was a blindfolded god with an old bent horn in his ear: Hodur, the greatest of all archers despite being blind. At the center of the table sat Frigg. Age only lent more credence to her reputation for wisdom, which was currently focused on knitting a fat pair of socks. Holding the wool for her was the mighty Thor, still a hulking figure although his muscles now sagged from his arms.

No one else was in the room. No warriors, no Valkyries, not even serving staff. The old gods went about their nose-blowing and napping without even glancing up at the newcomers.

John grasped for a properly formal way of addressing them. He cleared his throat and declared, "Norse gods! It is an honor to stand before you."

"Is it time for my bath?" Baldur asked.

Some of the gods snickered as John's face flushed.

"We bring greetings from Hell," he tried again.

"What's the old witch been up to, then?" Hodur asked.

"Not Hel," Frigg said patiently. "He means the place, not the goddess."

"Oh. Well, tell her we said hello," Hodur replied.

Dante stepped forward with an impatient sigh and produced a scroll that was burning with fire. "Just read this, will you? Which one of you is in charge?"

"I am." Thor's voice rumbled like thunder when he spoke. He stood and snatched the scroll out of Dante's hand, not fearing the flames. He unrolled the parchment and examined it, his brow furrowing in concentration. Half a minute later and he moved on to the next word. Eventually he grunted and shoved it toward Frigg.

The goddess took one look at it and tutted. "The writing is too small for these old eyes."

"Let me," Hodur offered. The blind god took the scroll and held it at arms length in front of him. "Mm-hm," he said after a moment's time. "I see. Hell wants to wage war."

"Against us?" Thor grumbled.

"No, no, against Heaven," Hodur explained. "They want our help."

"What care we of angels and demons?" Frigg asked.

"There are souls trapped in Purgatory, held there against their will," John said, stepping forward. "Not just Catholics, but souls from all religions. Some of your own people could be there, too."

"Most of our kind came here long ago," Frigg answered. "There isn't likely to be more on the way."

"There are the neo-Pagans," Baldur pointed out. "I rather like them, even if they don't have a taste for blood."

"Any of our kind could fight their way out of Purgatory!" Thor snarled, crossing his massive arms over his chest. "Nothing there but a bunch of fluffy birdmen. What are they called? Angels! Pfha!" The glimmer in his eye didn't go unnoticed by John. The thunder god was full of pent-up aggression. Enticing him into a war shouldn't take much more than a little creative description.

"Purgatory has changed," John told him. "Gone are the angels. In their place are giant spiders and glass wizards, cruel masters of their territory. Purgatory is surrounded by a barrier built from their victims, a monument to their skill in battle. They are indeed worthy foes!"

Baldur and Hodur were both bright red in an effort to hold back their laughter, but Thor was buying it. His eyes were alive with the idea, his great muscles twitching in anticipation. "And Heaven?" he asked.

"So deadly are the foes there that none have returned to speak of them."

The thunder god leapt to his feet. "We shall feed the ravens!" he bellowed. "We will wage war until Heaven is covered in wound-dew!"

Frigg delicately took hold of his elbow and pulled Thor back down to his seat. With an expression of limitless patience, she whispered into his ear. Thor flushed and pouted at her words. "We are too old to fight," Thor said in monotone. "Loki has stolen the golden apples that keep us young." He sounded as if he were reading from a script. "Go to Jotunheim, the land of the giants, and bring the apples and the traitor back to us, and we will join you. This falcon shall guide you." Finished with his speech, he sat back in his chair and glared at them.

A bird's cry echoed through the hall as a falcon swooped down from the rafters. The bird circled John until he raised his arm for it to perch on. He eyed it nervously for a moment before turning back to the thunder god. "What do we—"

"Go!" Thor yelled, cutting off his question.

They left the hall with haste, the sound of laughter bursting out the second the door slammed shut.

"There's something very wrong here," John said.

Dante nodded. "They're taking the piss. I reckon they're playing some sort of game with us. Asmoday said we weren't the first ones here."

"That's right. He said the others had been sent back in pieces." John frowned. "So what do we do?"

The falcon screeched shrilly and launched itself from his arm.

Dante shrugged. "Follow the bleedin' bird."

The falcon led them beyond the village to a hilltop, where a wooden bridge arched through the air, rising and twisting away into the distance. John marveled at this feat of engineering. The bridge had no supports and shouldn't have been able to stand, but physical laws didn't apply in the afterlife. Neither did the engineering limitations he had fought against his entire career. If he could build his own world, as Jacobi suggested, or even just create a few buildings in a realm that already existed, then John was sure he could work wonders.

Once on the bridge, they couldn't see much except the branches of the sky above and the occasional cloud. The falcon would fly ahead until almost out of sight, land on one of the rails, and wait for them to catch up. The temperature dropped steadily as they proceeded along the miles-long bridge. By the time they reached its end, the air was positively freezing and their environment had undergone a complete transformation. The grassy hillocks had been replaced by icy white mountains, all vegetation completely hidden beneath a heavy blanket of snow. John glanced at the dirt beneath his fingernails and sighed. It had been nice while it lasted.

He hoped they wouldn't have to stay here long. Not that John understood exactly what lay ahead of them. He said as much to Dante.

"You heard them," Dante said. "We're supposed to get their golden apples back."

"Right, so they can be young again. So we just sneak up on some guy and steal them back?"

"Not just some guy. Loki is a Norse god too, and a notorious trickster, one who always causes trouble for the other gods. He's a devious and cunning old goat, and we'll have to be on our guard."

"What do you mean?"

Dante smiled in a manner that wasn't like him at all. "Well, there was the time that Thor's magic hammer was mysteriously stolen by an ice giant while he and Loki were sleeping. Hardly a coincidence, nor was the ease with which Loki searched out the supposed thief, the chief of the ice giants. Loki returned to Asgard with news that the ice giant demanded the goddess Freya as his bride in exchange for the hammer. Loki had a grudge against Freya at the time, you see.

"Strong-headed Freya refused, even though the gods did their best to convince her. Loki enjoyed watching her being harassed before suggesting that Thor take her place. The old trickster promised Thor that the disguise would only be needed until they gained entry to the ice giant's stronghold, saying blood would flow soon after. Thor agreed, so Loki dressed the thunder god in a gown decorative enough to cover his muscles, and curled his blond hair so that it hid his face. Loki brought his rather ghastly creation to the ice giants, making Thor swear not to attack until he gave the signal. Poor Thor suffered through most of the wedding ceremony waiting for Loki's permission. Finally, during the vows, Thor couldn't take it anymore and went berserk, slaughtering every giant there. Thor got his hammer back, but I think Loki got much more out of the ordeal. Not only did he keep whatever the giants paid him for the hammer, but he took some revenge on Freya and was able to make a fool out of Thor in the process."

John thought of the beefy thunder god in drag and laughed. "Loki sounds all right."

"He has his moments," Dante murmured, "but he also has his dark side. As the myths go on, Loki's sense of humor becomes progressively wicked. Eventually he betrays the gods, unleashes Armageddon on all of creation in the form of Ragnarok, and is responsible for countless deaths, destruction, and the end of the world."

John shivered. "And this is who we are going to see?"

"As I said, we must be on our guard. It is no coincidence that we are being sent to see the cleverest of the Norse gods."

As much as John had enjoyed the story, something about it had troubled him. He realized that it wasn't the tale itself but the teller.

"What happened to your accent?" he asked.

"Hm?"

"Your Irish accent. It's gone."

Dante's face went pale. He looked shaken, just as he had in the coach. "Something's wrong with me," he whispered, his accent returned to him again. "Those things I told you, I didn't know any of them. I never read a myth in my life!"

John's skin crawled. Was this one of Loki's tricks?

"It was like being a captive audience in my own head," Dante continued. "How could I know those things?"

"If it makes you feel any better, I knew all the gods by name when I saw them."

Dante nodded. "Me too, but this was different. I wasn't in control. I wasn't me!"

The falcon screeched, making both men jump, but they soon

understood its warning. Ahead on the path was a giant. He looked mostly human, except that his skin was hypothermic blue, his white hair and beard covered in ice crystals. Even from a distance, his height was impressive, twice that of a normal man. The furs he wore were filthy and bloodstained, as was the giant, misshapen bone he carried as a club.

The giant noticed them too, roaring and raising his club with clear intent. Then the falcon shrieked in a manner that sounded oddly like "Run!" before it began swooping at the giant's head. Dante was first to act, grabbing John by the arm and pulling him into the pines off the path. They ran, dodging trees and casting fearful glances backward for any sign of pursuit, not slowing until the ground gave way to a steep drop that forced them to halt.

Peering over the edge, they saw only jagged stones slick with ice. At the very bottom was a small frozen stream. More rocks spiked into the air on the other side of the ravine.

"We could jump," John said. "Might hurt, but we can't die, right?"

Dante looked back the way they came. "I don't hear him coming."

"Come to think of it, why are we running, anyway?" John continued. "It's not like he can kill us."

"There are a number of unpleasant things that could happen to us here," Dante said, his accent gone once more.

"Like what?"

"Like that creature eating us. Being trapped in its stomach for all eternity as it feeds off our soul energy." Dante lost color, surprised again by the strange words coming out of his mouth.

They waited together in silence, Dante not trusting himself to speak and John no longer trusting Dante. He didn't know what to think of his companion's change. On one hand, Dante suddenly knew a lot more than he did before, and that was useful. On the other, who knew where this information was coming from. For all he knew, it could all be Loki's manipulative lies.

The falcon soon landed on the ground before them, its beak covered in blood. Everywhere the falcon hopped, it left red footprints in the snow. John was crouching down, concerned that it was injured, when the bird began to shimmer. The falcon grew and stretched, replaced almost instantly by a woman.

John knew her immediately, as he had the other gods. This was Freya, goddess of enchantment and poetry. Thick braids of honey oak hair wound in circles on each side of her head before resting on her shoulders. Her lips were red paint on porcelain skin, emerald eyes alive with intensity. She wore a long cloak made of falcon feathers that fluttered restlessly before settling. Freya raised a quizzical brow at them and frowned.

"It was only an ice giant," she said, recognizing the concern in John's eyes. She pulled the falcon cloak tightly about her and sat, motioning for them to do the same, her expression becoming determined. "The other gods may be content to play their games, but I tire of them. Diplomacy may be unfamiliar to us, but all other methods have failed. I am giving you a chance to earn our support, but only if you answer truthfully."

"You'll never meet a more honest bloke than I," Dante lied, eyes locked on the beautiful goddess.

"Good," Freya said and nodded. "Then tell me, where is Odin?"

The air reverberated with his name. Odin, king of the gods, the all-father, the one-eyed hanged man. Odin was the true chief of the gods, not Thor. John could mentally see the grizzled beard, the keenness of the remaining eye, the ravens that sat on each of the god's shoulders. What he could not see, unfortunately, is where this god was.

"I don't know," he said truthfully.

"Then tell me what has become of him," Freya demanded. "What did you demons do with him?"

John shook his head. "I don't know what you mean."

"Deceivers!" Freya hissed. "All was well until your first emissaries came. Shortly after their arrival Odin disappeared. You cannot tell me this is coincidence!"

"I admit it sounds suspicious," John said, "but I don't know anything about it. If Hell has your king, why would they ask for your support in the war? Wouldn't they use him to extort you into fighting for them?"

Freya's eyes narrowed as she thought over his words. "I will ask you one more time to tell me the truth."

"I already have."

She turned next to Dante.

"You're beautiful," he said, "but I can't remember the last

time a woman scared me so much. Not since my old mam. If I knew where Odin was, I'd point the way."

The goddess shook her head in frustration. "Then I leave you to Loki's whims."

Without another word, Freya's form shimmered and became the falcon, taking to the air. John thought she intended to abandon them, but the bird circled above until they got to their feet and began to follow again.

So the Norse gods had always meant for Loki to deal with them. The nonsense about stolen apples was only a ruse, this journey a long march toward a divine steel trap. Unless Loki was only to interrogate them. John wasn't that optimistic, but maybe the trickster god could be reasoned with. Perhaps Loki was a skilled enough liar to recognize when someone was telling the truth.

Freya left them at the entrance of a monumental ice castle. Transforming into a woman, the goddess asked them once more what they could not answer. John reiterated their ignorance and defended their innocence, and despite his certainty that she was on the verge of believing him, in the end she became a bird and swept away into the sky.

They were left to face the curiously constructed castle alone. The bricks of foggy ice gave only hints of colors and objects on the other side of the wall. John looked desperately for signs of movement, but the castle was as still as their frozen surroundings. The proportions of the building worried him. The massive door, the size of the windows, and the space he estimated between floors were all scaled to the size of a giant.

They saw no portcullis, drawbridge, or any other method of defense. Whatever lived here didn't fear intruders. In fact, the heavy door was cracked open, just wide enough for humans to pass through. They were expected.

"Nothing ventured, nothing gained," Dante muttered in a reassuringly thick Irish accent. He gestured for John to go first, as if he were being polite.

The entrance hall was a mess. Tapestries had been torn from the walls and suits of armor lay in pieces among shattered furniture. Perhaps the open door wasn't an invitation, but had been left that way by whomever—or whatever—had caused this devastation. Then again, maybe that was how things were supposed to appear. Was this all part of Loki's notorious cunning? They surveyed the surrounding chaos in silence before proceeding to the next room, careful not to slip on the icy floor. The large table, still laden with empty plates and goblets, showed it was once a dining hall, but everything else was in complete disarray. The remaining rooms in the castle would likely be in the same condition.

"Maybe this is the trap," Dante said. "They're going to pin this mess on us. Loki is probably on his way home, and is going to be pissed when he thinks we trashed the place."

"Seems like a lot of trouble just to frame us," John said doubtfully. "Unless the gods wanted to get back at Loki while getting rid of us at the same time."

They tensed at a noise in the adjacent hallway. A booming cough, a snort, and footsteps too heavy to be human. Dante and John took one look at each other before racing for the only cover in the room—the dining room table. Twice as tall as a normal table, it was easy to duck underneath.

Remaining silent was easier without a thudding heart or short breath, but they were still terrified to hear the footsteps nearing, one by one. A shadow cast across the floor as the doorway was filled by the very ice giant they had seen in the wild, its head now sticky with maroon goo. Dried blood clumped around the gashes on its face where Freya's talons had done their work. The giant surveyed the room, one of its eyes almost swollen shut, and sniffed.

John thought of *Jack and the Beanstalk* and almost burst out laughing, but clicking claws on the frozen floor distracted him. A dog was standing in the doorway where they had entered. Bolo! The dog's ears were perked, his eyes searching. Of all the times the dog could track him down, why now? John looked back at the giant, who was rummaging through a mess of pots and broken dishes on the floor.

Bolo spotted John and trotted toward him. John grimaced, knowing what was going to come next. The bark that had once saved him from Purgatory was now going to doom him in Asgard. Sure enough, the English Shepherd began yapping happily.

The giant swung around, and Bolo skidded to a stop, his

hackles rising as he noticed the monster. A low growl built in the dog's throat, one that was drowned out by the ice giant's roar. John thought of an eternity spent inside the giant's stomach and knew that would be the dog's fate if he didn't act. Already the giant was rushing toward Bolo, its feet sliding over the floor with the skill of an ice skater.

John was closer to Bolo and reached him first, despite the giant's speed. He crouched protectively in front of the dog, but Bolo scrambled to do the same for him. The giant leapt the final distance to them, grabbing John by the head and tossing him effortlessly across the room. John collided with a leg of the table, his body wrapping around it like a wet rag.

Bolo yipped as John grabbed the table leg to pull himself up. The giant had the dog by the tail, holding him aloft and dangling him over his maw as if he intended to swallow his prey whole.

Then Dante was there, gracefully moving across the ice, reaching the giant's feet in seconds. Dante's eyes glowed red and his chest expanded before his entire head lit up like a jack-o'-lantern. Fire exploded from his mouth. John used his arm to shield his eyes against the light. He didn't need to see to understand what was happening. The giant's screams of pain were deafening as he fled from the room, the noise moving toward the entrance and fading away in the distance.

When John uncovered his eyes, he saw Dante on his knees, white as a ghost. Bolo cautiously approached him and sniffed his mouth before turning to John for some sort of explanation. The dog's expression was remarkably similar to the Irishman's.

"We've got to get you to a doctor," John said.

"Why? You think I caught something?" Dante sounded panicked. "Maybe from the succubus, like some sort of demonic STD?"

John laughed. "I don't know, but it's proved convenient so far. As for you," he said to Bolo, "you need to stick with me. No more of these surprise appearances."

Bolo barked, hopefully in agreement.

After a brief reunion, they regained the urgency to fulfill their mission. The giant could come back, maybe with brethren. With this in mind, they began to cautiously explore the other rooms. Not all were trashed. A pattern began to appear, a path of destruction leading from the entryway, through the dining hall and half a dozen other rooms, before ending in the courtyard.

There, near the fountain in the center of the yard, a dozen ravens cawed in lustful abandon, pecking and tearing at the carrion beneath their feet. Bolo sent the birds flying, barking and leaping at them as they escaped.

"Well, we found the golden apples," Dante joked.

John saw nothing to laugh about. With the ravens gone, they could see what the birds had been working on. A man had been turned inside out, his muscle, entrails, and the raw red underside of skin spread out in a messy heap. The golden apples were scattered carelessly on top of it all.

The body was still identifiable. Like the other gods, it retained an aura that spoke its name and character. This was Loki, trickster god, dark and cunning—what was left of him anyway.

A falcon swept down from the sky and landed between them and the body. Bolo went after the bird, but quickly skidded to a stop when it changed into the goddess Freya. Her eyes were wide with shock. This obviously wasn't part of the plan.

"What happened here?" she whispered. "The other gods must know!"

And in an instant the gods were there, more of them than had been in the hall. And they were different now. Gone were any signs of age. Each was in his or her prime—Baldur indescribably handsome, Thor the pinnacle of physical fitness, and blind Hodur no longer senile, but grim and serious.

The names and natures of the other gods filled John's mind. One of them was Idhunn, goddess of immortality and keeper of the grove of golden apples. Of course the gods had a limitless source. How could Loki have stolen them all? Just as the gods had pretended to be old, Loki's theft of the apples had been part of the game, a ruse gone terribly wrong.

"You did this?" Thor demanded.

Before John could act, the thunder god grabbed him by the shoulders.

"You will pay," Thor hissed before tearing off John's right arm as if dismembering a paper doll.

John shuddered. It wasn't pain he felt... not exactly. Losing of a part of himself felt *wrong*, the disturbing sensation that he was no longer complete. Not just superficially, as in missing a physical part, but as if something had been stolen from the core of his being. John's head was reeling, but he forced himself to focus. The Norse god had ripped his arm from him effortlessly. If John didn't act quickly, he would soon lose more of himself.

"How could we have?" he whimpered. "Are we more clever than Loki? Is anyone?"

Thor hesitated before unstrapping his hammer. Lightning sparked along its rune-engraved surface. The hammer rose into the air, held above John's head and ready to strike. Bolo barked and snapped at Thor's legs, but the god paid him no heed.

"Freya saw us. She knows we didn't do this!"

John could see the goddess from the corner of his eye. She mouthed the word "Odin" to him and his stomach sank. She wouldn't vouch for them unless he told her where Odin was. She still believed he knew.

"I don't know!" John moaned.

Thor's face was grim. "You shall share Loki's fate."

"If I could kill a god, I'd kill you!" John snarled. "I'd take that hammer and shove it up your ass!"

Thor's eyes flashed with fury before giving way to amusement. He bellowed with laughter as he dropped John to his feet, clapping him on the shoulder and almost sending him flying.

"Now you are talking sense!" the great god boomed. "Here! Have this back!" He picked up John's arm and handed it to him.

John took it by the hand, feeling both grateful and repulsed.

"Just hold it to yourself," Dante said, suddenly next to him. His accent was gone again, the shadows deep across his face. Was that a glint of red in his eye?

John shuddered, the discomfort of being incomplete returning now that he was no longer in danger. Following Dante's instruction, he pressed the two severed parts together, trying not to focus on the perfect cross-section of bone and muscle visible where his limb had been torn. At least it wasn't oozing with blood. As soon as the torn areas reached each other, they snapped seamlessly together like two attracting magnets, and John's discomfort abated.

"Perhaps they are telling the truth," Freya said, a trace of apology in her voice. "Not only regarding Loki, but more. I asked them about Odin."

"You were not to speak of that!" Thor rumbled.

"But I did, and they know nothing. None who have come here since have known. Why have they made no demands? How could any of them have taken Odin against his will?" Freya nodded toward Loki's remains. "No visiting demon has ever held such power. A truce may be the only way to find your father."

"She has a point," Hodur said. The blind god was kneeling and examining Loki's body. "We've never seen anything like this before. Loki will pull himself together again, but he'll need time. Worship from his followers will help, but this isn't a state I would want to experience."

"A truce," Thor said musingly.

"Hm? What is this?" Hodur poked a finger into Loki's body, leaping away from it when something stirred. The flesh shifted and parted as a figure pulled itself free, rising from the remains like the dead from the grave. Covered in blood, its perfect features were sculpted crystal.

John's stomach turned as the glass man stepped toward them, glops of muscle and tissue sliding off its slick body.

"There will be no truce," the Minister of Order declared, raising a hand.

Dante threw himself at Loki's killer, his head aglow. This time John didn't shield his eyes as fire erupted from Dante's mouth. The flames cascaded around the Minister, the remaining gore on its body sizzling and popping. When Dante's assault ceased, the Minister showed no sign of damage.

The glass lips smirked as its other hand rose. The air began to hum, a terrible power building in the air that had the potential to destroy them all.

"There will be no truce," the glass man repeated.

Thor's hammer flew through the air, striking the Minister in the chest and shattering him into hundreds of pieces. The air fell silent after the tinkling shower of glass settled to the ground.

Relief only lasted a moment as the fallen shards began to spin and grow, their shape shifting, elongating, and unfolding at a terrible speed until each became a grinning glass skeleton. In the blink of an eye, an army of skeletons blossomed into existence.

Despite being outnumbered, the Norse gods didn't hesitate. They launched into battle. Thor's hammer returned to his hand, swinging in every direction and shattering translucent bones. Frigg moved gracefully, striking each opponent's weak point with two fingers and causing them to shatter. Freya became a falcon of enormous proportions, crushing skeleton after skeleton with her beak and talons while Hodur unleashed a barrage of arrows, each finding its target's joints and reducing the skeletons to piles of bone. Even Dante joined the fray, his fire more effective against the Minister's weakened form.

All John could do was duck and clutch Bolo as the battle raged around them. He had never seen anything like it. The skeletons barely stood a chance. If Hell wanted an army, they wouldn't need anything more than the Norse gods.

The battle was over almost as soon as it began. The remains of the skeletons were powdered, molten, and broken, but none of them moved anymore.

"Are there more of these glass creatures to be fought?" Thor asked, brow creased in thought. "Would joining with Hell mean more such battles?"

"I'm afraid so," John answered.

The thunder god's grin was victorious. "Excellent!"

Chapter Seven

The driver's seat of the steam coach creaked as Dante settled into place. With the Norse gods agreeing to join forces with Hell, all that remained was to report back to Hell, but how? As usual, Dante had chimed in with information he couldn't possibly have known.

"You're sure this will work?" John asked.

"Stop worrying," Dante said. "My soul will be ripped back to Hell, just like before, except now I'll be hauling you and the whole coach along with me. You can thank me by getting in the carriage and pulling the knob so we can return to civilization."

John didn't move. "You've taken it all in stride," he said. "The whole fire-breathing thing, I mean."

Dante shrugged. "I didn't hear you complaining when I was saving our asses. So maybe there are strange all-knowing voices coming out of my mouth, but they haven't done us wrong, have they?"

"I suppose not, but aren't you curious as to where these mysterious powers come from?"

"It's probably standard fare for the denizens of Hell." Dante crossed his arms. "Or maybe I'm just gifted. Take your pick."

"Right," John snorted. "Enough games. You can come out now."

Nothing happened, other than Dante looking at John like he was crazy.

"Come on, Rimmon," John said. "I know it's you in there."

Dante was about to retort when his eyes went wide and his face turned red. The Irishman groaned and fainted, his head lolling to one side, leaving Rimmon's head in its place. The demon stood, his body stepping out of Dante's as if he were stepping off an elevator. Unlike the unpleasant arrival of the glass man, Rimmon's exit didn't appear to harm Dante. The incubus hopped gracefully off the coach, flashing a wink at John and giving Bolo a pat or two before turning his attention back to Dante. Then he began strapping the unconscious Irishman into the driver's seat.

"Possession?" John asked as he watched.

"Yes. Very astute of you."

"Is he okay?"

"Fine." Rimmon nodded, as he finished his work. "He'll get used to this."

Rimmon moved to the coach door and gestured for John to enter, sweeping in after him and whistling for Bolo to follow. Once they were all seated, he pulled the lever that set the coach moving. John ignored the scenery whizzing by as he unleashed an onslaught of questions.

"So you were with us the entire time?"

"It would seem so."

The incubus smiled, causing mixed reactions inside John, but he refused to be so easily manipulated.

"Did he know?"

"Dante? Obviously not."

"So you were sent to spy on us?"

"My assignment was to bring back an accurate report of the situation in Asgard and to assist should your souls be endangered." Rimmon reached out to scratch Bolo behind the ear. "I'd say I did a commendable job, wouldn't you?"

John had to agree. He had made short work of the ice giant and helped finish off the glass skeletons. "Why all the secrecy, though? Why didn't you make yourself known?"

"You said it yourself. You aren't an agent of Hell, and we didn't know if we could trust you. Well, I did," the demon back-tracked, "but management wasn't so certain. Thus my orders were to remain incognito and to observe."

"And if I hadn't been trustworthy, what were your orders then?"

"Don't try to villainize me, John. I went out of my way to reveal myself to you. Do you really believe I can't fake an Irish accent?" Suddenly Rimmon sounded exactly like Dante. "Or do you think that all demons just happen to speak American English?" His voice sounded normal again. "As an incubus, I use the language and accent most appealing to you. All part of the seduction game."

Rimmon fixed John with a suggestive gaze that made his entire body smolder, but John gathered his willpower to resist. Eventually he managed to lock his arms over his chest and turn his focus to the window. If Hell was looking for a pawn to be played, they wouldn't find one in him.

"Forgive me," Rimmon said, the pressure abating. "As I said, I wanted you to discover the truth, and given your inquisitive nature, had no doubt that you would. Although I must admit, I hoped you would be a little more happy to see me."

John hid his smile. "Now that you're out in the open and I've proven myself trustworthy, you can go without possessing Dante on the next mission."

"Mission?"

"I thought there would be more. Asmoday mentioned multiple realms."

"Yes! Of course. I'm just surprised you are willing to continue. Your dog was almost eaten by an ice giant and your arm ripped off by a god, before you came face to face with your worst fear again."

"It wasn't so bad." John gave a nervous laugh. "Really, for the first time since coming here, I felt alive again."

And it was true. Purgatory was dull by definition, and even a night in Hell had left John feeling directionless. Unlike Dante, he wanted more from the afterlife than booze and sex. Their adventure in Asgard had been the first taste of something more. John had a purpose again, and he didn't want to lose that.

His only concern was knowing which side he was fighting on. As much as he despised the Ministers of Order, he wasn't truly convinced that Hell was the sort of realm he wanted to be associated with. As if on cue, the coach juddered to a halt, the glow of the red light district filling the cabin.

"That was fast."

"Dante belongs here much more than the previous driver did in Asgard," Rimmon said. "I'm surprised we weren't here sooner. Try to revive him if you can, and maybe explain about the possession. He may take the news better from you. Meanwhile, I'll give my report to Asmoday."

"But he's a *gay* demon!" Dante protested half an hour later.

Asmoday rolled all three of his eyes in response. "He's not gay or straight, you idiot! He's an incubus!"

Dante slumped in his chair and glared at John accusingly. John wished that Delilah was in Asmoday's office as she had been the last time. They could use her charms about now.

"Last time I checked," Dante said, "when a bloke sleeps with another bloke, it means he's bent. That's the only qualification. I think Johnny boy here can attest to that!"

"What does it matter, anyway?" John asked, trying hard to suppress a smile.

"Of course it doesn't matter to you!" Dante said, becoming more flustered by the minute. "How would you like it if a straight demon was inside of you? No, never mind. I can only imagine. Make it a female one. A succubus! How would you like that?"

Dante had him there. John didn't have much of a feminine side. Just a sense of style, if that even counted anymore. The idea of being possessed by a female entity would be disquieting.

"Are you saying you would prefer a succubus?" Asmoday asked.

"Yes! Well, no. Don't you have any straight demons?"

"I already told you," the Archduke snarled, "they aren't straight or gay. Rimmon has male and female clients. If it makes you feel better, Delilah has female clients as well."

Even this image wasn't enough to deter Dante. "Why does it have to be a demonic hustler?"

"This isn't open for negotiation," Asmoday growled. "Every soul in existence judges a book by its cover, especially when that book has red skin and horns. You make a nice little disguise, Dante, and you'll continue to convey Rimmon's expertise without spooking our would-be allies before we can even say 'hello.'" The Archduke glared to be sure his point was made, before turning back to John. "As I was saying, my superior is very pleased with your success."

The compliment made John uneasy. There was no mystery as to who Asmoday's superior might be. Learning that the Devil was pleased with John's work didn't exactly conjure warm feelings of contentment.

"You have a lot to gain if you keep working for us," Asmoday continued. "What is it you want? Power, money, an apartment?"

John didn't know what he would do with any of those things. All he truly wanted was something to do, a fact he planned on keeping to himself for now.

"We'll talk payment later. What's next?"

"A man of action! I like it!" Asmoday leaned back in his chair, making it groan. "The Norse gods may be good fighters, but they aren't the most powerful magicians. The Ministers of Order have magic in spades, but so do the Celts. We need the Irish gods on our side."

"Have you sent anyone to them before?" John asked.

"Yeah, and they actually come back in one piece, but they don't remember where they've been or what happened. You might want to avoid eating or drinking while you're there."

"Sounds easy," Dante said, doing his best to sound upbeat. "No problem at all. We should be able to handle this one on our own, just me and John."

"Nice try," Asmoday said. "Rimmon is going with you, and if I hear one more complaint about it, you're going to find out what it's really like to have a gay demon inside you, catch my drift?"

When they left Asmoday's office, they found Rimmon leaning against the coach. Bolo was at his side, tense with anticipation that broke into a full body wag when he spotted John. The coach already had a new driver, a rosy-cheeked, pleasantly plump old woman. How she ended up in Hell was hard to imagine. Maybe she cooked too many high cholesterol casseroles for her neighbors.

"What's her story?" John asked

"Converted to Catholicism in her old age to be absolved of her sins," Rimmon answered, "but that didn't stop her from sleeping with her husband's brother. Or the local miller. Or the miller's teenage son. She was a very busy lady until her final days and didn't make it to confession, although sleeping with the priest comes close."

"Off we go, then," the old woman said in an accent thick enough to rival Dante's. "I haven't got all eternity."

"Wait a minute!" Dante said as Rimmon neared him. "Just had an idea. Can't you possess John instead? Or how about the dog. Bolo won't mind!"

"Only works on denizens of Hell, sorry."

At least the process appeared painless. Rimmon simply stepped into the same space that Dante occupied before disappearing. Not that the Irishman took it well. He was instantly pale, but this time he didn't appear nauseous.

"It's nothing against you," Dante said once they were sitting in the coach cabin. "My brother is gay. Only came out to me, not that the whole family doesn't suspect, so it isn't if I haven't been around your kind. Truth is, I'd rather not be possessed at all, so it hardly has anything to do with what you or demon boy get up to."

"I was impressed you didn't mention it when I showed up with Rimmon the first time," John confided.

"I didn't pin you for the type, but it's no concern of mine."

"If it's any consolation, the moments Rimmon shines through you make you all the more attractive. When you aren't breathing fire I mean. Each time Rimmon talks through you, a lot of that incubus allure is there. If I find it attractive, then the ladies will too."

Dante mulled this over. "Not bad for a silver lining," he said, pulling the lever that sent the coach rolling. "Maybe Rimmon and I can reach some sort of agreement. There's bound to be some Celtic beauties where we're headed."

"I'll show you a good time!" the old woman cackled from the driver's seat as the coach reached escape velocity.

"Then again," Dante said, "maybe it's best not to mix business with pleasure."

Light glittered off the ocean below, white crests of waves breaking around lush, green islands. The coach veered sharply toward the smallest of these land masses, nose-diving at an alarming speed before righting itself in time for landing. With a thud the coach hit the ground, the driver toppling off the seat and onto the beach the second the straps released her.

"This is more like it!" she crooned.

Bolo agreed with her, launching himself out of the coach the moment the door was open and racing happily across the sand.

John smiled as he followed, enjoying the warm breeze on his face and the taste of salt in the air. Dante seemed to be enjoying it too, although his clothing made him appear out of place anywhere other than a city.

Instinct led them down the beach to a long narrow boat. The decorative prow and stern of the vessel twisted gracefully into curls; the colorful sails a mixture of turquoise, violet, and green. These sails puffed out proudly in the wind, but despite the force gathered there the ship remained motionless, not even rocking. Even the ramp that stretched from the ship to the beach was still and steady.

A god stood on deck, waiting near the ramp as if he were the captain and they the expected passengers. This was Manannan mac Lir, Celtic lord of the ocean and master over weather. The seas were his domain, as were the islands of paradise that lay beyond. Despite his status, the god's demeanor was casual, a half-smile playing about his lips. He pulled a pipe from his pale blue robe and raised it to them in greeting as they neared.

The old woman reached him first, a mixture of reverence and fear on her face.

"Marga, you treacherous thing!" Manannan said, his brow furrowing and his white beard bristling. His manner was so intimidating that they all took a step backwards. "What business do you have here?"

"Forgive me!" Marga pleaded. "All those stories about Hell spooked me good, so I figured converting wouldn't do no harm. I've suffered for what I done, but I don't expect no mercy from you."

A grin chased the ferociousness from Manannan's face. "There's nothing to forgive, you old fool! You could have come directly here if you hadn't been waylaid by such nonsense. On the boat with you!"

The sea god jerked his thumb over his shoulder, and Marga scrambled eagerly up the ramp. Bolo followed her, oblivious of the need for permission. Next Manannan turned to them, his penetrating eyes the subtle blue of the morning sky.

"What an interesting pair Hell has sent us this time," he said. "I can see why they specialize in temptation, as I'm almost persuaded to bring you along."

"We just want to talk," John assured him. "We mean no harm."

"And yet words can be the most harmful weapons." Manannan lit his pipe and took a deep drag. "I wonder, are either of you aware of your conditions?"

"Take us with you and you'll find out," Dante bargained.

"Our conditions?" John asked.

"Well, well," Manannan replied. "With the two of you along, this voyage might be interesting indeed, although it remains to be seen how much you will remember."

The second John and Dante were on deck, the ramp disappeared. John barely had time to look around before Marga took his arm and blinked her eyelashes in a way that he didn't find at all becoming. He tried pulling away, but Marga's grip was surprisingly firm.

"To think I could have come sooner," she said. "A demon let slip that my chains were of me own making. How's that for a thing?"

No mystery there, John thought. After all, they had needed a driver to the Celtic lands. What John didn't understand was what Manannan meant by him and Dante having a condition. If Dante's was the demon inside him, what was John's? He had thought the great secret in Asmoday's office had related to Rimmon possessing Dante, but now that he considered it, Dante had seemed just as surprised by that. Now John was back to wondering what was being kept from him.

Manannan pulled on his pipe and with a nod the boat slid forward, turning away from the beach and slipping into the ocean. Waves broke in two and parted for the vessel, allowing it to sail forward as if it were gliding across a perfectly still lake. The ship's wheel, turning of its own accord, steered them toward an empty horizon while Bolo scampered up and down the deck in excitement. Dante leaned against the rail a few paces away, leaving John, Marga, and Manannan to talk alone.

"Where are we going?" John asked.

"To Mag Mell," Manannan answered. "The land of promise where there is music, dancing, and storytelling in abundance. The souls there want for nothing, not food, company, happiness, or even youth."

Marga released John with a gasp. "Oh, would you look at that!"

John turned unwillingly back toward Marga, who was examining her hand in awe. The woman looked different now. She had lost some weight, and her features were tighter. As he watched the gray hair was chased away by a rich auburn, making her appear middle-aged. He didn't doubt that the process would continue until they reached their destination, leaving the woman in her prime. How easily he had become used to such wonders! John only hoped that his own age would remain intact. He had no urge to revisit his teenage years.

John returned his attention to Manannan. "Are you taking us there to meet with the other gods?"

"I am bringing Marga home to be reunited with her friends

and family," Manannan said. "It remains to be seen how far I allow you and your companions to travel."

"Well thank you for trusting us so far." John decided that now was his only chance to make his intentions known. "I don't know how much the other ambassadors told you, but we're actually here because we need your help. Are you familiar with Heaven?"

"Yes," Manannan said, "and now that I have answered three of your questions, it is time for you to answer three of mine."

"Oh." John wasn't sure if this was a custom or a challenge, but he saw no choice but to comply. "Okay."

"Are you trying to deceive me?"

Manannan's tones were casual. He didn't sound angry or defensive, but his penetrating eyes were locked onto John's as he waited for an answer. Were they deceiving him? John supposed they were intentionally hiding Rimmon, which did seem dishonest. But that wasn't lying, per say. That was simply holding back the truth. John had fought with more than one boyfriend over the intricacies of this philosophy, and had been on both sides of the argument at least once. In the current situation, he supposed they *were* being deceptive, but in the most harmless way possible.

"No, we're not deceiving you."

Manannan puffed on his pipe and exhaled, the dark smoke swiftly blown away by the increasing wind. John glanced away from him to notice dark storm clouds on the horizon, still far away.

Marga, growing bored with the conversation, moved over to join Dante. She looked as though she was in her early thirties now, and it was much easier to understand how she had been able to seduce so many men. She wrapped an arm around Dante, who didn't seem to mind.

"The help you seek from us," Manannan continued. "Do you feel the cause is just?"

The war against Heaven? John couldn't say it was, since he didn't truly know if Heaven was to blame. Asmoday had implied that freeing Purgatory was part of his campaign against Heaven, but John still had his doubts. Regardless, he wasn't going to earn Manannan's respect by saying they were here for an illicit purpose. John would sort out his misgivings later, but for now he wanted to avoid his memory being erased.

"Our cause is just," he answered confidently.

A sudden wind whipped John from behind, ruffling his clothing and hair. When he looked up, the storm clouds were now directly above them, a churning black maelstrom that grumbled and flashed. The winds kept ravaging the ship, sending it rocking back and forth. This was no coincidence. If Manannan's realm was the sea and the weather, then surely their environment was a reflection of his mood. John had lied twice, and only had one more chance to get it right.

Marga sidled up to them with Dante in tow. "We better get some shelter above our head," she said. She held up a hand to ward away the rain that had begun pelting down. "I'd be mighty thankful to go below deck."

"Of course. Off you go," Manannan said. "Not you," he added, when Dante moved to follow. "You stay here."

"What did I do wrong?" Dante asked defensively.

"You haven't answered my third question."

"Fine. Ask away."

Manannan's face was grim. "Is there a stowaway aboard my ship?"

Rimmon! Of course there was and they had to answer honestly, or else—

"Nope," Dante said, heading to where Marga had disappeared. "No stowaways here."

The storm above them exploded, an instant hurricane that sent the ship lurching. Torrents of rain washed across the deck as the winds howled. Dante was knocked on his backside and John stumbled, trying to find his footing on the now slippery deck. He grabbed hold of the rail and searched the deck for Bolo. Manannan was standing still as if the weather was calm, and Dante was smart enough to stay down, but John couldn't find the dog through the sheets of rain.

What he did see was the giant wave rushing toward the opposite side of the ship. The wave's height was tremendous, Manannan's ship a miniscule toy boat in comparison. John could only gape in horror before it came crashing down, clinging for dear life to the rail as his body was flung to and fro. Then he found himself slamming into the side of the boat, his feet no longer touching the deck. He was overboard, his tenuous grip on the rail his only lifeline.

John clung desperately to the rail, coughing up water as he readjusted his grip. He glanced down to see vicious waves lapping at his feet. He may be dead, but his fingers hurt like only the living could as he tried to gain enough purchase to pull himself up. Cold and numb, he could feel his fingers slipping as the boat kept lurching. In seconds he would be shaken free and lost to Manannan's angry sea.

Hands grabbed John's wrists, strong and red. They hoisted him upward, one hand releasing him so an arm could be thrown around his waist. John was pulled into Rimmon's comforting warm embrace.

"I am Hell's true ambassador," Rimmon yelled over the din as he held John protectively. "I will answer your three questions. Our only deception is borne out of prejudice, a cause is only as just as each man's heart decrees, and the only stowaway aboard this ship is me."

The rain, wind, waves, and thunder all ceased. The clouds dispersed within seconds, blue sky breaking through as sunlight reflected off the wet deck.

"Your honesty is appreciated," Manannan said with a twinkle in his eye. His pipe was still lit and his clothes bone dry.

Rimmon released John. As soon as John spotted Bolo and Dante, both soaking wet but still on deck, he groaned with relief and slid down the sideboard to sit on the deck. Rimmon moved away to speak with Manannan properly, while John tried to decide if he wanted to curl up into a ball or laugh. He allowed himself a few selfish moments, basking in the sunlight and enjoying the now smooth motion of the ship, before he stood again. He hadn't been honest with Manannan, and felt he needed to make amends by coming clean. The sea god was right. Their cause wasn't just, and John was no longer okay with that.

"Look at what tolerance toward the new religion has resulted in," Rimmon was saying. "Ireland has forgotten the Celtic gods completely and has been split in two. If you had fought against them from the beginning—"

"Some of us did fight," Manannan interrupted, his tone as steady as the boat's course, "but the wisest among us recognized that change is the one reliable constant in the physical world. We were once the new religion as well, replacing gods that truly have been lost to history. No, we old gods took our turn, basking in the light of believers until it was our time to move on, although many still discover us to this day."

"Comparing modern Paganism to that of old is comparing bread and water to a king's feast," Rimmon pressed. "You were once in the minds of an entire race! How can you truly be satisfied now?"

"And yet we are," Manannan replied. "Those who loved us in life are now with us here. That we are still remembered, our stories still told in the physical world, is the greatest of honors."

"It's your new followers who you should be worried about," John interjected, seeing his opportunity. He told Manannan of the situation in Purgatory, of how people were trapped there for all eternity. "Jacobi, a friend of ours, has been there since the changes began and when souls from other pantheons began arriving. I saw some of them myself. Have you noticed anyone missing? Anyone that you expected to show but who didn't?"

Manannan glanced meaningfully around the near-empty boat. "And how will warring with Heaven solve this problem?"

"It won't," John said. "The truth is, we don't know if Heaven is behind the changes in Purgatory."

Rimmon was clearly taken aback by this statement, but John had his own axe to grind. He no longer wanted to encourage a war against what might be an innocent realm. All he could be sure of was that the situation in Purgatory was wrong. If he played his cards right, he might be able to do something about it.

"Purgatory has always been under Heaven's jurisdiction," Rimmon said.

"Who is responsible doesn't matter," John said. "Good people are imprisoned, souls who need our help. Not all of them belong to your pantheon, but you can bet people there are silently praying for their gods to come free them. You say it's an honor to still be in the minds and hearts of these people. Well, maybe it's time to repay that love by doing something for them."

Manannan's eyes twinkled. "Are you sure you aren't a denizen of Hell? You have quite the silver tongue."

"I think that tongue could use some polishing," Rimmon smiled, "but he does make an interesting point."

"What is it to be, then?" Manannan asked. "Does Hell want to wage war against Heaven or Purgatory?"

Rimmon hesitated. "Hell only wishes to pool our resources,"

he said. "Together we can free the souls and return them to where they belong. Of course finding the culprit behind the recent changes is also a priority. Hell is interested in retuning balance to the realms, and dispensing justice is a crucial part of this plan. What say you, Manannan?"

"Such decisions are not mine alone to make. I speak only for myself and not the pantheon, but after hearing the impassioned words of you both, I will tentatively lend you my support. On one condition, which is that you must convince the other gods here." Manannan gestured ahead of them. "Gentlemen, welcome to Mag Mell."

The boat's journey over, they had reached an island thick with trees. The forest beyond was filled with the sounds of animal life. Marga, now young and buxom, squealed happily as she ran down the ramp toward the people gathered there. They embraced her enthusiastically, a tearful reunion that eventually moved into the trees.

"Her family?" John asked.

Manannan nodded. "I should have erased your memories and sent you away like I did the others," he said. "Although in your case, John, I wonder if I even could. Regardless, you've seduced me with your words, and I will allow you to continue your journey."

Rimmon clamped a hand companionably on the sea god's shoulder. "Your support is much appreciated."

"You may not find the others so easy to convince. I will summon a guide to take you further, although you had better slip back inside your friend. I can understand your fear of prejudice, and Cernunnos isn't fond of demons. He feels, perhaps rightly, that they stole his image."

Once Dante and Rimmon were joined again, Manannan placed his fingers to his lips and gave a shrill whistle. Birds erupted from the forest and took to the sky, not in reaction to the sound but what it had summoned.

At first John thought an elk was appearing from between the trees, for the antlers first drew his attention. They were a deep mahogany, stretching wide and tall from each side of the god's shaggy head. Stubble dominated Cernunnos' chin, the same dark shade of hair that covered his muscular torso, trailed down his stomach, and ended in a thick tuft just above his crotch. John didn't need the god's aura to explain that he was an avatar of fertility. If the nudity wasn't indication enough, his considerable endowment drove the point home.

Cernunnos moved like the animals under his domain, falling onto all fours to gallop toward them, his arms bulging with thick ropes of muscle that drove him forward with incredible speed. The god of animals came to a halt at the end of his territory, the point where the grass ended but before the beach began.

"Hail, Manannan!" he called in a gruff voice as he stood again.

"A pleasant day to you, Horned One," Manannan replied. "Against my better judgment, I've allowed two of Hell's ambassadors to take advantage of my good nature."

"They won't fare so well with me," Cernunnos promised.

John tried to leave the boat last, hoping if he lingered long enough he could speak with Manannan, to ask quickly what his condition was, but Dante stayed at his side like a Secret Service agent.

"We shall meet again," Manannan said, perhaps picking up on John's intentions. "After all, someone must bring you back to your coach."

John swallowed his frustration and disembarked. Bolo was one step ahead of him, as usual. The dog had already reached Cernunnos, but instead of his usual excited antics, he was sitting calmly with his full attention focused on the god. John couldn't help but join the dog in his admiration, feeling pulled in by the pure masculinity that seeped from Cernunnos.

He reeked of sexuality, of the irresistible primal urge to mate. Cernunnos carried the musky smell of animals and had a wildness in his eyes that was both mesmerizing and frightening. His very nature called to the beast in John's soul and made him want to rip off his clothes, cast off the starchy mantle of civilization, and be free again.

Without warning, Cernunnos turned and with an impressive burst of speed, shot toward the forest; John, Dante, and Bolo followed. The chase was on! Animal instinct whipped them into action as they raced after their prey. Two legs weren't fast enough. Bolo was already leagues ahead, but John's body knew what to do. He fell forward, landing painlessly on his knuckles and broke into a gallop. Dante had done the same. He was at

John's side, his eyes mad with exhilaration.

They broke through the line of trees and plunged into shadow. Obstacles were everywhere, but they didn't slow. Like possessed beasts they raced on, dodging around tress, sending leaves and twigs flying as they increased their speed. They were gaining on the horned god. John could see his flanks drawing nearer. He bared his teeth, overwhelmed by a terrible urge to bite into the flesh of his prey and draw it down to the ground.

The sun beat down on the clearing ahead that Cernunnos escaped into. The horned god stopped when he reached its center, skidding around in a circle to face them, his antlers creating a death trap. Bolo was the first to stop, then John before Dante collided into him. They ended up in a pile, just inches away from the fierce points of the antlers.

Cernunnos stood, towering over them. "Well? What words did you bring? What tricks did you think would turn us from our path?"

John struggled to find his voice as they regained their feet. The animal instincts had fled from him, but his mind hadn't yet recovered.

Cernunnos sniffed, his wide nostrils flaring as he sampled each of them before settling on Dante.

"What is that smell on you? An ox? A goat? Something with horns. Something close to me, but you aren't one of mine."

John waited for Rimmon to appear, but the demon stayed hidden. Cernunnos stomped a circle around Dante, guttural animal noises rising from his chest.

"You don't look like a demon." He took another deep whiff. "But there's no mistaking that smell. Your kind stole their scent from me."

"Don't go blaming me," Dante said. "Some friends you can't choose. Associations that you didn't ask for, if you catch my drift."

Cernunnos huffed, took a step back, and howled. The sound was terrifying, an immensely deep chord that made them shudder. Movement came from the trees. The first to step into the clearing was a bear, followed by a leopard and a boar. Then the stags came, at least a dozen of them. They were brawny creatures, their coats and hooves glossy with health, but it was the impressive racks that intimidated as they were lowered.

A low growl began in Bolo's chest, confirming the intended threat.

John swallowed. He needed a distraction. "These animals are yours," he said, "but is this where all animals go when they die?"

"Words," Cernunnos hissed as his beasts began to advance.

"How many stags did we see trapped in Purgatory?" John asked.

"Oh, I don't know," Dante answered smoothly, having caught on. "Ten? Twenty? Enough that it was hard to count."

"Empty and hollow words!" Cernunnos snarled. "Pots sculpted from liar's clay."

Bolo's growl broke into a whimper. They were done for. The dog could sense what humans couldn't and must have known no hope was left. Cernunnos meant to kill them, or whatever horrible condition he could inflict on them, except that the woodland god's complete attention was now focused on the dog. He growled at the dog and dipped his head in a feigned attack, but Bolo didn't back down. Instead he barked, dodging back and forth as if Cernunnos were a sheep he could herd. Cernunnos growled back, but Bolo continued to be a moving target. Then they both ceased this odd game.

"This hound vouches for you," Cernunnos said. "You freed him, but there were many more."

"That's why we want to go back and fight." John hesitated, wanting to say more but realizing that Cernunnos had little patience for words. The horned god thought. As he did so, the surrounding beasts relaxed and dispersed, disappearing back into the forest.

"Those before you had nothing to say about the animals," Cernunnos said.

"Maybe they didn't know," John said. "This is about freeing trapped souls, animals included. That's all you need agree to."

Cernunnos's eyes narrowed in suspicion. "I will free the animals, but no more than that."

John breathed a sigh of relief. "That's more than enough, but we'll need help reaching them. There's a barrier—"

"Come," Cernunnos beckoned them forward. "Save your words for the other gods."

One moment they were on trial, the next they had gained a new ally. John couldn't remember the last time he'd had so much fun! Maybe being an architectural engineer hadn't been the right job for him, when he could have sought his thrills as a hostage negotiator or something similar.

The woods Cernunnos led them through were full of life. Two foxes cut across their path, absorbed in chasing each other. Birds flitted from tree to tree, and the underbrush rustled with unseen activity. Squirrels chattered and deer grazed fearlessly, as if they were in the Garden of Eden.

"So, *is* this where animals go when they die?" John asked again.

"The animals go where they please," Cernunnos said. "They are not pulled to one place, as human souls are. Unburdened by religion, they are free."

"I've noticed Bolo does whatever he likes," Dante muttered.

Cernunnos nodded. "Dogs have no dogma."

"But what about atheists?" John asked. "Plenty of people aren't religious. What happens to them?"

The horned god shrugged. "They do not interest me. I tire of speaking. Let us run again."

John was all too glad to comply.

The sun was setting when they reached the edge of the woods and, soon after, the end of the island. Humps of grassy hills rolled along until they were interrupted by ocean-battered cliffs. The world was quiet here, the call of seagulls notably absent. Cernunnos led them toward a long, mounded hill broken by a dark opening.

A woman appeared out of the shadows. She was wrapped in a cloak of dark feathers, her slick, black hair a scarf around her neck. Her skin was the ivory of a moon set against the night sky, for that was what she was. Cerridwen, goddess of the moon, knowledge, magic, and transformation.

"Greetings, Horned One." Her voice was the breeze at midnight. "That you bring company suggests business instead of pleasure."

"I always seek your pleasure," Cernunnos answered. "Dispose of these visitors, and these silent cliffs shall be filled with our howls."

"Then I shall not let them delay me long." The goddess smiled. "Come gentlemen, come away with me."

They didn't need to move. The darkness from the hill's entrance spilled out and enveloped the world. Cernunnos and his woods, the sky above and crashing waves below, all were gone. John was barely able to see Dante and Bolo, their faces pale in the glowing light of Cerridwen's skin. The goddess glided away from them, and if they didn't follow, they would have no light left to see by. They chased after the goddess, who appeared to progress by a casual stroll, but they couldn't quite reach her. The glow of Cerridwen's skin intensified as they moved through the darkness, illuminating their surroundings.

The path they were walking twisted downward through a cave. The time-smoothed walls were covered in writing, strange chopstick letters from a language John didn't recognize. He tried to decipher words, to find meaning in the symbols, until the walls fell away. They had entered a large cavern, the echoes from their footsteps distant. Soon the goddess ahead of them was all they could see, their surroundings lost again to darkness. She was much further ahead than she had been before. The idea of losing her panicked them. Without her they would be lost in a void, deprived of their most precious sense.

"Hurry," John hissed, but there was no response from his friends. Desperately he cast his arms out to either side, but found no one there. Nor was there a reply when he called their names. Even Rimmon's name failed to provoke a response.

Cerridwen was little more than a slowly ascending ball of light in the distance. John's head spun with disorientation. Did the path ahead gain height? Was the goddess climbing? She continued to rise until she was far above his head. John stopped and stared. He could not follow. There was no possibility of reaching her. Cerridwen had become the moon, a solitary light in the endless night surrounding him.

The ghostly remnants of a song echoed in the distance, a multitude of voices harmonized into one that sounded familiar, although John couldn't quite remember where he had heard it before. Pressure on his shoulder caused him to gasp. He turned, expecting to find Dante, but found instead the goddess next to him, even though the moon was still shining from above. Cerridwen looked different now, older, but age had made her more dignified, more mysterious.

"Cernunnos brings out the girl in me," she explained,

unprompted. "The moon revolves around the earth, and such is my attraction to him, for he is very much a part of the land. In the same way the ocean waters strain to reach me, the tides rushing back and forth in the hopes of entrancing me, Manannan's eyes burn bright for me. We are balanced, you see? Earth, sky, and water, but it will not always be so."

John stared, fixed by her words and unable to find any of his own as she continued.

"The war you propose has already begun, triggered by your actions. The Ministers of Order felt the death of their own in Asgard. Already they move to silence the other pantheons. They mean to break us down like pieces of a stone, dividing and separating us until we are gravel, sand, dust. You must bring us together. Seek out the other dark gods, those who understand the depths of the underworld. Prepare them to move, to slither beneath the roots of the world tree and into the warmth of the fiery pits. Whether they agree to fight or not, they must come."

The goddess placed her pale hands on his forehead, and John's mind filled with names, dozens of them. They settled there where he could always find them, even though he wasn't sure what purpose they held. He turned to ask, but Cerridwen was gone.

John looked at the moon, now sallow and heavy on the horizon. He took a few steps forward, encouraged when it did not move away from him. The moon was stationary as he continued to walk, although he noticed that its shape wasn't right, too rough around the edges and flat at the bottom.

Sounds came to him, conversation, chairs skidding on the floor, and the crackle of a fire. John rushed forward, recognizing that what he mistook as the moon was a doorway. He burst into a cavern, warm with heat and the scent of food. Seated around a large round table were dozens of gods. John focused on them only momentarily, feeling overwhelmed by so many powerful auras in such a small space.

"Where'd you get to?" Dante asked, approaching with Bolo.

"I was—" John hesitated, unsure of how to explain it. "Well, how did you get here?"

"We followed her." Dante nodded toward the table.

Cerridwen was seated there. Her eyes met his momentarily and were filled with meaning before she turned back to the proceedings. Cernunnos was to her right. Further down the table, Manannan was deep in thought.

"I think they're going to join," Dante whispered. "Assuming she doesn't up and slaughter us in her excitement."

There was no question of who he was referring to. The Morrigan was standing now, vehemently outlining the reasons they should go to war and occasionally striking the table with her fist. The war goddess had the attention of everyone in attendance. She radiated authority and power, and yet somehow John knew she was not the leader of this pantheon.

John searched the table, trying to determine who the leaders were in order to gage their reaction. Lugh was nearest to the Morrigan, a capable warrior in his own right. Next to him was Brighid, threefold goddess of poetry, smithcraft, and healing. Her face, framed by fiery red hair, wasn't as convinced as some of the others. The Dagda was the next in line, and for a moment John thought he was the leader. The older god watched the proceedings with confident experience. Perhaps he had once led his people or was often looked to for guidance, but he wasn't an exact match. The next chair was empty.

John stared at it, a name calling out to him but too muddled for him to understand. Whoever sat there, the one person missing, was their leader. But who was that person, and why were they absent? He strode over to the chair in a dream state. Nothing had felt quite real since he walked through the night, chasing after Cerridwen. John reached the chair and placed his hand on its back, pulling it back slightly as if to sit. Whoever had sat there was divine, and their aura still clung to it. He could almost feel the missing god's warmth. John moved his hands along the chair, exploring the surface and earning himself a splinter in the process, but the pain was just enough to send him over the edge.

A goddess, mother to most of the deities here. The wife of the Dagda, she was a goddess of fertility and wise leader of her people. And then it came to him, the name on the tip of his tongue.

"Danu!" he said out loud.

The room was suddenly quiet. All eyes were turned on him, some questioning, others accusatory until someone cleared his throat. It was Manannan.

"We have decided to go to war," he said.

* * * * *

Manannan's ship was waiting for them when they exited into daylight again. The tides had risen high enough to swallow up the once-steep cliffs, and John knew better than to wonder at this improbability. Instead he considered how Manannan could have dropped them off here in the first place, rather than making them chase through the woods with Cernunnos. Just more evidence of the gods and their games.

Much to John's surprise, he found a private moment with Manannan. Dante was making himself scarce as possible, no doubt because of the golden goblet he had pilfered from the feast table, and Rimmon was stuck with him. Another of the Celtic deities had decided to see them off: Brighid stood at the ship's stern, her freckled face upturned to the sun. Even though the Celts had agreed to join with Hell, revealing now that a demon had been hiding in their midst would appear dishonest.

This was the perfect opportunity to find out what everyone conspired to keep from him. John decided to approach the issue with tact, even though he feared his privacy with the sea god might not last, and asked instead another question that had been troubling him.

"Cernunnos mentioned that religion determines where we go when we die."

"Belief more than religion," Manannan corrected.

"So what happens to people who don't believe in anything?"

"Any number of things. An atheist, for instance, might cease to exist if determined enough. That is, the soul will revert to the ether that we are all created from. Not necessarily though. Faced with new information, an atheist might become agnostic and find himself wandering, trying to understand the situation better or find the realm best suited to him. Visits such as yours weren't so rare at one time."

"But now they are?"

Manannan nodded. "We thought there was some form of campaigning, another afterlife venturing out and recruiting these souls to their own cause, but now we know that Purgatory is to blame. Any lost soul is now drawn to Purgatory and imprisoned there, but for what purpose?"

"I don't know," John murmured. "Do you think my condition is what drew me there?"

Manannan was silent for a moment. "Your friends seem to think that you aren't aware of your unique properties."

John tensed. Dante, maybe even Rimmon, had gotten to Manannan first. "It doesn't seem fair that they know something about me that I don't."

"They have your best interests at heart, or at least they feel they do."

"And you?"

"I think you are stronger than any of them realize."

Bolo began barking, his front legs against the starboard bow so he could see over the edge. The English Shepherd had been watching the water the whole trip, but now a school of dolphins had noticed him and were putting on a show. Brighid laughed and Dante's caution was forgotten as he approached to see what all the commotion was about.

"Tell me what it is," John pleaded. "Quickly."

"I'm afraid I promised not to," Manannan said, "but perhaps if you took a seat and gave it all a good think, you might find yourself drawn to the answer. Oh, look! Your coach!"

John stared blankly at the little island and their ride home before it clicked. What if he took the driver's seat? The steam coach was supposed to take any soul to where it belonged. He wasn't sure how this would answer his question, but it was the biggest lead he had.

"Thank you," John said.

"There's nothing to thank me for," Manannan replied. "We all deserve to know where we belong, but be warned, some journeys are more difficult to return from than others."

Chapter Eight

John waited in the coach, absentmindedly petting Bolo while Rimmon strapped Dante in the driver's seat. With Manannan's boat having set sail, Rimmon could show himself again, and John was eager for the chance to talk to him alone before they reached Hell.

So much was happening so quickly. Being trapped in Purgatory seemed a distant event of weeks or months ago. John still didn't understand how time functioned in the afterlife, but he knew that if he were alive, he would be desperate to crawl into bed about now. As it was, John felt great, especially since he had more to do than ever.

The tip Manannan had given him, the key to the secret that was being kept from him, was far from his most immediate concern. Instead he kept thinking of what he had said to the other gods, how Heaven wasn't their target. Purgatory was. Standing up for his convictions had been easy at the time, but soon Asmoday would hear a full report. John could only imagine that the Archduke's reaction wouldn't be pretty.

The coach door opened and Rimmon climbed inside. He gave John the sort of look reserved for meeting a date. Not a first date, but a few later when the sex was really gearing up and getting exciting.

"We have to stop meeting like this," John teased.

"Oh, I don't know." Rimmon ran his fingers over the brass-tipped lever before grasping it and giving it a healthy jerk. "A little alone time could be just what the doctor ordered."

John braced himself as the coach lurched forward, barely managing to get an arm around Bolo to prevent him from sliding off the bench. "Then again," he said, "this van is rocking enough as it is."

Rimmon stretched himself wide on the bench, arms and legs splayed open in a very clear invitation. "Maybe we can counteract that motion."

"Sounds good. Just show me written permission from your boyfriend and we'll get started." John meant it as a joke, but Rimmon looked pained, if only for a second. John wondered, not for the first time, what the true story behind their relationship was. "Sorry. I guess that was a little below the belt."

They both considered the potential humor in this expression and grinned.

"Nothing to worry about," Rimmon said. "The mistakes of the past are mine to bear."

John hated to cause the incubus further pain, but he had to know. "If this job causes so much strain between you and your boyfriend, why don't you do something different? I know you said it's your nature, but surely your line of work only makes it more tempting."

Rimmon sighed. "You were born a human, but why did you never strip off your clothes and live among the apes? I don't mean to insult you or the origin of your species, but would you be happy living in the trees, picking lice from your neighbor as a snack?"

"Oh, I don't know," John said. "Beats working in a cubical."

"My point is that either of us could try to change our nature and be something that we're not, but neither one of us would be happy. I'm very good at what I do, and I enjoy it. I've found my calling, just as you seem to have."

"What do you mean?"

"You didn't need my help at all with the Celts, and you've found a cause worth rallying behind. It's been a pleasure watching you work. Hell should gracefully step aside and allow you to carry on with your goals."

"Really? What do you think, though? About going after Purgatory, I mean. Do you think it's the right thing to do?"

"Not many people worry about what an incubus thinks, and to be honest, I prefer it that way." Rimmon paused. "But since it's you, and I know that questions plague your mind like fleas on a dog, then yes, I think what you're suggesting is much more sensible than Asmoday's plan."

"Do you think Asmoday will feel the same way?"

Rimmon laughed much longer than John liked. "No," he said. "No, Asmoday won't like the idea at all, but let me worry about him."

"Thanks, but don't think I didn't notice you changing topics."

Rimmon crossed his arms and legs, looking sidelong out the coach window. "Very well. The reason I don't quit my job to please my boyfriend is because it is already too late. He refuses to see me, and no matter how often I try, he never answers my summons. There's no sense in stopping what I do now, because it has already driven him away."

"I'm sorry."

"Don't be. I'm the one foolish enough to still give him such a title, to refer to him as a boyfriend, lover, or any other self-deluding term of endearment that helps keep my sorrow at bay."

John didn't know what to say, but he hated to see the incubus miserable, so he tried flirting. "Hey, at least I don't need that permission slip now."

Rimmon rewarded John's attempt with a sporting smile, but the incubus was still troubled. The remaining trip to Hell passed mostly in silence. John wished he could find comforting words to make up for those he had already spoken. Manannan was right. Words could be the most harmful weapon, and perhaps Cernunnos was right to mistrust them so deeply.

As soon as they returned to Hell, so did John's anxiety. He waited outside with Dante and Bolo, but even the sights of the red light district didn't distract him. Despite Rimmon's assurance that he'd handle Asmoday, John couldn't help feeling nervous. He wasn't sure what the Archduke would do in his anger, and he wasn't eager to find out.

"Shit," Dante said, holding up his stolen goblet. The cup had lost its gold sheen and was now an unbecoming brown color. The smell wafting from it wasn't pleasant either. "I mean that literally! This has turned to shit!" He tossed the goblet to the street, where it landed with a wet splotching noise. Bolo ran over to sniff it eagerly.

John laughed. "That's what you get for stealing from gods."

"Irish gods, at least. I think they call that fairy gold."

"You're lucky that's all that happened to you. Stealing from the gods seems risky, even for you."

"If you haven't noticed," Dante said defensively, "my particular afterlife isn't the cheapest place to live. I have to make a living somehow!"

"I just hope I'm not around when you get caught." John hesitated. "When this is all over, do you think you'll be happy here?"

"Here in Hell? No doubt about it. Fits me like a glove. Seeing those farmers and sleepy villages in Asgard made me shudder, and the Celts were just too weird. At least this realm feels like what we knew back home."

"I suppose. You know it's not all like this though. Rimmon showed me. There are people who want to be punished, and in those places it really is fire and brimstone."

Dante shrugged. "I'm not one of them. The only problem I see is that we've gotten caught up in intrigue. Nothing worse than intrigue." He stubbed out his cigarette on the coach. "As soon as this whole mess is over, I hope to be beneath the notice of someone like Asmoday. When you get to the top, all the people below become a threat, and that's everyone. Guys like Asmoday have everything to lose, and they'll cut off your bollocks if they think you have designs on their position."

John eyed the entrance to Asmoday's office. Right now Rimmon was in there telling the Archduke that John had taken matters into his own hands, and more likely than not, Asmoday would find that threatening.

"Me?" Dante continued. "Give me a couple cold ones, good friends, and the occasional woman. That's all I need."

The simple life sounded good right now. John could imagine whiling away a few decades, leisurely exploring the different realms with Bolo and meeting Dante at night for a drink. What was stopping them from walking away right now, leaving the whole idea of war behind and never looking back?

Except John knew it wasn't in his nature, just as monogamy wasn't in Rimmon's. John could climb into that coach seat right now and fly away to wherever he was meant to be, but doing so would take him off the job. He had started something, and he intended to see it through. John wouldn't be able to rest otherwise. People like Dante who found it so easy to release their cares and simply relax, they were the lucky ones. John had never been good at letting go.

The red-lit cabinet swung open, Rimmon's perfect form filling the frame. He smiled seductively, whether he meant to or not, and motioned for them to follow. John braced for the worst. What he didn't expect was for Asmoday to stand and start clapping.

"There's my boys," he said, grinning around the cigar trapped between his onyx teeth. "The heroes of Hell! Have a seat, make yourself comfortable. Delilah!"

The succubus came from the backroom, carrying a tray loaded with all manner of drink. John shook his head at her offer, but Dante didn't hesitate to grab two.

Asmoday leaned forward, splaying both hands flat against his desk. "Good news! The war with Heaven has been called off."

"Called off?" John asked more incredulously than intended.

"Called off," Asmoday repeated. "The idea has weighed heavily on my heart, and I've decided it's not right. We just don't have enough to go on. For all we know, Heaven could be in the same boat as the rest of us, am I right?"

"Could be," John admitted, "but what about the Norse gods? And the Celts?"

"Don't worry, we need them as much as before. Purgatory is still in plight, after all."

John glanced at Rimmon, who was concentrating on the ceiling. Asmoday's change of heart was much too convenient, an obvious ruse to ensure that John kept recruiting for them. No doubt Asmoday had recognized Purgatory as a selling point for coming together and had decided to use it, but the Archduke's true intentions were all too easy to guess.

"So it's business as usual, then?" John asked.

"Onwards and upwards!" Asmoday rubbed his hands together. "We have the warrior skills of the Norse and the magical prowess of the Celts. What we need next is raw power."

The man strapped to the coach's driving seat was a Roman solider, possibly an officer, judging from his highly decorated armor. The arrogant scowl on his face was permanent, refusing to disappear even after John greeted him, and was still there when the coach kicked into motion. The military discipline did not allow any sign of fear or enjoyment on the soldier's face as they picked up speed and left Hell behind.

"I thought you would be happier. Maybe even grateful."

John spared Rimmon a glance. The demon had chosen to stay outside Dante for this part of their journey and was sitting next to John, the heat of his body radiating against his arm.

"Asmoday is playing me," John said. "Why should that make me happy?"

"Because it allows you to do whatever you please," Rimmon replied. "You can continue telling the gods the real reason you want them to join you."

"True, and I like that, but in the end Asmoday still gets his army."

"An army that has been told that we're warring against Purgatory, not Heaven. Asmoday will still try to turn this to his advantage, but I have faith that your will is stronger than his."

John thought about this for a moment. "So you've pit me against an Archduke of Hell, and you expect me to be thankful?"

Rimmon grinned and leaned against John. "I assure you, I have your best interests at heart. Poor Asmoday doesn't know what he's up against."

"Get a room, you two," Dante said across from them. "Or wait until we're in Greece before commencing with the buggery. At least there they'll appreciate it."

John laughed but Rimmon took the comment seriously.

"We're not headed to Greece," he corrected. "The Olympus we're visiting isn't the mountain in the physical world, although it is related. The Greeks knew Mount Olympus wasn't really the home of the gods. They could view the top of the mountain on a clear day and see there was no marble palace there. Instead, Olympus was allegorical, a symbol for a higher realm represented by the highest land known to them. In the afterlife, that symbol became the Olympus of their stories, the actual home of the gods."

"But we have a Roman officer guiding the coach," John said. "Shouldn't we have a Greek philosopher up there or something?"

"Finding a repentant philosopher is no easy task," Rimmon said, "but there are two roads leading to our destination. The Greek myths were so popular with the Roman people that they adapted many of the stories to fit their own deities. Jupiter inherited Zeus's history and attributes until they became more or less indistinguishable. This was the case with the other major gods as well. Even though the concept of Olympus wasn't officially recognized in Rome, the blending together of group belief spread across two cultures created phenomenal metaphysical anomalies that—"

The lecture was cut mercifully short as an explosion shook the coach. A dusty landscape had appeared beneath them, filled with soldiers, horses, and catapults. On each horizon were organized formations, but for the most part the battle had descended into chaos. Olympus was at war.

The coach shuddered and spun, Rimmon snarling in frustration. This could barely be heard over the driver's furious shouting. The officer was desperate to join the battle below, his intent so strong that it threatened to send the coach crashing directly into the fray. Poor Bolo was sliding back and forth along the floor of the coach, his claws skittering for purchase. John wanted to help him, but it was all he could do to not fall over himself.

"His mind is almost as stubborn as yours!" Rimmon cursed as he tried to stand but ended up tripping over the dog instead. "Damn it! I'll be right back."

"Where is there to go?" John spluttered.

As an answer, Rimmon opened the coach door, swinging out dangerously with it. He managed to maneuver himself to the other side of the door before it slammed shut again. John watched in fascination as Rimmon steadily gouged his way toward the driver, his normally well-groomed nails now extended into deadly claws.

The coach dropped abruptly. Outside the window, an enormous beast with a hundred heads and just as many arms towered over the landscape. John stared with terror and revulsion, his gaze met by a dozen pairs of eyes as their comparatively small vessel was noticed. The beast roared from a multitude of mouths, a hundred hands reaching out to crush them when the coach lurched and gained altitude again.

Rimmon was shouting something at the driver, most of his words lost in the wind, but "Olympus" and "gods" were among them. Finally the demon lost all patience and grabbed the officer's head, forcing him to look farther along the plains toward a great, cloud-covered mountain.

The coach shot upward at an angle that sent them directly into the clouds, and for a moment they seemed to have escaped the chaos. Rising to the very top of the mountain, they could see a number of white-columned palaces, decorative gardens, and fountains. The sight was serene until sunlight glinted off moving figures scattered among the buildings. John's stomach sank. They were men made of glass. The Ministers of Order were already here.

The coach lurched again, the officer sensing that something

was amiss. Rimmon struggled with him, forcing him to focus on a large, domed temple. The direction was achieved but stability was not. A crash landing was imminent. Dante and John both covered their heads, an instinct left from life.

The collision was painless but confusing. By the time the coach had skidded to a stop, John's face was buried in Bolo's stomach with Dante's body keeping it pressed there. John tried unsuccessfully to push Dante off until he realized that his world was upside down. Bolo was on top of him and they were both crushing Dante.

After enough struggling and swearing, they managed to push open the coach door—which was now above them—and clamber out, except Bolo, who was stuck. They found themselves inside the domed temple. The coach had made it through the huge open entrance before crashing and skidding a fair distance into the building. The ceiling was high and constructed out of white marble, like everything else in sight. All around them, placed rather randomly, were statues of the gods. The Roman officer frantically prayed to one before determination returned to his features, and he ran toward daylight.

"So eager to fight," Rimmon murmured. The demon placed his hands on the coach and heaved, muscles flexing until it rocked back onto its wheels, allowing Bolo to hop out.

"Did you see the glass men?" John asked.

"I saw them," Rimmon grunted, "and their handiwork." The incubus gestured to the statues around them.

"No!" John breathed, approaching the nearest. The sculpture was of Venus, her feminine beauty and aura of love unmistakable. On touching the statue, John could tell something was wrong. The sculpture wasn't made of marble. The stone gave to his touch, like skin that had turned gray and stiff. He could feel something just below the surface, an emanating life force.

"These statues are the gods?"

Rimmon nodded.

"Can we help them?"

"Maybe. I'd like to get them out of here before the Ministers return to finish the job."

"Nice chair," Dante said from across the room where a massive throne sat upon a dais. "Even nicer hat." Sitting on the throne was a crown made of white gold, encrusted with long flat diamonds.

"Don't you dare!" John said.

A defiant look crossed Dante's face, but before he could steal the crown, a new voice spoke, making them jump.

"Is the coast clear?"

One of the statues began to tremble, the stone flaking off piece by piece to reveal the god beneath. The shrewd eyes under the winged helmet made Mercury instantly recognizable. He shook the remainder of the stone off his body like a dog drying itself and looked around.

"Ministers still gone, then? I sent them on a wild goose chase. Conjured up images of gods that don't even exist and set them loose in the city."

"So nobody is hurt?" John asked. "The stone thing was all a ruse?"

"Only for me." Mercury frowned. "I stoned myself, so to speak, to avoid detection. The others here weren't so lucky. The Ministers came wielding gorgon heads, waving them around like incense burners. Not nice, turning our own mythology against us." Mercury raised an eyebrow when he noticed Rimmon. "Who let the demon in, and more important, does he know anything useful?"

"Plenty," Rimmon answered, "but I don't think your trick will keep the Ministers at bay for much longer."

As if on cue, a strangled cry came from outside the temple. One scream sounded much like any other, but John suspected it might have been the Roman officer.

"Time to move," Mercury said. A staff entwined by two serpents appeared in his hand. "Luckily the Ministers have yet to grasp the true nature of our pantheon."

Without further explanation, Mercury began swinging his staff in a wide circle, whipping up a wind that made their skin buzz with electricity. Raising the staff high, he struck it once on the floor.

Everything changed.

And yet it was exactly the same. Almost. The temple appeared identical, but the steam coach was gone and the statues were now living gods. As for Mercury, his hair was longer and curled, and a new name came to mind when John focused on him: Hermes.

"From the Roman pantheon to the Greek," Hermes explained. "We are very much the same. Two sides of one coin, if you will."

"Do you bring news, messenger?" spoke Hera, queen of the gods.

"Yes, why this feeling of weakness?" sun god Apollo asked, his features so fair they appeared feminine.

The deities gathered around Hermes, desperate for answers. As Hermes explained what had transpired, John took stock of his friends. Bolo was nearest to him, and Dante was loitering next to the throne, which was still empty except for the crown. There was no sign of Rimmon, but a subtle red glint in Dante's eyes suggested he had hidden himself.

"And which of you will complete this story?" Hera's voice rang out.

John sighed, knowing it would be up to him again. He slowly worked into his best speech yet, detailing more than ever the horror of the situation in Purgatory and citing the three realms, including Hell, that had banded together to free the trapped souls. When he finished, the faces around John weren't moved or impassioned. Instead they were cold or incredulous.

"What good will this union of pantheons do us?" snarled Ares, the god of war. "The Ministers have already assembled an army. They've managed to recruit the Titans and turned the hundred-handed giants against us again. Where are these would-be allies? Can you summon them now to join us in battle?"

The other gods soon took up this angry cry, all of them demanding an explanation. John had to shout to be heard. "We never expected an attack like this! There was only one Minister in Asgard, not an army."

"So you provoked them by attacking one of their own kind." Ares glowered down at him. "You probably thought this would force us to join you, that we would tremble and beg for your assistance. Only a fool would leave his allies isolated, to be picked off one by one! No doubt Hell's forces are nearby, ready to sweep in and save us once we've given in to your ridiculous demands."

John stared. "There is no army. Even if you agree, there's only us."

Ares snorted in amusement, but his smile soon faded. "But you can summon them, surely. You can call Hell's armies to our aid."

John shook his head.

"No means of communication?" Ares roared "No contingency plan?"

"No!" John shouted back. "Why are you so desperate? I thought you were gods!"

Ares appeared to grow in height as the shadows of his face deepened. "Don't try me boy, or I'll pound you back into the clay Zeus sculpted you from!"

"You can hardly expect us to fight," Apollo whined, waving a golden fan in his face and appearing on the verge of a dramatic swoon. "Our Roman counterparts failed to carry their half of the burden, leaving us much too fatigued to fight."

John suspected Apollo was never in a state to do more than lounge around his temples and be admired. The other deities shared this air of self-appointed royalty and weren't likely to be useful in battle, all except Ares. Or perhaps Hermes, which gave John an idea.

"They call you a messenger," John said to him. "Could you travel to another realm? Ask the Celts and the Norse to come here?"

"Easily," Hermes said, "but I don't think they'll make it in time. The Ministers are clever. They might not enter the Greek realm as directly as we did, but they'll find a way."

John supposed that if Hell could strap a Roman man to a magical coach, then the Ministers probably had similar means. Ares was right. They should have had a better plan. If John could get them out of this mess, then maybe Hermes could be the one to establish communication between the pantheons. Ares would be useful too, since he had the tactical knowledge to organize the alliance of pantheons into a proper army. Perhaps the other Greek gods had talents John hadn't yet recognized, but he would never find out if couldn't get them back to Hell.

A memory surged to the forefront, one of the names put there by Cerridwen. Hel, Norse goddess of the underworld. How interesting that her name was so similar to Christianity's word for their version of the underworld. That couldn't be coincidence, nor could the fact that the Celts, Norse, and Christians all embraced the concept of an underground realm. Did every religion have such a place? John's mind ran over the list of names, stored there in perfect recall, searching for one that sounded Greek.

Pluto. That was the name of a Roman god, which was only

one step away. Mythology wasn't his strong suit, but John was certain that Hades was the Greek equivalent, and that name conjured up all sorts of underground imagery. Cerridwen was the Celtic goddess of the underworld, her realm the darkness of caves as well as the night. John felt it was a fair bet that every god on the list was an underworld deity. What had Cerridwen told him?

"Seek out the other dark gods, those who understand the depths of the underworld. Prepare them to move, to slither beneath the roots of the world tree and into the warmth of the fiery pits. Whether they agree to fight or not, they must come."

John understood now. Cerridwen had handed him the solution to their problems. His eyes darted around the room, looking for the god in question. Of all the names and personalities that impressed themselves upon him, Hades was not among them. John looked to Hermes, who wore an expectant expression.

"How quick can you get a message to Hades?"

Hermes blurred for a split second, like film snagging in a projector before returning to normal.

"Brothers, sisters," a deep voice intoned as a new god joined their ranks. Hades was dark in almost every regard. His pitch black hair was thick and coiled, as was his beard, which blended in with the dark material of his robe. His skin was the deep olive color of the Mediterranean, the corneas of his eyes deepest onyx. "Is this a call to arms?"

"No," John answered. "It's a request for sanctuary."

Ares turned even redder. "You expect *us* to cower in Hades' realm? Trembling among the rotting dead as if we'd already fallen in battle?"

"No one said anything about trembling," John retorted. "If I'm not mistaken, Hades' realm connects with the underworlds of other pantheons. We can travel through them like a sort of underground escape route."

The Greek gods turned expressions of disbelief and suspicion to Hades, who ignored them in favor of sneering at John. "Your mouth is dangerously free with secrets."

"Desperate times," John said, refusing to be intimidated. "Ares had a point about organizing our resources. Hell has allies, but not where we need them to be. We need to get everyone to Hell."

"And what of our realm?" Hera asked. "The people we will be leaving behind?"

"Are you sure your armies aren't sufficient?" Hermes asked of Ares.

"They've already lost in the Roman realm," the war god replied. "If the battle plays out here, it will only be history repeating. If I had somewhere to call them to, a safe haven where we could regroup and develop a plan, then victory could be ours."

"Which would mean joining with Hell," Hermes said. He turned to his fellows, who shuffled uncomfortably but didn't protest. John had a feeling that this was as close to agreement that they would come.

Hera gathered her robes about her and stood tall, reestablishing her status. "Is it true, Hades? Can we make our way through your realm to Hell?"

Hades nodded grudgingly. "Charon can boat us down the Styx to the river Acheron. An offshoot of water there will lead us to the Hvergelmir spring in Hel's realm. The Christian Hell isn't far from there."

Hera considered this in silence before nodding.

"What will happen to your Roman selves?" John asked. "They're still trapped on the other side."

"They will enter Pluto's realm there at the same time we enter mine here," Hades answered.

"But they're statues. How can they move?"

"Do not burden me with the reasoning of man," the dark god replied. "I have no patience for it. Are we ready?"

"My brother's crown!" Poseidon, god of the oceans cried. "It is no longer on the throne! The Ministers are already here!"

John gritted his teeth. Dante was innocently petting Bolo on the opposite side of the room, having put as much space as possible between himself and the throne.

"Don't be an alarmist," Ares growled. "The only enemy here is your imagination."

"Then where has it gone?" Poseidon said. "We dare not leave it to our enemies."

"Time's up!" Hermes eyes had grown wide. "The Ministers have returned to the Roman temple. They sense our presence here."

"The steam coach," John exclaimed. "We need it on this side!"

Hermes shook his head. "The glass men swarm over it like ants on sugar. There is no possibility of recovering it. You are stuck here."

"You are coming with us then," said Hades. "You troublesome humans and my arrogant brethren, all of you, coming to my domain where I reign supreme." The dark god smiled. "I'm beginning to warm to the idea." He snapped his fingers and the floor disappeared beneath their feet, plunging them all into eternal darkness.

Chapter Nine

Falling became standing. The black void became shadow. Dim light outlined a barren river bank and cold cave walls. The few visible paths shifted if John looked away, making escape impossible and getting lost a certainty. The Greek gods muttered to each other and shuffled uncomfortably, all but Hades, who wore a serene smile. The river before them was so dark that not even light reflected off its surface. Without its bubbling song, no one would know it was there.

A small boat made a subdued appearance, a figure standing at its bow. He was everything John expected Charon to be, a nautical version of the grim reaper, holding a long punting pole rather than a scythe. The skeletal features peeking from beneath the dark hood were filthy and worn with age. As the boat came to a standstill at the shore, its captain didn't even lift his head in interest at the gods gathered there.

"Surely you have a more appropriate ship than this with which to convey us," Poseidon complained.

"I concur," Apollo said. "You can hardly expect me to stand for the entire voyage."

"I shall require a cabin of my own," Hera commanded. "It isn't fitting for the queen of the gods to travel like a lowly fisherman."

"Oh, very well." Hades snapped his fingers again and the little pontoon, without the least bit of fanfare, was suddenly a large, floating home. "A house-boat on the Styx. Happy now?"

Placated, the gods began boarding.

"Come on, Bolo," John called, but the dog's attention was focused on the shadows further down the shore.

John kept calling to the dog but was steadfastly ignored. He rolled his eyes. How easily dogs became the master when they so desired. Giving up, John went to Bolo to coax him away and flinched when Bolo began to growl. Loose gravel skipped across the cavern floor toward them as something massive shifted and stood. Bolo began to bark, and out of the shadows, three canine heads appeared to return the challenge.

John stared upward. Cerberus, the legendary three-headed dog and guardian of Hades, was larger than a two-story house.

The beast could easily swallow them whole or crush them with a single step of its mighty paws, which were already stomping closer. The three canine heads growled, foamy drool splattering on the ground.

"Come on, Bolo," John whispered, tugging on the scruff of the dog's neck.

Cerberus took another step forward, growling again. The three-headed beast sniffed at them, knocking John over with a slimy nose, before dismissing them as unimportant. Instead it turned its attention toward the boat. All had boarded except Hermes, Hades, and Dante.

Dante! Could Cerberus smell the demon inside? Or was it the stolen crown that attracted its attention? The revelation of either could prove disastrous. Hades appeared more interested than agitated by his pet's behavior, his eyes narrowing with suspicion as they sought out Dante.

"What's wrong with your dog?" Hermes asked, wincing every time the great beast barked.

"Cerberus feels there is a stranger in our midst," Hades murmured.

"I would rather you think of me as a brother than a stranger," a new voice said.

Emerald light flooded the cavern as a god manifested. Osiris was nothing like the other gods present. His skin was pale green, and the cut of his robes exotic. The Egyptian god wore a tall white crown with large plumes to each side, and held a crook in one hand and a flail in the other. Both were golden, reinforced by blue copper bands. Osiris crossed these instruments over his chest and bowed his head.

"I hope I am as welcome in your realm as you would be in mine," the green god said.

Cerberus barked again, sparing only the attention of one head for this new arrival, but Hades snapped a finger, silencing the dog before commanding it to leave. The great hound retreated back into the shadows, all three heads casting sullen gazes toward their master.

"I delight in your presence as if you were my son, brother, and father," Hades responded with sincerity.

The aura surrounding Osiris was similar to Hades' own, since he was a god of the underworld in his own pantheon, but there was more to him. There was life, a promise of something more than death's finality. Fertility, not only of the earth, but of the soul.

"What reason has compelled you to honor us with your visit?" Hades asked.

"We, too, would meet with these curious envoys," Osiris answered. "We would hear of their war and how it can benefit us. They are to accompany me back to our realm immediately."

Hades' indulging smile faltered. "That is a shame, for I am not quite finished with them."

Dante, who was already moving toward Osiris, quickened his pace.

"Trg'kl det srogyln en p'gered dehrk," Osiris uttered in a strange tongue.

Hades responded in the same indecipherable dialect, to which Osiris replied in turn. The two gods locked eyes, a battle of wills playing out, until Hades smiled and nodded. An understanding must have been reached, for Hades turned and boarded his boat. Hermes followed, pausing only to raise his eyebrows meaningfully at John. His silent warning was unmistakable.

"Come." Osiris walked backwards toward an opening in the stone wall that hadn't been there moments before. He beckoned for them to follow. "We must travel the length of the night to reach our destination."

John looked at Dante, hoping to see a glint of red in his eyes, to glean some indication from Rimmon if this was the right thing to do. There was nothing. Was the demon even in there anymore?

John sighed. "Come on, Bolo."

They followed the Egyptian god into the dark passageway. As they walked, John pondered the reason behind this means of travel. Osiris had arrived surrounded by light, and Hades had transported his entire Pantheon to his realm with a snap of his fingers. The gods were capable of these feats and more, and yet Osiris expected them to walk. Like the Celts, was the god using this journey as a test? If so it was a strange one, for the Egyptian god showed no interest in engaging them in conversation, nor did their environment prove to be a challenge. But as they moved through mile after mile of stone tunnel, this began to change.

The darkness here was death. Cold, it brushed against their skin, whispering of their graves and the eternal silence of night, because here dawn never came. But there was more. This wasn't just the realm of the dead, this was the pathway of gods, ancient beings from a time so long ago it was almost incomprehensible. This was their footpath that no man, living or dead, was ever meant to walk.

You do not belong here, the void around them intoned. *You are small, insignificant. Only the gods tread here, gigantic and eternal. Turn back now before your souls shrivel into dust and blow away.*

A hand reached out to take his. John gripped it back. The idea of holding hands with Dante would have made him laugh any other time, but here it was different. Here they were two terrified children, trespassing somewhere they were never meant to be.

John tried to silence his fears by focusing on the god leading them. Unlike Cerridwen, Osiris didn't glow with the light of the moon, and yet he remained visible. The effect was unnatural rather than comforting, for little about Osiris was familiar. He may have had the shape of a man, but his strange clothing and green skin made him alien. Even the scent of him was unusual: a mixture of cloves, incense, and honey.

This wasn't working. John needed something else to take his attention away from their journey or he feared he would snap.

"Dante?" he began, unsure at first what he intended to say. It didn't take long to find a topic he wanted to broach. "I need you to tell me what everyone is keeping from me."

"What are you talking about?"

"Come on, you know what I mean. What Asmoday told you in his office. What Manannan mentioned before you asked him not to tell me."

Dante's chuckle was loud in the stillness surrounding them. "It's nothing bad. The opposite really, since it made all that stuff you could do in Purgatory possible. We never would have made it out otherwise."

"Then why can't anyone tell me?"

"It's like one of those Zen things. If you don't know, it's a good thing, but if you did know it would be bad."

John gritted his teeth. He had never enjoyed riddles, meaningless answers hidden behind deliberately obtuse questions and thinly veiled jokes. He realized that some people reveled in their challenge, but they always left John feeling stupid.

"What's bad if you know it, but good if you don't?" John said, not hiding the sarcasm in his voice. "When is a door not a door? What gets wet when it's drying?"

Dante was silent for a moment. "The truth, when it's ajar, and a towel."

"I hate you."

"Sorry, mate."

In his irritation, John shook Dante's hand off and immediately wished he hadn't, for the moment he did everything disappeared. Everything in this case was Osiris, who could no longer be seen, Dante who he could no longer feel next to him, and Bolo's steady panting, which he could no longer hear.

John clamped down on his rising panic. So this was the test? They wanted to see how he would fare when alone in the dark? Bring it on! What child hadn't grappled with and eventually conquered this fear?

John stood motionless, waiting for his eyes to adjust to light that wasn't there. When it became clear that he wasn't going to regain his vision, he systematically began exploring his surroundings with his hands. Each stone wall was still there, separated by about thirty feet of space. He was still on the same path. Maybe the others had disappeared while he remained.

He stayed close to one of the walls, keeping his hand in contact with it as he walked. What had Osiris said? The trip would take the length of a night? Another riddle. Who knew what that really meant, but John was going to find out. The sound of gravel beneath his feet was the only sign of his progress as he marched blindly forward. He disciplined his mind, dismissing fears and focusing on the light he hoped to see, *had* to see eventually, at the end of the tunnel.

When his hopes became reality and that light finally appeared, it didn't come from ahead as it should have. It came from behind, a strong yellow floodlight that ripped away every shadow and rendered the tunnel in stark detail. The light roared and rumbled like a train, and as John turned to look, what he saw terrified him more than darkness ever could.

A raging yellow sun came rolling down the corridor, its rays instantly transforming the rock around it to molten lava. But it was much, much more than that. This was god. Order, power, creation, direction. Ra.

The other gods John had met couldn't compare with Ra. The

chief of Egyptian gods was on an entirely different level. If gods had deities of their own, this is who they would worship. The idea of a power greater than this was incomprehensible.

John screamed as the sun rolled nearer, at first unintelligibly, before screaming the god's name over and over again like a deranged cheerleader. "Ra! Ra! RA!" He wanted to be noticed, desperate for the giant to look down at the ant below him before he was crushed, before his soul was incinerated into oblivion. John wanted to turn, to run, but the sun was all there was now and its heat—glorious and life-giving—held him in place like a physical force. Had John's eyes still been flesh, they would have been overwhelmed long ago, but here they were wide in rapt attention even as the sun was just a hair's breadth away.

Then John burned.

Pain.

John's body ached so much that he felt certain he was alive again. A pleasure came with the pain, a positive association that took him back to days on the beach lazy as a full-bellied cat. He shifted, his skin stinging with sunburn.

"I'd touch you, but I fear it would only hurt you more."

John opened his eyes, marveling at how his eyelids had been burnt as well. The sight that greeted him was worth the pain. Rimmon's handsome face loomed above him, his golden eyes wet with concern. John would have stolen a kiss, if his barbecued lips weren't aching.

"I take it we're somewhere safe," John rasped, "otherwise you wouldn't be outside Dante."

"Quite the contrary," Rimmon replied. "Can you sit up?"

"Yeah," John said, not knowing if it was true. As it turned out, he had nothing to fear. His chaffed skin smarted as his clothing shifted, but aside from discomfort he appeared unharmed. He winced as his palms pressed against the floor, the tender skin burnt there, too.

"I don't suppose you can heal me?"

"Heal you?"

"Like you did in Hell, from the glass man's touch."

The incubus shook his head. "That was an emotional wound. What you are suffering from now is something different altogether."

"Might be worth a shot anyway." John's grin was suggestive.

Rimmon matched it. "And to think I was once sent to seduce you! As tempting as you are, I prefer my men rare rather than well done."

"That bad?"

"Could be worse, but I hate to imagine how. Tell me exactly what happened to you."

John related the details, the demon's face growing serious but then reflecting surprise when Ra's name was mentioned.

"Then consider yourself lucky," Rimmon said. "Most souls would have been atomized back into the ether by an experience like that."

"Which means?"

"Which means that it would have taken you a very long time to find yourself again, if ever." Rimmon's eyes were smiling. "You're just full of tricks, aren't you?"

"A magician who doesn't know his own secrets," John said with a sigh.

"The burns are already fading, which is promising." Rimmon offered his hand. "We need to go. The others are waiting for us."

"Why didn't they come with you?" John asked as he stood.

"They were needed as collateral. Osiris was much more surprised by your sudden disappearance than he was by my appearance."

"Then they knew about you?"

Rimmon nodded. "Cerberus tipped them off. Hades said something to Osiris about my presence, but I couldn't understand much of the archaic tongue they were speaking. Regardless, your vanishing act wasn't part of the plan. Osiris wasn't willing to leave the path to come find you, so it was up to me."

They began walking. John was glad that the soles of his feet hadn't been roasted as well. "Do you think Hades could be behind this? Any reason he would have a grudge against us?"

Rimmon grimaced. "Against me and all of my kind. The Christian Hell is based on his realm more than any other. One of his territories in particular, Tartarus, is a great flaming pit where evil souls are sent to suffer. This concept was a part of Greek religion before the Christians adapted it to their own needs. Since then, the Christian Hell has become much more prevalent than Tartarus, something Hades takes personal offense to."

"Divine plagiarism?"

"Something like that." Rimmon chuckled. "But to answer your question, no, I don't think Hades is behind this. He wanted to know what we were hiding, but he wouldn't interfere with the gods of another pantheon to find that out."

"I can't blame him for being suspicious," John said. "If you had been open with them from the beginning—"

"Then they wouldn't have listened to a word we had to say. Hell's reputation is darkly tarnished and for good reason. We embrace every sin, vice, and despicable trait with open arms. Honest as I may be, truth rarely touches the tongues of most demons."

"Fine, but why didn't you reveal yourself later? We were sending them on a boat to Hell, after all, and Mercury didn't seem to mind you being a demon."

"Maybe I should have, but I think you underestimate the level of mistrust felt for my kind. It certainly doesn't help to be hidden in the body of a kleptomaniac."

"Dante stole the crown, didn't he?"

Rimmon nodded. "Quiet now. We're almost back to the others."

"One more thing," John said. "How did you find me?"

"We have a connection."

"A connection, eh? Next thing I know you'll be asking me to move in with you. Not that I would mind."

The demon's lips turned up at the corners. "The connection exists because when we slept together, an emotional bond was created between us. I was able to follow the remnants of this bond to find you. This is a natural ability of the incubi, and not at all romantic or indicative of fondness, although I do consider you my friend."

John rolled his eyes. "I bet you say that to all the guys."

"No, usually I have to explain to them that nothing more will come of our association together. I must confess, I enjoy not having to worry about that with you. My ego may be bruised, but it's good to finally have a friend."

John couldn't help smiling.

Familiar barks echoed down the tunnel. Bolo performed his usual ritual of greeting while Dante looked impatient for them to continue, perhaps fearing that a pantheon of Greek gods was on his trail. Osiris' expression was harder to read. Whatever his thoughts were, the god's eyes remained fixed on John as if he would disappear again at any moment.

John felt like he owed them explanation, even if he didn't understand the reasons himself. He willingly told Osiris what had transpired, but hadn't been prepared for the reaction. Osiris, who had been stoic and distant, was suddenly animated, his eyes wide with hope and emotion.

"Come!" Osiris urged them on. "We must leave these dark passages and exit into the world above. There the skies will testify to the truth of your story!"

"Were you telling the truth?" Dante whispered as they followed.

"Yeah. Can't you see the sunburn?" But as John touched his own face, he realized it was already gone. Only the very back of his neck still felt raw.

"Did anything happen while we were away?" Rimmon asked. "Interrogation? Intimidation?"

"No, it was boring," Dante said. "I tried striking up a conversation, but Kermit the Frog over there has never heard of football before."

"We have arrived," Osiris declared.

The phonics of the god's voice were different now, due to the large chamber they had entered. Every flat surface was covered in hieroglyphics. A disturbing number of them showed green men holding human hearts aloft like trophies. An altar was the room's only decoration, four stairs leading up to its apex where a set of gleaming, golden scales sat. Shining even brighter behind them was a pair of massive ornate doors, golden too but decorated with a jewel-encrusted mosaic that depicted a fertile land.

"Here the souls of the living are judged, to determine if they are worthy of joining the gods in the fields of Aaru," Osiris declared.

"And if they're not?" Dante asked.

Osiris brought his crook and flail together with a clang. From beneath the altar, a pile of scales, fur, and weathered skin slithered out into the open. The beast had the head of a crocodile, but the rest of its body was a mesh of a lion and something gray and leathery. The creature gaited to its master's side, where it waited in anticipation.

Osiris reached down to stroke its head affectionately. "The hearts of those judged unworthy are fed to Ammit."

"We are visitors here upon your request," Rimmon said cordially. "Surely such trials are unnecessary for us."

"The humans and the hound are welcome," the Egyptian god responded, "but it remains to be seen if a creature of Hell can be trusted."

"I can vouch for him," John said.

Osiris shook his head. "Such decisions are not for you to make."

John did his best to swallow his anger. "You want to join Hell in their war, but you won't let one of their kind enter your land?"

"I say only that he must first be judged."

Gut instinct told John what was happening here. "Is this what you want, or is this what Hades told you to do?"

Osiris didn't respond. Instead he turned his eyes on Rimmon and waited.

"What's he have to do, exactly?" Dante asked.

"If I remember right," the demon sighed, "my heart will be removed and placed on the scales. If it is too heavy, it gets fed to the beast. If it is light enough, then my existence will continue."

"What is your heart weighed against?" John asked.

"This." Osiris took a single feather from his crown and placed it on one of the scale's plates.

"Forget it." John took hold of Rimmon's arm to pull him away, but the demon didn't budge.

"I warned you of their prejudice," Rimmon said. "There have been too many demons and devils before me whose fame has tarnished all of our names. When my brethren choose to do evil, they excel beyond what any other race is capable of, and history has not forgotten."

"Don't do this!" John pleaded.

"I will be fine."

"It's not like any of us need a heart," Dante pointed out. "There's no blood to pump."

"The heart is merely a symbol," Osiris explained. "It is the essence of his soul that will be measured and destroyed if need be."

"Oh, well, that's fine, then," John snarled.

"Easy now," Rimmon gently removed John's hand and

stepped forward. "I am ready."

At least there was no satisfaction on Osiris' face, no reaction that a victory had been won. If this was indeed Hades' desire, then the Egyptian god took no pleasure in it.

Rimmon's shirt had disappeared in the strange way that all clothes here were ideas rather than objects. In John's imagination, Osiris would take a great curved knife and cut open the demon's chest, or perhaps claw into the flesh with his bare hand and remove a spasming heart. Instead the green-skinned god placed the palm of his hand against Rimmon's maroon chest. The contrast in hues was beautiful before Rimmon gasped in surprise.

Osiris slowly withdrew his hand, and out from Rimmon's chest came a crystal, pulsing with rose-colored light. The heart resembled a gigantic snowflake, rounded out in three dimensions instead of being flat, but it wasn't cold. The heart's warmth could be felt throughout the entire room, radiating with the heat that always accompanied life.

As the final outstretching arm of the crystal slipped from Rimmon's chest, the demon's body collapsed to the floor. The red skin faded to pink before becoming transparent, the edges of the body fuzzing and losing definition like a chalk drawing in the rain. John had the terrible revelation that the body, much like their clothing, was nothing more than an idea, a memory to be held on to lest it fade away. How much longer until the incubus disappeared entirely, until he was forgotten?

Helplessness ate at John as he tore his eyes away. Already Osiris had placed the heart on one of the scale's golden plates. Ammit was at his feet, drooling uncontrollably in anticipation of its meal. John wouldn't allow it. He would grab the alligator jaws so they couldn't close down on Rimmon's heart. His fingers might be pierced by those sharp teeth, but his blood would choke the beast before he ever let its mouth close. John stepped forward in anticipation, his own teeth clenched painfully together, when a short but loud squeak echoed in the chamber. The scales had shifted.

"I'll be damned!" Dante exclaimed.

John looked up. The plate with the feather had sunk lower. It might only have been a fraction of an inch, but it was lower.

"Judgment has been passed." The look on Osiris' face was slightly puzzled, but not at all displeased.

John's joy disappeared when he noticed Rimmon's flickering body. The demon didn't have much longer. John rushed the altar, heedless of the shouted warnings as his hands wrapped around the crystalline heart.

The moment John's fingers touched the heart's surface, he knew Rimmon. Neither his memories, nor the details of his life, but his essence. The warmth flowed through him, filling every inch of his body. He knew then the demon was good, that he could be trusted, that he had never willfully wronged someone. Rimmon was noble and honest, and yet there was so much of him that was lonely and torn between who he was and what others wanted him to be. And the hunger, the constant desire for sex and intimacy. John inhaled all of this. He could smell Rimmon around him, taste the pomegranate flavor of his kisses. The feeling was like their first night together but a hundred-fold stronger. John was both filled with and surrounded by the incubus, possessed by him in a way that Dante could never be.

The sensation ebbed away as his hands parted. He gasped in surprise, finding himself kneeling on the floor over Rimmon's body. The heart floated gracefully down, rejoining its host. The body became solid again. Rimmon's eyes fluttered open, turning at once to seek John's.

Did he know? Had he felt it too? The essence had fled from John, everything of Rimmon now back where it belonged, but something remained. The intimate comfort that came with being with someone for a long time, of knowing who the other person was, even if the full story of his life hadn't yet been revealed. John had touched his incubus heart and been burnt by its love. But if Rimmon had come close to John in a similar way, the demon's eyes betrayed nothing as they broke contact.

Chapter Ten

The world outside the mosaic door was Egypt as it had never been seen before. Luscious green grass carpeted the gentle hills, each rise cresting with a fine crease at the top before sloping downward again in the manner of all sand dunes. Pyramids populated these hills, each a different color. Jade, onyx, ruby, sapphire—the great bricks were hewn from impossibly large precious stones. In the distance were four great sphinxes in cross formation, their backs turned to the powerful geyser fountain in their center. The water rained down and pooled around their massive paws. Children laughed as they splashed each other in the fountain, the adults among them distinguishable only in size as they joined in the revelry.

"I had such hopes. Despite the beauty of Nut my heart yearns for something different." The voice of Osiris was sad, his dark eyes fixed on the star-swept sky. "You have either deceived me, or you were mistaken about what you saw."

John needed a moment to understand what he was talking about. "My neck is still sunburned," he said, half turning so the god could see. "I saw the sun beneath the ground."

Osiris sighed. "Perhaps the same reason that compelled Ra to leave us continues to keep him away, for I don't believe there is any being who could impede him against his will."

"How long has it been?" Rimmon asked.

"Weeks, months, an eternity. The passage of time means nothing without night and day to gauge it by." Osiris still searched the horizon, not having given up hope. "Do not tell the others what you have seen. It will only turn them against you."

They were led to the largest of the pyramids, the light of the moon playing along its diamond surface. The pyramids John had seen on television were always silent, the decaying bodies of giants, but here throngs of people crowded the pyramid's base. Many were on their knees, bowing and chanting prayers. Others were delivering food or fulfilling other duties.

Navigating the crowd would have been difficult had Osiris not been leading them. People moved willingly out of his way, their eyes filled with love and admiration for the god who walked among them. John and his companions were as good as invisible, weeds growing next to the most beautiful rose in the garden.

The interior of the pyramid also defied expectation. No passage was dark or dusty, nor was there a mummy or sarcophagus in sight. The outer areas of the pyramid were illuminated by light filtering through the diamond bricks. Further in, golden bowls blazing with pure white fire hung from the ceiling at regular intervals. The crowds thinned as they journeyed deep into the pyramid's interior; only the occasional priest in decorative robes crossing their path.

Here in the pyramid's inner sanctum, a number of cats made their home. The felines were everywhere, lounging in fur-lined beds, lurking at the tops of shelves, or peering out of small cat-sized tunnels in the wall. When they saw a priest respectfully step aside to allow a cat to pass, it became clear that the cats were treated as royalty.

Bolo was terribly tempted by all he saw. John said his name in warning tones, the poor dog whimpering and fighting to obey against his instincts. Eventually overcome, Bolo broke rank, racing toward a Siamese cat carrying a kitten in its mouth. The feline obviously hadn't seen a natural predator in many centuries, for it simply stared in wonder instead of fleeing.

"Bolo, no!" John cried out, wishing desperately for a leash. His arm almost jerked out of its socket as the leash went taut, Bolo's front paws airborne momentarily as he was yanked backward.

John stared. He would have let go of the leash he was now holding had it not been wrapped tightly around his hand, just as he had envisioned. The leash matched the one belonging to his childhood dog, even down to the same worn leather. If he checked the matching collar on Bolo's neck, John wouldn't be at all surprised to find the name "Dipsy" stamped into the rawhide.

"Nice one," Dante said, producing a lit cigarette from thin air. "I knew you'd get the hang of it eventually."

John felt as though he had performed a miracle, but Dante had already lost interest and Rimmon appeared amused. John wished he had more time to experiment. What else could he create? What else did he need?

The chamber Osiris led them to might have been large, but the treasure, art, and servants that filled every available space made it appear small. Two mammoth statues of pharaohs sat stiffly at the far end of the room, their heads touching the ceiling. Between them was a throne, occupied by a skinny man whose lazy posture was the opposite of the statues'.

The court was filled with gods. With only a few exceptions, each had the head of an animal. Reptilian, canine, and avian eyes all focused on John and his friends as they entered. Human emotions lurked eerily behind each gaze, sly and suspicious rather than the frank honesty of animals. The auras of each god reached toward John, overwhelming him with names and histories, so he turned his attention back toward the man on the throne. His soul didn't carry the divine presence of the deities assembled before him.

The man's eyebrows were raised expectantly until Osiris formally announced him. "His majesty Pharaoh Den, the embodiment of Ra."

Every being present turned to face the throne before falling on both knees. John followed suit, Bolo licking his face excitedly as if this were all just a game. *The embodiment of Ra?* John pondered this as their names were announced. He thought he understood. While living, the pharaoh would have been considered the earthly incarnation of the chief god, but in the afterlife there was little sense to this. If this man were Ra, would they still be trapped in eternal night?

Just as everyone else stood again, Bolo decided to sit. John held back a chuckle as he was addressed by the pharaoh.

"Your skin is so very pale," Den said. "Only once before have I seen one of your kind, from lands far away. I remember feeling surprised that day, to learn that the Egyptian Empire had borders. I had thought the entire world to be Egypt. Now I find myself equally perplexed to learn that there is another religion."

Tons of them, John almost said, but the gods around him shifted. He glanced over at the nearest to meet piercing falcon eyes. Horus, sky god, master of war, and the god of kings. No Egyptian deity was more important, aside from Ra, and his powerful thoughts had a presence of their own.

The existence of other religions was no secret to Horus, but the sudden pressure in the room insisted that John humor the pharaoh. For negotiation purposes, he supposed Hell should be acknowledged; Purgatory too, since speaking of an alliance would be impossible otherwise.

"Tell me again," Den said. "What is the name of this place where men are white and dogs are revered in place of cats?"

"Hell," John said.

"And this man who is red and horned like a goat, where is he from?"

"Also Hell. We come in all colors there." John thought a moment about history. "But most devils are white."

"Ah. Is color indicative of class? Is this goat man your servant?"

"No. Rimmon is Hell's ambassador, a native to his pantheon. I only represent the mortal men who travel to his realm in death." There. Let Rimmon do all the work this time.

The pharaoh, unabashed at having mistaken an ambassador for a servant, turned his attention to Rimmon. "Were you well treated on your journey here?"

"Of course," Rimmon said graciously.

"Except for having his heart cut out and thrown on butcher scales," Dante said. "Not the best way to make new friends."

"I'm very sorry to hear that." Den frowned at the collected gods, who managed to look somewhat ashamed; all but one who had a dark bestial head like a nightmare version of an aardvark. Set's eyes were furious black spheres with blood-red pupils that glowed with anger. The chaos god seemed to barely restrain his fury at being treated in such a manner. The situation at court was tense, that much was clear.

"No harm was done," Rimmon insisted. "Your people have every right to be cautious in these troubled times."

"Ah, yes," the pharaoh breathed. "I understand there is a war of some sort? Hm, well, I'm sure it will sort itself out. Now then, tell me what has transpired on Earth since my death. My name is still revered, I am certain?"

"There isn't a man in the world who hasn't heard of the pharaoh," Rimmon answered smoothly.

"Of course," Den looked rather pleased despite his alleged certainty. "I have noticed though, that not as many souls come here as before. Scarcely any at all."

The gods shifted uneasily again, but Rimmon had an answer ready. "Egyptians live much longer than they once did."

That much was true, John supposed. They might not worship the old gods anymore, but life expectancy was double if not more than it had once been.

"Of course," the pharaoh said again. "And have many pyramids been built since my time?"

"I could not count them," John chimed in, eager to play the game. No one could count what wasn't there.

"Of course," came the standard response.

"There's even a pyramid in far-away land called Las Vegas," John said, getting carried away. "A great beam of light that pierces the sky shoots from its center. Every year millions of people visit to—"

Rimmon cleared his throat meaningfully just as a delicate bell tinkled from another room.

"Ah!" Den was instantly alert. "You will, of course, join me in my feast?"

"I believe, sire," Osiris stepped forward, "that the lady Nefaru was hoping to dine alone with you tonight."

"Nefaru! Of course!" The pharaoh's dinner date must have been special, for in a matter of seconds he and his serving staff had vanished from the room. An intentional silence fell as his footsteps faded away. Then the atmosphere in the room changed entirely.

"This is how you want us to appear?" Set snarled. "Sniveling cowards who answer to a buffoon? Let him stuff his belly before I devour it whole! His feast shall become my own!"

"You would rather our pantheon be known for dissidence among its ranks?" Horus chided. "There is good reason that Den is sitting upon the throne of Ra."

"Then let us explain our foolishness to our guests," Thoth suggested, earning his reputation of a god of council and wisdom. The long ibis beak turned toward them. "In the time of our rule in Egypt, the pharaoh was often considered the embodiment of Horus. This varied over the many centuries, and for one brief period, the pharaoh was associated with the great god Ra. Our dear naïve Den is from this era."

"Ra finally came to his senses and abandoned these fools," Set interrupted, "and they feel that replacing him with a clown will bring Ra back rather than alienate him further."

"The gesture is one of reverence and respect," Horus shot back, "although maybe Ra would prefer a sacrifice. I, for one, would revel in the sight of your foul head bleeding on an altar."

"And you would be the one to cut it off, no doubt," Set growled. "You'll find your visage plucked of every feather and roasting over a flame before you lay a hand on me!"

Violent energy crackled around them as the gods argued, a prickling penetrating sensation that John imagined radiation would feel like. One by one the other gods joined in the shouting as they each took sides. Soon the air felt on the verge of exploding. Bolo whimpered and Dante hit the ground. Rimmon threw his arms around John to shield him from the coming war between gods. Then the voice of Osiris rose above all else.

"Take it to the astral heavens, or may Ra curse you both!"

And just like that, it was over. Both Set and Horus disappeared, and reality was no longer in danger of tearing at the seams. The only remaining evidence of conflict was an ominous rumble of thunder in the distance, caused by the two gods continuing to battle elsewhere.

"Talk about a dysfunctional family," Dante said as he stood. "Papa's run off, and the kids are duking it out in the backyard."

The Egyptian gods hissed and glared in response to Dante's words, but he was right. Another pantheon was in turmoil because they had lost their leader. The pattern was now undeniable. In each realm they were sent to, the chief deity had gone missing, leaving the remaining gods disorganized if not desperate.

This couldn't be a coincidence. If anyone stood to benefit from the resulting confusion, it was the Ministers of Order. How they had caused each realm's leader to disappear was still a mystery, but this tactic was a grave miscalculation. With the leaders gone, recruiting the desperate pantheons to Hell's side was even easier.

John's stomach sank. Of course, Hell could be behind all of this. John couldn't deny the existence of the glass men, but for all he knew they could be some sort of demon. Maybe Hell had kidnapped the leaders and sent the glass men to cause panic, blaming it all on Heaven.

"I am greatly embarrassed by Horus's and Set's behavior," Thoth said to Rimmon. "At least they have made clear that these are difficult times for us. We understand that we are not alone in this situation, which brings us to your war."

And just like that, they were playing into Hell's hands. John had to say something.

"Joining Hell in a war against Purgatory, possibly even Heaven, won't do anything to bring Ra back. Maybe we should focus on discovering the truth behind Ra's disappearance. He could have been taken against his will."

The laughter of the other gods was unanimous, except for Thoth, who was thoughtful. John supposed he was being foolish, since he had seen Ra free and rolling through the underground, but that didn't mean some magic wasn't keeping him from returning home. Perhaps the Egyptian gods were too confident in Ra's invulnerability.

"Our reasons for joining this war may differ from your own," Thoth said, "or they may very well be the same. Before discussing our own desires, we invite you to see what we can offer you. If you leave here, you will find the Nile on the other side of the Sphinx quartet. Following it downriver will bring you to the pyramid of jade. We shall await you there."

And with that, the gods disappeared from the chamber, leaving the companions alone, except for the beautiful goddess Isis, wife of Osiris. This mistress of magic directed them to the entrance they had come through, but when following her they found the long halls and public areas were gone. They were outside almost instantly. The goddess bid them farewell, her colors taking on those of her surroundings, before she faded into the background and disappeared entirely.

"Something's fishy," Dante said. "If they had something to show us at the jade pyramid, then why bring us here in the first place?"

"To meet the pharaoh?" John suggested.

"Or maybe he insisted on meeting us," Dante replied. "Otherwise I think they would have preferred to keep him out of sight."

"Regardless," Rimmon interjected, "they could have brought us instantly to our destination with their magic, if they so desired. Unless I'm mistaken, they want us to see more of their realm. I suggest we take our time and enjoy the sights."

This was an easy idea to embrace. The grass was so soft that John took off his shoes as they strolled. Despite the evening hour, people were everywhere, calling out to each other, chasing their children, or lying as lovers together beneath the stars. A group of old women sat in a circle next to a cylindrical clay oven and gossiped as they pounded dough into flat discs. One flashed them a toothless grin before downing what resembled beer out of a worn mug.

"First time I've seen old people since Purgatory," Dante commented.

John smiled. "An ex-boyfriend of mine used to say that everyone was twenty-one in Heaven."

"He wasn't far from the truth," Rimmon said. "Only in the beginning does the mind cling to the former physical self. As time goes by, the silent wishes of the heart come true. 'I wish I didn't have this paunch on my stomach,' or 'I wish my hair was as thick as it once was.' With no physical laws saying it should be otherwise, all souls soon achieve the appearance they find most ideal. More often than not, this is an age before forty. This effect doesn't exist in Purgatory, which is why it is only recently that you have both begun to change."

John looked over at Dante and was startled. The difference was subtle but it was there. Gone were the lines beneath his eyes and the pallor of his skin. The years spent drinking—and whatever else he had gotten up to—had mostly been erased, although he still appeared to be in his thirties. Even his hair had a healthier shine.

"Do I look different?" John asked.

"A little bit closer to being jail bait," Rimmon said, "but still old enough to be taken seriously."

"I better not return to my teenage years," Dante warned. "I was a walking zit until I hit my twenties."

"Don't worry," Rimmon assured him. "Age is always based on your personal ideal, the appearance you felt most confident about. Old age wasn't common in ancient Egypt and was an achievement that brought great respect. That is why some women here choose to wear their wrinkles as a badge of honor."

"I like that," John said, "but if a hot enough guy comes along, I bet they start getting younger."

When they reached the Nile, they stared in wonder at its dazzlingly clear water, despite its great depth. Here people swam or paddled small wooden boats. A passing sailor offered them a ride, which they declined since the jade pyramid was now near enough to see.

Next they passed through a small village, and a group of

children abandoned their games to run after them, fascinated by the lightness of John's hair and amused by Rimmon's tail. Bolo was in paradise, chasing off in all directions, greeting everyone, and creating laughter wherever he went.

John could imagine staying here. The only thing missing was a clear blue sky and the warmth of the sun. He wanted to return that light to these good people, to give them back their god. He didn't know how, but he felt he was meant to find the reason behind Ra's disappearance. Why else would the sun god have appeared to him?

Even more animal-headed gods were waiting outside of the great jade pyramid, but they weren't the biggest surprise. In their midst was the unmistakable shape of the steam coach.

"How did you get it back?" John asked, running to it and placing a hand against the cool wood. "Hermes said it was covered in glass men."

"It was." Set handed a cloth sack to him. The chaotic god looked as though he had been severely beaten, as did Horus, who was standing further away, but both of them appeared satisfied rather than angry. "These men of glass are nothing in battle compared to my nephew."

John took the heavy bag and peered inside. It was filled with powdered glass.

"You see what we have to offer," Thoth spoke. "We Egyptians have always understood the secrets of creation. When one understands how something is built, destroying it is only a matter of snipping a single thread."

"Hell would be honored to have your support," Rimmon said, "but I know better than to think it will come free."

"Souls," Osiris said, thumb and finger on his green chin. "Travel between realms has all but ceased. All of us are like puddles separated from the sea, growing more stagnant by the day. Our hope is that the actions of this war will start the rivers flowing between us again, but until then our realm is the most drastically affected. Our culture is so ancient that all who would come to us have done so long ago. Thus we need the invigoration of fresh life. Our price is ten thousand souls."

Rimmon nodded thoughtfully. "I have no doubt that after the war—"

"Now, not after the war." Osiris said. "The surplus of souls caused by Purgatory's fall is another matter. Ten thousand souls and you have our loyalty."

Rimmon launched into negotiations, but he faced tough competition. John felt uncomfortable with the entire proceedings. He didn't understand why they needed the souls, or how those souls would reinvigorate the gods' lives. Whatever this meant, John didn't like people being treated as currency. He watched distractedly as Bolo tried in vain to attract the attention of Anubis, jackal-headed god of mummification. John supposed it was lucky that the dog hadn't noticed the cat-headed goddess in their midst. Then the negotiations were over. Rimmon hadn't gained any ground. The number of souls would not be reduced.

"Ten thousand souls," the demon said, extending his hand to Osiris.

"No."

The gods turned as one to look at John.

"We're fighting to free souls from Purgatory," he said. "I won't let you treat them like poker chips!"

"What is this chipped poker that he speaks of?" Set growled.

"I believe his concern lies with the fate of the souls in question," Thoth said gently. "This is why we wanted you to see some of our land, so you would know that existence is good here, as it will be for those who come."

"The souls will be volunteers," Rimmon added, "those who wish to move on. Nobody will be forced to come here against their will."

John knew he could trust Rimmon, knew to the very core of his being since touching his heart, but that didn't mean Rimmon couldn't be mistaken. A piece was missing from this puzzle, some vital information they weren't being told, and John wouldn't budge until he found out what.

"If you want us to work with you," he said, "then you have to come clean. Otherwise, no deal."

Rimmon tried to intervene. "John, I'm sure there is nothing to be concerned—"

"Very well," Thoth said, nodding with a dip of his bird beak. "Too often a blind eye is turned to those details of life considered unpleasant. Our realm isn't the paradise we've led you to believe. Extend your trust in us once more and journey to the onyx pyramid of the north. There you shall find your answers."

* * * * *

"You just had to open your big mouth, didn't you?"

John ignored Dante and focused on their destination. He could see the dark pyramid on the horizon. Gone were the fountains, the lush green grass, and the winding Nile. In their place was only sand and silence. What this had to do with the ten thousand souls, he didn't yet understand, but the answers were only moments away.

"John," Rimmon said, removing Bolo's leash so he could run free. "Slow down. We'll be there soon enough."

"You're one to talk," John replied.

Rimmon digested this. "You feel I was too hasty in my negotiations."

"Yes. Ugh. I don't know. The whole thing sounded like human trafficking. What if I hadn't challenged them? We never would have learned the real reason they wanted the souls."

"I'm sorry. I should have asked more questions. I feel as though I've betrayed your trust."

"You haven't. I know I can trust you, but that doesn't mean that you can't be wrong, especially if you're being lied to."

Rimmon took hold of John's arm and stopped him. "This isn't only about the Egyptians, is it?"

"No," John admitted, "it isn't. The leaders of each realm go missing, the Ministers of Order arrive, and all the pantheons fall in line. It's all too convenient. The chess pieces have been perfectly arranged on the board, and when I ask myself who really stands to gain from all of this, the arrows keep pointing to Hell."

Rimmon was silent.

John's jaw dropped. "You know something!"

"I know a good many things, but I have never deceived you. You are right that there is a game being played, but I don't pretend to understand the rules. There are two halves of the board, and I promise you Hell and the Ministers of Order are on opposite sides."

"And the missing leaders?"

"That is a question I cannot answer, but if you trust me just until we return to Hell, then I'll make sure you hear the truth from the horse's mouth."

"Does this horse have three eyes and chain-smoke cigars?"

Rimmon smiled. "Yes."

John nodded. "Okay. Not only do I need answers, but the other pantheons do as well. If we expect them to fight alongside us, the least we can do is tell them the truth."

The demon agreed before breaking into laughter. "Oh, how you remind me of him! Always so serious, so earnest in your duty. Look around you, John! You're in immortal Egypt, surrounded by the old gods and their pyramids. Drink in the details and allow yourself to become intoxicated!"

"Yes. It's very nice," John said, hiding a smile.

"Very nice?" Rimmon shook his head, before grabbing up John in his arms and spinning him around, as if they were dancing. "I would show you so many wonders, see that stoic face of yours light up like a child's. There are red sands in the second circle of Hell that flow like a river, pulling you down into their warmth, but the sensation isn't uncomfortable. The way your body bends and moves, like a snake across the ground, is pure ecstasy."

"Yeah, yeah," John teased as Rimmon set him down. "We have yoga back home." But there was nothing like Rimmon on Earth. As the demon shook his head ruefully, John's heart was beating, not out of habit, but because of the feeling that came from being this close to the incubus.

The moon caught Rimmon's eye and he began to sing in a voice that sounded like many, a chorus both haunting and beautiful. And then they really were dancing as John was swept up into his arms again. Like a whirlwind Rimmon spun them back and forth along the sands, his song and movements enchanting John and erasing every worry from his mind. John felt they could go on like this forever, letting time pass by as they forgot everything in the world except each other.

"When you gents are finished." Dante's voice could barely be heard over the song, but Rimmon stopped singing and set John gently on his feet. "Sorry to break up your Village People moment, but there's something you might want to see."

Dante disappeared over the dune in the direction of the pyramid.

"I've heard that song before," John said as they followed, his blood still racing with excitement. "In Cerridwen's cave, when I thought I had lost you."

"I was singing to the moon," Rimmon said, the light in his

eyes growing distant. "I always serenade the moon, because that's where I met him."

"You met your ex-boyfriend on the moon?"

"In its essence, yes. It's difficult to explain. I was symbiotically resonating with moon's light, basking in the glory of its existence. There's so much you haven't experienced yet, John, but you will. Regardless, I must have been singing then as well, because that's how he found me."

John studied his face, the subtle longing, the barely concealed affection. All the signs of love, and even though they weren't for him, seeing their effect on Rimmon made his legs feel weak.

"I always sing when I see the moon, hoping by doing so that he will one day hear and come back to me."

John could have cried for him, sensing the pain that was so well hidden. Part of him hated this other man for hurting Rimmon, for not answering his song, but the other part felt a strange sort of hope.

"Maybe it's time I stop," Rimmon said with a shake of his head. "It's been so long now."

"Keep singing," John said, feeling a rush of passion. "He might not come, but someone else will. I promise." And he was starting to realize who he thought that person should be. All of this was so new, but was it a part of touching Rimmon's heart or something more? John needed to know if Rimmon had felt the same connection or at least understood what had happened. "There's something I need to ask you—"

But they had crested the dune and found themselves in the shadow of the pyramid, the scene there chasing all thoughts of hearts from John's mind. The onyx stones were unpolished, flat black that seemed to make a pyramid-shaped hole in the world. Not far from its base sat two old women in front of a huge pile of thin bricks.

No, not bricks. Bread. The old women were seated next to a bread oven, just as elsewhere in the realm, but the sense of communal joy was absent here. The old woman pounding the dough flat did so mechanically, with the dull precision of a machine. Her companion stared, unmoving, as if she had grown as stale and inflexible as the countless loaves piled beside her. The sand had built up around her, evidence that she hadn't moved for a long time.

Bolo snuck forward and stole the fresh dough from the first woman's hands, gulping it down in two swallows, but the old woman didn't react. She simply reached into the flour bucket next to her to begin again.

"It doesn't matter how much you talk to them," Dante said. "They don't respond."

What did any of it mean? John didn't understand what was wrong with them, or what he was supposed to do. He wondered for a moment if he could help, as he had done for Bolo in Purgatory, but these women weren't frozen against their will. Somehow they had become machines.

"The pyramid entrance is just over here," Dante said.

John was all too eager to leave the strangely disturbing scene, until he saw the unlit rectangle leading to the pyramid's interior. The dark entrance was barely distinguishable from the onyx stones. Whatever awaited them inside, they wouldn't know what it was until they ran headlong into it.

"I don't suppose you can see in the dark?" John asked. "Demonic vision or something?"

"No," Rimmon said, "but there's always my flame breath."

"Right, then you're going first," Dante said. "I don't fancy getting roasted from behind."

Of course they had one more option, one that would allow John to put his skills to the test. All he needed was a little motivation, which wasn't hard considering the pitch-black maw they were about to enter.

The torches appeared in John's hands, three of them that he had been wise enough to visualize as unlit. They came as easily as Bolo's leash had, John's need summoning them into existence.

"Well done," Rimmon said, taking one and lighting it with a gentle puff of his flame breath before passing it back.

"I don't know why you always steal," John said, handing the freshly lit torch to Dante. "If you'd practice creating more than just cigarettes, you could literally make your own money."

"Don't give him any ideas," Rimmon said. "The merchants in Hell have no trouble spotting a counterfeit. Besides, it's the essence of an object, the energy and history imbuing it that holds value. A pile of conjured gold holds no more worth than mud."

"The money Asmoday filled my pockets with in Hell didn't seem so special," Dante said, not willing to give up hope.

"Because they had Asmoday's mark on them," Rimmon explained, "and his favor is extremely valuable. Now let's see what awaits us inside while John is still concentrating on keeping these torches in existence."

Beyond the entrance of the onyx pyramid were stairs leading down into the earth, but never upward into the pyramid itself. John wondered if anything was to be found in the structure above, or if the black pyramid was one huge gravestone.

Their path ended in a large chamber full of people, the four walls covered in hieroglyphics. Only the occasional shuffling of feet gave the people away as being more than statues. John was reminded of the animals in Purgatory, except here the people weren't in stasis. They were free to move, so why did they choose to stay here in the darkness?

"I thought mummies were supposed to wear bandages," Dante said.

His voice echoed through the chamber. The reaction was subtle at first. A few heads turned to look at them, followed by surprised murmurs. This attracted more attention, and soon bodies began to jostle each other for a better view. Then everything exploded. The crowd rushed them, eyes wild, teeth bared, and hands outstretched. John panicked as the first wave of people hit them, their fingers clutching, tearing at him as if hungry for his flesh. His mind was filled with the need to survive, leaving no room for the torches he should have been concentrating on, which disappeared and left them in complete darkness.

But the hands continued to explore. Bolo was barking, and Dante's screams were unintelligible. Where was Rimmon's fire? He needed to burn these people before—*before what?* The hands, while intrusive, weren't doing any harm. In fact, John could hear excited voices discussing details. Rimmon's horns, or the strange fabric of John's suit. These weren't brain-hungry zombies. They were curious spectators, no matter how overzealous they were.

"Be calm, my people, and remember to show restraint!"

The commanding voice of a god was followed by a soft blue light that filled the chamber, restoring their vision. Crane-headed Thoth was at their side, and with his appearance came a wave of calm. Even Dante stopped shrieking.

"What is this?" John asked.

"Stagnant water, people who have long since lost their passion for existence. For eons they have experienced all that we have to offer them, until they became weary with time."

"Thus the behavior of the bread-makers outside," Rimmon said, nodding in understanding. "They've been performing the same actions for so long that it's become mechanical."

Thoth nodded. "The passion has been extinguished from their souls."

John felt his anger rising. "So you bury them under a pyramid and leave them to rot?"

"The properties of the onyx pyramid brings them what comfort we can provide," Thoth answered. "We gods use our magic daily to give them rest, but this is no solution. Even before the other realms became suspicious of each other, we Egyptians preferred a secluded existence. The price of this is what you see here. These people long for new experiences outside of this realm, which is why we ask Hell to send us fresh souls. You can see the reaction your presence alone has caused. Tell them a story."

John's brow furrowed. "Sorry?"

"A story from your life. Let them hear of matters unknown to them."

John looked at the crowd, their faces eager as children on Christmas Day. What could he possibly tell them? The contracts he struggled to fulfill in business? The malls he helped build, or the boyfriends who one by one tired of his working hours and left?

"There's the first time I killed a man." Dante was speaking, looking rather sheepish. "I never really talk about it, so it would be good to get it off my chest. Not that I'm confessing, mind you. Being born Catholic doesn't make you one, no matter what anyone says. That was only on my father's side anyway, and he ran off long before I was a teenager."

John looked at their audience, expecting to see confused faces, but they were enraptured. Thoth raised the staff he was holding, and suddenly John could see Dante's father in his mind as clear as day, a stern man with small, suspicious eyes and a chin covered in black grizzle.

"I dropped out of school not having learned much," Dante continued. "At least nothing that could earn me a wage, so me and my mates would drink and try to find women dumb enough to waste their time on us. Pints don't come free, so I took to stealing. At first from my mam, later from neighbors. As soon as they left the house, I'd let myself in by one means or another. If I was lucky, I found money and a little something to drink. Otherwise I'd have to find valuables, which was never easy as I couldn't care less about antiques. Eventually I attracted the attention of one too many pigs, and it was in my best interest to leave Dublin.

"I decided to go to England. My mam always said that the streets of London could go from civilized to sinister in the beat of a heart, and I suppose that appealed to me. It didn't take long before the East End was my second home. No surprise to anyone I fell in with a bad crowd. That's how I met Filthy Henry, who had more than one neighborhood under his greasy thumb. He fancied himself a regular duke of the streets, which I suppose he was. I didn't like him much, but he had money, so I started working for him. Henry always knew the right houses to rob and the most valuable things to take. He cased jobs for me, and even after he took his cut, I was still making more than I ever did on my own.

"Henry had a small army of lads running jobs for him, but that didn't stop him from coming along occasionally. He wasn't scared to get his own hands dirty, which is where his name came from. He was good, too, made short work of any lock, and was a vicious bastard in a fight if anyone got out of line. Things were good for a while, until Henry started getting into drugs and weapons. I didn't mind the drugs so much, but the army surplus he was picking up I avoided like the plague. Who wants to pick up a crate of shoddy grenades from a shifty bloke bristling with weapons? Filthy Henry respected this, so I would only do the occasional drug run.

"I was supposed to push some heroin on a new buyer, but I smelled him out as a pig. He didn't look comfortable in his coat. I know that sounds crazy, but a man should be used to his own coat. I played it cool, said I could get him what he wanted in a week, even though the boot of my car was loaded down with the stuff. Picked the man's pocket as he left, and sure enough, the badge was tucked in right next to the wallet."

Dante paused to make sure his audience was still listening, and shrugged when he saw they were.

"I suppose I shouldn't have told Filthy Henry, but I had to

give a reason for why the deal went sour. If I hadn't mentioned the wallet, everything would have been fine, but Henry snatched it away. There it was, Constable Warren's home address right next to all the photos of his kids. You should have seen them. Each one was a different color, like a United Nations meeting or something, all squeezed in between him and his Yoko Ono wife. I'll spare you what Filthy Henry's plans were, but they involved using some of those surplus explosives to make sure Constable Warren and his family would never sing Kumbaya again."

"I thought you were going to spare us?" John interrupted.

"Yeah, well, I didn't tell you where he planned on shoving those explosives. Anyway, I tailed Warren the very next day and watched him take his kids to church, stopping along the way to talk to a beggar. Didn't give him a thing, or so I thought, but then Warren pops in a bakery and comes out with some food and gives it to the bum, along with the change. All the while his family is watching patiently as if they'd seen it a thousand times before. Constable Warren was a good man, and his kids would probably grow up right with someone like him around. If he lived long enough."

"So what did you do?" John asked.

"I decided to kill him," Dante said, causing the audience to gasp. "No! Not Warren. Filthy Henry. I figured it was either him or a gaggle of goodwill kids, so the choice wasn't so hard. I bought some rat poison and put it in Henry's tea that very day. Even with his cuppa drowning in milk, he could taste something was wrong. Of course I had been dumb enough to make his tea for him, like I was suddenly his mother. Filthy Henry had a suspicious mind, you see. Before I could blink he had two of his favorite pistols pointed at me, his eyes all blood and murder. I was a goner! But then that little bit of rat poison hit his stomach, and before you know it, Henry was keeled over and puking up his guts."

The audience groaned, Thoth's magic conjuring the smell of the puke along with the lumpy visual details.

"All he ever ate was fish and chips," Dante explained. "Anyway, I've never been handy with a gun, but I figured it was time to learn, so I grabbed the pistols and started pulling the triggers. Nothing happened. They didn't budge. Might have been the safety but I didn't know where that was, and Henry was getting to his feet. So I used them as clubs instead. Worked a treat, really. Before long, Henry was filthier than he'd even been before."

The audience was horrified, except one twisted soul who cheered.

"After the deed was done, I took what I could from Filthy Henry's safe and hightailed it back to Dublin. Funny thing is, if I hadn't saved Warren's life, I probably would have gone straight to Hell. Would have saved me a lot of trouble, come to think of it."

With the story having mercifully reached its conclusion, the chamber full of people began talking, their gestures animated. Seeing them like this, John could not believe they were once nearly comatose.

"He's a hero!" one man said emphatically.

"He could have warned the constable instead of committing murder," an old woman complained. "They could have arrested Filthy Henry."

"There was no time!" another insisted.

Where debates weren't raging, others were discussing the modern wonders that had been the backdrop of the story. Pubs, cities, and cars: All were concepts that must have seemed like something out of Star Wars to the people of ancient Egypt.

Thoth led John and his friends from the chamber while his people were distracted. He had no need to speak, as his point had been made. The souls that came from Hell would have a captive audience and possibly enjoy celebrity status. After all, no other realm's citizens had more interesting stories to share. John didn't know if they would be a good influence, but anything was better than boredom.

Outside the onyx pyramid, the other Egyptian gods awaited them, along with the steam coach.

"Ten thousand souls?" Osiris asked.

Rimmon turned to John. "Many people in Hell feel the urge to move on as well. This could be good for them, but I leave the choice to you."

John nodded. Why not? Wasn't this what they were fighting for? Not just to liberate Purgatory, but to return free movement between the realms. With the deal finalized and the amount of souls agreed upon, it was time to return to Hell. Once the coach was airborne, the view outside the window was a sea of animal heads, waving goodbye with human hands. With Dante in the driver's seat, the land of pyramids, sphinxes, and pharaohs was soon far behind them.

Chapter Eleven

Asmoday's office was empty, the only sound the ticking of an antique clock that normally couldn't be heard over the Archduke's heavy breathing. John was tense with anticipation. Rimmon had promised him answers when they returned to Hell, but he couldn't imagine what form they would take. Truth could be an amazing catalyst for change. Once a perspective had been altered, there was no return. John was tempted to grab Rimmon and say he had changed his mind. After all, wasn't he happy enough? He had goals keeping him busy, and he enjoyed the freedom of moving between the realms and exploring. But if he stopped himself now, John knew he would no longer be happy. To live in fear of the truth was so much worse than knowing it.

So now they stood in an empty office, Asmoday's absence ominous. In what initially appeared to be a rebellious gesture, Rimmon leapt onto the vacant desk and kicked at a snow globe that sheltered a plastic melting snowball beneath its glass surface. The snow globe tipped over, revealing a hinge where it was attached to the desk. There was an audible click, then the desk rumbled and shook.

The incubus held out his hand as the desk began descending. "Come."

By the time John recovered from his surprise, the desk's surface was even with the floor and sinking further. John jumped for the desk, allowing himself to be more clumsy than necessary so that Rimmon would catch him. The demon's stabilizing hands were warm on John's arms, but flirtatious desires were swept away when John saw what lay below Asmoday's office.

This was the Hell that foam-mouthed preachers and maddened Bible-thumpers always promised. The world spiraling out below the desk was all flames and sulfur fumes. The heat waves were so great that they were visible, like wavering ghosts. A geyser of lava erupted just inches from the desk, sending John recoiling. Only Rimmon's grip saved John from tumbling over the edge.

"Take it easy."

Rimmon's voice was calm, making John feel as though he were a Neanderthal reacting to something as common as city street traffic. He thought up a smart reply, but before the quip could leave his lips, a dark shadow slid over them as something enormous passed above their heads. A moment later, a bloodcurdling scream sounded from the direction it had flown.

"What was that?" John asked, voice harsh with fear.

"The flying creature I've never seen before, but the scream came from an escapee," Rimmon said without emotion. "They usually don't get this far."

"An escapee? From what?"

"Whatever tortures they were suffering." The light from the surrounding fires made Rimmon's skin appear even redder than usual and cast his face in deep shadows. Never had he appeared so demonic. "Keep in mind that these tortures are purely of the sinner's own design, a manifestation of his or her guilt. Sinners create the very scenarios they feel they deserve. Occasionally one will allow himself to escape, to experience a moment of release before suffering crushing defeat when caught."

A monstrous squawk and a tearing noise came between screams. John felt so repulsed that he moved away from Rimmon.

"I explained all of this to you when we first met, John, and even showed you a vision."

"You did, but that felt like a dream. Seeing it in practice is entirely different. You can't tell me that person down there *wants* to be—" He broke off, his imagination filling with gory possibilities.

Rimmon sighed. "We could go down there, forcibly drag the sinner onto this desk, and take him up to the surface to freedom, but the second we take our eyes off him, he would be right back down here again. They believe they should be here and so they are."

"But the steam coach drivers—"

"Felt they had earned redemption, had worked off whatever sins they committed in life. I promise it isn't all like this. Some parts of Hell are drab and boring, people milling around and unable to be with the ones they love. In other places liars lose the ability to speak or hateful people suffer an unending barrage of ugly truths. Each of these souls works through the issues they didn't resolve in life, and none of them remain here forever. They leave better people, because deep down we all know what is right for ourselves." Rimmon frowned. "Then there are the real sinners, the child molesters, murderers, and rapists. They are in a category all their own. They are the ones who suffer in places like this one or worse. The little sinners, they move on soon enough, but big sinners aren't so lucky."

John swallowed. "But you said some of those people don't feel guilty or ashamed of their crimes."

"And they are usually happiest here, torturing the souls who feel they deserve it. Hell isn't a perfect system. None of creation is. There is real evil out there on the astral plane, unapologetic and uninterested in games of torture, but we try to contain as much of it as we can here."

"Do you guys have Hitler?" John asked, regaining some of his sense of humor.

"Oh, yes." Rimmon smiled. "Hitler is a keeper. There's a whole region dedicated to him and his friends."

The desk finally thudded to a stop below the level of the molten pools of lava and eternal blazes. Stalagmites glowed with crimson veins, and the floor beneath their feet steamed like freshly laid blacktop. Ahead was a mansion hewn directly out of the surrounding stone. Ornamentation was carved into the exterior, scenes both carnal and violent. The windows were wide and slanted, like angry eyes, each lit by a single violet flame that appeared to follow them as they neared the massive wooden doors.

With an ancient creak, the great doors opened, revealing a corpse dressed smartly in a butler's uniform. A permanent smile was on its face, the mummified skin having pulled away from the teeth long ago. The lack of eyelids gave the butler a look of constant panic.

"The master is relaxing in the hot tub," the deceased creature rasped.

The butler needn't have informed them. John barely had time to take in the heavy concrete stairway or the obscene tapestries covering every wall before Asmoday came wobbling into the room.

"What is it?" he sputtered. "Are the other pantheons here early? Did you greet them?"

Seeing Asmoday naked had never been on John's wish list, and the steaming yellow chunks that were sliding off his chubby curves certainly didn't help sell the idea. What had the Archduke been bathing in, puke?

"Nothing to worry about," Rimmon soothed. "We're just here for a debriefing."

Asmoday's three eyes narrowed, the undead butler already shambling toward him with blanket-sized towel that he had conjured up.

"Then why'd you bring him along?" the Archduke snarled as the towel was stretched around his waist.

"Because, thanks to him, the Greco-Roman pantheon will join us. Asmoday, it's time we bring John inside, tell him the full details of the situation. If we don't, then we stand to lose his support."

"We never needed it to begin with," the Archduke snorted. "There are plenty of—" He hesitated. "—his sort who can get the job done."

"Could any of them bring the Egyptians to our side?"

Asmoday barked one humorless laugh. "Of course not! We'll all be dust in God's nose before those elitist mummies crawl out of their tombs."

Rimmon raised an eyebrow. "And yet they are poised to join us in battle. That is, if John chooses to call on them."

"Him?" Asmoday pointed a stubby finger at John. "The Egyptians are at his beck and call?"

"Yes," Rimmon lied, "and if we don't show him some respect, we stand to lose everything they could bring to your war."

"I've always considered John a part of our inner circle," Asmoday oozed without missing a beat. "I just never wanted to burden him with details he would find boring. Still, if he insists. Come on in! *Mi casa es tu casa, compadres!*"

John shook his head ruefully as they were led through the gaudy mansion to an open courtyard devoid of flora. Only humanoid sculptures were there as decoration, usually in pairs, sometimes in threesomes. The statues were twisted into positions even the Kama Sutra had failed to depict, mostly because half were physically impossible if not downright deadly. The hot tub in the center of these statues was filled with a bubbling, thick substance that really did resemble vomit. Asmoday slipped in, inviting them to join him. They declined, which was just as well since his considerable bulk took up the entirety of the tub.

Instead they sat on two doggy-style statues that served as

benches. Rimmon went through his debriefing. Asmoday already knew of the success with the Greeks, thanks to a message from Hermes, but his eyes glittered greedily when he heard the deal made with the Egyptians. He barely blinked at the sum of ten thousand souls, a sure sign that the Egyptians could have asked for more. The only detail Rimmon left out was the cause of John's sunburn, although the topic came up in its own way.

"No sign of Ra, then?" Asmoday asked.

"He wasn't with the assembled gods," Rimmon answered smoothly.

The grimace on the Archduke's face was the final piece of the puzzle for John. He could think of only one reason Asmoday would look disappointed instead of happy that a competing pantheon was left without its chief. Now it was only a matter of getting him to admit it.

"I know you boys have worked hard," Asmoday said, rubbing his hands together eagerly, "but there's one last place I need you to go. We have more than enough generals and majors, but what we lack now are troops."

John listened half-heartedly to the details of their next trip, waiting for his chance to speak. Once it came he said, "I'll go, but first I would like a meeting with Satan."

"Satan?" Asmoday floundered.

"Satan, the Devil, Lucifer, whatever you call him. I need to speak with him before this goes any further. Seeing as how I'm on the inside now, this shouldn't be a problem."

Asmoday tried to stand and ended up slipping in the sludge, but this didn't stop him from shouting. "Who do you think you are? You think the Devil has time for you? Do you realize how miniscule and unimportant your existence is to him? You're nothing! Beneath his notice! Plankton begging for the attention of a shark!"

"Just one minute? Ten seconds even?"

"No!"

John smiled. "How long has he been missing?"

Asmoday glared accusingly at Rimmon.

"He didn't tell me anything." John stood to draw attention to himself. "Every pantheon we visited has been without its leader. Why would Hell be any different? How long has he been gone?"

Asmoday's look of fury melted into one of misery. "Linear

time is for humans, but you could say he's been gone more than a century in living years."

John nodded. "And did the other leaders disappear at the same time?"

"I don't know!" Asmoday wailed. "Lucifer vanishing was a dream come true! For millennia my single ambition was to supplant him. Once I took his place, I was too busy reveling in my new power to pay attention to the other realms. Oh, it was wonderful, *wonderful* at first! What I didn't realize is that the previous king had spent a millennia shitting on his throne, leaving me sitting on nothing more than one giant pile."

John grimaced. "Please tell me you mean that metaphorically."

"By the time I had finished binging on power," Asmoday continued, "the pantheons were all pointing accusatory fingers at each other, most of them aimed at us. They always blame Hell, when everyone knows it's never the most obvious suspect."

"And the real reason you want to wage war on Heaven?" John pressed.

"Lucifer's plan," Asmoday said. "Before he disappeared, he was secretly organizing this war. He hadn't told any of us about it, but the plans were left behind when he went. Gathering the pantheons together, the strategic advantages they each had, all of it mapped out in careful detail. He knew what he was doing."

"Well, that's no surprise," John snorted. "That's what the Devil does, right?"

"In fact, it isn't," Rimmon said. "Lucifer had more power in Hell than he ever did as an angel by God's side. That God still had more power never bothered him. Lucifer wasn't a fool. Second place out of billions was more than enough for him."

"But he was still scared of something." Asmoday's chins wobbled with greater velocity as his panic increased. "Why else would Lucifer plan a war that repulsively shares the glory with other pantheons? He knew his days were numbered!"

John sighed. "Did it ever occur to you that God may have whisked the Devil away *because* of this plan?" The Archduke squirmed uncomfortably, and even though he knew it was cruel, John couldn't help but continue. "Maybe Lucifer got bored after all those millennia and decided to shake things up, have another go at that celestial throne. God caught wind of it and decided to deal with him once and for all. And now you are walking in those very same footsteps. Why, any minute now…"

Asmoday's chins ceased quivering and his jaw set in anger. "Then explain the other pantheons, mongrel! Why would God run around kidnapping all of their leaders? They were even less of a threat than Lucifer! Or do you really think they were all planning the same war?"

John didn't, but he liked seeing Asmoday get his back up like this.

Rimmon cleared his throat, his instincts as ambassador kicking in. "We believe that even God may have abdicated his throne. There may have been a coup for power. The Ministers of Order began appearing seven human centuries ago, around the end of the crusades, and have been growing in prominence ever since. There was a dramatic increase in their numbers around the time of the disappearances. God has often been silent, but never so much as in the last century."

The news hit John like a stone. The idea that even God had gone missing was incomprehensible. He pictured kidnappers shoving an old, white-bearded man into the trunk of a car. The image was ridiculous, but so was the idea that something could overpower the most powerful deity in all creation. Nothing was greater than God, right? Unless the issue wasn't as simple as who was strongest. Maybe the position held the power and not the person. Asmoday had spoken of the great power he received once Lucifer was gone. Had the same happened elsewhere?

"Does this mean that someone else is the leader of Heaven?" John asked.

"It could," Rimmon said. "Even so, we suspect it will take time for the usurper to step into the void of power left by God. But once he does, it will be too late for any of us to act."

"We fight now," Asmoday said, "or we spend the rest of eternity as slaves."

John stirred his drink with a thin cocktail straw and wondered why it smelled like cinnamon. He had asked for a hot tea, but what John received was foamy with cream and resembled a latte. Rimmon had said something about chai as he brought it to the table. John gave a cautious sip. If anyone but the incubus had chosen it for him, John would have sent it back.

They sat together at a street side café, their table in view of the steam coach parked further down the alley. Dante had been glad for some downtime when they had gone to visit Asmoday, but he was supposed to take care of Bolo. Instead they found the dog tied to one of the coach wheels. Bolo was happily watching the parade of people walking by, wagging his tail and occasionally getting petted for his efforts.

Now Bolo dozed under the table as they waited. They would only be able to reach their next destination with Dante's help and were stranded until he reappeared, but John was glad for the chance to think things over. Asmoday had known less than John would have liked. The Archduke was only following instructions left by his predecessor, which wasn't encouraging. John couldn't help feeling that they were all playing at soldiers without knowing the war, and that the generals had abandoned their troops to an unseen enemy.

"Penny for your thoughts," Rimmon said.

"Fine, but you're getting a bargain. I don't like that we're following instructions purportedly left behind by Lucifer. That's like finding a treasure map with a big black 'X' on it. Way too convenient. Someone was cunning enough to get the jump on the Devil, but they left his secret plans behind? I'm starting to think they were placed there by whoever did the Devil in, which would mean we're operating under the enemy's instructions."

Rimmon smiled around the edge of his coffee cup until he had finished sipping. "I don't think I've ever met such a suspicious mind," he said with a chuckle.

"I'm just getting started. If someone *is* strong enough to take down the most powerful gods of each pantheon, why stop there? They could have finished the job and taken down the smaller gods, if that's what they wanted. Then there's Ra, who certainly appeared free to me. No, we're still missing a piece of the puzzle, which means we don't know if what we're doing is right or not."

"I think it is," Rimmon said without hesitation. "Whatever we're up against had reason for wanting the realms separated and at each other's throats. The glass man in the Norse realm only revealed himself when a truce became imminent. Bringing the pantheons together is the first step in the right direction. What we choose to do once we're all together is another matter."

John sighed. "I hope you're right. Whoever is in charge of Purgatory probably wants to shape the rest of the afterlife in its image, and that frightens me. Being dead should mean having more freedom than we had in life, but something out there wants to make us all prisoners."

Rimmon set his coffee down and considered John carefully. "You're an old soul, John, but don't let them sell you their fear. We won't fall. Not as long as we're together."

That "together" no doubt referred to the different pantheons rather than the two of them. Which was a shame really, because he wouldn't mind exploring that particular avenue. John felt, and not for the first time, like asking Rimmon if he even stood a chance.

"I know the question on your mind," Rimmon said.

John refused to blush, and for once the rest of him complied. "Do you?"

"It's the same thing you asked Dante."

Uh, no. Rimmon definitely didn't know what John was thinking.

"You want to know what it is that makes you special," Rimmon continued.

"Is there enough time in the day?" John quipped, earning him a smile.

"I mean what Asmoday kept from you that first day in his office. Dante was telling you the truth when he said that it's something good. I hope one day to tell you everything you deserve to know, but doing so means we will have to say goodbye."

John cocked an eyebrow. "And you aren't ready for that?"

"None of us are, but I believe what you said about freedom. You should choose for yourself. If you insist on knowing, I will tell you now, but please heed my warning."

"If you tell me, I won't be able to see you again?"

"Not for a very long time, I suspect."

"And Dante or Bolo?"

The dog grumbled from beneath the table.

Rimmon smiled. "I doubt there are many places Bolo couldn't follow you."

And it was that smile that was terribly unfair, because not seeing it anymore was the price of learning the truth, and Rimmon had to know that John wasn't willing to pay. Wasn't interest always obvious? Emotions like these were always visible to the naked eye.

"Dante's back," John said, nodding at the steam coach. "And by the look of things, he's very, very drunk."

John wouldn't have minded joining him. He was glad for the distraction. This way he wouldn't have to tell Rimmon his choice, wouldn't have to acknowledge that he was— What? In love with the demon? John knew so little about Rimmon. He didn't even understand what an incubus was. Not fully. He didn't know if demons were born or somehow created, if they had families, went to school, or even experienced childhood. He didn't know Rimmon's past and barely knew any details of his present. Logically, John shouldn't feel anything for him but friendship.

Except that he had touched Rimmon's heart, his essence, and had unequivocally known in that moment that Rimmon was good. That he was also handsome and intelligent had been obvious from their first encounter. Everything else was just details. Love wasn't blind, but it was very, very stupid, and John was having an increasingly hard time ignoring its call. But he had an escape plan. If his feelings ever became too much to bear, then he would ask Rimmon to tell him the truth, and they would be parted.

"Let's do this," John said, pushing away the bastardized tea and standing. "Getting Dante to play dress-up will be easier while he's drunk."

Dante had opened the coach door and was resting his upper body on one of the velvet cushions while the rest of him was still in the street. A series of miserable groans accompanied their efforts to get him upright again.

"We have something for you, Dante," Rimmon said as they leaned him against the side of the coach. "Something valuable."

"Goodies?" Dante asked.

"Oh, yes." Rimmon took a long, thin box from his cloak and opened it. Even in the limited light of the alleyway, the contents glimmered.

"What's that?" Dante asked, some sobriety returning to his interested eyes. In the center of the box lay a necklace, its gold band wide and thick in order to support its six apple-sized jewels. To each side of this necklace were two smaller bracelets, each sporting one large gem.

John couldn't say much for their style, but their worth must have been phenomenal. The jewelry had a presence of its own, as if it were a living being. This is what Rimmon had meant regarding true value in the afterlife. The resemblance of precious minerals meant nothing; it was their power and singularity that gave them worth. Asmoday's eyes had been greedy and reluctant when he had handed them over, but he had no choice if they were to reach their next destination. These three pieces of jewelry were called the Regression Regalia, and their power was about to be demonstrated.

"Take a look at these beauties," Rimmon said to Dante. "There isn't anything else like them in all of existence. Their value is incalculable. Wouldn't you like to wear them?"

"I'd rather pawn them, but whatever gets your rocks off," Dante slurred.

"You'd better help him," John said after Dante made a clumsy swipe at the box.

He watched as the demon adorned Dante with each piece, resisting the urge to crack a joke. No matter how special the Regression Regalia might be, they were still tacky. Dante looked like a child playing dress-up in grandma's old costume jewelry. The innocent image was somewhat ruined when the Irishman passed out.

"Do we need him awake to do this?" John asked.

"It's probably better if he isn't. Are we ready?"

John hesitated. They hadn't even explained to Dante what they were about to do. On the other hand, there was a good chance that Dante wouldn't have immediately understood. John hadn't at first. He never had much faith in the idea of past lives since everyone turned out to be Cleopatra, Caesar, or some other glorious historical figure, but according to Asmoday, reincarnation was real. Now John had a chance to see proof.

He reached for the bracelet on Dante's right wrist, the one set with a gigantic diamond, rather than the bracelet with the dark stone. Once touched, the diamond began to glow, sending a chain reaction across the jewels of the necklace. Soon Dante was invisible behind their bright light. When the light eventually faded, Dante had undergone a complete transformation. He now was in his late fifties, his red hair thin and his beer belly huge compared to his skinny arms and legs. He opened his eyes and glared up at them.

"Is there a reason you two poofs are staring at me?" he said in a thick Australian accent.

"Not particularly," Rimmon said, reaching down to touch the diamond again.

"I thought he was supposed to be Chinese?" John said as the Australian man was lost to the light of the gems.

"Must be one life further back," Rimmon said. "I sensed it while possessing him, but this is hardly a perfect science."

John sighed. This seemed a tremendous effort just to hitch a ride to the Taoist realm. Their normal method of using a redeemed soul wasn't possible, since no viable candidates were available in Hell. Rimmon had suggested using the Regression Regalia to bring Dante back to a previous life, hopefully one with a connection to the realm they were trying to reach.

The lights cleared a second time, revealing a small Asian woman with white hair fashioned into a bun. She had lived a much longer life than either of her successors, and had likely died of old age. Shrewd eyes considered each of them before she stood up. When she spoke, she chose her words carefully.

"You are not my ancestors."

The first impression was that she spoke English with an impossibly thick accent, when in reality she was speaking her native Japanese. But language is universal in the afterlife, and John could understand her perfectly. He did a mental double take. *Japanese?* He didn't know the language, but he'd seen enough subtitled anime to differentiate it from Chinese.

"She's not—"

"I know," Rimmon said.

"Maybe we need to go back another life?"

The demon shook his head. "This is the one I sensed. What religion are you?" he asked the woman. "Shinto?"

She nodded briskly, her eyes darting down the alleyway in each direction. Was she thinking of running? John changed his position, keeping her between him and the coach. Rimmon picked up on this too and moved closer to her.

"All you need to do is hop in this seat and you'll be reunited with your ancestors."

The woman's eyes widened. She took a tentative step backwards, but Rimmon matched her by stepping forward. He placed a hand on each arm, muscles flexing as he lifted her. "Allow me to help you," he said politely, even as the woman began struggling and kicking. Once in the driver's seat, chains extended from the steam coach to hold her in place.

"Nice seatbelt," John murmured as they took their seats inside the cabin. "Is it just me or is she not looking forward to going home again?"

"We'll soon find out why."

The coach lurched forward, accompanied by the usual indignant shouting as the denizens of Hell were knocked over in the street. Bolo hung his head out the window and observed, barking in response to the loud insults.

"Will Dante remember any of this when we restore him?" John asked. "For that matter, does she remember being Dante?"

"It's hard to say. This sort of past life regression is almost unheard of. We don't know what purpose the Regression Regalia was invented for or its origin. One story claims that a demon lord invented them for his own entertainment; another is your standard romantic tale of lovers chasing each other across time. The Regalia is truly unique. That Asmoday allowed us to borrow it is a strong sign of his desperation."

John nodded. They weren't travelling to recruit other gods this time. They were after an army, one made of terracotta in fact. John remembered seeing a documentary about it once. Qin Shi Huang, the First Emperor of China, had been buried with an army of more than eight thousand soldiers and a good number of chariots and horses, all made from clay. The idea was to give Qin his own army in the afterlife. Presumably it had worked because Asmoday was sending them to hire this army.

Of course, now they were off track, guided by the Japanese religion of Shinto rather than Chinese Taoism.

"We should be able to reach our intended destination," Rimmon said, predicting John's question. "At the very least this will get us nearer to where we need to be."

Bolo moved away from the window to lay his head in John's lap. John could see why the dog was bored with the view. Nothing was visible outside except darkness. He looked at Rimmon for answers, but the demon appeared just as perplexed.

The coach stopped. With no reference point, they sensed this rather than felt it. Rimmon left the coach first, stepping down onto ground that could not be seen. John followed, feeling vertigo from being suspended in a void.

"Home," the woman in the driver's seat moaned. "Why did you bring me home?"

"Fumiko!"

The voices came from all around, booming in unison.

"Fumiko, you have returned but you have not changed!"

"They don't sound happy," John whispered. "Maybe you better get her unchained and turned back into Dante."

But the coach had already released the little old woman, who hopped down and began to run.

"You cannot escape from your ancestral home."

In the darkness, shapes began to form. Cabinets, couches, paper lanterns, and tidy wooden floors. These were monochrome at first, but colors soon flourished as reality solidified.

"You were to reincarnate, Fumiko, to learn from your mistakes. You are still a liar, a thief, instilling the confidence of strangers before taking from them!"

"So what?" Fumiko shook her fists at the air. "I'm not ashamed of what I am! The people I stole from were too stupid to deserve their money. If I hadn't taken it, someone else would have!"

"That's Dante, all right," John muttered.

Faces began to form all around them. People of all ages were there, young and old, so many now that it was impossible to count.

"You will return to Earth. You will live many lives until you are worthy of joining the family spirit."

"Amaterasu!" Fumiko cried. "Amaterasu! Goddess of the sun, I beseech you. Take me into hiding, take me away from these spirits that trouble me so. Hide me from my family as you once hid from yours!"

"You will reincarnate!"

The faces descended, moving for Fumiko, but a beam of sunlight cut through the room, surrounding the old woman in its glow. She cackled victoriously as the light intensified, becoming so bright John had to close his eyes. When the light disappeared, Fumiko was gone.

"No," John breathed. "Wait! Wait you idiots, that was Dante! It wasn't Fumiko at all!" He ran forward, waving his arms for attention, but the faces, the house, everything faded until nothing was left but the black void. They had lost Dante.

Chapter Twelve

The darkness was unforgiving and impenetrable. How vision was still possible was, like most of the afterlife, beyond reasoning. John gripped one of the coach's brass lanterns stubbornly and scowled.

"We can't leave. If we do we'll never see him again."

"Staying here serves no purpose," Rimmon said. "We will find Dante, perhaps with the assistance of another god, but staying in place won't bring him back. He's Fumiko now, a woman who has no warmth for us and won't willingly return to this place."

"There has to be something we can do!"

"We can move on." Rimmon snapped his fingers and the wheels of the coach began to turn, following the demon as he walked away.

John released the lamp and decided to protest by staying in place, Bolo waiting loyally at his side. But as the coach began shrinking into the distance, they ran to catch up. Rimmon was decent enough not to act smug.

"We'll get him back," he reassured John once more.

As they walked, John promised himself a hundred times that he would set things right with Dante. He would enlist the entire army he had raised if need be.

"Neat trick," he said eventually, nodding at the self-propelled coach wheels. "Why didn't you do that before?"

"I was busy possessing Dante."

"Will it cause trouble here, you being out in plain sight?"

Rimmon shook his head. "I'm just another *kami* here, a spiritual being like any other. Ironic that the denizens of Hell are welcome here when there's so little to see."

"It's creepy. I could see a sort of house back there before it faded."

That wasn't all. Objects faded into existence before disappearing again, like icebergs in a fog-drenched sea. No rhyme or reason seemed to govern what would appear. An old stone well, a wooden cart, once even an acre of farmland appeared suddenly below their feet before vanishing again.

"I'm beginning to suspect existence here is more private than what we are used to," Rimmon said. "As we saw with Fumiko, the souls here cluster together into an ancestral spirit. Not being a part of these families might mean we cannot see their homes, but I wonder if they can see us."

Like ghosts, passing through the walls of their homes, John thought as he watched Bolo bounding along ahead of them. The dog had an amazing knack for knowing the direction they were headed in, which was more than John could say for himself. Without any visible landmarks, at least any that stayed in place for long, he couldn't tell if they were walking in a straight line or going in circles.

"Do you know where we're going?" he asked. "We were aiming for Taoism, but this is Shintoism, right? Can we walk from one afterlife to another?"

Rimmon nodded. "Here we can. Religion isn't divided here as it is in the Western world. Shintoism, Taoism, Buddhism, each is different and yet complimentary. The people take what they need from each. Reincarnation, for instance, isn't part of the Shinto faith. Shinto has very little to say about the afterlife. There's a saying in Japan, 'Live Shinto, die Buddhist.' The philosophy of Shinto guides them through life, but the more gentle traditions of Buddha are what they turn to when a loved one departs.

"Believe it or not, the Western world wasn't so different once. Just look at how much the different religions have in common. Flood myths aren't limited to just Noah. During Ragnarok, the Norse version of Armageddon, the world is flooded and everyone dies except for two people, a man and a woman. End of the world scenarios, both past and future, are found in most mythologies, a time of peace and repopulation often following destruction. Who's to say that Noah and his wife weren't the survivors of Ragnarok? Am I losing you?"

"No, I think I follow," John said. "You're saying that most religions tell the same story or at least borrow heavily from each other."

"Exactly. There are countless examples of this. The Norse have the Haminjur, and the Greeks have Erotes, both of which are remarkably similar to guardian angels. The Greek gods fought the Titans just as the Norse fought ice giants, and we've already established that the original concept of Hell was Greek by design. The Greeks were influential in the concept of Heaven as well, if you consider the sky home of the gods on Mount Olympus.

"As for the deities themselves, the Hindu gods Brahma, Shiva, and Vishnu form a triad that represents creation, preservation, and destruction. Is that so different from the Holy Trinity? Then there's the son of God, champion of Earth, and born of mortal blood, but that could refer to both Hercules and Jesus. Religions often deny these comparisons, unwilling to acknowledge that their beliefs are rooted in many different cultures, but I've always felt these similarities to be complementary.

"There was a time, in this world at least, when these connections were celebrated. But now all is separated, the similarities forgotten in favor of differences. Suspicion and mistrust have deteriorated the pathways between realms, and soon they will be destroyed altogether. We are confined to our rooms, forbidden to go outside and play, and why?"

Rimmon turned to John, who shook his head, surprised it wasn't a rhetorical question. Perhaps Rimmon didn't know the answer himself because he remained silent, lost in his own thoughts.

The void around them became oppressive, objects no longer appearing as often as they once had. Aside from a comment that they were between realms, Rimmon didn't speak. John had never been much for idle chitchat himself, but the void didn't provide his mind with any entertainment. His thoughts turned to Rimmon, as they seemed too keen to do lately, and of Rimmon's estranged boyfriend. John knew very little of the man. There had been the breathtakingly handsome bust in Rimmon's dining room and the story of how they met, but nothing more.

"Tell me more about your ex-boyfriend," John said.

"Hm?"

"I'm curious about him. Is he a demon like you?"

Rimmon smiled. "It's complicated."

"So? We have time."

"You know that I miss him, and that he isn't happy with who I am. The rest is unimportant."

John pictured the bust in his mind again, except this time it was smirking. *Nice try, chump,* he imagined it saying, *but I beat you to the punch. Besides, what makes you think you're good enough for him? What are you to an incubus?*

John's subconscious wasn't normally so self-depreciative,

but he supposed it did have a point. In life John did just fine for himself, but here, surrounded by gods, demons, and other strange creatures, what was he? John was still a fledgling, learning the ropes. Rimmon possibly perceived him as being ridiculously young. His frequent questions were probably nothing more than baby talk to a being who may have existed for centuries.

Then again, John was moving gods with his words. Lowly human he may be, but the afterlife was dancing to his tune as of late. He was playing ambassador for Hell, a role that Rimmon shared, and their mutual success could only bring them together. They were partners in crime, so to speak. Gentlemen of equal standing, sharing the same footing, two peas in a pod, and a bunch of other silly metaphors.

"We have company," Rimmon murmured.

John's thoughts evaporated as he saw his mother. The yearning in his heart drowned out even thoughts of Rimmon, but the emotions soon sputtered and died. This woman was thin, tan, and had short blond hair, just like his mother, but her eyes were vacant. She had the same easy smile she always wore, but this wasn't her. His mother was still alive in California. She couldn't be here with them now. John didn't want her to be, not until it was her time.

"What do we do?"

Rimmon spread his arms and closed his eyes. "We make her welcome."

A world sprang into creation, filling the emptiness around them with color and light. Trees heavy with ripened fruit appeared first, forming a grove where they stood. An azure sky bled through the dark above, white cotton ball clouds coming next. Green grass unrolled like a carpet, stretching out to the stranger and halting just in front of her feet.

John had felt accomplished when creating Bolo's leash, but this demonstration of skill was pure mastery. Rimmon only needed seconds to create a miniature world. Rolling hills covered in tiny white and purple flowers now stretched as far as the eye could see. Bolo was already racing across these hills, barking gleefully. This is what Jacobi had spoken of, the ability to craft a new world in the dark and empty spaces between realms. If one person were capable of such a feat, he could only imagine what an entire community could do.

Their guest hardly reacted, having eyes only for John as she came nearer. He wondered for a moment if this wasn't his mother after all. Why else would the woman not be looking at Rimmon, whose beauty was greater? Her vacant eyes never left his, even when Rimmon greeted her.

"John," she said, and he was certain this wasn't his mother. She had called him Johnny since the day he was born. "John, I have such important news for you. Such wonderful news!"

"Who are you?" he asked but she shook her head, eager to continue.

"I've been sent to find you, to tell you what they don't what you're—"

Rimmon snarled, thunder exploding and drowning out her words. John flinched, still trying to read her lips, to decipher their movement, but Rimmon's back obscured his vision as he leapt upon the woman and punched at her face. The woman's mouth stretched wide, her features lost to a gaping orifice that enveloped Rimmon's fist.

Rimmon stumbled back, but the woman followed, not allowing his fist to leave her mouth and taking in half his arm. He began struggling to dislodge her, but the woman sank her fingers—now pointed claws—into his sides and pulled him close. Rimmon howled as the lips around his elbow began inching forward like a caterpillar, progressively taking in more and more of him. A horrible sucking noise came as wisps of light were pulled from Rimmon's arm and into the creature's mouth. The woman was eating him, absorbing his life force.

Fire exploded from Rimmon's mouth, both figures lost in the inferno, but when the torrent of flame cleared the woman was left unscathed and determined to finish her meal. John rushed forward and grabbed Rimmon's shoulder, hoping to help pull him out of the creature's mouth, but the incubus shrugged him off and ordered him to back away. As soon as he did so, Rimmon lifted his legs and braced them against the woman's torso. The scene was ridiculous: the entire weight of a large, muscular demon hanging off a slight woman who wasn't even struggling to support him.

Rimmon groaned and strained before a loud popping noise sounded and his arm pulled free. From the elbow down it had lost all form and color, a gray mass of dead material. Rimmon didn't hesitate; he leapt off the ground and threw his arms around the woman, whose huge, gaping mouth was gurgling in anticipation of more. To John's horror, Rimmon shoved his nose, mouth, and chin into this inverted face like some sort of disgusting kiss. Then the demon's fire roared down the creature's throat. The woman's eyes bulged outward, lights playing behind them before they exploded and streams of flame poured out the empty sockets. Soon the entire body exploded into flaming chunks that were quickly reduced to ash and disappeared.

"Are you all right?" Rimmon panted, his eyes wild and proud as they looked him over. Then he collapsed onto the grass he had so recently created.

John fell to his knees, rolling the demon over on his back while saying Rimmon's name over and over again. There was no response. Normally Rimmon's skin was warm, steadily radiating the gentle heat of a blush. There was comfort in this aura of heat, but now the warmth was gone, his body as cold as the grave, his skin color washed out.

John's mind warred between panic and indecision. Checking for a pulse, mouth to mouth, all of the emergency protocols John had been taught in life were meaningless here. How did one heal a soul, if that's even what Rimmon was? Was there such thing as a soul who had never lived a physical life? John knew so little and feared his ignorance would cost Rimmon his existence. Panic won. John began pounding on Rimmon's chest.

"Wake up! Wake up! God damn it, wake up!"

The demon groaned. His eyes fluttered open, looking lost and confused before steeling over with determination. John laughed, pounding him a couple more times for good measure and near tears with relief, even if Rimmon was glaring at him. The incubus pushed himself up, his right arm still a malformed, colorless stump. John did his best to help him rise, wincing at his body's frigid temperature. If a hot demon was a healthy demon, then something was still very wrong.

"You need to rest," John said. "Let's get you inside the coach and comfortable."

"No," Rimmon grunted, pushing John away to show he could stand on his own. "I'll be fine. We should continue on."

"You're not okay!"

"I'm fine!" Rimmon snarled. The fury in his eyes shifted to

hunger, bestial and urgent.

"The woman who attacked us, what was she?" John hoped the question would reach Rimmon, kick-start his intellectual processes again, but the demon responded by grabbing John by the arm and pulling him close.

"A vampire. The truth behind the legends." Rimmon's answers had an edge of a growl. "A creature that feeds off souls, feasting on their essence until they are lost to oblivion. Exceptionally rare. An honor… to… kill one." Rimmon's eyes lost their focus as he swayed. His flesh was the pink of new skin rather than its usual ruby tone, the hand that gripped John as cold as ice.

John thought of vampire stories, of how one bite could change someone into a pale, hungry version of their previous selves. "Is that what you are now? A vampire?"

Rimmon's laugh was cruel. "Oh, I feed! I love to feed, but not on souls. Only lust can satiate my craving. The crashing wave of climax, the slapping together of sweaty flesh. That is my banquet and I am hungry. I'm always so damned hungry! Only with him did I have my fill, stuffing myself to contentment on his sighs."

"Let me be him," John said, clenching his jaw. "That's what you need, right? You want to eat? Then let me be him for you."

Rimmon's frozen lips slammed into John's mouth, but they soon thawed as they slid down his chin to his neck, where teeth scraped against his skin teasingly. Clothes disappeared into the ether in response to their mutual desire.

"This might hurt," Rimmon whispered, before he spun John around. The demon's bare chest was cool against John's back, but warmed gradually as Rimmon slid inside of him. Had this been physical reality, John would have been in the greatest of pain. Rimmon's desire manifested in size, and right now the demon was bigger than John could normally handle. But here, in this strange world of form without physical limitation, all John felt was pleasure.

Rimmon growled into John's ear as he pumped, a beast driven by heat and instinct. John let him take everything he needed, which was more than just pleasure. John could feel the energy draining from him and into Rimmon. At first this frightened him, but when Rimmon's other arm came around to embrace John, no longer was it colorless and misshapen. The arm and hand had grown back, fully restored, which meant that John was healing Rimmon. The last of his resistance faded as John poured everything he had, every emotion he felt, into their love-making.

Soon Rimmon began to reciprocate, his tail sliding up John's leg before wrapping like a spring around his cock. John moaned in pleasure as their union became what he had known the first time with Rimmon—intellectual, a transcendental voyage across higher planes of the spirit and mind. No longer was Rimmon feeding. Now they were sharing their energy, passing it back and forth in waves of pleasure, the emptiness inside replaced by utopian totality.

When they finished, arms the color of ripe cherries gently lowered John to the ground before wrapping around and holding him. They lay in fields, warmed by a sun created from a shared dream, John resting his head against Rimmon's chest. His thoughts were formless, his mind fuzzy as he basked in an opiate haze of endorphins. If this was how you saved the life of an incubus, John was determined to become a doctor.

"Feel better?" John murmured, his cheek pressed against Rimmon's skin, which now held the reassuring warmth of an incubator.

"Much," Rimmon said and chuckled, "but I wish you hadn't seen me like that."

"No regrets here. I'd buy the vampire a drink if you hadn't killed it." John shifted. "The Ministers must have sent her."

"I have no doubt." Rimmon sighed. "A being with so much power, and its only instructions were to speak to you. This worries me. If the enemy knows your secret, then it's only a matter of time before they find a way of telling you."

"And then I go poof," John said.

"And then you go where you belong, which isn't so bad. You've done so much for Hell already that I think it would make little difference. The enemy either doesn't realize this, or they fear you for reasons we haven't yet considered."

"Sounds good to me," John yawned. "Just get me some earplugs until this whole ordeal is over."

"There may be something we can do. I'll consult with Asmoday once we're done here. Perhaps he will have a solution."

"Just as long as we get Dante back first," John reminded him, feeling guilty for taking an after-sex nap in the sun while his friend was still held hostage by a previous life.

The sound of galloping paws fast approached them, accompanied by happy panting. John sat up, tense until he saw it was only Bolo returning from his run. At least he'd had the good sense to disappear while they were getting it on. He even managed to find a ball of some sort.

"Hey, boy! Watcha got? Watcha got?"

The dog trotted up to John and dropped it next to him. The small head rolled a few times, but when it stopped, its eyes were staring up at John. And they blinked.

Chapter Thirteen

The head was made of terracotta, its worn face defined by shallow lines. Its expression was rather pensive as it stared up at John, unmoving. Had he only imagined the eyes blinking? The head was much smaller than he expected, small enough to pick up and hold in one hand. John turned it, taking in the two twisted braids on top of its head and the tidy little mustache. His fingers traced the uneven base where the neck had been broken off from the rest of the body.

"You did it!" Rimmon exclaimed, looking over John's shoulder. "Good boy, Bolo!"

"Good boy! Good boy, Bolo!" the head parroted.

John almost dropped it. He turned it upward again but the face was still.

"It looks like a terracotta figure," John said, "but how did Bolo know what we were looking for?"

"I asked him to find the terracotta warriors," Rimmon explained. "We've been following him the entire time."

John looked at Bolo, whose attention was fixed on the head, as if it were a tennis ball for him to play fetch with. "You can talk to the dog?"

"So can you," Rimmon replied.

"Right, but can he understand you? Aside from 'sit' and 'wanna treat?' I mean."

Rimmon nodded. "Animals have their own means of communication, a mixture of body language and telepathy. Reaching through to them is much easier on this side of the veil. You should try it sometime."

John looked back at Bolo, who met his eyes. The dog's expression was frank, as though he were open to the idea of polite conversation. "How did he know where to find the terracotta soldiers?"

"The same way he managed to find you in the Norse realm, even though he left you in Hell. Like the vampire that tracked you here, he has the gift of the seeker."

"But he's a dog."

"A dog with the gift of the seeker," Rimmon said patiently. "I'm just pleased that it worked, although I thought the soldiers would be larger than this."

The terracotta head spoke again. "You're thinking of Qin's army. Tall fellows, heavily detailed, outfitted in armor and accompanied by great chariots, yes?"

"Precisely," Rimmon said. "Do you know where they are?"

"Oh, no, you don't want them." The head smiled. "My brothers are closer and don't take up nearly as much room. We're much more economical."

"I have no doubt that your family is charming," Rimmon replied, "but we have specific instructions to seek out Qin's soldiers, not an army of dolls."

"None of us can help how we're made." The little head frowned. "Had I known that my destiny after centuries of being buried was to be dug up and insulted, I would have remained a lump of clay."

"Sorry," John began, but the head cut him off.

"Oh, it isn't you! I like how comfortable your hand is. I haven't felt this cozy since my potter fashioned me. It's him—" the head glared toward the demon, "—who is obsessed with size! Well I'm sorry I didn't live up to your expectations! You might as well bury me again so I don't cause you any further disappointment!"

Rimmon shrugged. "Bury it."

"Don't listen to him!" the head pleaded with John. "I'm still a soldier, and I'm still made of terracotta. That's what you were looking for, right?"

"True," John said with a nod, "although I hope your brothers have been better cared for. What happened to your body?"

"Somebody dropped and broke me long ago. What happened to your clothes?"

"Whoops!" John turned the head away from him, and hastily conjured up his clothing. This time he left off the suit jacket, opting instead for a tightly cut, forest green dress shirt, a charcoal tie, and gray slacks. If he had time later, he would put some effort into creating a mirror, but from what he could see, John felt like he was getting the hang of this.

"Very nice," Rimmon said, filling out a white button-up shirt with brown tweed slacks.

"Congratulations!" the head said. "You have found some clothing! Now we find my body. It's not far from here, not far at all. Bolo, find my body!"

"Wait!" Rimmon protested, but Bolo had already barked in agreement and run off.

"Well, let's go find Asmoday's army." John laughed as he ran to follow.

Without lungs or blood that needed oxygen, John could run as far as he liked without becoming winded. He felt like a kid again, full of infinite energy. Rimmon kept pace as they chased Bolo over the green hills.

The landscape began to change, the hills becoming steep, the grass making way for more rugged plants and weeds. On the horizon lay a village, and behind it a tomb built into a large hill. They stopped before reaching these landmarks and watched as Bolo circled the ground and began digging.

"You didn't create all this, did you?" John asked.

"No. We must have finally reached the Taoist realm."

"Oh, yes," the head confirmed. "We are home. Oh, it will be nice to have a body again! I barely had a chance to enjoy it before I was broken."

"What happened?" John asked.

"The family went into a panic after the king killed himself. There was very little time, you see. He wasn't really supposed to have an army."

"Maybe you'd better start at the beginning," John replied. "You belonged to a king?"

"Oh, yes, Liu Wu, king of the Chu state, the largest of seven territories." The head beamed up at him proudly. "He was a wonderful king! His reign was prosperous and peaceful. Everybody loved Liu Wu. I love Liu Wu. Do you? Do you love Liu Wu?"

"Of course!" John said, trying not to laugh. "I haven't met him, but you don't have to meet the king to love him, do you?"

"Oh, no, not at all!" the head agreed.

"So why would such a universally loved king kill himself?"

"When the Emperor's mother died, he decreed that all should mourn her passing, and for a while, Liu Wu did. Just a little while, but he tried. Then Liu Wu returned to his rightfully joyous life: the celebrations at court and all the wonderful meals. When the Emperor found out, he was furious. He wanted Liu Wu dead, but this was his brother—if only by marriage—so instead the

Emperor punished him by taking away some of his land. How cruel!"

"Harsh," John agreed, "but he still had a kingdom, which is more than most people have."

The head considered John for a moment, weighing how treacherous these words were before continuing. "Some time later, another of the seven kings came and suggested they rebel against the cruel Emperor. All seven kings agreed, including Liu Wu, but the war didn't go well. If only I had been alive then as I am now! I surely would have won the war for my king."

"But that's not what happened," John said. "Unfortunately," he added when the terracotta head scrutinized him again.

"No. The king was so ashamed of his defeat that he took his own life, a very brave decision, I feel. His family wasn't so brave and rushed to make peace with the Emperor, but they hadn't completely forgotten their love for the king. They knew the Emperor would never allow a rebel to be buried with his own personal army, or he might defeat the Emperor in the next world. So they rushed to bury the soldiers before the Emperor discovered us. They weren't so careful with me, I'm afraid."

Bolo whined for attention, having finished his excavation. The partially revealed body was indeed the size of a large doll. John didn't dare say it out loud, but he was beginning to share Rimmon's misgivings. They needed the best possible army, not a bunch of toy soldiers. John set the terracotta head down so he could lift the body and brush off the excess dirt. When he was finished, he placed the head on the severed neck, turning it until the jagged pieces lined up. Immediately they melded and became whole again.

The little soldier ran forward and wrapped his arms around John's leg, his head barely reaching John's knee. "Oh, thank you, gentleman of flowering grace, thank you!"

"Please, just call me John. Do you have a name?"

"Yes, the potter gave names to all of us. He named me Yi Yi!"

"Well, Yi Yi, I think you should take us to Liu Wu. There's an awful lot we have to discuss with him."

John looked to Rimmon, who shrugged his agreement.

"Oh! I'd like nothing more!" Yi Yi gushed. "I hope Liu Wu hasn't been lonely without me!"

As the little warrior turned to leave, John noticed the basket sculpted onto its back. Once it had probably held small arrows, but now it was empty. If the other soldiers were missing their weapons too, then they would be all but useless.

The entrance to Liu Wu's tomb was a long stone hallway chiseled out of the hillside. Guarding it were two of the little terracotta soldiers, their tiny hands devoid of weapons. John was very tempted to step over them when they blocked his way, just to test their defensive capabilities. Instead, Yi Yi rode forward and greeted them enthusiastically. John had to admit Yi Yi looked rather dashing, just like a little general on a steed, except it was on Bolo's back he rode.

"I have returned and am ready to serve!" Yi Yi announced. "These nice people dug me up. Liu Wu will surely be happy to see me!"

"Liu Wu hasn't been happy in two thousand years," the soldier on the left grumbled.

"And there's nothing for you to do anyway," the soldier on the right complained. "Liu Wu hasn't waged a single war in all this time. We're lucky to have guard duty, not that there are ever intruders. Not proper ones, anyway."

John had assumed that Yi Yi's eager disposition came from being built to serve, but it appeared this wasn't so. Perhaps the soldiers here had also started out excessively happy before boredom had taken its toll. Then again, Yi Yi had spent two millennia as a buried head and hadn't let it get him down.

"We should probably kill the demon," one of the soldiers said, sounding a bit more optimistic. "Can't imagine the boss wanting him around."

"Yes, I will help you!" Yi Yi chirped happily.

"Rimmon is my friend," John said gently. "You are my friend too, and I'd hate to see anyone attack either of you."

He didn't think it possible, but the little statue's cheeks blushed momentarily. "No!" Yi Yi said to the other soldiers. "We will not attack the demon, for he is a friend of my friend."

"Whatever," one soldier grouched as both returned to their posts.

"Hey, Chi Pu!" the other called out. "Let the boss know he has company!"

A soldier further down the hall sprang to life and scuttled away.

"Right," the soldier on the left puffed up his chest. "The coach stays outside. Once you enter the tomb, do not touch any of the items on display or deviate from the main hallway. Make sure the dog doesn't urinate anywhere and don't allow the demon to curse any items. You will show respect to the king at all times. His majesty should be dressed in his ceremonial costume and ready to receive you now. You may proceed."

"Next time, I will help him to dress!" Yi Yi said, his little fists shaking with excitement at the idea.

The interior of the tomb was palatial, both in size and décor. Yi Yi led the way, instinctively knowing where his master could to be found. Without him, they would have been lost. Hallways gave way to more hallways, extending in all directions, the walls of each decorated with tapestries and treasures of all kinds. Before each stood a little soldier, most appearing disenchanted. They had been built for war and were clearly unhappy with their duties as museum curators, no matter how impressive the treasures were.

John snorted. "If Dante were here, the guards would have something to worry about."

But his humor was forced. In truth he was worried they would never find Dante. How could they, when they weren't even in the same realm? Worst of all, none of this had been accomplished with Dante's consent. They had used him to get here, changing him into a person he wasn't anymore without explaining to him why it was necessary. As soon as they were finished here, they had to find him, but how? An idea occurred to John, followed by an unhappy realization.

"You said there was nothing we could do."

"Hm?"

"To find Dante." John stopped and turned to Rimmon, his anger rising. "You said there was nothing we could do, but you knew that Bolo was a seeker."

Rimmon snapped his fingers. "Bolo! Go find Dante! Seek boy! Take us to Dante!"

Bolo turned, took a step forward, and turned again. His sharp eyes scanned the ceiling, then the floor. He sniffed, whined, and walked in another circle, before sitting. Yi Yi almost slid off his back.

"You see," Rimmon said. "Bolo isn't able to find him either. If seekers could find gods in hiding, there wouldn't be so many missing leaders."

John's face flushed. "Sorry. It's just that the guilt is really starting to eat at me."

"I know. I'm concerned about him too. Even if I weren't, Asmoday will have my head if I return without the Regression Regalia. The goddess that Fumiko called on to escape, Amaterasu, is unfamiliar to me, but we might be able to learn more here. We just need to give it time."

"Master isn't far now," Yi Yi said impatiently. "We shouldn't keep him waiting!"

A few more twists and turns, and they entered the throne room. A dozen tall pillars, each painted either red or gold, were evenly spaced throughout the chamber to support the ornate ceiling. In the center was a raised dais covered in golden sculptures of lions, dragons, warriors, and birds. In the middle of these inanimate beasts was a throne. Lengths of maroon and yellow fabric swept away from the throne's high back to the ceiling before falling and rising again, looping continuously toward the rear of the room.

On this ostentatious throne sat a suit constructed from small jade squares, the corners of each connected to thei neighbors by golden thread. The style of the suit was reminiscent of fencing gear, especially the mask. It covered the head fully, devoid of human features except a raised area for the nose.

The head of the jade suit turned to face them. John jumped, not expecting anyone to suffer such suffocating armor. Then he noticed Rimmon and Yi Yi kneeling on the floor, their heads touching the ground. Even Bolo had respectfully lain down with his head between his paws.

"Kowtow," Rimmon whispered.

John's mind caught up with his body, and he fell to his knees. As he lowered his head, his heart filled with rebellion. Why should he bow to another man, for beneath the jade suit that's surely all there was. Just another soul, like any other, who had drawn the long straw in life. Had this king ever done anything to earn the position he had been born into? Even if he was a good ruler, the time of monarchies was long over. John brought his head close to the floor, but his forehead didn't make contact. Had they not needed something from Liu Wu, he wouldn't have even done this.

"You may rise, travelers."

They stood, and John waited for Rimmon to take command, but all the demon did was clear his throat meaningfully. John, the victim of his previous successes, began as he always did.

"Your majesty—"

"You can't borrow, buy, or in any way employ my terracotta soldiers," the king interrupted. "No exceptions."

"You anticipated our request?" Rimmon asked.

"Dreaded is more like it." The king sounded bored. Indeed, the jade suit wasn't even considering them anymore. It was looking around the room as if hoping to find something more engaging. "If only you knew how many people came here with the very same idea. Of course, this is usually their second stop. Most of them start with Emperor Qin, who humiliates them. Then they come here with injured pride, hoping I'll raise my army against him. Thieves!" The king's attention was suddenly focused on their group again. "Where did you get that? Give it back! It belongs to me!"

"Your greatness!" Yi Yi ran forward, stopping to kowtow every few steps. "Your Excellency, I belong only to you! These nice people dug me up and brought me back to you. I am your Yi Yi!"

"My... Yi Yi?"

"That's his name, your grace," John said helpfully.

"My aunt was called Yi Yi," the king said, his voice distant. "She was— Oh, for goodness sake, get this damned mask off me!"

Yi Yi complied instantly, leaping artfully onto the king's lap and climbing onto his shoulders before removing the mask. It split into two halves, front and back, which Yi Yi had no trouble in carrying even though the pieces were almost as large as he was. Perhaps the soldiers were more capable than they appeared.

For the first time, they looked upon the face of Liu Wu. Nothing about his appearance was particularly distinguished. He wasn't attractive, nor was he ugly. John estimated that he was about the same age as himself.

"The rest of it, too!" Liu Wu ordered. "I don't know why I bother anymore. More a curse than an honor."

Yi Yi had the armor off him in no time, despite having never handled it before. Liu Wu was left in nothing but a swath of cloth tied around his groin. He stood before them with no shame or embarrassment, scowling at them with displeasure. Two more terracotta soldiers appeared from a doorway carrying a yellow robe that they draped Liu Wu in by leaping into the air a few times. Once dressed, the king sat back on his throne and continued as if nothing had happened.

"My aunt was named Yi Yi and was a fine advisor. The potter did you a great honor by giving you her name. You shall remain by my side."

"Oh, thank you, exalted one!" Yi Yi practically swooned. "Today is a day of a thousand blessings!"

There was no doubting the little soldier's excitement, but John noticed something curious. Yi Yi's attention seemed divided between his king and the jade suit of armor. His gaze kept returning to it. The robe-bearing soldiers had given it more than one glance as well.

"Is that all?" Liu Wu asked. "No pleading, begging, or bribing? Good, we can call it a day, then."

"Your grace, if we could just—" John began, but Liu Wu clapped his hands. Within seconds, the room was filled with the little soldiers, all of them eager for action.

"We will take our leave now," Rimmon said, retaining his dignity. "We thank you for honoring us with your presence." He knelt to bow, but this time John refused to join him.

As they left, John looked back at the throne. Yi Yi's face expressed regret, one of his little hands waving goodbye, but before they had even left the door, Yi Yi was gazing with wonder at the suit made of jade. John gave it one last glance as well, recognizing what could be their key to victory.

In a tiny village nestled in the shadow of a mountain was an inn. It didn't have a bar, or restaurant, or a long hallway leading to a number of rooms. The quaint wooden house with its paper windows and doors had only one small space to serve all purposes. The occupant of this home would, in exchange for money, give up his bed and sleep in the adjacent corner. This was the only inn the village possessed.

Twice as much money was needed to convince the owner to leave them and stay with family in the village. Before he left, he prepared the table with salted fish, rice, a bottle of rice wine, and two miniature cups. His smile was fixed in place until they sat at the low table and thanked him. This triggered a series of bows that continued until he backed out the door and disappeared. Once left alone, John was finally free to ask Rimmon all the questions that crowded his mind.

"An inn in the afterlife? Really? Are there so many tourists who come here?"

Rimmon smiled. "Obviously not, or they would need a bigger inn."

"But why does this even exist?" John pressed. "The man who lives here, this is his eternal reward?"

"I'm sure he was proud of what he had in life and desired to have just as much in death," Rimmon answered while pouring the rice wine.

"So you *can* take it with you when you go." John chewed his lip. "Couldn't you have just made us a house? It took you seconds to create those green pastures."

"That was in a void. This is an established realm, and we don't belong here. Imposing our own perception of reality would be impolite." Rimmon raised a glass in salute before taking a controlled sip. "Now, if you don't mind reversing roles, I have questions for you. Why did you insist we stay here instead of continuing on to Emperor Qin or returning to Hell?"

"You heard what Liu Wu said about Qin. He's just as unlikely to help us. Besides, Wu's army will soon belong to us."

"Oh?"

"I think so. Did you see the way Yi Yi and the others reacted to the jade suit? They couldn't keep their eyes off it. Any idea why?"

"A jade burial suit is an honor reserved for emperors and only some kings. Liu Wu must have been very respected in life. The suit is the ultimate symbol of this, thus the reverence the soldiers show for it."

"Interesting history lesson, but the suit isn't something new to the soldiers. They've seen it for thousands of years now. As disenchanted as they've become with their positions, surely they should be just as blasé about the suit."

"Possibly," Rimmon conceded, "but the soldiers are crafted to venerate their king."

"Exactly, and it's clear that they associate the suit so strongly with their king that they are almost one and the same."

"Ah." Rimmon began working on his fish.

Not interested in eating, John moved his fish to the floor where Bolo was begging and waited for the demon's reply, certain that his plan was clear.

"This is risky," Rimmon said eventually. "Even if we manage to steal the suit, there is no guarantee that the soldiers will obey whoever is wearing it."

"But you think it might work?"

"It might. The soldiers are so eager for action that they might be willing to deceive themselves. Your idea is good," Rimmon shook his head to the contrary, "but how do you propose we steal the suit?"

John sighed. "We need Dante."

"Even I am beginning to miss him," Rimmon admitted.

"What about Bolo? He fetched a terracotta soldier for you. Let's send him in!"

"Even if he were able to get past the soldiers, I don't see how he could carry the armor back in one piece."

"Think he could seek out another entrance? Some sort of secret passage?"

"Tombs were built to have one entrance and for very good reason." Rimmon considered the jug of rice wine before pouring himself another cup. "No, I think our best option is to create a diversion, something to draw the soldiers out. Any ideas?"

John played with his rice while he thought. It was sticky and clumped together easily, so he molded it into the shape of an igloo. Next he smooshed it down and fashioned a little man out of it while thinking of the terracotta soldiers.

"Yeah, I think I have an idea."

Three decoratively armored soldiers stood before John, each the height of a man. Only the soldier in the center moved. Unlike its companions, this soldier had a number of gaps in his armor plates and shifted uncomfortably.

"How do I look?" Rimmon asked from beneath the terracotta armor.

"Passable," John replied. "More convincing than Bolo."

The dog was rolling on the ground, trying to dislodge the clay plates they had tied to him in order to disguise him as a terracotta horse. Together with Rimmon in his armor and the two decoys, they hoped to strike terror into the hearts of the villagers. Seeing his plan actualized, John was beginning to have his doubts.

They had retreated back to the void to fashion these costumes from the ether. Rimmon had done a commendable job creating the extra soldiers. They couldn't compare with the fine detail and craftsmanship put into Qin's terracotta soldiers, but if placed strategically they should get the job done. Three soldiers and a pint-sized horse weren't much, but Rimmon assured him this would be sufficient as long as they created enough panic.

John continued to worry as they loaded the statues into the steam coach in preparation for their journey. By the time they returned to the village, the moon was high. They paused briefly on the outskirts so that Rimmon could sing to it, causing uncomfortable feelings to stir inside John that he hurriedly pushed away.

Life in the village closely resembled that on earth, and like Hell, this was a realm where souls could sleep. They put their plan in motion by choosing two silent homes on the far corners of the village, furthest from the tomb. They placed a statue at each one, positioned just far enough outside each front door to be visible while still allowing the residents to escape.

"I still feel guilty," John whispered.

"I know," Rimmon replied, "but we are running out of time. Sunrise isn't far away, and we need the dark of night if this is going to work. You'd better get into position."

John made his way out of the village to Liu Wu's tomb, climbing to one side of the entrance where he could observe without being seen. He eyed the two motionless soldiers there before focusing on the village. Already orange flames licked the sky. Rimmon had used his demon breath to set the first house on fire. With any luck, the occupants would notice the fake terracotta soldier on the way out. Rimmon would then set fire to the second home, before parading around town in his costume and causing as much mischief as possible. Bolo would be out there with him, one more decoy for the villagers to report.

The flames from the first house grew, sending another surge of guilt through John. Rimmon had promised him that the occupants wouldn't be harmed by the fire, and that the homes would return to normal after the crisis. This realm was based on memories of what had existed in life, and in theory those memories should undo the damage once the flames died out. If not, John couldn't stay behind to help rebuild since they would soon be on the run.

Before long the fires had the entire village roused from sleep and bubbling with panic. A young man and woman were the first to approach the king's tomb. John crept closer to the entrance to better hear. The beginning of their panicked speech was lost to him, but what he did understand involved fire. As they continued speaking, the couple did not mention Qin's soldiers at all.

John sighed. *If you want something done...* He descended the hill, circling away from the tomb and then approaching it directly, working himself into a frenzy as he neared.

"Qin's army!" he panted. "They're attacking the village!"

"It's only a fire," one of the soldiers yawned. "We've already sent a platoon to assist."

"I saw them!" he insisted.

"More likely you saw your own shadow."

They turned at the sound of footsteps, John hoping Rimmon had arrived to draw more soldiers out, but it was only a hobbling old woman. "Why are the soldiers attacking?" she demanded. "They are burning our homes!"

"What did they look like?" John asked. "Tall? Short?"

"As tall as you," she pointed a finger in his direction, "and breathing fire!"

"I told you!" John exclaimed. "Qin's army! Go help your fellow soldiers! This is the fight you've been waiting for! I'll sound the alarm. Go! Go! Go!"

The soldiers hesitated only a moment before running off into the night. John dashed inside the tomb, shouting that Qin's army was raiding the village. Soldiers streamed around his legs and out the entrance as he made his way through the halls to the throne room. By the time he reached it—after making a number of false turns—no soldiers were left in sight.

The throne room was unlit, the dark silhouettes of the pillars an ideal hiding place for anyone who might have heard his approach. John imagined the king awaiting him, tucked behind a pillar with a golden knife in his hand. John tensed as his footsteps echoed, giving away his location to this imaginary foe as he moved toward the throne. He gasped when he saw that it was occupied, the king dressed once again in his jade suit.

"Your majesty?" he whispered.

The figure on the throne didn't react to his voice. John spun around, suddenly certain that he was looking at a decoy, but he was alone in the room. Perhaps, when it was not in use, the jade suit was left on the throne. John approached cautiously; the suit remained motionless as his shaking hands reached for the helmet. He held his breath and pulled it off in one smooth motion. The suit was empty.

"In here, your greatness!" came Yi Yi's unmistakable voice as light moved down the hallway. "We must get you dressed and prepared for battle!"

"Qin wants a war," Liu Wu ranted, "I'll give him one. Size isn't everything, you know. My soldiers will swarm his troops like hornets!"

John searched for a place to hide. In the far corner of the room was a huge decorative jar, more than large enough for him to fit inside. He ran to it, too short on time to be stealthy, and hoped the king couldn't hear anything over his own grumbling. Just as he reached the pot, John realized he was still carrying the jade helmet, but he didn't have enough time to return it. He removed the lid of the jar and threw the helmet in first before climbing in, thankful that the pot was heavy enough to be stable.

John had found the perfect hiding place, but the lid was on the floor outside. He had gone from careless to sloppy, but all he could do now was remain still and hope Liu Wu wouldn't notice. John's breathing was loud in his ears until he remembered it was optional. He stopped and strained to hear what was happening outside.

"It must be here somewhere," Yi Yi was saying. "I placed everything on the throne, just as you commanded. Maybe the helmet fell off and rolled away."

"Hurry, you idiot! Emperor Qin could be here at any moment!"

"That's no way to talk to your Yi Yi!"

There was a thick moment of silence.

"I'm sorry," Liu Wu said quietly. "I'm just excited."

John needed all of his willpower not to laugh. To think that little Yi Yi had tamed the king so soon! His amusement didn't last long. There were only so many places they could search in the room, and it was only a matter of time before—

"Why is the monk's jar open?" Liu Wu asked.

The pitter-patter of tiny terracotta feet came closer. He heard a grunt before Yi Yi's hands caught hold of the rim and his face peered over the side. John alternated between pressing a finger to his lips and pressing his hands together to beg. Yi Yi looked torn, but to his credit, he pulled himself over the edge and into the pot without announcing John's presence.

"You shouldn't be here!" the little soldier whispered. "Why do you have the master's burial mask?"

"Take it!" John pleaded. "Put the lid back on the jar, and I'll sneak out later. I promise."

"But what are you doing here?"

"Well?" Liu Wu boomed. "Is it in there or not?"

Yi Yi frowned but accepted the jade helmet. He gripped it with a hand the size of cat's paw before leaping and landing on the rim of the pot. "I have it, your excellency! One of the other soldiers was playing a trick on Yi Yi!"

Liu Wu was barely listening, having launched into another rant. Above John the lid of the pot slowly slid over the opening, the circle of light fading to black like a solar eclipse. Blanketed in darkness, he listened to the muffled voices outside and wondered how he was going to get out of this. He was safe, for now, but the plan hinged on him taking control of the terracotta army. Rimmon and Bolo were currently facing them alone, greatly outnumbered. The longer he delayed, the more likely they would be hurt or captured.

"What am I going to do?" he sighed.

"There are only two mistakes one can make along the road to truth." The terribly loud voice manifested from inside the jar as the darkness began to glow with an orange light. "Not going all the way, and not having started."

"Who asked you?" Liu Wu bellowed.

"Please," John whispered. "Talking jar or whatever you are, please be quiet or I'm going to be in very, very big trouble."

The orange light congealed into the form of a bald monk in orange robes who pressed a finger to his smiling lips. "Of course," he whispered. "My apologies."

"Thank you." The atmosphere was suddenly awkward. If John had just appeared out of thin air, he would certainly offer an explanation to anyone he appeared next to, but the monk seemed content to hover in the air with his legs crossed beneath him. "So what are you, some kind of genie? Do you live here?"

"My name is Kenjo," the monk answered. "I am follower of the teachings of Buddha, and this is my burial jar."

"So, no granting wishes then? I could use a little help here."

"No one saves us but ourselves. No one can, and no one may. We ourselves must walk the path."

John stared at the monk, whose face remained passive and tranquil even though John was sure he was being mocked. "I'm sorry, did you say burial jar?"

"Yes, a ritual common to the temple I lived my life in. I was buried in the earth above Liu Wu's tomb long after it had been swallowed by the hill. Because of that, our destinies have become intertwined in this world."

"Can you leave?" John asked. "I mean, you know you don't have to stay in this jar, right?"

"I am content to rest here and contemplate the teachings of Buddha before the winds of reincarnation bring me to my next life."

"And you never get bored?" John pressed.

Kenjo smiled. "Occasionally Liu Wu and I engage in conversation, which is always delightful. For me at least."

"Then maybe you can help me. I need to get Liu Wu's jade suit. If I don't, my friends are going to be in trouble."

"Then why don't you ask him for it?"

John hesitated, but the monk appeared to be serious. "Uh, it would be nice if things worked like that, but if you haven't noticed, his highness is a bit of a hot head."

"The Buddha says that 'Friendship is the only cure for hatred, the only guarantee of peace.'"

"Yeah, great. I'd love to buy him a beer sometime, but my situation is a little more urgent than that. Is there anything you know that could help me, any way I could convince him, bribe him, even trick him into giving me that suit?"

"Do not dwell in the past, do not dream of the future, concentrate the mind on the present moment."

"What does that—"

The monk pressed a finger to his lips again and smiled. John listened.

The throne room was silent. Had Liu Wu left for battle?

"Master," Yi Yi said quietly. "You are fully dressed in your suit."

Liu Wu's voice was even quieter in its response. "Yes. I am."

"Then why do you not go to battle?"

A sigh echoed throughout the chamber.

The monk floated even nearer to John and whispered, "He who experiences the unity of life sees his own self in all beings, and all beings in his own self, and looks on everything with an impartial eye."

In other words, try looking at things from someone else's point of view. For all of his bravado and bluster, Liu Wu had no desire to go to war. He hadn't since his death. No surprise, since losing a war had been the cause of his downfall. These thoughts must have weighed heavily on his mind for centuries.

Inspiration struck John so suddenly that he wanted to shout 'Eureka!' He knew a way to get the armor while allowing Liu Wu to regain his honor.

"Thank you!" John said to the monk. "You're really very good!"

"My delight is yours, your happiness my own!" The monk bowed his head and disappeared.

John stood and slid aside the lid of the burial jar.

"Victory!"

A roar followed this declaration as dozens of doll-sized soldiers marched into the throne room.

"We have vanquished the enemy, your highness!"

Two motionless masses were held aloft by dozens of tiny hands. Rimmon and Bolo were both bound in glowing ropes of white light. The plates of their makeshift terracotta armor were mostly broken or missing. Both looked dead, or at least unconscious. Tiny glowing arrows and the occasional spear were buried in their flesh. The little soldiers, whose hands had always been empty, were now bristling with various weapons made from this same light.

Liu Wu stood in his excitement and removed his jade mask, but now his face was puzzled. "These aren't Qin's soldiers! These are the fools from yesterday!"

"Allow me to explain!" John said.

He ducked back into the pot just in time to avoid a swarm of arrows.

"I can give you what you most desire!" John shouted.

"Your head on a pike?" Liu Wu shouted back. "I think that belongs to me already!"

"You leading a war," John said, "at the front of the battlefield, in full view of every realm in the afterlife. All will witness your glory and name you victorious! All this, without you having to leave your tomb!"

The king's footsteps echoed in the huge room as he moved toward the jar. Two jade gloves grasped the rim before Liu Wu glowered over the side. "Go on."

"We're about to wage a war against Heaven," John explained quickly. "We have dozens of gods on our side, but we need your soldiers. Give me your armor and I will lead your soldiers in battle. I will only respond to your name and won't remove the mask. If I win, you can claim the victory as your own. This isn't dishonest, since they are your soldiers and the jade suit a mark of esteem you earned in life."

Liu Wu shook his head. "If you win, I win, but if you lose, then I suffer a humiliation ten times greater than before!"

"If I lose, which I have no intention of doing, then you will confront me on the field of battle. You can tell everyone there how I stole your armor, and you can take my head. A victory in itself, wouldn't you say, decapitating the leader of a renegade army?"

Liu Wu scowled as he considered the idea. By the time he was finished thinking, his eyes shone with the idea. "Me, leading an army, victorious against Heaven itself while Qin and his army rot in their tomb." He glared at John. "If you lose, my soldiers will cut your soul into a hundred pieces and scatter them across the realms, all but your head, which I shall keep and do unspeakable things to."

John stood cautiously and offered his hand. "Then I think we have a deal."

Chapter Fourteen

Fists of clay pummeled the demon's back, striking the exposed skin without mercy. Rimmon lay face-down on the ground, a vanquished foe powerless against the brutal onslaught. He moaned in pleasure.

"Don't ever stop," he pleaded. "The massage parlors in Hell can't compare with your skills, Yi Yi. Not that much massaging takes place in such establishments."

Next to them, Bolo was playing tug of war, his jaw clenched firmly on a rope pulled by six terracotta soldiers on the other side. The soldiers—who were clearly humoring the dog and could easily win—were in high spirits. The recent battle had dusted off their cobwebs, and news of a full-fledged war had them feeling nearly as optimistic as Yi Yi. Most of them were in council with Liu Wu, who began formulating strategies as soon as he had been briefed about the enemy. The king was determined to be as involved as possible with the battle, even though he didn't intend on taking the field himself.

Rimmon and Bolo had made quick recoveries, the arrows that penetrated them disappearing the moment the soldiers willed them to. The demon admitted that he had been captured swiftly and efficiently by the soldiers, an experience that had earned his full confidence in their abilities. The arrows were an effective weapon. Not only were they painful, but they rendered the victim's body immobile while causing the mind to enter a delusional state. All in all, the mission had been a complete success. Except for one crucial aspect.

"Dante," John said meaningfully.

"Yes," Rimmon said. "I was just giving some thought to that. Someone in the village might have a connection to the goddess Amaterasu or at least know something that could help us. Perhaps Liu Wu could send soldiers out to the villagers to ask on our behalf. It would be much faster than going door-to-door ourselves."

"It's worth a try," John said. "I'll ask him right away."

"Never heard of her," Liu Wu grunted when John found him. The king was pouring over an ancient book that had diagrams of soldiers in various training exercises. "I could send men out to survey my people, but you should ask Kenjo first. All he ever did in life was read. It's as if someone crammed an entire talking library into a jar. There's a reason I had him moved to my throne room. You can't imagine how useful that is."

John thought wistfully of the Internet as he made his way back to the throne room. Were there more monks in burial jars? If John could find a way to network them, he could be the afterlife's version of an Internet tycoon.

He felt somewhat awkward when approaching the jar, wondering what the standard protocol was. Should he knock politely or simply crawl inside like he did before? In the end he decided to remove the lid and call Kenjo's name. Orange light collected into the shape of a man again. Now, with only his upper torso visible, the monk really did resemble a genie. Kenjo patiently waited for him to speak, a serene smile on his face.

John explained what had happened to Dante. This went much smoother than he expected since the monk was already comfortable with the idea of past lives and reincarnation. Kenjo listened closely and without interruption. When finished, John braced himself for another existential quote from Buddha, but instead the monk began to tell him a story.

"What do you know of Japanese mythology?" Kenjo asked first.

"Nothing at all," John admitted.

The monk nodded and began his tale.

"Amaterasu was the goddess of the sun. Her twin brother, Izanagi, was god of the moon. Both of them were renowned for their grace and fair appearance. The twins had a younger sibling, Susanoo, who was neither fair nor graceful. Susanoo was known for his temper and lack of manners. How fitting, then, that he was god of storms and the temperamental sea.

"Izanagi, tiring of his little brother's rude behavior, went to great pains to banish him from the heavens. Susanoo eventually agreed to go, but insisted first on visiting his sister Amaterasu to say goodbye. Susanoo went to her home and made himself a guest there. Soon it became clear that he had no intention of leaving, so the sun goddess decided to challenge him to a game. If Susanoo lost, he would leave, but if he won, he would be allowed to stay in her home indefinitely.

"The contest was to see who was more skilled at bringing

life into the world. The sun goddess took Susanoo's sword and fashioned from it two men. Drawing inspiration from this, Susanoo took Amaterasu's necklace and divided it into three women. He delighted instantly in his victory, only to be quelled by his sister.

"'The necklace belongs to me,' the goddess said, 'and thus so do the women. I have won the contest and you must go!'"

"That's not fair!" John interrupted.

"Susanoo felt the same and was so outraged by his sister's trickery that he refused to leave and made a nuisance of himself, chasing away the goddess's animals and terrorizing her servants. Eventually Amaterasu could take it no more and fled to a cave, where she sealed herself away from the world. The earth suffered in her absence, for there was no more light and the crops could not grow. Without the goddess, the world grew dark, hungry, and cold.

"All the other gods gathered outside the cave and begged Amaterasu to come out, but she wouldn't heed their cries. Finally, clever Uzume, goddess of happiness, devised a plan. First she placed a mirror in a tree across from the cave. She then dressed herself in flowers, turned a wash bucket over, and started to dance on top of it. Then she began to strip off her clothes, which had the other gods cheering and laughing in amusement. Amaterasu heard the music and merriment and asked what was happening. How could they be enjoying themselves with no sun in the sky?

"'There's a new sun goddess,' Uzume replied. 'One of indescribable beauty!'

"Overcome with curiosity, Amaterasu came out of her cave. The first thing she saw was her own face in the mirror and was flattered. Then she saw the silly dance that Uzume was performing for the other gods and was herself overcome with laughter. She left her cave and her sorrows behind, and once again blessed the earth with her light."

John appreciated the monk's story, but he didn't see how it would help him get Dante back. His puzzlement must have been clear, because Kenjo spoke further.

"Legend says that the *kagura*, the spiritual dances performed by those of Shinto faith, take their origin from Uzume's dance and are performed at the Imperial court by the descendants of Amaterasu."

"And you think one of these *kagura* dances might attract the goddess to us?"

The monk smiled. "If it is sufficiently amusing."

"If dressing in drag and dancing around is what it takes to get Dante back," John said, "then count me in."

"Forgive me," Kenjo said, "but your features are very fair. I feel you would make an attractive woman, rather than one that invokes mirth."

"Then what do you suggest?"

Villagers shuffled excitedly, the crowd at least six deep. The object of their attention was an overturned water barrel centered on a bare patch of dirt. Chatter filled the air, occasionally interrupted by laughter. When the soldiers of the king arrived, waving banners ten times their size, the crowd fell silent and parted to let them pass.

Rimmon scowled as he entered the clearing, looking as ferocious as a chained beast, an impressive feat considering his attire. His wig was woven from field grass and decorated through with white lilies, and his makeup was atrocious. White paint covered his face, sharp arches of pink running from his eyelids to his temples. Only the natural red of his lips was left exposed to simulate lipstick.

As for his clothing, the tops of two pumpkins had been cut off and fashioned into a bra, the stems pointing upwards like bizarre nipples. A skirt of bamboo and elevated wooden sandals completed the look, with the extra touch of silk bows tied along Rimmon's tail.

John led Bolo to the front of the crowd as Rimmon climbed onto the barrel. Convincing the demon to do this hadn't been easy, especially when word of mouth spread and the entire village expressed interest in being there. John assured him that they were coming to see a demon and a goddess for the first time, not to laugh at him. Besides, John felt they owed the villagers something for terrorizing them and burning their homes. As Rimmon had promised, all had quickly been set right again, but compensation for their troubles in the form of entertainment seemed fair.

They required the villagers' assistance too, since they needed music for their dance. Liu Wu arrived in a *jiao*, a chair mounted on two poles and carried by four men. In this case, four of the little soldiers were holding the king effortlessly aloft, giving him the best—and only—seat in the audience. Liu Wu gestured with his hand, and a number of villagers came forward with drums.

Rimmon climbed onto the barrel and gave one hopeful glance at the sky, as if the goddess might appear without him having to dance. Shapeless gray clouds were all that could be seen.

The musicians began drumming, and the audience cheered, eager for their show. Rimmon stepped to the left and then to the right. He was moving to the beat, but his dance was hardly inspiring. He continued to shuffle back and forth, his eyes not meeting the now-grumbling crowd.

"Come on!" John yelled. "Show these people what a real incubus can do!"

Rimmon's gaze rose to meet his, and John nodded encouragingly. A slow cocky grin spread across Rimmon's face as his torso began to gyrate, a movement that wound down to his pelvis, which pumped just enough to be suggestive. His forked tail began to thump against the barrel, setting a new beat that the musicians quickly picked up. Rimmon's steps were twice as fast now as he turned and whirled, showing off every angle of his body.

There was laughter from the men in the audience, but most of it was drowned out by appreciative catcalls from the women. Eventually the men grew quieter, and when John tore his eyes away from the strangely erotic display, he found most of them looking confused. The men hadn't expected to find Rimmon so sexually appealing, but the incubus was turning the ridiculous costume to his advantage, rubbing his hands over the pumpkin breasts and hiding them so the men were forced to use their imaginations.

The air was getting tense with confused passion when the clouds parted enough to allow a beam of sparkling sunlight through. Rimmon kept dancing, but one by one he lost his audience to the glimmering beauty that now stood in their midst. The goddess was difficult to see clearly, light moving along her skin, the sun's reflection on water. Every part they could see—a hint of eyes, a little bit of leg—was perfection. The goddess turned to watch Rimmon, laughing in delight.

She was given a good show, as piece by piece, the demon took off his costume without missing a beat. Soon he was revealed in all his glorious masculinity, even managing to wipe away the makeup in a becoming manner. The skirt was the last to fall away, and after an appreciative gasp from the audience, Rimmon snapped his fingers and was dressed in contemporary clothing again. Then the audience began to drift away, all of them in pairs. The men had something they wanted to prove, and the women were in the mood to let them.

"Amaterasu," Rimmon said. "You honor us with your presence."

"I've never seen a *kagura* performed like that before," the goddess said, her voice the sound of wind chimes on a summer breeze.

"I hope it was still to your liking."

"Oh, it was," Amaterasu breathed. "I shall commit the details to my memory for all eternity."

Rimmon smiled as he hopped off the barrel. "You flatter me, sweet sun goddess. It pains me to ask for anything more than your generous presence here, but I believe you recently rescued a friend of ours. We'd very much like to be reunited with her."

The light of the goddess dimmed suddenly, revealing her frown. "You mean this?"

There was a scream from the sky that grew louder as it neared, ending with a thump. Fumiko pulled herself up from the dirt and scowled. "What was that for?" she demanded. "This is how you treat your guests?"

"Not since my brother Susanoo overstayed his welcome has my home been made so miserable," the goddess complained. "In fact, I rather prefer Susanoo's company to that of this witch! You will do me a great favor by taking her back into your care!"

"My only wish is to serve you," Rimmon said solemnly, " but I can't help notice that she is no longer wearing the jewelry she left with."

The Regression Regalia! Without it they couldn't transform Dante back. For all of his shortcomings, at least the Irishman wasn't as treacherous as the old woman before them.

Amaterasu cupped her hand, and the jewels appeared there. "I took them as payment for the generous accommodations I provided, although a mountain of jewels wouldn't have been enough!"

Fumiko didn't have a retort. She was eying her surroundings with an all-to-familiar air. Escape was her intent. Rimmon must have sensed this, for he stepped forward and grabbed her arm.

"As much as you deserve compensation for your troubles," Rimmon addressed the goddess, "those jewels weren't Fumiko's to give."

"You would take them from me?" Amaterasu sounded surprised.

"Not without giving you something in return."

The full force of Rimmon's allure hit John like a wall. He was nearly overcome with the urge to run to him, until he realized that he wasn't the intended target.

The goddess's eyes sparkled as they grew wide. "What would you offer?"

Rimmon's reply was quick. "I'd show the sun how to move through the night."

John's stomach sank. Was he serious? Was he really going to sleep with the goddess just to get the Regalia back? He could barely stomach what happened next: Amaterasu handed him the jewels, her hand lingering on Rimmon's and moving up his arm.

John tore his eyes away, pulse beating in his neck. The green-eyed beast inside him stirred, refusing to be silent this time. Just the thought of Rimmon being with the goddess was enough to make John shake with anger. When had this happened? When had he decided that Rimmon belonged to him? John never should have touched his incubus heart, but until now, he hadn't fully understood the ramifications.

"John."

The demon stood before him, a knowing expression on his face. John met his gaze with difficulty.

"Take these," Rimmon said, handing him the jewels. "Use them on Fumiko, but not in front of anyone. We dare not reveal their value. I'll be with you again in the morning."

John couldn't answer. He looked away to where a number of terracotta soldiers were holding Fumiko in place.

"When I see that expression," Rimmon sighed, "it's like seeing his face again."

John turned away. It was bad enough that Rimmon was prostituting himself. The reminder that his heart had long been taken by somebody else was too much to bear. By the time

John gathered the strength to raise his head, the demon and the goddess were gone.

The old woman growled and launched herself at him again. She had recovered surprisingly fast from the piledriver John had subjected her to. She came at him with splayed fingers, her nails whistling past John's nose before he ducked and shot an uppercut straight into her chin. The old woman spun in a complete circle before falling to the ground.

Doing battle with a senior citizen was hardly his proudest moment, so John was relieved no one was around to witness it. Obtaining privacy hadn't been difficult. Liu Wu had raised his eyebrows when first seeing Fumiko squirming to get loose from John's grip, but had shrugged in a manner that suggested it was no concern of his. He probably thought John had taken an unwilling lover, but the truth couldn't be explained without revealing the Regression Regalia.

Fumiko now lay on a floor that was just as bare as the walls. Only a bed furnished the room, on it the priceless jewelry. John grabbed the Regalia before pouncing on Fumiko, punching her a few more times after she spit in his face and bit his arm. After a couple more amateur wrestling moves, John managed to get the necklace and bracelets on her arms and neck. He stabbed at the onyx jewel on the left wrist, glad when the venomous old woman finally disappeared in a lightshow. The potbellied, ginger-haired man appeared next. John didn't give him a chance to speak before he pressed the dark gem again.

He sighed with relief when Dante's familiar form reappeared.

"Get these things off me!" he spluttered. "And then you get off me, too!"

"Sorry!" John said, doing as he was told. "For all of it, I mean. We should have explained the plan, given you a choice."

"It's just as well you didn't," Dante grunted as he stood. "I never wanted to be her again. Not in a million years!"

John paused, unsure if he had understood. "You mean you knew about Fumiko even before all of this?"

"Her and everyone else I've ever been, yeah." Now it was the Irishman who expressed surprise. "You mean you don't?"

"No," John said flatly. "Why do you think that is?"

"Side effect of the big spooky secret, I suppose," Dante said, wiggling his fingers theatrically. "It's not as interesting as you'd think, remembering past lives. They're just the numbers that add up to the sum of who you are. I'm sure you noticed that Fumiko and I share similar morals. She was just me a few steps back, that's all. It's like remembering what an awkward twit you were at twelve."

John thought of how he had been all teeth and legs back then. "You're right. That doesn't sound like fun."

"It wasn't all bad. At least I got to spend time with the goddess. Not as a man, unfortunately, but that had its benefits. She even asked me to help her get dressed once. Can you believe that?"

John's stomach sank, the idea of Rimmon sleeping with the goddess causing a dull pain in his chest. Logically, he knew he shouldn't be bothered. He'd known what Rimmon was since they first met. Call him incubus or ambassador, when Rimmon's profession was boiled down to the basics, he was first and foremost a hustler. In a way, all politicians were whores, doing everything to please the right people in order to get what they want. Rimmon was simply more honest and direct in his methods. And he had always been honest with John—right from the beginning—by never making any false promises.

If only John could make his stupid heart understand that, maybe the pain would go away. He thought of the goddess's hand on Rimmon's arm and shook his head. What a terrible way to realize he was in love.

John wasn't helpless though. He could leave. His work was mostly done anyway. The most powerful gods had been gathered together, and now they had an army to command. All that remained was the inevitable victory, and they didn't need John for that. All he needed to do was climb into the driver's seat of the steam coach, and he would be free. John thought he knew his destination. Rimmon had hinted about it being where he belonged, a place where Dante or the incubus couldn't follow. Where else could it be but Heaven?

"I'm leaving," John said, heading for the door. "When Rimmon gets back, tell him to find someone else to wear the jade suit. It won't make any difference to Liu Wu. He doesn't even have to know."

"Jade suit? Wait, leaving?" Dante followed John into the

hallway. "What do you mean?"

"I'm taking the steam coach for a spin. Or you could save me the trouble and tell me the big secret."

"Couldn't if I wanted to," Dante said. "Asmoday has some sort of spell on me, but I don't see how the coach is going to help you any."

"Manannan thought it might. If I take the driver's seat, then it will take my soul to where it belongs."

Dante's eyes widened. "You think that will work?"

"Why wouldn't it?"

John picked up his pace. The chariot was just outside the tomb, moonlight glistening off its black finish and brass pipes. John climbed the two small steps to the driver's seat.

"Wait up!" Dante shouted.

"You can't stop me," John said, taking a seat.

"No, but you'll need someone to pull your lever." Dante grinned at him. "Besides, someone should see you off properly."

John smiled back and gestured for Dante to climb inside. He probably wouldn't be able to complete the journey anyway. Once John was in Heaven, Dante's soul would be kicked back to Hell, which was where he was happiest.

Even though it didn't need to, John's heart thudded in his chest while he waited for Dante to pull the lever. The steam coach lurched, first forward, then backward. It spun to the left in a full circle before launching forward and halting, tipping forward dangerously on two wheels before it fell backward again. Clearly the steam coach was confused. Then it went still, and just when John thought they wouldn't be going anywhere at all, the coach began to fade.

He looked down at his own hands to see they were now transparent as well. They disappeared entirely as he watched. He couldn't see at all anymore, not even the world around them. There wasn't black, white, gray or any other color. There was nothing.

Then they arrived, the world exploding back into existence. The room was dark, the orange street lights outside just bright enough to illuminate the details. Two beds were in the room, a flat-screen television mounted on the wall across from them. A utilitarian dresser sat next to each bed, a curtain separating the two, although it wasn't pulled far enough to provide complete privacy.

They had arrived on Earth. John resisted a laugh, thinking how much that sounded like a line from a cheesy sci-fi movie. He could probably turn on the television and watch one of those films if he wanted, and despite the inevitable commercial interruptions, the idea sounded blissful.

"A hospital," John murmured. "St. Francis Memorial by the look of it."

"All the answers are right here," Dante said, appearing around the side of the coach. "I can't say them until you know them, but—" He gestured to the beds.

John stood, walking with deliberate care down the steps of the coach, which didn't even fit in the room. Most of it had disappeared beyond the walls, sticking out into the hallway, although John doubted it was visible to the living.

The sights and smells weren't lost to the dead. The drab furnishings and sterile smell took John straight back to the time his grandmother had been in the hospital, shortly before she died. He had walked right past her bed the first time, no longer recognizing her because of the cancer that had ravaged her body.

John didn't need to choose which bed to look in; he was drawn to it, almost pulled across the floor. And there he was, sleeping on his back, his mouth open and slack. John looked at John, and felt dizzy, delirious, horrified, and excited. He saw a heart monitor, and while it didn't beep like they did on television, a steady green line jumped across the screen.

"I'm not dead," he said, and his feet left the floor as he floated toward his body.

"Whoa, whoa, whoa!" Dante said, grabbing one of his feet. John stopped like a balloon tethered by a string. "See, they told me this would happen. You're drawn to your body like a moth to a bug zapper. That's where you belong."

John's feet slowly returned to the ground as he regained control of himself. With considerable effort, he turned to face Dante, even though he wanted to dive into his body like it was the only pool on a scorching summer day.

"I'm not dead," he repeated.

"That's right. You're still alive and kicking. Sort of. Your body is in a coma. No idea if you'll wake up from it or not, but with your willpower, I wouldn't be surprised." Dante gave him a playful punch on the arm. "So this is it, then. Whenever you do get around to dying properly, I hope we see each other again. Not that I want you to go to Hell," Dante backpedaled. "I just mean, you know … Look me up, all right?"

"We left Bolo behind," John realized suddenly. "And Rimmon." For the first time since entering Purgatory, John felt like crying. He wouldn't have a chance to say goodbye to them, wouldn't see them again for a lifetime.

"I'll take care of the mutt," Dante promised. "The demon can take care of himself, no doubt, but I'll keep an eye out anyway."

Dante would need to watch out for all of them because a war was coming, one of John's own creation. He had gathered enough forces for Asmoday to do whatever he pleased, and John didn't believe for a second that the Archduke would stop at Purgatory. Asmoday's fear of Heaven would lead him to attack there next, perhaps even first, and John's friends could be lost or hurt in that battle. And yet, as much as he didn't want to turn his back on all of this, his body was calling him home, urging him to return to life.

"You have a choice," a new voice said. "You always have a choice."

The god stood next to the coach, dwarfing it in size. He was much too large to fit into the already cramped hospital room, but somehow the ceiling made way for him. The large elephant ears wiggled in greeting, as did one of the four human arms. Like all gods, he was wrapped in his own name, his history radiating out from him. This was Ganesh, the breaker of barriers, the destroyer of obstacles.

Similar to the Egyptian gods, he had the head of an animal—an elephant with a trident tattoo above his deeply intelligent eyes. Ganesh had the body of a man, aside from the four arms that blossomed like petals around the rotund belly. Despite his size, he carried himself gracefully, his movements delicate.

"Talk about an elephant in the room," Dante murmured.

Ganesh's eyes remained on John. "You are not yet at the pathway between reincarnations," he said, "so you may not know me as you once did. You have worshipped many deities in your lifetimes, John Grey, but more often than not you have found your way to me."

John hesitated. There was something familiar about Ganesh, but it was the nature of the gods to be known when in their presence.

"So you are my—"

"Friend," Ganesh said. "High caste or low, man or woman, I have always found you to be pleasant company. How amusing that I stand here before you as a stranger. Would you care for a sweet?"

The god stepped forward and held out one of his arms. Resting in his hand was a bowl filled with small dumplings. They, like the elephant god, were very familiar.

"You've heard of taking candy from strangers, right?" Dante warned, but John paid no heed.

He popped one of the dumplings into his mouth. They were sweet and tasted of coconut. Modak, that was what they were called. The dumpling melted in his mouth, memories accompanying the pleasing flavor. He remembered being an Indian man who spent most of his time at the temple because he enjoyed the camaraderie so much. He remembered the joyful statue of Ganesh that filled one wall of the rectangular room, always present as he talked and laughed with friends.

John remembered another life too, as a housewife in North Carolina with six children. Oh, how she had lived for those children! A neighbor had loaned her a book about Eastern religions, and she had been instantly drawn to the black-and-white photograph of Ganesh. She had researched this strange god with a passion, even attempting to bake her own modak that ended up sticking to the pan.

He remembered even more lives, other connections to this god, but they faded as John swallowed the last of his treat.

"I know you!"

Ganesh smiled and snatched up one of the treats with his long trunk. "What a unique time to meet again," he said as he snacked. "A man who is living but walking among the dead. We all do occasionally in dreams, but as a distant audience member who can only make-believe their role in the play. These aren't dreams, John. You've set a great many events in motion."

"Have I done wrong?" John asked urgently. "I only wanted Purgatory to fall, but I fear for Heaven's safety, even though I don't belong there."

"Rarely is there ever a single place we belong," Ganesh said, "and even rarer is change for the worse. But you haven't finished your task. You've merely pushed a boulder down a hill without yet chasing after to see where it rolls. You may even find the strength to guide its path."

"Or?" John asked, knowing there were choices to be made.

"Or you may sleep again in your body until you reawaken to the real world."

John turned to look at himself. The car wreck hadn't been kind. There were cuts on his cheek and stitches on his forehead. Dark circles ringed his eyes; his lips colorless.

"If I stay out of my body, can I still come back to it when I'm done?"

Ganesh cocked his head, long eyelashes fluttering. "The body is not meant to be without a soul, not for so long a time as this. But if you act quickly and wisely, you might just make it back in time."

John nodded. "Then I look forward to the day when we walk together again."

Ganesh smiled. "No matter what paths we choose, in the end we will all be together. Do not forget that. No choice you make will separate you from those you love."

Headlights from the street cut through the room, and Ganesh was gone. John turned back to his body, the gateway to so much that he knew and loved. He wanted to see his family again, to sit in his mother's kitchen while she baked and listen to the latest gossip. He wanted to call a friend and talk for hours, laughing about their latest misadventures. Or simply sit at his drafting desk in the morning, staring out the window and enjoying the morning light while nursing a tea. John missed all of this and more, and before him was the chance to return to it all.

But behind him was an unresolved conflict, not just Purgatory but his emotions for Rimmon as well. He could run from that, or he could face it before returning here.

"We're leaving," John said.

"Yeah?" Dante stopped slouching and gave John his full attention. "You mean it? Where are we going?"

John regarded the steam coach. "To Hell. And then we are going to war."

Chapter Fifteen

A marble glowing with blue light. A lonely planet set not against space but countless swirling colors and shapes. Purgatory imitated Earth's appearance from afar just as it had on street level, but the gentle blue glow didn't come from azure skies. The glow came from souls, locked into stasis, sizzling with energy that numbed and paralyzed. Like Earth, Purgatory only appeared a place of tranquility when seen from a distance.

John was pensive, observing all of this from inside the steam coach, which had been chained to countless other vehicles. Viking ships, chariots, wagons stuffed full of soldiers—all manner of vessel and vehicle were bound together in one massive convoy. These were flanked and protected by innumerable beasts, all scale and wing, creatures from the deepest pits of the inferno.

Hell had its own army. Of course it did, but John had never stopped to consider the possibility. Asmoday behaved as if Hell had little power of its own, when really he was just adding to its already considerable resources. Among the numerous gods and wagons of terracotta soldiers were demons of more variety than John had ever imagined. He had to admit he was impressed. At first he was angry, as if everything they had gone through to gain Liu Wu's army had been for nothing, but Asmoday assured him that the terracotta soldiers had the skill his brutal demon forces lacked. John considered these creatures, the bizarre number of eyes and appendages holding his attention only momentarily before he began searching their ranks for Rimmon.

John knew the incubus had returned to Hell because the jade suit was in the coach next to him. A less-than-casual inquiry to Asmoday revealed that the goddess Amaterasu had transported Rimmon and the terracotta soldiers back to Hell, but the incubus hadn't made any effort to seek him out, and John had no idea where to find him.

He reached over to stroke Bolo's head. At least the dog had found him, almost instantly. John thought of the countless animals they had seen trapped in Purgatory's depths. If they managed to free them today, then they too would run free across the realms as Bolo did.

"Looks like we were expected," Dante said. "Think that's

some sort of weapon?"

The massive structure floating ahead of them resembled a construction vehicle rather than a weapon. John had seen plenty of excavators on construction sites for buildings he had designed, except they usually had only one arm. The monstrosity before them had four arms with spoon-shaped scoops. The strange device was facing away from them, nestled up against Purgatory's dome. As they watched, one of the scoops dove into the surface, dislodging a handful of souls who soon disappeared, called away to whatever realm they belonged to.

"I'd say it's on our side," John said, "but I don't remember it being part of the plan."

The excavator must have been at it for some time, for a notable dent had been made in the dome's surface. As another scoop delved into this barrier, it penetrated deep enough to break through and create a hole. John was about to cheer when insects started spilling out. The featureless Props, transformed into their arachnid forms, hatched like spiders from a nest. Their numbers were incredible as they spread over the machine. An elderly voice carried across the distance, yelling in panic from inside the excavator's cabin.

"Jacobi!" Dante exclaimed.

The old man must have been here the entire time, working on building a device that could free the other souls. John felt a rush of affection for the man and his determination, but now Jacobi had gotten himself into serious trouble.

"Defend that vehicle!" John shouted out the coach window. "The pilot is our ally!"

Help was already on the way, countless demons swooping in and pulling the spiders away. Not all of the demons were humanoid. Some were strange mixes of animals; others resembled nothing remotely known to Earth, great balls of sinew and hair or creatures made entirely of vapor. "We are legion!" was their battle cry. One that resembled a loop of sharp teeth with neither head nor eyes flew past the coach door. Fascinated, John watched as it reached a spider and began spinning, tearing the creature to shreds.

Soon the entire scene was nothing but demons and spiders, the construction vehicle lost completely in the chaos. John felt trapped and useless in the comfort of the coach. He wanted to leave its safety, but was unsure of how he could help or even survive in the fray. He would be on his own, too. If Dante tried to leave the coach he would be pulled back to Hell, just as he had been when they had first escaped from Purgatory. Only the specially trained demons had a chance out there. The rest of the troops were useless until they reached Purgatory's surface.

They heard a thud on the roof of the coach. Dante and John grabbed each other for comfort while Bolo began to growl. Something was up there, crawling around. They were being attacked from above! Then Bolo ceased his growling and stood, his tail thumping enthusiastically. A red face appeared upside-down in the window closest to John, the features more handsome than monstrous.

"We need to talk," Rimmon said.

The demon swung down from the coach roof, wings flapping. They were huge, segmented into four sections like a butterfly's but visually similar to the wings of a bat. Purgatory's blue light reflected off their black surface, shifting hypnotically as the wings pumped.

Rimmon opened the coach door and extended a hand. "Come."

John took his hand and was pulled into Rimmon's arms, but the incubus's face was stern, not seductive. The wings pumped hard, and they flew upward with startling speed. The battle below disappeared and soon even Purgatory was nothing more than a star, a distant pinprick of light. When they stopped, Rimmon held John at arm's length, his face no more friendly than it had been before.

"How can you be out here without being pulled back to Hell?" John asked.

The stony expression softened slightly. "Always the questions. You never change." The hint of a smile showed when he realized that John was waiting for an answer. "My soul, like yours, is mostly in balance. Remember the test of Osiris and the scales? And before you ask, I have wings when I need to have wings."

"They're beautiful," John murmured.

Rimmon frowned. "I don't know how to convince you that nothing will come of your attraction toward me."

John swallowed. "Don't flatter yourself."

"I know, John. I've known since after the vampire attacked

me. I felt the intensity of your emotion, and it healed me more than simple sex would have. I know that you love me, and I'm sorry." Now the demon's voice was gentle. "I should have told you then, given us both time to talk it through rather than let you be hurt the way you were, but I suppose I was in mourning. I was so happy to find a friend in you and so sad to think that emotion would drive you away. And it did, but much sooner than I expected."

"It's not fair," John said.

"No, it isn't," Rimmon agreed, "but then love rarely is."

"No, I mean the reason is unfair. You don't know why I love you, do you?"

Rimmon shook his head.

"When Osiris weighed your heart, I was stupid enough to touch it. Before then I was reasonable and sane. Sure, I found you attractive and cared about you, but the second I touched your heart, I knew you. You must think my feelings are superficial, considering how little we know of each other, but they run much deeper than you might expect, and it's not fair. I wish it could be undone, that there was some way for you to take these feelings back from me."

"Do you?"

John sighed. "No. Not really. But I wish you felt the same way about me."

"But you also wish I was different," Rimmon said.

John was momentarily confused. "You mean my reaction to the goddess? Yeah, I blew it. I wanted to play it cool, to show you that I could handle your occupation, but it's hard to feel secure when you've never belonged to me."

"To be fair, having my affection didn't make my boyfriend feel any more secure than you do," Rimmon said.

John rolled his eyes. "Him again? Can't it be just about me and you for once?"

"I'm just as much a victim of my emotions as you are."

At least some satisfaction could be found in that. Rimmon didn't have the superior position here. Both of them were heartbroken, unable to be with who they truly wanted.

"Look," John said, "he's going to love you no matter what. As much as he might hate your profession, or your nature, or whatever you want to blame it on, he'll still love you. If you and

I can't change the way we feel, then neither can he. Find him again, Rimmon, and then for god's sake, change."

"Sorry?"

"Change who you are. I know, everyone thinks that they should be loved for who they are, but that's not how it works. Every relationship is dysfunctional, because no two people are a perfect fit. The ultimate expression of love is to come together as much as possible, to change for each other. You need to resist straying as much as possible, and he needs to find new ways to satisfy your needs. The love is already there between you two. You might as well make the best of it. Do anything you can, absolutely everything in your power, Rimmon, but never give up."

"You're phenomenal."

"I know, and it's your loss. Now if you don't mind, I'd like to go back to feeling sorry for myself." John gave his best smile. "Long-distance relationships never work out anyway. I could hardly expect you to wait until I finally get around to dying."

John reveled in the shock on Rimmon's face.

"They told you?"

"No. Asmoday doesn't even know that I know. I didn't just take off in the steam coach to spite you. I wanted to see where I belonged. Now I know."

"But how did you manage to come back, to resist the allure of your body?"

"How can *you* resist, that's the real question." John grinned. "No, I was very tempted to stay, but there was too much unfinished business. That, and I wasn't quite ready to say goodbye to Dante, Bolo... you." John felt his emotions rising. "Look, I'll probably always find you irresistible. Once love is there, you're stuck with it. The best I can do is try to tame it into being the love of friendship. It won't be easy, but if you're willing to forgive the occasional relapse, I think we'll be all right."

Rimmon shook his head. "You never cease to amaze me. I'm looking forward to seeing what becomes of you, John, both in life and in death."

John broke his gaze, unable to handle his feelings anymore, and looked to his feet. Far below a blue star awaited them.

"The old man who created the construction vehicle is a friend of mine, and he's in trouble. I think I can help if you can get me close."

"Getting close has never been our problem," Rimmon said.

Before John could retort Rimmon grabbed him and flipped in the air. Soon they were nose-diving, not slowing even when Purgatory became planet-sized again. Demon and spider alike leapt out of the way as they plummeted toward the excavator. Rimmon's aim was good, the cabin of the vehicle directly ahead and nearing. The only obstacle in the way was one stubborn Prop whose arachnid arms were raised, ready to attack.

"Go!" Rimmon said, tossing John aside before tackling the creature.

John fell the rest of the way, crashing painlessly into the excavator, just inches from the cabin door. He looked up to where Rimmon was fighting, relieved to see the battle going in the demon's favor, before returning his attention to the task at hand. John threw open the cabin door and was promptly beat over the head with a baseball bat.

"Ow! Stop that!" John scolded the old man who was still in the midst of a battle cry. "And next time try a sword or something sharp."

"I'm sorry!" Jacobi stuttered, the bat disappearing from his hand. "Bless my stars! I can't believe it's you!"

"Long time no see." John grinned as the old man threw his arms around him. John hugged him back before pushing him gently away to examine the cabin. "You built all this?"

Jacobi nodded enthusiastically. "It took a few attempts, but I think I've got the hang of it. I'd never seen an excavator before, but other souls in Purgatory told me of their times and I did the best I could. It functions primarily off will and desire, but intention is also crucial or else the actual purpose is lost to form, or at least—"

"Maybe you could explain later. Right now it's important that you keep going. We need a hole big enough to bring our army in. We'll take care of the rest after that."

Jacobi hurried to the seat, which didn't include any sort of controls. Instead he sat perfectly still, sticking his tongue out in concentration. Slowly an arm of the excavator moved forward and dislodged a few more souls. Demons and spiders in battle occasionally blocked their view, but the arms continued to work, one at a time.

"Can't you use all four at once?" John asked.

"I had hoped to," Jacobi admitted, "but it's rather more difficult than I anticipated. That terrible numb feeling from the dome conducts along the arms like electricity and makes everything more difficult."

"Let me try," John offered. "I always had an easier time with that."

And it felt good to know why. He was a soul half in this world, half in another. John understood his advantage now, and as far as Purgatory was concerned, there would be a reckoning.

John hopped into the seat. "How does it work?"

"That's what I was trying to explain earlier," Jacobi complained.

"I guess now would be a good time, then."

When wanting something done in life, the process began with the brain, which then told the body what to do through a series of electrical impulses. There was no such system here, so the will had to be flexed as muscles once were. Simply desiring an arm of the excavator to move forward wasn't enough. John also had to imbue his desire with intention. Otherwise the arm might move through the souls without ever touching them, for outside a realm's borders, physical law did not exist. John made a couple of false starts, but when he did get it right, he sent dozens of souls flying.

Buoyed by his success, he tried again, this time with two arms. Simultaneously, they tore into the blue barrier, freeing more souls than ever. The spiders were left behind, grabbing at nothing before being set upon by demons.

John dug back into the barrier, adding more instructions to his intentions and more oomph to his will. He was an engineer. He understood concepts like structural integrity, how an entire building could crumble with enough damage to just the right area. John called on these principals, willing all four arms into motion and focusing on his goal. The hole was large now, revealing the gray mist below. All four arms of the excavator reached into the hole, hooked onto the edges of the dome, and pulled.

And it happened. The entire barrier crumbled into pieces and dissolved, millions of souls coming alive again for the first time in a century. Voices filled the air, excited, puzzled, and babbling about the different realms they each saw before disappearing. They had done it! They had breached Purgatory's defenses.

The gray sky above was a bandage wrapped suffocatingly tight around the soul. Purgatory had only one park, a space devoid of fauna or flora. Once an old man pretended to be these things, but he had disappeared long ago. Some still gathered here, weary individuals who could no longer bring themselves to rush mindlessly along the streets or play games that earned useless points. They came here to stand in silent defeat, to let time wash over them.

But today there was something new. For the first time in decades a breeze blew through this concrete garden. A few looked up, awakened by memories of leaves skittering across the ground, of autumn, a time of death and a harbinger of change. Boats and wagons came from the sky, some pulled by beasts, others guided by chariots. A dark wooden coach, covered in bronze pipes that hissed with steam, was the first to alight. Then the coach was still, waiting as its companions chose places to land.

The cobwebs of the mind were brushed away as once dull eyes took in the joyous sight of something new. Many gasped as the door of the rickety old steam coach swung open and a figure stepped out. He was dressed in a suit of jade that covered every inch of him, even his face. The jade helmet turned as it swept the crowd before an arm shot into the air.

On this signal, thousands of clay soldiers poured from the wagons and boats to gather around him. Gods and goddesses threw back their cloaks, revealing themselves fully, the power of their auras changing the air around them. Sunlight, love, passion, rain, soil: Each embodied something long-since absent in Purgatory.

Led by the man in jade, the army began to march. The citizens of Purgatory fell in behind them, laughing and leaping with joy as bards from the Celtic tribes began playing their songs. Flowers began to rain from the sky, summoned by the goddess Flora. Demons swept through the air on leathery wings, nipping at the flowers playfully and spinning around each other like dancers in the air. Next the sun came to Purgatory in the form of the goddess Amaterasu, who glided above their procession like a beacon of hope. In only moments the visitors had won over the people of

Purgatory, awakened them from their lethargy and rallied them to their cause.

The parade of people and cultures flooded the streets, an unstoppable display of unity and strength. Purgatory would fall this day and the voice of humanity would be heard! Nothing could go wrong or stand in the way of the crowds, who cheered their support as they continued to join the procession.

Then the buildings began to tremble, and all hell broke loose.

Chapter Sixteen

Being back on the streets of Purgatory felt like returning to school as an adult. John had once been sent to pick up his niece at school, and walking along the rows of beaten-up lockers had felt surreal. Memories had come pouring back, some good, many bad, but mostly John had felt relief that the whole ordeal of public education was behind him. He only wished he could say the same for Purgatory. John had returned to this school not to visit, but to burn it to the ground.

Their plan was a good one, devised by the god of war himself. To John's surprise, Ares had not suggested brute force, but a strategy that involved subterfuge and cunning. They were facing an unknown enemy here. The extent of Purgatory's forces and the preparations they had made for invasion were both unknown. The best Hell's army could do, Ares insisted, was to walk straight into the most obvious trap.

John's part in this plan was to lead his terracotta troops in an attack on the administration building. As the only centralized source of intelligence on Purgatory, it was the most public locale they could advance on. This was, no doubt, exactly what the enemy expected them to do. Newly arrived souls were led through administration to reinforce the belief that this was their headquarters, but Ares felt this was only a farce, a false target designed to attract attention. The real battle would be fought elsewhere, but in order to keep their true plan a secret, they had to show the enemy what they expected to see.

The parade wasn't a spontaneous celebration. They wanted to make their presence instantly known, a show of their numbers and diversity. As calculated as this move was, getting lost in the spirit took little effort. The delight of being outside their realms, of mingling with other cultures, made the gods feel elated, and their joy was contagious. John hoped that they wouldn't be met with resistance, that the light they had brought to Purgatory would be enough to liberate it completely. He wished even more that his friends were there to share this moment with him, but they had a more important mission and he was alone.

Aside from Yi Yi, that was. The little soldier beamed and waved at the crowds when not looking back at the man in the jade suit. All of the soldiers did this, their fixation on John not allowing them to look away for long. As long as John wore the suit, he was their leader. He felt enormous responsibility, even though he didn't understand if they were souls, too. Perhaps their potter imbued them with life as they were sculpted and given individual details and names. John wasn't sure, but he was determined to take care of them and not to treat them like toy soldiers. Nor would he let the people of Purgatory stand by while his army took all the risks.

"Do you want freedom?" John shouted to the crowd.

The answer was less than impressive, so he repeated the question until he roused a healthy chorus of "Yes!" from them.

"What do you want?" John roared.

"Freedom!"

The crowd was falling in line, becoming part of the army.

"What you want?"

"FREEDOM!"

"What do you want?"

"FREE—"

A tearing noise filled the air, the buildings on either side of the street trembling. Facades that housed nothing resembling their outsides began to crack and split. From out of the dark crevices, Props appeared, only a few at first before they began to flow like water onto the street. At first the Props remained humanoid, but soon they shifted to other forms. Many became spiders, but others took on new shapes, thin arms forming skeletal wings that flapped and lifted the creatures into the air. Some remained upright on two legs, but their hands were replaced by stingers, buzzing with stunning energy.

The nearest of these struck out, stinging a citizen and a terracotta soldier simultaneously. The citizen went still, instantly subdued, but the soldier wasn't affected at all. As one, the little clay faces turned to look at John, awaiting instruction. He hesitated no more.

"Arm yourselves!"

Weapons of light blazed into the hands of the terracotta men. Some held bows and arrows, some swords, others long staves with curved blades on the end. What to do now? Citizen after citizen was falling, the Props having turned their attention away from the soldiers they couldn't affect. Other Props had become four-legged creatures that were rushing toward the rear.

"Protect the people!" he shouted.

His army leapt into action. Three, sometimes four soldiers at a time would attack a Prop, cutting off limbs. They dismembered as quickly as they could before moving to their next target, but still more Props poured from the facades. Screams filled the air as panic increased, the citizens of Purgatory running in all directions. This was good. Word of the battle would spread, which is what they wanted.

Behind John all manner of magic was being unleashed. Too many of the four-legged Props had made it through their defenses. The power of the gods was supposed to be reserved for another enemy, not this initial wave of assault. Some of the citizens tried to fight, but they weren't prepared, their bare hands ineffective. Most of them retreated to the middle of the army for protection.

John needed the archers to take down the flying Props and those scuttling toward their flanks. To John's surprise, all it took was a thought from him and his troops responded. Half the archers turned their attention upward; the others began picking off Props as soon as they began to shapeshift. The arrows didn't have a tranquilizing effect on the Props, but they could sever wings or pin those earthbound to the wall.

Bodies began to stack up, to block the rifts in the buildings. New Props couldn't rush them anymore. The tide had slowed enough that John was able to lead his troops forward to another block. Continuing with this strategy would allow them to reach their target.

The buildings here also ruptured, but they were prepared this time and able to stem the flow of Props much quicker. John was about to give the signal to move forward when gravel rained over him. A smacking noise followed, and more gravel showered down. The Props had changed their strategy. Instead of stingers, their hands had become mallets that they swung wildly. Whenever these hammers connected with a soldier, his terracotta body shattered. Some lost their heads or an arm and kept fighting, but these were easy targets for the Props, who soon reduced them to rubble.

More Props were coming from the street ahead, pouring unchallenged out of the facades as more and more soldiers fell.

John commanded half the troops to rush out to meet them, but one of the Props broke through the ranks and headed directly for John, hammers knocking soldiers aside. The Prop intended to smash the jade suit, but there was still one soldier between it and John.

Yi Yi! The little soldier's attention was focused on a Prop flying overhead, unaware of the coming hammers that would shatter him to pieces. John would never reach him in time. Even calling out would attract Yi Yi's attention in the wrong direction before he was reduced to pottery shards.

Yellow robes collided with the Prop, sending it to the ground. A golden katana swept down, amputating its hammer hands before slicing sideways and severing the head. Liu Wu turned, wild eyes focused on John.

"Yi Yi, get him out of my suit!" he commanded.

"Master!" the little solider responded. In a ridiculously short time, John was stripped of the jade armor and was watching as Yi Yi efficiently dressed its rightful owner.

"Have you no knowledge of battle?" Liu Wu complained. "Have you never studied Sun Tzu's *Art of War*? I'll not have my name further tarnished by an incompetent buffoon!"

John couldn't feel insulted. He had made a mess of things and was glad that responsibility was taken from him. "What do we do?" he asked as the mask was placed over Liu Wu's face.

"We retreat!" the king said.

"We can't!" But the troops were no longer his to command. They swarmed around and past him as if John were no longer of any consequence. He had to run to keep up as the progress they had made was lost.

"Archers to the rear!" Liu Wu commanded.

They formed ranks, neat little lines that John had failed to will them into, and began a backward march at an impressive speed. One by one they began unleashing arrows at the Props that pursued, felling them effortlessly. The army's flanks were effectively protected now, but they were heading in the wrong direction.

Liu Wu appeared back at John's side, an imposing figure in his jade suit. "At the next crossroads we make two rights and travel up the side street. This city is a grid, is it not? We need to choose an indirect path, one that keeps the enemy guessing. Can you do this?"

"Yes," John said. This shouldn't be hard. He had roamed these streets for weeks and knew them all too well.

Liu Wu used his soldiers efficiently. The ground troops remained at each side of the army, engaging the Props enough that the army could keep moving. The archers at the rear slowed the pursuing enemy so that they were never overcome. John and Liu Wu were at the front now. When enemies appeared ahead, the army would turn down a street to avoid them. In this manner, they soon reached the administration building. A huge army of Props was now in pursuit, but this was a dead-end street and only so many Props could attack them here at once.

Unknown to Liu Wu, the outcome of this battle didn't matter. The goal was only to draw enemy fire while the true battle was fought elsewhere. John scanned the building as they approached, awaiting the enemy he knew must come and feeling a tingle of fear when he saw them. The doors to the building were guarded by men made of glass, the Ministers of Order.

But only two of them stood in front of the door. This wasn't right at all! According to Asmoday's intelligence, more than a hundred of the glass men were in Purgatory. Most of them should be here, ready to spring their trap.

John stared, dumbfounded, as the gods Anubis, Artemis, and Baldur rushed forward to engage the glass men in battle. The Ministers didn't last long. Even as the shattered pieces became an army of glass skeletons, John felt they weren't resisting enough. Could they possibly know about the gods who had dulled their auras and disguised themselves as citizens? His mind went to the park where they had been left behind, his friends among them. Dante was to show them the sewer entrance to the true heart of Purgatory.

This was a trap. They had always thought they were intentionally walking into one, but they had misunderstood its nature. They had expected to be ambushed, but now they were simply wedged between an army of Props and the administration building. John rushed past grunting gods and shattering skeletons to the doors. They would not open. He pounded on them and tried to will himself inside, but he couldn't. Nothing was there. The masters of Purgatory had changed their realm, created a true dead-end that they couldn't escape. And while they were stuck here, the full force of the Ministers would attack the few who had been left behind. Rimmon. Dante. Bolo. John needed to get to them, to warn them, if he wasn't already too late.

He looked upward. The only clear path was the sky. John had lost track of Amaterasu, but a little skyward searching revealed a glow coming in their direction. John did his best to wave her down, jumping and calling out her name, even trying a bit of a dance. She landed in front of him and he was struck by her beauty.

His beauty.

"I'm sorry," John stammered. "I thought you were—"

"A beautiful goddess?" Apollo smirked. "Honey, I get that all the time." The sun god squinted toward the other gods who were finishing the battle and casually said, "I'm here for reinforcements. Which three should I pick?"

"Reinforcements? What happened?"

"What hasn't?" Apollo sighed. "Ministers everywhere. Can't say I like the look of them. True beauty shines, wouldn't you agree? They look like cheap diamonds, and that's only because it's *my* light reflecting off them. Then there's the massive—" Apollo wiggled his fingers, "—thing."

"What thing?" John asked through gritted teeth.

"Ugh. Well, I can't describe it." Apollo rolled his eyes. "Do you know if any of these deities are good in a brawl? I see Aphrodite over there, but she's always a little gropey. What about the guy with the beard?"

"Take me with you," John said.

"Well, he must be," Apollo continued. "Look at those arms!"

"Take me!" John commanded this time, stepping into Apollo's line of vision.

"You aren't even dead," the sun god said distastefully. "That means you are heavy. If I take you, I won't be able to carry any others."

"Then get me halfway there, out of this street at least! I can help!" He didn't know if this was actually true, but John was desperate to check on his friends. "One block," John pressed. "It won't take you long, and then you can get back to chasing Norse tail."

Apollo glared at him before offering his hand. "Well, come on then!"

John took the glowing hand, the fine, narrow fingers not

escaping his notice. Apollo's delicate beauty would be quite striking if it weren't for his attitude. The sun god behaved as though he were the center of creation. John supposed the entire solar system did revolve around him, but he could still show some humility.

The sun god's warmth spread over John as they rose into the air, but they remained just as they were standing. John didn't dangle from Apollo's arm or press against him to fly over the city like a scene from a Superman movie. They simply moved through the air, Apollo with a bored expression, John's brow crinkled in worry as he surveyed the city.

Then he saw the "massive thing" Apollo mentioned. The description was surprisingly apt, since John wasn't sure what else to call it. Cthulhu came to mind. So did Godzilla. The creature loomed over buildings, swarms of tentacles swaying in all directions. It had a head—of sorts—long, segmented, and deformed. Eyes were everywhere, scattered across the dark, slimy skin like freckles. The beast filled the block where the park had been, the place John had last seen his friends.

"Get me as close as you can," John pleaded. Apollo must have felt his desperation because he complied.

John searched the streets as they flew for any sign of Rimmon and the others. Glass men were everywhere, attacking those who had been left behind. The Ministers wouldn't find the battle easy. The best of each pantheon, the most powerful magicians and fighters, had been selected to travel into Purgatory's depths and face its masters, but none of them had been prepared for the gigantic creature below. Was it the mind behind this spiritual prison or just its guard dog?

"Athena!" Apollo cried.

They plummeted toward the ground like a plane shot down, but Apollo was in full control and they landed smoothly. Ahead of them, seven Ministers of Order circled a heavily armored goddess wielding a sword in one hand and a double-bladed axe in the other. Shards of glass lay scattered around her, previous victims of her skill in battle, but already these glass pieces were trembling, ready to transform into an army that would surely overwhelm her.

Apollo's posture changed completely as he rushed forward with hands extended. Gone was his bored, exhausted-with-life expression. Now his face wore vicious offense that anyone should try to harm one of his kind. Apollo's hands began to glow red, and soon so did the glass shards before they melted into powerless puddles. One of the glass men turned to focus on Apollo, but the sun god pressed his hands together, creating a beam of light that struck the nearest Minister. The beam passed into its glass body and stayed there, light ricocheting back and forth like a laser beam, gaining in momentum. The Minister flailed as the light flashed and flared until the glass body exploded from the inside.

Apollo reached Athena's side and they bumped fists before turning their attention to the remaining glass men. Together they clearly had the situation under control, so John left to find his friends, heading toward the park and the giant creature there. He scanned the streets, searching for Dante's spiky hair or Rimmon's red skin. Citizens were running everywhere, seeking the shelter that Purgatory didn't provide. The panicked crowds helped camouflage John as he ran past countless Ministers, a platoon of them heading toward Apollo and Athena.

The world shook as a tentacle from the massive Cthulhu beast fell into the street, writhing and twitching. John leapt aside just in time, but a young man ahead of him wasn't so lucky. The tentacle passed through his midsection, and the man exploded into sand. One moment he was there, the next he was a cloud of dust. John pressed against one of the buildings as the tentacle continued to slide through the street, bursting more souls into miniscule pieces. John realized this wasn't dust or sand, but tiny fragments of soul now floating through the air like soot. How could they ever hope to recover from that? This disintegration was the nearest thing to true death that John had ever seen.

Fear twisted his stomach as he wondered what would become of him at the tentacle's touch. John pictured his body, his true body, lying in the hospital, the heart monitor emitting a high-pitched whine as his soul was reduced to dust. He swallowed and prayed to every god he had met that this wasn't the reason he couldn't find his friends.

Then Set was there, strolling down the street as if window-shopping on a Sunday afternoon. The beast's grotesque appendage writhed again. Set, heedless of the danger, didn't flinch as the tentacle rolled over him and back again. Set was still standing, as if he hadn't been touched. Then he began to chant.

Set's words were terrible, dark and eldritch. John had to press his hands to his ears lest the words drive him insane. He watched as the tentacle began to tremble and wither. Soon it was nothing more than a dried husk, curling in on itself like a leaf in winter.

Those few souls remaining in the street chose this time to flee. John had to wonder if they were actually running from Set, and if he should do the same. The chaos god turned his dark eyes on John, the glowing red pupils fixing him in place before Set spoke.

"I know where your friends are. Come with me."

The Cthulhu creature wasn't faring well on its eastern-most side. There, four gods and an incubus attacked, systematically burning, hammering, slicing, and working arcane magic to gradually cut away its flesh. The goal was to remove enough of the beast to access the entrance to Purgatory's lower levels, which was somewhere beneath the monster's ugly bulk. This was very messy work. Thor was the most enthusiastic, knocking away great chunks of flesh with his hammer. Rimmon had to duck as one went flying over his head, before he turned his flame breath on the creature again.

"It's nice to be useless sometimes," John commented.

"That was my life philosophy," Dante replied.

"So it just appeared here?"

"Not long after you left, it sort of materialized. We could see it coming before it showed up and just barely managed to move our asses out of the way. Then the Ministers followed, and it's been chaos ever since."

They both winced as Manannan sent a dozen lightning bolts into the creature's side. The flesh liquefied and began to ooze away.

"I think they've found the right technique," Dante said as Thor contributed lightning bolts of his own. Good thing they were watching from a distance because the area was beginning to flood with the creature's flesh. John was pondering whether monster ooze would conduct electricity like water did when Bolo began to growl.

The hair on John's neck stood on end. He turned to find two dozen glass men, all as beautiful as ice, coming toward them. The deities on the outer perimeter had been charged with keeping them at bay, but the gods must have fallen. That, or the Ministers had found another way through.

"Into the ooze!" Dante said, bolting toward the gods.

John followed, calling out warnings. To his relief, he saw the gods had found the entrance, which still looked like a simple manhole. They were struggling to open it, something that John could finally do to help. He slid through goo, pushing away Rimmon's ineffectual hands.

"Hurry," Rimmon said. "There isn't much time."

Ares growled and charged toward the glass men, Thor at his side. Set followed coolly, dark shadows spinning around his hands.

"What are they doing?" John said as he flipped the manhole open. "We can all escape through here!"

"They're buying you time," Rimmon said before fire exploded from his mouth.

A Prop crawling out of the hole fell back in. John looked over the edge to see it colliding with dozens more.

"The tunnels are full of Props! We'll never get through!"

"Stand back!" Manannan commanded. With a sweep of his billowing blue robes, Manannan was at the hole and thrusting his hands inside. Then came the roar of water and the smell of salt as the sea god flooded the tunnels, washing away the Props.

"Watch yourselves!" Ares snarled from the front line.

Half a dozen glass men had broken through and were headed for them.

"Into the hole," John said, shoving Dante forward. "Keep the water going, Manannan! We won't drown, and it will get us there quicker."

Manannan nodded, taking a few steps back so they could enter while oceans continued to pour from his hands.

"You realize that we'll end up wherever the Props do," Dante said.

The Cthulhu creature gave a terrifying wail. If it shifted even a few feet, the gods would be crushed and he and Dante would be dust. "Go!" John shouted.

Dante pinched his nose and jumped into the hole. Next John shoved Bolo in. He felt cruel doing so, but had no other option.

"You next," Rimmon insisted.

"And then you," John said, locking eyes with the demon.

Rimmon clapped a hand on his shoulder, his eyes intense as he struggled to find words. The world around John faded away as he waited to hear what the demon had to say.

"Go, John. End this, if not for all the souls trapped here, then for me. And if we never see each other again, just know that every moment spent with you was a reward worthy of Heaven."

John opened his mouth to respond, but Rimmon shoved him forward. Manannan's waves picked him up, sweeping him into the hole and away from the surface. The last thing he saw before the water rushed over his head was Rimmon breathing fire toward the advancing glass men.

As John fell, he tried to remember where he would land. Ages had passed since he and Dante had made their escape attempt. Dozens of Props were already ahead of them, and John hoped to remember which direction they should run once they gained their footing. An elephant trumpeted just before he hit bottom. He definitely didn't remember that!

John landed with a splash, a thick gray leg almost trampling him as it walked by. Animals were everywhere, sloshing through the knee-high water, many swaying groggily. The animals they had discovered in stasis had revived. Whether that was a result of the conflict above or a side effect of Manannan's magical water, John didn't know, but thousands of them filled the area. Props were scurrying to fulfill their programming and recapture the animals, but not all of the animals were sleepy. A lion leapt over John's head, engulfing a Prop's head in its jaws. The elephant nearest to him became enraged as a Prop tried to sting it, knocking it and others aside with its trunk before stomping on them.

"John!"

Dante, drenched and panicked, was beckoning toward the doors. John imagined he didn't look much better as he sloshed through the water toward him. Only one Prop noticed him as he made for the exit, and it was dragged underwater by an alligator.

"Where's Bolo?" John asked as he reached Dante's side.

"Over there."

The Irishman nodded to where the dog barked and bounded through water around different animals. The lethargic beasts were soon aggravated or panicked by his behavior, their reaction causing even more problems for the Props.

"I think he's helping," Dante said. "Or having fun. Either way, he's better off here."

John didn't like leaving him behind, but they didn't know what they faced ahead. The worst that could happen to Bolo here was being put back into stasis. They reached the doors, John's heart heavy as he gave one final glance toward the dog. First Rimmon, now Bolo. He could only hope this wasn't their last goodbye.

Together John and Dante ran down featureless gray corridors, and here the plan fell apart. They didn't know what they were looking for or what they would do once they found it. Had things gone according to plan, ten of the most powerful gods would be here instead of John. They would have divined the correct path and confronted whatever lay at the maze's center. John had nothing to go by, no godly sense of direction, and no magic to defeat a being powerful enough to control an entire realm.

Still they ran, for they could do nothing else. The halls were silent and empty, as if the battle raging above had been a fleeting dream. That is, until a loud thrumming noise attracted their attention. John remembered it. When they had fled with Bolo to the edges of Purgatory, he had heard the sound of a machine. He hadn't thought much of it at the time, but now it was the only clue they had.

"Think that's it?" Dante asked as they paused to listen to the deep thrum, its steady rhythm hypnotic.

"Must be."

They followed the sound as best they could. Before long the floor was lost in fog, and soon after so was everything else. The world became a gray cloud, forcing them to slow to a walk. They squinted into the fog, jumping occasionally at shadows passing before them. The thrumming noise was their only beacon, growing in volume as they stumbled after it, a vibration that filled their very being. The floor below slanted so steeply they often slid and fell. Wherever they were headed was deep underground.

When the ground leveled again, they saw something new in the fog. Blue flickering light, rectangular. They paused, taking it in and debating if it was a trap. Eventually they crept closer, and John saw it was a door. They could taste the electricity on their tongues as the blue light hummed, and the taste was familiar. This was the poison Purgatory used to numb its victims, except stronger than ever before. The door ahead of them was a barrier that could turn away any kind of soul, be it god or human.

Except John was no ordinary soul. His ties to the physical plane would allow him to pass through. He felt this with absolute certainty. The masters of Purgatory didn't fear the army he had raised or the mighty gods in this realm or any other, but they would fear a person who could pass through this barrier to reach them.

Something stood, silhouetted in the blue light. The shape was humanoid, and for one brief moment John thought one of their friends had beaten them here. One of the clever gods or maybe even Rimmon by some miracle, but then he noticed the unnaturally long appendages. Where the tips of a person's arm would normally end was a second elbow, another forearm attached to it. The being bounced on elongated legs as it approached, leaning forward through the fog to see them better. It was a glass man, and yet it wasn't. There was something inexplicably feminine about the long, narrow head that bobbed on the end of its stretched neck. The eyes were huge and penetrating, devoid of life one moment and mad with interest the next. The mouth was a long comical "O" and inside of it something moved. Fingers, teeth, worms. John couldn't bear to look any longer. He knew it wasn't good. The creature, having finished its examination, began advancing again, its long arms extending outward.

"So that's the guard dog, huh?" Dante grimaced. "Ugly bitch, isn't she? Think you can get through the barrier ahead?"

"I know I can," John said. "If you hold my hand I think I can pull you through."

"I told you I don't swing that way," Dante said, but he wasn't smiling. "You go. I'll hold her off. We'll never both get past her."

"If we both feint—"

"It'll never happen. Besides, what's the worst she can do to me?"

A memory of pain throbbed in John's abdomen where the glass man had played inside him. If a normal Minister was capable of such atrocities, he didn't want to know what the abomination in front of them could do. He wouldn't leave Dante to face that alone.

"I'm about two seconds away from betraying you to save my

own ass," Dante snarled. "You either go now, or I turn tail and run, leaving you as a snack for this thing. Go!"

But it was Dante who ran forward first, leaping on the creature and wrapping his arms and legs around its torso. John didn't hesitate. He ran for the barrier, mentally bracing himself to pass through it. The glass creature turned as he passed, but its hands were full of Dante, who was doing everything in his power to be a nuisance. Dante managed to free a leg and kick the thing in the face, sending its head bobbing backward, but it recovered quickly, turning an angry eye on its prey.

John couldn't watch further. The doorway was directly ahead of him, unobscured except for the electric blue light that sizzled and snapped. The thrumming was deafening now, but John focused only on the barrier ahead.

I'm alive, he thought. *I'm alive and Purgatory is nothing but a ghost to me. There is no obstacle in my way. Only light that I can, will, pass through.*

John closed his eyes to express his apathy toward the object he refused to acknowledge. Given more time, he might have passed through it effortlessly. Instead he slammed into the barrier, only half of him squeezing inside like he had run into a wall of electrified gelatin. His body arched and burned, the light coursing over him and demanding he submit, but John's will was true, his mind clear. An inhuman roar sounded from behind him; stomping followed. John could imagine the creature dropping Dante and reaching to pull him back out. John utilized that fear, let his mind burn with it, and shoved the rest of the way through the blue light.

The thrumming changed, the difference between hearing a muted song outside a nightclub and stepping inside to discover the full force of the beat. John heard it all now, and it wasn't pleasant. A million drums pounded in unison, their rhythm dominating, enforcing only one subjugating sound, one tyrannizing tempo, one bullying beat. This was the heartbeat of Order, and it made John want to go running, crying, whimpering back to his comatose body.

The walls were crystal. Everything here was crystal, mathematically perfect in shape and form. The room was small, a triangular chamber without decoration except for three hideous sculptures, one set on each wall. John barely considered them, turning his attention to the middle of the room and searching for the reason he was here. He saw nothing. He walked to the center and turned on the spot, looking for another door, a mysterious item, the magic button, anything.

"John Grey," many voices said in unison. *"You do not belong here."*

The voices were coming at him from every side. John flinched at the sound before giving the sculptures on the wall fresh appraisal. They were like the other Ministers of Order, except they weren't beautiful men or crystalline skeletons. What hung on each wall were glass corpses, emaciated bodies the color of muddy water and run through with cracks. Their bony arms and legs were splayed wide, as if they had been crucified to the walls. Their zombified heads were fixed in place, too, the dull red points of their eyes straining to keep up with John as he examined each of them in turn.

"Rejoice!" the voices continued, eyes flaring. *"Rejoice and be free, John, for you are not dead! Your physical body is in a coma, but you may return to life. You can go home."*

"Already been there," John murmured. "Decided to come back. Nice try though."

Something inside each rotting sculpture beat to the head-splitting rhythm. No! They were the rhythm, the source of the sound. Inside of them something pulsated, throbbing like a heart and in the same location, but they weren't the right shape at all. The hearts were rectangular. What were they?

"You meddle in affairs beyond your comprehension," the creatures intoned. *"A child kicking angrily at the parent who has its best interests at heart."*

"Best interests?" John scoffed. "How was being locked up in Purgatory good for me? Or how about being a brick in a wall of souls? That was in my best interest as well?"

"It was not your destiny to remain there. We saw that, as we see everything. We foresaw you gaining your freedom, and it pleased us."

John scowled. "So why didn't you let me go in the first place? Why all the struggle if I was never meant to stay here?"

"No human willingly embraces predestination. Your egos demand the false belief that every path taken is forged by your own will. The fragile ego deludes itself, clinging to its perception of singular importance."

John walked as they talked, looking at each of the beating hearts and trying to ignore the uneasy feeling that he wasn't being lied to, that his story had long ago been written from start to finish. How else had they predicted his arrival, trapped his army, and dealt with the gods in such short order?

"You were meant to bring them here," the voices continued. *"The end of the disorderly realms began long before you came. Cut off from each other and from the minds of men, their demise has been slow but steady. Through our grace we allow them to die here, to embrace their destiny now rather than fade away."*

"Gods aren't human," John countered. "Even if I believed in predestination, which I don't, you can't tell me that gods are subject to it as well."

"They will die in battle or they will kill the last child of Chaos. Either occurrence will mean the undoing of their kind."

John stopped. "The creature above, that's the child of Chaos?"

"The last of its kind. Destroying it is beyond our capabilities, so Purgatory was requisitioned to contain it. Purgatory isn't a prison for human souls. Their only function is to enforce the barrier of souls. Purgatory is nothing more than a cage for the child of Chaos."

John shook his head. "I don't understand. That creature is the only thing that can kill you? Is that what you're afraid of?"

But it was more than that. John was standing in the stronghold of Order. If the child of Chaos was the only thing they feared, they never would have remained with it in Purgatory. He realized that the creature's title wasn't simply a creepy name. The beast above was literally the child of Chaos, the embodiment of all that was unpredictable, inexplicable. They had said the gods would undo themselves by killing it. Only order would remain. Their strange natures, their magic, their wonderful realms; all that couldn't be pinned down, dissected, and explained in the universe would cease to exist. Maybe even love.

John turned to the door, intending to leave and warn those above to stop their fight, but the exit was no longer there. He had been so distracted that he hadn't noticed his own imprisonment.

"What are you?" John demanded. "You aren't God! You can't be!"

The Wardens, for that is how John now thought of them, chuckled in unison. *"The fool mistakes his son for his father."*

"What is that supposed to mean?"

"We are your creation."

"My creation?"

"The creation of all mankind. Since the beginning of time you have desired security, predictability, assurances against the terrors in the night that dragged you from your caves to eat you. You formed tribes, finding protection in numbers, but with so many personalities there were conflicts. The only true resolution was to allow the strongest personality to lead. There was always dissent, but for the most part, the rest of humanity was content to follow and serve. Anything rather than returning to those dark days when nothing was certain.

"The tribes grew in number while the leaders became fewer and fewer. Laws became necessary to keep the order. At first they were basic. Thou shall not kill. Thou shall not steal. But eventually there were rules for everything. Thou shall not stand too close when speaking to another, thou shall not belch at the dinner table, thou shall not accelerate thy vehicle above the posted speed, thou shall not utilize inside information in trade. Rules govern every aspect of your life, how you appear, smell, move, behave, everything. These rules were your choice, your desire. Without them you would return to being the weakest animals on the planet. Without us, you would be nothing."

John walked to the nearest Warden, bringing his face as close to its chest as he could without touching it. He peered in at its rectangular heart, stared hard until he was certain that he was seeing it correctly. Then he understood.

"We took it further than that, didn't we?" John said. "We made rules for the things we couldn't see, for worlds we could only guess at. Our entire lives were governed by rules, but we needed more, and so we made rules for the invisible, for when we are dead." He tapped on the Warden's chest without thinking. His finger clinked on warped glass the first few times. The fourth and final time it passed partially through, and with that came hope. John walked to the next Warden on the wall and bent to examine its heart, just so he could be sure.

"Tell me something," he said as he squinted. "If all of this is part of some grand plan, then what am I doing here? What reason did you have for bringing me to this room? The first thing you told me is that my body is in a coma. You were hoping that the shock would send me zooming back to Earth, far away from you. And why the guard outside? Don't you want me here?"

The resulting hesitation told John all he needed to know. He reached into the glass Warden's chest. It wasn't difficult. In fact it was the easiest thing he had ever done, because John suddenly believed in free will and this is what he wanted to do. His fingers wrapped around the spine of the book. It throbbed under his hand like a living heart as he pulled. The Warden screamed, its eyes flaring with so much light that the entire room was cast in eerie red shadows. John pulled it the rest of the way free, and two things died at once: The fire in the Warden's eyes disappeared first and then the book stopped pulsating.

John held the Bible up. "These aren't rules," he said to the two remaining Wardens, "These are stories, parables that teach morals. This isn't the word of God! It's the word of—"

"MAN!" the Wardens shouted. *"We serve man, not God! These are your words that we obey, your will that we carry out."*

"This isn't my will," John said, approaching the next Warden, "and I'm glad to hear it isn't God's will either."

He tore the next book free and placed the Quran with the Bible in his left hand. The Wardens moaned and wailed, but John ignored them. He considered the tomes in his hand and shook his head, amazed at how simple words could cause so much trouble. The books were just well-meaning manuals of morals from a time long past, not something evil. No book in the world was evil, no matter how many people used them as justification for their actions.

John was reaching for the third and final book when the only remaining Warden spoke.

"We pray for you, John. Every Minister, every angel in Heaven. Sleeping priests see your face before waking up in the morning, and they pray for you. We have this power and man has another. They pray for your swift recovery. Your body will awaken, and you will be taken from this world before your work is done."

"Then I better not waste any time," John said as he pulled the Tanakh, the last beating heart of Order, free from the glass chest and returned it to what it truly was. Just a book.

Chapter Seventeen

"We should run!" Dante said for the third time.

John sighed. "There's nothing to run from and nowhere to run to."

Purgatory had begun fading away the moment John had taken the last book. It would have been satisfying to see the crystal walls crack, for rubble to rain down around them as this realm was reduced to nothing. Instead the walls had grown transparent before simply disappearing. This phenomenon was spreading outward, starting from the room John had been standing in. He was reunited with Dante as soon as the walls disappeared. The Irishman looked pale, and while he behaved like his usual self, John knew some injuries were invisible.

"Are you all right? Did that creature hurt you?"

"Me?" Dante puffed up his chest. "Nah. Stung me a few times and gave me some nightmares, but I came to as soon as the walls started fading. Saw that thing running away too, and let me tell you, the back of her was no more pleasant than the front. Like a catwalk model gone wrong."

"But she wasn't fading too?"

"Nope. Solid as can be."

This worried John. With the Wardens defeated, he had hoped the remaining Ministers of Order would fade away with the rest of their realm, but it seemed this wasn't the case. With Purgatory soon gone, the Ministers would be forced to flee, but to where? The final Warden had said every angel was praying for John. Unless it was being poetic, maybe Heaven really was involved in some way, and yet the Warden had said that they didn't serve God.

Around them Purgatory continued to fade away. Cross sections of hallways were left exposed, as if the world were made of cake and someone had taken a slice. Layer after layer disappeared, the process quickening as it continued. John wondered if this would soon happen to him, if the well-wishes of his enemies really could heal his body. He'd heard of the power of prayer, of names passed around in churches and the subsequent recoveries. If this was possible, John would soon be drawn home when his body awoke. But he wasn't ready to go. Not yet.

"Hey, check out the animals!" Dante said.

Exposed far above them was the endless warehouse that had once been filled with animals of every kind. All were free now. Many ran through empty space; others began to disappear to wherever they wished to go. Bolo chased those that he could, barking with joy. Scattered among the animals were Props, no longer moving, that began to deteriorate and fall apart. They were only constructs, soulless manifestations fading away with the rest of their realm.

"Come on," John said. "We better get you to the steam coach as quickly as possible."

"Why?"

"Because you'll be pulled back to Hell. Purgatory won't exist for much longer."

The floors had already disappeared, leaving them standing on nothing, so John willed himself to rise. It worked. He snagged Dante's jacket on his way up, pulling the other man behind him.

"I've figured it out now!" Dante complained half-way up. "I can do it myself, so let go of me."

By the time they reached the animals, the streets of Purgatory were exposed before they too dissolved into nothing. They saw no sign of the child of Chaos. Perhaps it, like so many others were doing, had disappeared back to its proper home. Only the invading armies remained behind. Deities were cheering in celebration, clapping each other on the back and boasting about their feats. John rose to their level, but he couldn't join in their gaiety, not yet. He found the coach and shoved Dante inside, but someone was still missing.

"Thank the inferno! You're okay!"

John turned and resisted the urge to throw himself into Rimmon's arms, but only just. The incubus didn't share John's reservations. He pulled him into a hug, and John let himself enjoy the moment, since it wasn't of his doing.

"I knew you would manage," Rimmon said as they separated. "John Grey, liberator of Purgatory. How does it feel?"

"Not bad," John laughed. "Are the gods okay?"

"Mostly. Some received serious injuries, but I think they learned a little humility in the process. Tell me what happened to you!"

John told him, and as he did so his audience grew until every being present was listening to his story. When he reached its end, the cheering began anew, except now the cheers were for John. He felt very much like a hero, and oddly enough the feeling was mostly embarrassing.

"I was down there too, you know," Dante's muffled voice complained from inside the coach.

"We have much to thank John for!" a voice boomed over the crowd. Above them was Asmoday. The portly demon had been completely absent from the battle, probably waiting somewhere safe until the whole ordeal was over. He was here now though, and John knew why.

"John's actions were brave," Asmoday continued, "but so was the decision all of you made by coming here today. We have shown that no force in existence can stand against us when we are united, not even Heaven! No, not even Heaven, for they were the puppet masters behind the blasphemy of Purgatory. Heaven held the souls of our people hostage, hoping to drain and weaken us, and it is Heaven that must be made to pay!"

The crowd roared. The sound was deafening. Many more pantheons had arrived, John noticed. News about the battle had spread. He saw African gods, wild and powerful in appearance. Then there was a woman dressed in white with a coyote at her side. Behind this pair was an army of Native American warriors. There were many other beings John had not met before, but he pulled his attention away and looked at Rimmon.

To his surprise, the demon nodded without John saying a single word. Rimmon snapped his fingers and turned away. The steam coach followed behind him as the crowd parted. No one took much notice of their departure. All attention was riveted on Asmoday, whose speech was continuing to gain momentum. Once outside the crowd, John was finally free to speak.

"You know what I want to do?" John asked Rimmon.

"Does it involve Heaven?"

John nodded. "We have to warn them. I don't think Heaven is behind this, at least not entirely. I want to see the truth for myself, preferably without an army at my back."

"We should hurry, then."

"But how will we get there? We don't have anyone to take the driver's seat."

"I've given that some thought." Rimmon whistled. From

out of the crowd Bolo came bounding toward them, his tongue hanging out one side of his mouth.

"Bolo?" John asked.

Rimmon nodded and smiled. "All dogs go to Heaven."

There were clouds. Big, fluffy, and edged with a hint of blue reflected from the surrounding sky. John hadn't expected Heaven to be anything like this, mostly because it was exactly what he expected. Hell hadn't been a pit of flames, at least not most of it, so on their way here John prepared himself for anything except the pearly gates below.

The bank of clouds they landed on was filled with people, throngs that put summer crowds at Disneyland to shame. Emotional greetings and hugging were the predominate activities. John was sure that many of these newly arrived souls had just come from Purgatory, and allowed himself a moment of pride as the coach landed.

Their arrival went mostly unnoticed. John stepped out of the coach and went to the front seat to set Bolo loose. The dog had done well. He didn't belong in Heaven, any more than he did any other realm, but his natural seeking ability had led them here well enough. Rimmon had simply talked to the dog, and Bolo had done the rest.

"You realize we could have used the dog to get to Chinatown," Dante complained as he jumped out of the coach.

Dante's eyes turned red, and in a voice similar to Rimmon's he said, "I didn't know if it would work. We could have ended up back in Purgatory or anywhere else for that matter."

"Well, you could have tried, rather than unleashing Fumiko on the world," Dante said in his own voice again.

"We could only risk it once Purgatory had fallen," came the demonic response. "Otherwise a neutral soul such as Bolo would probably have been pulled—"

"You're attracting attention," John interrupted, smiling at a chubby woman who was staring at Dante with some concern.

"Sorry," Dante/Rimmon said to her, a wisp of smoke escaping from the side of his mouth. The woman had the good sense to continue on through the crowds, not looking back until she was a safe distance away.

John sighed. "There's no point in you possessing Dante if

you're going to constantly talk through him." He waited for a demonic comeback and nodded with satisfaction when it didn't come.

The importance of Rimmon remaining incognito was driven home when a Minister of Order passed through the crowd, just three people away from them. The glass man was clearly flustered by the unexpected number of arrivals and didn't notice John, although it did spot the coach and move toward it. Luckily they had already walked some distance away, but now their transportation was lost.

"What do we do now?" John whispered as they joined a stream of people moving away from the edge of the cloud bank.

"I don't know; ask directions!" Dante hissed back.

"On how to get to God?"

"Why not!"

John looked around for a friendly face, a description that applied to every person he could see. Since they all appeared nice, he settled on the most handsome. That turned out to be a tall man with well defined cheekbones and brownish-blond hair. He was dressed in a pilot's uniform and was holding a gray cat that he was kissing as if they had just been wed.

"Excuse me," John said as he approached, glancing at the name tag. "Jace? Are you new here too, or do you know your way around?"

Jace noticed him and smiled. Suddenly John's feelings for Rimmon felt more distant. "I've been here a little while," Jace answered. "I was just picking up my cat. You have no idea how long I was waiting for him. I think he got lost on the way."

"He was probably stuck in Purgatory with the other beasties," Dante said. "We just set them all free, so you owe us a pint."

"Nice," John muttered.

Jace chuckled. "It's all right. They say there are no lies in Heaven, so I suppose I really am in your debt."

John felt relieved. "We were just wondering if you could point the way to God."

Jace's face fell. "That's not as simple as you might think."

"He's gone missing," John said. Just like all the other pantheon leaders, God would be gone, too. He had been so caught up in their recent victory that he hadn't thought of the one remaining mystery. If the leaders of each realm weren't trapped in Purgatory, where were they?

Jace's eyes darted through the crowd. His smile was natural, the perfect show for anyone watching, but his tone was serious. "Let's walk."

John followed along, waiting for him to say more. As the crowds thinned, so did the clouds, revealing green grass below their feet. Wildflowers grew in abundance, their colors as varied as their scents, but the smells were complimentary, a perfumist's dream of perfection.

"The clouds are only for show," Jace said. "People need a clear signal that they haven't shown up in the other place, if you know what I mean. The rest of Heaven doesn't look that way, which is a shame because I really like the clouds. Couldn't get enough of them in life, and it's no different here."

Majestic mountains appeared before them as they entered a valley.

"How beautiful," John said. "I'm sure we'll be very happy here."

"No, you won't," Jace replied. His cat was riding on his shoulders now, while keeping a wary eye on Bolo. "You don't belong here. Not that you aren't welcome, but there's something different about you. Both of you. Did you really liberate Purgatory?"

John nodded. "Purgatory had become a prison, and a lot of people blame that on Heaven. Powerful people. We don't have much time to find out if there's any truth to their claims."

"Things are good here," Jace said, "but something is wrong. Everyone asks about God when they arrive—who wouldn't—but they soon learn not to. There are these things, men made of glass, and they say that no one can look upon God. These men say they are the word of God and his representatives. They're handsome as hell too, but they make your skin crawl."

"I've seen them," John said, "and I don't think they have anything to do with God. In fact I think they might have done something to him."

"I can believe that," Jace said. "Most of us try not to worry about it much, but you hear things sometimes. There's a place—"

"That'll be it then," Dante interrupted. "Anywhere no one is supposed to go. That's where we'll end up. There's no getting around it."

"Can you take us there?" John asked.

Jace nodded.

The world around them had changed yet again. The grass was still under their feet, but the mountains had been replaced by structures of light. John marveled at them, overwhelmed by designs beyond reasoning. Glowing girders were the basis, while the walls were made of harmony, held in place by pieces of song and finished by the resonation of the correct vibrations. These concepts were alien to John, but here they made instant sense. They just felt *right*.

"Beautiful, aren't they?" Jace said. "That's just the beginning of it all. The transition into Heaven is gradual. The lands beyond are even more abstract and utopian. Once you're in there, you never want to leave. I've only gone so far myself, but always come back before it's too late."

"Why?"

"Oh, I suppose I'm not ready yet. I was waiting for Samson here, of course." Jace's expression was wistful. "There's someone else I'm waiting for too. The both of them, if that's what makes them happy. There's a lot more room for love in Heaven than there ever was on Earth."

John didn't fully understand, but felt it wasn't his place to ask. "So what do people do in there? Sing hymns all day, play harps, that kind of thing?"

"No," Jace laughed. "Well, there are people that are into that. *Those* sorts of people. They have their own place in Heaven. Most of us just enjoy our lives. I know, we're dead, but it doesn't feel like that. In fact, it feels more real here than it ever did back on Earth, as if we were all only dreaming of life until we finally woke up."

"But what do you do?" John considered the outfit Jace was wearing. "You were a pilot in life, right?"

"A flight attendant actually, but seeing how this is Heaven I figured I'd give myself a complimentary upgrade."

John smiled. "Fair enough, but don't you miss having that job to do everyday? One of the worst times in my life was when I lost my job and didn't work for months. For the first few weeks I tried to treat it like a vacation, but soon I was going crazy to actually do something with myself."

"Type A personality." Jace nodded. "I can understand your

concern, but there's no limit to the things that can be done here. I've only experienced the very first level of an infinite array, and my mind is constantly being blown away by each new activity. You can create here, not just buildings like those on the horizon but entire environments. You can also compose multidimensional music that makes instruments back home sound like cheap toys. Then there are these strange emotional raft rides, relivable life experiences that you can share with others, but you see them from every possible perspective at once. Or you can just eat ice cream and watch the living."

"Is that what you do?"

"Sometimes," Jace said. "You watch the people you love, and when they feel joy, so do you. When they face conflict, you try to guide them as best you can. I like playing guardian angel, especially for him. I've always been patient, so some of us wait until we no longer have to."

There was a moment of silence in which John felt he had been taken into Jace's confidence. He liked this man. John couldn't imagine that he'd had many shortcomings in life and was exactly the sort of guy that John would have been thrilled to meet.

"Plus you can see into locker rooms," Jace added, causing John to laugh.

The horizon had changed again. No longer were there mountains, or strange structures. The horizon was only a perfect blue sky. The field they were walking on had grown more wild, countless species of flowering plants all thriving happily together.

"There aren't many people in Heaven," John commented. "We haven't seen anyone since we left the crowds behind."

"That's how it works here," Jace explained. "If you are lonely and desire company, you find it instantly, but because we currently need to be alone, we are."

"Funny," Dante said, "I keep getting the feeling that you two want to be alone."

Jace smiled. "That would explain why the walk has taken this long."

"You mean it's optional?" John asked. "I've enjoyed talking with you, but time is of the essence."

Jace nodded. "And so we are there."

Ivy crawled over the worn, rounded stones of the cottage, a thatched roof covering its single story. Thick glass filled the round windows on either side of the entrance, while ancient yellow paint peeled off the wooden door, the color matching the sunflowers growing around the cottage. A pathway of flat stones led to the door, passing first a small herb garden barely distinguishable from the wild brush that filled the valley.

The cottage was surrounded by a swarm of angels. They flew in a cylindrical formation, stretching from the ground to higher than the eye could see. The dozens of angels, each winged and robed, looked just as they were usually depicted, but rarely did any artist capture their colors. Every angel's wings had a different shade of feather, some sporting a single color such as cobalt blue or chartreuse, while others had wings like tropical birds, orderly patterns of feathers in multiple colors.

"They're beautiful," John said.

"They are," Jace agreed. "This is the only place in Heaven where you see angels. Old souls say that it once was different, that angels and even God would walk among the people. But now they circle that cottage. Anyone who comes too close is always carried away by the angels. They're sort of intimidating, like the glass men are, but more like a big brother or parent. The glass men are just—"

"Monsters," John said when Jace failed to find the right word.

"Yes, monsters. Anyway, I think he's in there. I think that cottage is God's home."

"Then this is where we part ways. It's going to get dangerous from here on out."

"I'm not afraid," Jace said coolly. "I believe the angels are good, that they're protecting God, as ridiculous as that might sound. Besides, I'd like to meet the big guy, too."

"This isn't a social call," Dante said. "There's a bloody huge army hot on our heels, and we have to get past those angels and warn God as quick as we can. Once we're in there, I'm going to ask him why no one in the afterlife ever does anything heroic but us because it drives me mad."

"Okay," Jace said, taking it in stride, "but I still don't see what makes you any more qualified than me."

"I'm still alive, and he's possessed by a demon," John said.

"And the dog?" Jace asked without blinking an eye.

"He's the team mascot." John grew serious. "You're right that we don't belong here, and there truly is a tsunami of trouble rising up behind us. It's best if you go somewhere safe, if only for your cat."

"Ah, the old 'concern for others' trick," Jace said. "Very well, I'll respect your wishes, but it was a pleasure to meet you. And thanks again for springing Samson out of jail."

John offered his hand and Jace accepted it. "Awkward timing, I know," John said, "but if this were Earth, I'd ask you for your phone number."

Jace raised an eyebrow but smiled. "Good luck, John. If you do find God, give him my love."

With his cat dozing contentedly on his shoulder, Jace returned to the flower-covered valleys they had passed through. John watched him leave before the importance of their mission came rushing back.

"We have to hurry," he said, marching toward the cottage. Bolo barked in excitement and bounded ahead of him.

Before they even reached the garden, two angels dropped from the sky. One had black and gold wings striped like a bumblebee, which complemented his ebony skin. The other, slight and female, had narrow wings of pale blue. Both angels were smoking hot, like supermodels who had just finished a heavenly photo shoot.

"This area is off limits," the female angel said.

"Look closely, Zophiel," the male angel said, a golden spear appearing in his hand. "These souls aren't from Heaven."

"Well spotted, Sariel. We shall escort them to the astral plane."

"We have to speak with God," John said, taking a step back. "It's important! There's an army coming at this very moment."

"No one is allowed to see God," Shields appeared on Zophiel's wrists. "You will return to your own realm."

John shook his head. "Aren't you listening? We're here to warn God, to save him! Or are you holding him hostage rather than protecting him?"

"Enough," Sariel said, stepping forward.

Rimmon leapt out from Dante and pounced on the male angel, snarling like a wild animal. He turned his head to spit fire at Zophiel before shouting at them to run.

Dante tried to flee away from the cottage, but John caught his arm and pulled him along. More angels were beginning to descend. Bolo leapt off the ground, barking and snapping as if he were trying to catch a small bird. Another angel landed directly on top of Dante, but John couldn't stop. One of them had to make it into the cottage. He was so close now, just a couple more paces to the unguarded door. John was reaching for the worn wood, his fingers inches away, when it opened.

An angel stepped out of the cottage, his beauty stopping John in his tracks. His hair was auburn and barely reached his shoulders. His face was perfection: a strong brow with dark, delicately arching eyebrows and eyes like serene sapphires. Full lips carried the slightest touch of arrogance, his well-defined jaw flexing against his strong neck. The chestnut wings spread wide, obscuring the door from view as the angel drew a flaming sword from his belt. His eyes lingered on John, who stared stupidly back. Deciding John was of little consequence, the angel turned his attention to the yard.

John followed his gaze. Dante was still pinned beneath an angel, and Bolo was being pursued by two more, wearing a look of glee as if this game had been invented for his amusement. Rimmon was the only one truly fighting. Three angels were on the ground around him, as he raised another above his head and threw it at an angel who was descending.

"Hello, Rimmon."

The angel guarding the door had spoken, his voice soft, but the demon heard him regardless. Rimmon stepped out of the way of a new attacker, his eyes locking on the angel.

"Uriel," he breathed.

A dozen angels dropped from the sky, but Uriel raised his hand and they withdrew. Rimmon marched toward John, showing no signs of stopping, so John stepped out of the way and watched, fascinated, as Rimmon wrapped his arms around Uriel and kissed him deeply. They were smiling when they pulled apart, faces beaming as they examined each other, eyes hungry.

Seeing their impossible beauty together, John knew this was the person to whom Rimmon belonged. He saw before him an immaculate union. They were crafted, quite possibly by the being in this very cottage, to be together. To try to step between them would be wrong, and rather than feel any sense of loss, John felt honored to witness such perfect happiness.

Uriel shoved Rimmon away and pointed the flaming sword at his throat.

Okay, so maybe it wasn't *that* perfect.

"Imposter!" Uriel snarled. "You are not my lover!"

Rimmon was pained. "How could you say that?"

From his crimson robe, Uriel pulled free a necklace. Hanging from it was a small, single horn that looked exactly like those on Rimmon's head.

"He gave this to me," Uriel said, "and yet you have two horns. What is your excuse, imposter, that Rimmon would hide his love in shame?"

"Did I feel like an imposter when I kissed you?" Rimmon pushed the flaming blade aside and stepped close to the angel, whispering something in his ear. Uriel's eyes widened briefly before narrowing again.

"And why should I believe such a ludicrous claim?"

Rimmon smirked and began to sing, his serenade just as haunting in day as it had been at night. Uriel's face softened before he joined in with his own melody. His voice was a gentle angelic choir, the purity of light, that soothed as much as Rimmon's song stirred. The two voices that sounded like many met and harmonized, blending together seamlessly, the beauty of the sun complementing shadow.

"I heard you," Uriel said when they had finished their song. "Every time you thought of me and sang, your voice was carried to me by the grace of His will."

"But you did not answer."

"I wanted to," Uriel promised. "My anger at you faded long ago, but by then the Ministers had come, and I could no longer leave His side."

"We must speak with Him," Rimmon said.

"Are you certain?"

As Rimmon nodded, one of the angels cried out in alarm. An army had been seen on the horizon, one very familiar to John since he had helped raise it.

"Return to formation," Uriel commanded, eyes fierce as he turned back to Rimmon. "I must do my job, as you have always done yours."

There was uncomfortable emphasis on these words, reminding John that Rimmon's profession was still a point of contention between the two. Uriel took to the sky, leading a formation of angels to battle.

Rimmon watched him go with concern. "Let's end this quickly, before anyone gets hurt."

John nodded and placed his hand on the door, anything but ready to meet God face to face.

Chapter Eighteen

The fireplace in the corner crackled and spit. A bundle of fragrant pine needles had been tossed onto the fire, filling the cottage with an earthy, comfortable scent. An old man with wild eyebrows, a long beard, and mane of white hair slumped contentedly in a chair upholstered with fabric so worn that stuffing stuck out of the arms. The fire was reflected in his eyes as he watched it, his face serene until panic crossed his features and he hopped to his feet.

"I forgot to make tea!" he declared.

"Then why is there a cup beside your chair?" asked another old man from behind a book. He hardly had any hair at all, but his cheeks were warm and red.

"He means for the arriving guests," another elderly man answered. His skin was dark and wrinkled, his eyes stern as he pondered the chess pieces before him. "If they wanted tea, you would have made it already. When have you ever gotten it wrong? Or I, for that matter."

"More than once," mumbled a younger man. He stroked his short brown beard worriedly as he peered out the window.

"Well I made cookies to go with the tea," the white-bearded man said. "Not enough for the armies though. Do you think that's rude of me?"

"Considering that they are here to kill us," said the chess player's opponent, who positively glowed with light, "I hardly think they are expecting tea or cookies."

"I always liked giving them the unexpected," the book reader said.

"At least I made enough for the first three guests."

"When do they get here?" the younger man asked.

"Right about now," every voice in the room said in unison.

John stepped into the cottage to find half a dozen faces staring at him. As with the other gods, he knew their names and natures instinctively. Allah was playing chess with the Holy Spirit. Jehovah was sitting up in bed and reading a book while Jesus was waiting by the window. Directly in front of them Yahweh was holding a tray laden with a humble tea service. Each paused in their activity to regard John and his friends.

John licked his lips and swallowed before asking his question. "Are you God?"

"Yes," they all answered.

"Close the door, would you please?" The Holy Spirit said.

"Tea?" Yahweh offered. "Or perhaps a cookie?"

John fought back a smile. He liked all of these gods instantly, and felt like he was meeting a father, an old friend, and a complete stranger all at once. Bolo must have shared his sentiment because he hopped onto the bed with Jehovah and settled down for a nap with his head on the old god's leg.

"There's an army at your door," John said, forcing himself to look away from the inviting scene.

"It's your army, isn't it?" Allah said pointedly. "Tell them to go away."

"Don't tease the boy," the Holy Sprit chuckled.

"There's time for us to talk," Jesus said. "Time enough for us to do what is necessary."

"No tea, then?" Yahweh asked again. "Very well." The tray and service disappeared. "Let us get down to business. It would be best if John hears it from someone he trusts."

"Me?" Dante said. "What do I know?"

"I think he means me," Rimmon said, turning to John. "Go on then, hit me with your usual barrage of questions."

John didn't need to be asked twice. "These are all aspects of God?"

"Yes."

"And we were expected?"

"More or less."

"We hoped you would come," Jesus said. "But few things in life, or death, are certain."

"I was certain," Allah said.

"And the army outside," John said, "they aren't really a threat?"

"I imagine they are," Rimmon said, "but we hope to defuse the situation with your help. Before you narrow your eyes any further, I never deceived you, John. I was only ever there to help you, never to manipulate you. I stood by and let you make your own choices, and my instructions were not to hinder you if you decided to act of your own accord."

"I trust you," John said, but his mind was already spinning. It seemed to John that God wanted him to come here, and yet his actions had resulted in the army waiting outside the cottage. How could he be both the problem and the solution?

"One must think many steps ahead," Allah said. "But you haven't been given all of the pieces. Let him unpack."

"Unpack?"

"I believe Dante would be the best one to show you," Yahweh said.

Dante crossed his arms. "Again, what do I know?"

"It's not what you know, it's what you have stolen," Jehovah said.

"You're going to have to be much more specific than that," Dante snorted before he could catch himself. He squirmed under the combined gaze of the deities. "Oh, fine. I knew it was special the moment I laid my hands on it."

From out of his jacket he pulled a crown, glistening with jewels. John recognized it as the crown Dante had stolen from the Greeks. He handed it to Yahweh, who placed it on the floor and spoke.

"We gods have always delighted in disguising ourselves. A swan, a burning bush, or a humble beggar. That's always a popular one, but we needed to be even more subtle this time. Not that our colleague here shares our definition of that."

The crown slowly rose into the air, pushed from below by hair and soon after a head. The effect was like watching a man being poured from a bowl. The process continued until Zeus stood before them, white hair bristling with electricity. The missing leader of the Greek gods adjusted his toga, glared at Dante, and wordlessly walked to the window.

"You stole something everywhere we went?" John asked accusingly.

Dante held up his hands innocently. "If I was supposed to, then we're screwed."

"The rest is up to John and his stowaways," Yahweh replied. "The lead deities were quite clever about getting here. By travelling with John, who is unique, they avoided detection from the Ministers. Hold out your hand, John."

John held out his right hand, and as he did so the splinter there stung. He had nearly forgotten about it, how he had placed his hands on Danu's chair in the Celtic realm. The pain from his finger disappeared as the splinter left. It spun in the air, growing in size and changing, one moment the size of a plank, the next the shape of a woman. She initially appeared to be made of wood, before her features colorized and softened.

Danu wore a practical emerald-green robe and a belt with a number of items hanging from it. Her red hair held just a hint of gray, and the light lines around her eyes and mouth spoke of amused wisdom. She turned, regarding the rest of the gods in the room.

"You really must get in touch with your feminine side," she said.

"That has always been a shortcoming of mine," Yahweh said, "which is why we are so glad to have you join us."

Danu took a seat on the bed's edge. "Any guesses as to what is next, John?"

"My sunburn!" John exclaimed. "I knew it was Ra I saw in the underworld, and it never left completely."

The skin of his neck flared in pain, and with it came a light so bright he was forced to close his eyes. When he opened them again, Ra was standing in the room. He had the head of a noble falcon, and was clad in a simple white skirt. His upper torso was bare, the muscles of his dark chest impressive.

"I hope the pain I caused you has since fled from your memory," Ra said, his voice deep. "You have done all of us a great service."

"Yes, at least he didn't steal you," Zeus growled as Ra joined him.

"Examine your right hand, John," Yahweh said. "I am especially proud of how subtly Odin chose to travel with you."

John turned his hand over a few times. It looked as it always did, except for his fingernails being a bit dirty. They had been ever since he had touched the ground in the Norse realm, happy to see nature again for the first time since his supposed death. As John watched, the dirt spilled from his fingers, grain by grain, until the air was filled with much more than his nails could have carried. The soil swirled in front of them, becoming a solid brown traveling cloak.

Odin wore a floppy hat that dipped low over one eye, almost obscuring its absence. His white beard was speckled with gray, and a number of battle scars crisscrossed his face. A line of runes was carved into the simple walking stick he carried.

"They're coming," Odin said.

"He's right," Zeus confirmed. "Just in time, too."

John rushed to the window. The scene outside was chaos. His army of gods and demons had broken rank and were rushing the cottage. Angels attacked them from all sides, landing in front and behind while even more attacked from above. The angels had a tactical advantage, but the powers of the gods were mighty. Flames rose from the ground to sear any angel who came too low, and storms were brewing above that would soon make being in the air a liability.

"You have to get out there and stop them," John said. "You're their leaders!"

"Watch," Ra said, nodding to the window.

From further afield came a new army, rows and rows of glass men, all in perfect formation. They marched in precise rhythm toward the cottage, but the battling armies hadn't seen them yet. Then an angel sparing with a demon did see them, alerting his combatant to the new threat. They ceased fighting each other to turn on this new foe, launching themselves at the front line.

One of the terracotta soldiers—John was certain it was Yi Yi— cried out in a loud and clear voice, attracting the attention of both good armies. Soon they had all turned and merged together, the battalion of angels, demons, and pagan gods becoming one. The Ministers of Order had numbers on their side, but they were uniform, predictable drones. The combined army they faced was wild, creatures from the entire history of man and religion, each with its own strange and wondrous abilities.

"The Ministers don't stand a chance," Zeus said, echoing John's thoughts.

"Regardless," Ra said, "I think the reappearance of their leaders will drive them to an even swifter victory."

"To battle, then," Odin said, sweeping toward the door.

One by one all of the gods filed out of the cottage, all except Yahweh. A roar from the army welcomed their arrival. As the door closed behind them, the cottage was returned to relative silence, the crackling of the fire the only sound. Yahweh regarded Rimmon with a subtle smile. John looked between them, wondering what was to come next.

"That leaves us with just one," the old god said.

Rimmon reached up to his right horn and snapped it off. He didn't wince in pain. The stub left behind looked as though it had long since healed. Rimmon tossed the horn into the air, where it stuck. The horn lengthened at its base, its curvature increasing. A matching horn bloomed into existence next to it, followed by the rest of the god.

His hair was messy waves of black silk, two ebony horns sticking out in an upward salute. Below the horns his eyebrows scowled. His ethnicity was ambiguous, his skin a shade of brown that could be anything from a deep tan to natural pigmentation. His age was difficult to determine. He wasn't young nor was he old. Only tired almond eyes hinted that his lifespan had been eons longer than that of any human.

"My dear Rex Mundi," Yahweh said, opening his arms.

"You know I prefer to be called Lucifer."

"Of course," Yahweh said, dropping his arms. "Your part in this was unexpected but crucial. I think my kingdom would have fallen had you not come forward with this plan."

"All of our kingdoms would have fallen," Lucifer replied, "and in that regard my actions will surely be labeled as selfish, as they always are. Still, I might have seen your kingdom fall first, before I took action."

"And why didn't you?"

"Because I've always labored to show you why there must be more than one, that all of your children deserve freedom, not just mankind."

"It was your freedom I was giving you," Yahweh said softly. "The curse of any parent is to set their child free. So rarely can it be done gently. A bird must push its child from the nest if it's to fly."

"The metaphor would carry more weight if you hadn't created the birds," Lucifer retorted. "They are merely a reflection of your own philosophy."

"Then I look forward to the day when you have children of your own." Yahweh smiled. "It is good to see you again."

For a moment, Lucifer wavered. John was sure a hug was in the making, but the Devil regained control of himself before that could happen. "I must see to my people," he said, turning toward the door. "Dante, Rimmon, excellent work. You will be rewarded."

"I have a few things in mind," Dante said, following him out the door.

"I must check on Uriel," Rimmon said, pausing on his way out to look at John, "Are you coming?"

"In a moment."

Yahweh waited patiently, knowing that John wished to speak with him. He had so many questions, so many things he wanted to know. Was there a limit? Was it like a genie's wishes where he would only get three?

"Why do things this way?" John began. "The different leaders were always on your side. Why not have them bring their armies here, rather than the disappearing act?"

Yahweh's smile was kind. "The Ministers of Order took advantage of rifts that had long ago formed between religions and cultures. The plan of my very clever son has made it possible for those rifts to be bridged, once and for all. Had I called the other pantheons here, some may have come grudgingly, others not at all. Instead we asked the leaders to step aside. Without the leaders of each realm, the remaining gods were forced to make their own decisions. Now those gods have come, even more than we expected. Had it not been for your efforts, the outcome of the current battle may have been similar, but the aftermath would have been vastly different."

John nodded, even though he didn't fully understand. "When I was in Purgatory, the creatures in charge, their hearts were—"

"I know," Yahweh said sadly. "Man learned long ago to give his own words credence by claiming they were mine. Many of them meant well, and some good has come of it, but there are those who search for meaning through cold words instead of the warmth of their heart. Just as there have been divisions here, there have been many on Earth. Too many. Perhaps the effects of today's events will be far-reaching enough to change things there as well. As above, so below."

"Can't you just, I don't know, fix everything? I mean, you're *God!*"

"Even if I could, I wouldn't, for what would I fix it to, and for whom? Myself? There is never one singular path, never one lonely truth. That is the biggest lie ever told. Existence is wonderfully strange, frighteningly varied, and above all, beautiful. No, I am much happier to let the story play out on its own, to truly feel proud when my children choose to do what is right."

John smiled, another question ready on his lips, but then his head swam. He fell to one knee and inhaled, really breathed in, for he could feel his lungs. They were still far away, but close enough that he could smell the sterile hospital air. His body was coming out of the coma, waking up, calling him home.

"Not yet, not yet," Yahweh said, placing a hand on John's head. "Don't you want to stay for the ending?"

John's world stabilized again, his awareness returning to the cottage.

Yahweh put an arm around him and guided him to the door. "Come, Bolo!" he said.

The snoozing dog instantly awoke and hopped off the bed to join them.

Outside the battle had run its course. A couple of glass skeletons had yet to fall and a number of Ministers could be seen running for the hills, but the worst of it was over. John scanned the crowd, hoping no serious losses had occurred. He saw Liu Wu—little Yi Yi riding on his shoulder—being clapped on the back by Ares. The king's features were proud as he and the war god exchanged congratulations. Elsewhere, Hermes zipped through the crowd, shaking hands with the surprised deities he appeared before. Thor was one of them, interrupted in his attempts to flirt with Amaterasu. Not far away, Cernunnos watched a group of animal-headed Egyptian gods with interest.

There didn't seem to be any mourning, or fallen allies. In fact, the only unhappy face John could see was Asmoday. The Archduke stomped through the crowds, trying to rally tempers toward Heaven again until he spotted the Devil himself. Then Asmoday fell to his knees, his many chins quivering as he spluttered a mixture of apologies and pledges of loyalty. John smirked and searched the scene for his own demon. There, in the center of the battlefield, stood Rimmon, an angel at his side. Rimmon laid a hand on Uriel's shoulder, and the angel placed his palm against the demon's cheek. As they kissed, John allowed himself one last sigh.

Then the land beneath his feet began to rise, taking the cottage with it. Soon all eyes were on him, Bolo, and Yahweh. The old god clapped his hands in joy, as if he had witnessed a wonderful play, before he beckoned for the others to join him. One by one the different aspects of God, along with the leaders of every realm, walked up the newly formed hill. There were even more pantheons represented now, deities from other realms who had decided to join late in the battle.

"There are many reasons why we have come together today," Yahweh addressed the crowd, his voice loud enough for all to hear. "The enemy vanquished here was more than an army of glass men. The true enemy was division taken too far. What we have conquered today is fear and suspicion, and now they must be replaced with respect and unity. As our differences benefitted us on the field of battle, so can they enhance our everyday existence, for diversity tempered with love instead of hate is infinitely giving and supportive. The time has come for our many islands to join together, to create a world of many different roads and bridges, one where all are welcome and where every soul is home."

The crowd cheered as the different aspects of God moved to join one another. Yahweh, Jesus, Allah, Jehovah, and the Holy Spirit stepped into each other, becoming one deity instead of many. The leaders of the other realms followed next: Ra, Odin, Danu, one after the other merging and becoming a being of the brightest, purest light. Finally only Lucifer was left, cockily motioning for the being of light to come to him instead. It did, wrapping its arms around him lovingly and taking him in.

Then everything changed.

They had all gone home, which is to say, they hadn't gone anywhere, since 'here' was all there was. From the cottage on the hill they could see it all. The strange lights of Heaven wavered on the horizon. Behind them was majestic Mount Olympus. To the south could be seen the cities of Hell, and to the west a glimmering blue ocean filled with the Celtic isles. Other places were out there, too, exotic buildings and strange environments John had never seen or imagined. The realms were connected now, separate but without borders, and beyond them was the wild astral plane where dreams had yet to be born. John wanted nothing more than to explore all of this. Except he didn't have much time left.

The leaders had separated again, their display of unity over, but the significance behind their gesture would be remembered for all eternity. One by one, they guided their people home, although many chose to move on to other realms, to experience something new. Yahweh had been the last to leave, conjuring up patio furniture in front of his cottage before giving John and his friends their privacy.

Yahweh had promised John just enough time to see the results of his efforts and to say goodbye to his friends. That moment had come. Soon John's body would come out of its coma, returning him to the land of the living, but not quite yet. Rimmon sat closest to John, the demon's expression content, while Dante struggled with the awkwardness of the situation. Bolo was there too, sleeping on his back with his four legs spread wide.

"Did you manage to get much out of Lucifer?" John asked, hoping to jump-start the conversation.

Dante grinned. "Actually, yes. I wanted a place to live, preferably in demonic Amsterdam, and he mentioned a sprawling apartment above a pub. It barely took any begging at all to have him include the pub as part of the deal."

"So you're going into business, then?" Rimmon asked.

"No," Dante said, "I'm selling it for money and on the condition that I can drink there for free whenever I want. I'm not going to spend my afterlife working!"

John chuckled. "What about you?"

"A promotion," Rimmon answered. "One that doesn't require the use of my natural talents, which should be enough for Uriel to fully forgive me. I'm looking forward to a new challenge, but I believe I'll take some time off before I begin."

John gave him a knowing look. "I heard the angels have been given time off, too, since they've been patrolling nonstop for so many years."

Rimmon smiled. "That is very convenient, yes."

"And, uh, what are you going to do?" Dante asked, not making eye contact.

"I don't know," John said. "Wake up, shower, eat, go to work. The usual things, I suppose. It all seems a little unreal, to be honest, which is crazy considering where I am. Jace was right. Being here makes life sound like a fairy tale."

"You'll get caught up in it soon enough," Rimmon said. "Physical existence can be wonderfully distracting."

"Just don't go starting any creepy cults," Dante said. "Unless they worship me, that is. Hey, maybe we can work something out! I hear believers are as good as cash over here!"

"What about Bolo?" John asked, reaching down to stroke his belly. "Do you think—"

John slipped from his chair and fell, but he couldn't stop falling. There was nothing to grab hold of anymore, nothing solid. The world around him had disappeared.

"Best of luck, kid," he heard Dante say, but his voice was far away and distorted.

"We can't choose who we love," Rimmon's voice was barely a whisper, "but if we could, I would love—"

John awoke with a gasp, the tube in his throat jostling painfully in his esophagus. Every nerve screamed with sensation and his body felt terribly heavy, but John's mind was still elsewhere. He thought of Dante, his schemes and sarcasm. He saw Bolo's happy face in his mind. And of course he thought of everything he loved about Rimmon. John willed himself to return, just for one minute more, just to say goodbye properly and to have one last laugh.

"John?"

The voice belonged to his mother.

John managed to open his eyes. The world seemed much too bright.

"John! You're awake! Oh, thank God, you're awake!"

She threw herself over him and together they cried, each for very different reasons.

Epilogue

"You're a silly old fool, John Grey."

He said this to his reflection in the mirror, and it had never been truer than today. John was old. He scoured his image, searching for a single square inch of skin that wasn't covered in wrinkles or hadn't been stretched by ninety-two years of gravity. He remembered those first gray hairs, how upsetting they had been, which was laughable now that his hair was wispy and white. A hair hearty enough to be gray would have been a welcome sight. Even the color of his eyes had grown pale and misty.

John stopped scrutinizing himself and turned away from the mirror. Seeing his reflection only made him feel more ancient. His body had enough aches and pains to remind him of how many long years he had lived. Almost all of them were good, he considered as he hobbled down the stairs of his home, taking one at a time. So many years full of life and love.

He paused halfway down the stairwell, as he always did, to look at the framed photo of Scott. He had been John's physical therapy coach, helping him recover from the weakness left by the coma. Scott had been there from the beginning, kindly guiding him back to health. John had barely noticed him the first week they worked together, his mind lost in everything he had left behind and so desperately wanted to return to. But when John finally focused on life again, Scott's bright smile won him over completely. Suddenly, John's heart found a new adventure, one that had lasted all of these years.

John brought a shaking hand to his mouth, kissed the tips of his fingers, and pressed them to Scott's lips in the photo before continuing down the stairs. He and Scott had seen so many interesting times together. There were wars, as there always were, but there was also a subtle change. Religion once again became a comfort in those hard times. Not just one faith, but all of them, for believers began to open their arms to each other, to embrace the ideas and opinions of their fellow human beings. As one pope famously said during this period, you can never have too much of a good thing. There were still divisions among people. There always would be, but no longer were they created by the spiritual institutions meant to provide hope.

John reached the bottom of the stairs, gripping the banister with gnarled fingers until he caught his breath. His body was giving him a harder time than usual today. He could hear Scott's voice in his mind, crystal clear even though it had been two years since he had passed, chiding John for not getting enough exercise. He would be right, of course, as Scott always had been. Lately John had been content to sit and think of the past, often drifting off to sleep no matter the hour.

John gathered his strength and moved to the couch, sighing with relief when he was finally seated. His old bones shifted and settled, grateful for the comfort the thick cushions provided. On the coffee table was a scrapbook, the corners of the pages curled from so much use. John pulled it onto his lap and opened the worn cover.

Inside was everything he had been able to find. A newspaper clipping for Dante Stewart's obituary was on the opening page, the first piece of evidence John had found that proved he wasn't crazy. Scott hadn't known back then, but had humored John when they took their trip to Dublin. John spent an entire day at the public library, searching through old newspaper obituaries until he found it. Dante Stewart had died on October 16, 1983, in what the paper described as a "violent incident outside a pub." Scott had blocked him from the librarian's sight as John tore Dante's obituary out of the paper. A few days later, they visited the home of Dante's mother.

That had been awkward. John had been a toddler when Dante died, and despite lying about his age, it wasn't easy to convince his mother that they once knew each other. He didn't dare explain where they had met, but he knew enough of the Irishman's quirks to convince her in the end, even though she remained puzzled. Before John left, she gave him a photo of Dante, which was now in the scrapbook next to the obituary. Dante was younger than John had ever known him, his constant stubble absent, but the ornery eyes were unmistakable.

John turned the pages. Little else was as personal as this first page. There were clippings about religion and mythology, an excerpt from Milton's *Paradise Lost* that mentioned Rimmon, and different artistic interpretations of an incubus—anything John could find to help remind him of the memories he had made.

When John had finally told Scott everything, years later of course, the scrapbook was his biggest piece of evidence. John was never completely sure if his husband believed him, but Scott loved him enough not to say if he didn't. John supposed that Scott was seeing all of it for himself now.

Toward the back of the scrapbook was a photo of Bolo. Not the English Shepherd, naturally, but a yellow lab they had named Marx. In the sixteen years that Marx was a part of their lives, John was reminded of Bolo nearly every day. He often wondered if the dog hadn't found his way back to him, as Rimmon once promised he could.

John sighed and closed the scrapbook, which felt too heavy on his lap now. The morning sun had slowly moved across the floor and reached part of the couch. John set the scrapbook aside and stretched out, laying his head in the warmth of the sun and pulling his favorite quilt over the rest of him. Funny that he should still need a blanket, even in the middle of summer.

For a moment, as he was dozing off, John thought he heard Scott's voice calling him, could feel his husband's fingers interlocking with his own. With his touch, John didn't feel old anymore. The aches and pains had gone as memories returned clearer than ever. Buildings made of light and sound, gods he had once fought alongside, and the friends that had journeyed with him through colorful realms. He could see their faces now and hear their voices, because they were all around him, everyone he had missed from this life and the other, welcoming him home again.

Also by Jay Bell:

The Cat in the Cradle

To set out into the world, to be surrounded by the unknown and become a stranger. Only then would he be free to reinvent himself. Or fall in love.

Dylan wanted one last adventure before the burden of adulthood was thrust upon him. That, and to confront the man he hadn't spoken to since their intimate night together. Stealing a boat with his faithful companion Kio, their journey is cut short when they witness a brutal murder. A killer is loose in the Five Lands and attacking the most powerful families. Dylan—a potential target—seeks sanctuary from an unpredictable bodyguard named Tyjinn. Together they decide to turn the tables by hunting the killer down. Along the way, everything Dylan thought he knew about himself will be challenged, but if he survives, he stands to win the love he never dreamed possible.

The Cat in the Cradle is the first book in the Loka Legends series and features twenty-five original illustrations created by Andreas Bell, the author's husband.

For more information, please visit:
www.jaybellbooks.com

CPSIA information can be obtained
at www.ICGtesting.com
Printed in the USA
LVOW11s0835280317
528733LV00001B/246/P